S/A

D1509576

The
Easiest
Thing
in the
World

The
Easiest
Thing
in the
World

The Uncollected Fiction of
GEORGE V. HIGGINS
Edited by Matthew J. Bruccoli

Carroll & Graf Publishers
New York

THE EASIEST THING IN THE WORLD
The Uncollected Fiction of George V. Higgins

Carroll & Graf Publishers
An Imprint of Avalon Publishing Group Inc.
245 West 17th Street
11th Floor
New York, NY 10011

AVALON
publishing group incorporated

First Carroll & Graf edition 2004

Library of Congress Cataloging-in-Publication Data is available.

ISBN: 0-7867-1474-3

Printed in the United States of America
Distributed by Publishers Group West

CONTENTS

INTRODUCTION

by Robert B. Parker

GEORGE Higgins wrote like no one else had written before him. He told his stories in the voices of people talking. Not so much a master of dialogue as of monologue. The alternate monologues of people recalling. The recollections are often presented to us second or third hand. Recounted by people who had participated or had heard of the event, or heard someone tell of the event. The resulting work of fiction is both leisurely and immediate. His first novel begins thus:

"Jackie Brown at twenty-six, with no expression on his face, said that he could get some guns."

We are in the story, smack up against it, in fact, with no warning. And yet there's nothing hurried in the pace. The conversation proceeds. One of the men tells a story. The other man responds. It is not clear what the larger story is about, but the moment is compelling, and we learn things. We are witnessing a story as it unfolds, almost narrationless, entirely dramatized. The writing is both deliberate and quick. It is the hallmark of George's best work.

People trying to learn how to write (which George and I always agreed was not a learnable skill) often ask how prose style is developed. It probably isn't. It is probably the verbal manifestation of who you are—and, maybe, to write like George Higgins, you might have to become George Higgins. This is not to say that George was like his characters or that reading his books will allow you to understand him as a person. It is rather that George's self, filtered through the shaping mechanism of his imagination (along with discipline, the *sine qua non* of fictionists), found a voice unlike anyone else's. You can learn from George. Relax. Let the story tell itself. Don't be literary. Dramatize, dramatize. You can copy George, but you can't write like George. You can only write like yourself.

George was excessive. He worked excessively. He had served time as a journalist, prosecutor, defense attorney, teacher. He wrote not only fiction but newspaper columns, magazine articles, television criticism, current history, and a ton of other things, some of which are herein. He loved Loretta and his children excessively (my favorite thing about him). He was full of opinions, which he articulated loudly and at length (often wrong, I used to tell him, but never uncertain). He was a fierce enemy and a wonderful friend (I was, praise God, the latter).

The Friends of Eddie Coyle, the first novel he published, was both the best and worst thing that could have happened to him. It was a huge bestseller. It made him famous and affluent. It became a big movie starring Robert Mitchum, and it was the most successful book he ever wrote.

There are those—I am not one of them—who think my early books are the best, the truest to the old pulp action tradition of detective stories. Someone asked me once when I was speaking at a writers conference, why so many writers wrote less and less action as time went on. I gave a literary (which is to say evasive) answer at the time, because, in truth, I didn't know. But in retrospect I realized that I at least, and probably most writers, get bored writing about fights and shootings. We get more and more interested in the characters, and, for lack of a better word, the process. Did this happen to George? Maybe.

Maybe he wished to go where his imagination and his talent took him, and it was a place where some readers didn't want to go. Maybe he was badly published (it happens). But his talent did not diminish. As this collection demonstrates, there are few people who write as well as George, and no one who writes quite like him. We were often linked, because we both set novels in Boston, and wrote them about people who did bad things. In fact we were entirely dissimilar writers. When we were together we talked about the things most writers talk about; advances, film deals, agents. We rarely talked about writing. Because, in truth, we never had anything to say. We pretty much agreed it was a thing done, not talked about.

And few people have done it better than George V. Higgins.

Robert Parker
Cambridge, MA
May 10, 2004

EDITOR'S NOTE

THE big risk with a posthumously published collection is that it may resemble a grab-bag of left-overs. *The Easiest Thing in the World* is a strong volume that combines previously unpublished work from the Higgins archive at the Thomas Cooper Library, University of South Carolina, with a selection of the short stories he published.

The novelette is an uncommercial form—unless written by John O'Hara, Higgins's idol. "The Easiest Thing in the World" and "Slowly Now the Dancer" were declined by publishers because they are too short for a separate book and too long for a magazine. This volume provides the right venue for them. "The First of the Year" is included as the prequel or sequel to "The Easiest Thing in the World."

The only volume of Higgins stories, *The Sins of the Fathers* (London: Andre Deutsch, 1988), was not published in America. Three of the stories collected here are taken from that book. "The Habits of the Animals: The Progress of the Seasons" was reprinted in *The Best American Short Stories of 1973*. "Old Earl Died Pulling Traps" was published in a collector's edition limited to 300 copies.

Given Higgins's extraordinary skill with American speech and dialogue, it is perhaps surprising that he did not persevere as a dramatist—probably because he found the play format restrictive. "The Last Wash of The Teapot As Told by Cornelius McKibben, Esq." is subtitled "A Book for a Play" but is not written as a play script: the key words in the title are "As Told by." Higgins's narrative technique customarily utilized the narrator—either as protagonist or as partially involved story-teller. The movie or television treatment for "Jack Duggan's Law," though not a first-person narrative, is in story form. George V. Higgins was a natural story-teller. There are very good ones here.

George was my friend. I'll never find another one like him.

The previously published stories are reprinted from their first appearances. The texts of the new novelettes and stories are set from Higgins's typescripts, with correction of typing errors that do not affect meaning. Obvious missing words have been supplied, and a few editorial emendations are inserted in brackets.

Matthew J. Bruccoli

The
Easiest
Thing
in the
World

THE EASIEST
THING IN
THE WORLD

BARBARA Harkness Kendrick asked me to handle her divorce because, she said, I was a friend of the family. If this had been true, it would have been the worst of all possible reasons. Since it wasn't true, it was merely the worst of available explanations.

The fact was that I had known her and Miles since the summer of 1962. Since 1967, I had acted as his attorney, which is to say that I had performed certain legal services which he requested, in the belief that I was affording professional service to him. Until very recently I did not suspect that our relationship might include rather more than that.

This suspicion had not arisen when I met Barbara, at her request, for drinks in the skyroof lounge at Logan Airport one hot, still, August evening last year. Accordingly I knew very well, before I saw her once more, after six missing years, that I would be obliged to decline her offer to hire me.

I did not utter my refusal at once. To be sure, I had it all prepared: a dignified, somewhat regretful, explanation of the implications of professional ethics, perhaps somewhat confusing to a layman but binding nonetheless, precluding the termination of one's legal relationship to a client of some standing in order to assert opposition to that client in behalf of another. This omitted mention of the substantial fees I would renounce by ending my services to Miles. I justified this selective silence on the grounds that the factor concealed did not conflict with the judgment expressed, but tended rather to reinforce it.

Still there was nothing in my professional duty to Miles which obliged me to seem heartless, unsympathetic or even mildly disapproving when I saw Barbara again. She was, after all, an acquaintance of many years and an extraordinarily beautiful woman. Even allowing for taste, and the improvement of memory by nostalgia, she had seemed to me in 1962 the most beautiful girl in the world. Six years later, when she was five years shy of thirty, she was well on her way to becoming the most beautiful woman in the world. Irritated, uncomfortable, fatigued and upset as she was on that August evening, she sat among the ordinary women in the airport lounge like a princess unconvincingly disguised. "I'm glad you could come," she said. "I was beginning to wonder if I had a friend in the world."

She had no other friends in that saloon. She was wearing a tailored black suit and her honey hair was long. She was the entirely ornamental woman she had been born to be, and the other women in the lounge, their hair cut short and their cotton dresses comfortably loose-fitting, glanced slyly at her and despised her. They resented her for the soft curves of her breasts and the impressive extent of good thigh she displayed. They were angry because she had chosen to interest men by wearing that suit on an evening discomforting enough to excuse a woman from the obligation of pleasing men. They despised her for the scant good jewelry that she wore, and they believed they knew how she had gotten it, incurred the unremitting duty to please men, and lost her standing in their sisterhood. They surmised the part those breasts and thighs had played in the acquisition of her status, and they were right, and they were hostile. But most of all they despised her for looking unhappy about the world she had obtained and the place she held in it, for that meant they had been right to play the game their way; on the shag end of a wearisomely humid August day, bored in the fatigue of waiting for their husbands to arrive on the next shuttle from New York or Washington, they hated their worlds also, and needed to be able to wonder if the worlds inhabited by Barbara Harkness Kendrick were not better. She denied this need.

She provoked another. While I made some modest, restrained noises of concern for her, and understanding, I strenuously resigned myself to the immediate resurrection of the feeling of mingled lust and frustration I had experienced during the summer of our introduction, and sat down to order whiskey and listen to her sorrows.

We talked for nearly an hour, waiting for Miles to fly in from the Bahamas—she was waiting, and we agreed that I had met her by chance after delivering a client to a plane. She told me of her fear of Miles. She said she did not know what to do, although she had plainly decided. She said she loved another man.

It is now nearly two years since she told me that, and I am no longer sure that it was true. I am convinced that she believed it and, with Milton Mallus since deceased, has almost certainly been confirmed by grief and hatred in the certainty of the love that was torn away from her.

At the time I was not so skeptical, not skeptical at all, in fact. Disregarding the fact that I had never taken the time, in six years, to sort out what I had learned about her during that enduring summer and to make an estimate of her personality and character, I listened to her carefully while she talked of Milton Mallus, and of Miles Kendrick, and was very much impressed. With my judgment of her muddled as before by the urgency of my desire for her, I compared her report of her thinking in 1968 to the way I had seen her behave in 1962, and found her unexpectedly mature. Even insightful. She described the temperate man who had inherited the Continental franchise in East Hartford, Connecticut, comparing his considerateness, thoughtfulness, substance and manifest decency to what she had come to perceive as the coldness, violence, and remorselessness of her husband, Miles Kendrick.

"I'm afraid of Miles now," she said. "I don't mean he beats me. He doesn't need to. He doesn't need to hit anybody. He just makes it so plain that he could beat you up if he wanted to. He makes you feel as though you weren't worth killing. He pays attention to me and he buys me everything I want and we always go nice places. He gave me a Thunderbird for my birthday. But I always have the feeling, you know, that if he decided I wasn't what he wanted any more, well, there would be somebody else. With Milton I feel secure, that he really wants me. He's rich, of course. He's got at least as much money as Miles, and I like that, I like being pampered. But he cares about me too, and I need that. . . . Well, I almost think I could get along without the money if I had to, if I couldn't have money and feel the way I do when I'm with Milton."

Let me be precise. I do not say that I completely admired everything she said. I am still a bachelor, at age thirty-one, partly because I have met a great many materialistic women whose avarice, very similar to my own, offended me nonetheless. I was neither delighted nor disarmed by her appetite for luxury. I did not find it startling either.

What impressed me was her realistic appraisal of herself, the comparative clear-sightedness of her self-analysis, even the very fact of that self-analysis. I had not, I suppose, thought her capable of it. To see that capacity was so unexpected that I did not question its exercise.

Now I do. My knowledge of the girl she had been in 1962 should have made me cautious about the woman she seemed, in 1968, to have become. Of course I had not observed the process of development, if in fact there had been one: her apparent—and unaccustomed—competence hit me all at once. Nor had I received any substantial inkling of a change in her; Miles seldom spoke of her to me. His formidable reserve discouraged questions of a personal nature. I had no family about whom to ask questions. To the best of my recollection, he offered only one hint of a transformation during the two years of our business which preceded my meeting with her at the airport, and it is only in hindsight that I recognize it as a clue.

It was late on a May afternoon. We had spent the bulk of the day acquiring title to some rather extensive holdings in Dennisport. There remained too little of the day to accomplish anything at our offices, mine in Plymouth, his in Boston. We stopped for a drink at the Wychmere Harbor Club in Harwichport. In the harbor beyond the windows, white sailboats leaned back and forth in the tidal current, and we swallowed fresh clams and drank Lowenbrau. On the dock opposite the club, a man and a woman, both in white Levi's and blue sweatshirts, were marshalling three children, a dog and a cooler aboard a small cruiser in the soft sunlight.

"You did well today, Miles," I said, expansive because our association was new and I had not become habituated to fees of the size I had earned in that placid afternoon. "Hang onto that land three years and you can sell it, as is, for sixty thousand easy."

He didn't answer immediately. He waited until the family across the inlet had made themselves comfortable on deck chairs, and the father backed the cruiser carefully away from the mooring. The exhaust muttered in the water as the cruiser headed for the Atlantic beyond. When it passed the window, the children waved to us.

"I wonder if you can do that," he said, when the wake of the cruiser had died against the pilings of the club. "Three years is quite a while to maintain anything as is, no matter what you can sell it for. Land, whiskey, dogs and people: nothing stays as is. You take your chances on a woman and you take your chances on wood-lots. What goes on around them, that changes them. Nothing you can do about it."

It seems to me now that I thought of Barbara then, and wondered if something might be going sour, changing what had seemed certain to survive, that summer at the Light. But I am not sure.

The world in the summer of 1962 was encompassed by Plymouth on the north, Route Three on the west, the Cape Cod Canal on the south and the Atlantic on the east. It was called Martin's Light and was full of time.

The center of this world was Clay's Inn, two and a half wooden-frame stories painted gray with white trim, crowded in against a stand of oaks at the edge of Winslow Street. It was presided over by a man named Bruno, Jim Bruno. Later he became the manager of a fairly plush steak house on the Lynnway north of Boston. Recently he was sentenced to two years in the Middlesex County House of Correction at Billerica, for receiving stolen goods. The State Police found forty portable color television sets in the panelled basement of his home in Reading.

The Inn was a cocktail lounge in his eyes. In fact it was a roadhouse. *Was*, incidentally, is the proper tense: the Inn was torn down eighteen months ago, and a shopping center catering to the summer people—groceries, hardware, greeting cards, coin laundry, liquor store—erected with impressive cinderblock speed in its place.

When the Inn was running, it served food (sandwiches) to those of extreme hunger and intestinal fortitude. Of these there were not a great many. The Inn also served drinks—I served drinks—to a large number, of whom a substantial minority were underage. There was a band on Thursday night, Friday night, Saturday night and Sunday afternoon. The leader weighed three hundred pounds, played the saxophone, took nitroglycerine every time the door slammed, and taught civics in the winter at Fall River. He was known as Tiny. I don't know what became of him.

It was not a particularly attractive place, although I suppose it had a certain raunchy charm about it. The door to the men's room opened away from the plate glass window at the front of the building, and after nine o'clock almost none of its visitors remembered to shut it. The middle-aged people were generally coarse; the younger, but legal, drinkers were ignorant bores, surfeited with Daddy's prosperity, Mummy's neuroses, and their own aimless ambitions and importunate tumescence; and the youngest drinkers were just what young drinkers usually are: boys and girls of moderate bravado, alternately too noisy and too subdued, horny, and afflicted by uneasiness of digestion brought on by drinking done in disregard of experience and capacity. The customers in their forties and fifties frequently fought over one another's women, primarily to settle disputes about which was whose. The college graduates became maudlin toward the end of each evening. The teenagers left by eleven to attempt fornication in parked cars, unless sooner disabled by the debilitating need to vomit in the scrub which fringed the rocky parking lot in the back. Almost all of these people lived in the Light in the summer, in cottages purchased in 1946 with overseas pay, poker winnings obtained on troopships, and overtime wages earned in defense plants. It was not a classy town, and the Inn was not a classy joint.

I was there because being there was the best I could do, in the summer of 1962. I was a very tense fellow that year. I had left Cleveland—Shaker Heights—for the Air Force in 1955, not because I preferred the service to college but because I preferred anything to four more years of tacit approval, expressed by participation, in my parents' vaulting satisfaction taken from their hard-won prosperity: eight drugstores, secured by sacrifices Siberian in their severity. Thirteen years later, after earning my dogged way through college, law school, and the early installments due on debts thereby incurred, I grew inclined to the view my father had had in 1955, but had common-sensibly failed to express to me: that I had been unusually silly. But in those days I had a fiercely protective attitude toward my independence, which engendered necessarily the completely untrue presumption that someone or something meant to make me dependent, and a similar jealousy of what I believed to be my integrity, without being too sure of what that was. I was further handicapped by having almost no judgment at all.

For material possessions, in the summer of 1962, I had a 1956 Ford Crown Victoria, one of those turquoise and white hardtops with the big chrome belt at the midsection. It had a turquoise and white vinyl interior, cold as a plastic toilet seat on a winter morning, a hooded instrument panel which probably furnished to me some subconscious consolation for being unqualified for flight training in the Air Force, and a large Thunderbird V-8 out front. It consumed premium gasoline copiously, partly because I drove it hard, and this expensive appetite, satisfied on an airman's pay, was a major reason for the fact that I had had to allocate much of my mustering-out pay to discharging the lien I had put on the car when I bought it three years before.

This improvidence constituted much of the reason that I could comfortably carry all of my other possessions in the trunk of the Vic. Those consisted of shaving kit, the books accumulated during my four years at Boston University, and the clothes I had bought cheap, worn out fast, and lacked the money to replace. I also had a portable radio, a red plastic Westinghouse that looked very much like a lunch-box, and administered a mild shock to him who touched the metal hardware.

I had no debts. In 1962 that was a source of considerable pride to me. I believed it demonstrated my prudence. But this was balanced by the fact that I had no capital either.

To inspire me, I had the fact of my acceptance as a member of the class entering law school in September of 1962. To worry me, I had a clear enough estimate of my abilities to know that if I attempted to work my way through three years of law school on my undergraduate job tending bar six nights a week at the Pastime Grille on Boylston Street, I would flunk out. My inspiration, therefore, was dampened by the sure and certain knowledge that its implementation would exact the tribute of my other principal satisfaction: I knew, in that summer, that I was about to get into debt, and had to if I ever hoped to gain enough margin to keep all of my future satisfactions in at least precarious security. Late in the rainy summer mornings I awoke in the hot, heavy air of the room provided by Jim Bruno, over the bar, and I focussed my eyes on the dark brown creosote stains on the wallboard, trying without much success to occupy my mind with the interdependent natural processes which dropped the acorns and leaves of the sheltering oaks into the gutters of the silent Inn during autumn, stuffing the downspouts with the winter snows that melted in the spring to flood the walls through the eaves. I also prayed that I would not get sick.

In this anxious state, ignored by the college graduates who might have taken time in their patronage of the Inn to offer some companionship (which I almost certainly would have disdained) but didn't, I was in no position to discriminate among potential friends. When Miles initiated our acquaintance, by mere desultory courtesy, I responded gratefully. Possibly, even, excessively. Definitely without a reflective assessment of his faults and virtues, his overall suitability as a friend.

Miles, I learned in the course of that summer, might have belonged to the Inn's group of fat college grads, but had decided not to. He had been in the Light every summer back to 1947 or so. In the summer of 1962 he was twenty-one, halfway to a bachelor's degree at Brown, in physics.

According to strict educational timetables, of course, Miles ought to have had the degree in his hands by then. But at eighteen he had driven out of Providence one December night in 1959 in a 1957 black Olds convertible (given by his father in consideration of high grades earned as a member of the Class of 1957 at Weston High School), and disappeared into the dark, rolling fields of the Republic. He vanished for a year, and I don't know what he did in that time because he never told me. But whatever it was, it paid him enough to permit him to limit his correspondence with his parents to reports of persisting good health. These he had remailed, for twenty-five cents, by a man in Fairbanks, Alaska, who advertised his services in *Popular Science*; the envelopes carried no return address.

Miles, he told me, had emerged from the country in September of 1961, having arranged some sort of cease-fire with himself and looking toward a similar truce with his family and their values. He achieved that also: he let them alone, they left him alone. In the summer of 1962 he stood five-eleven, weighed a hundred and forty or so, had black hair and an agreeably sallow complexion, and drove the Fifty-seven Olds. He was spending the summer reading, a *droit de seigneur* which I coveted, and he presented an air of purposiveness, a manner which I envied. He was doing, of course, precisely what was open to me, if I had had the wit to see it: he had made both his point and his peace with his family, and was allowing them to support him while he did what they believed they desired him to do: develop his abilities. At the time I did not make this connection.

In the summer of 1962, Barbara Harkness, without meaning it, seemed to resemble Miles to a considerable degree, and in fact had a great deal in common with me. Which meant that in the most important respect she resembled neither of us: Miles had attained his nonchalant condition of existence by action taken on reflection; I grimly behaved according to the strictures of my own irrationality; Barbara inhaled and exhaled on a regular basis, resembling Miles in her apparent unconcern, and me in the fact that she had a very long way to go.

She came from Auburn, Massachusetts, which is a nice place to come from if you have a fighting chance to get somewhere else. Her father was in the roofing business in the Worcester area. She had four older brothers. One was in the Army. Two were in the construction business (and occasionally, I gathered, in jail, as the result of getting into quarrels in bars on Friday nights). One was officially unemployed, most likely supported by a modest horse-book. She had a sister, Julia, also older than Barbara, married to a cop in Chelmsford. Her mother clerked in a five-and-ten.

It was clear that none of these people had ever perceived anything unusual about Barbara, and were by long custom habituated to treating her as one of themselves: an undistinguished human being with no prospect whatsoever of anything beyond a life the color of oatmeal, and about as appetizing. Barbara, in the summer of 1962, appeared to share this view, a fact perhaps attributable to her practice of doing no thinking at all.

This was not the misfortune which it might have been. While it went a long way to explain how she happened to have spent the second week of September, 1960, as a freshman on the campus of the University of Maryland, leaving at the end of that week because she was just smart enough to know she wasn't smart enough, her absence of intellection was in the general picture no more of a shortcoming than fear of high places would be to a sandhog. Barbara being what she was, the most beautiful girl in the world, it was foreordained that someone would take an interest in her which would effectively remove her from listless days of movie magazines, and vague ideas of going to beautician's school. Whether angels watch over drunks and little children is matter of some doubt to any man who ever tried a driving-under, or brought a case in tort. But most will concede the invariable chivalry, not to say protectiveness, which flies to the assistance of a notable piece of ass.

In the summer of 1962, this noble broad, late of an evening in June, entered Clay's Inn for the first time through the door that led to the parking lot. She was followed and attended by a human afterthought, albeit an afterthought well-pleased by the circumstances in which he found himself, named Joe Geoffrey, who played hockey for Dartmouth, drove a red MGA with a Chevy V-8, and answered to the name of Jeff Joefree. She wore a white sweater and white hiphuggers and she had a fine tan. The people in the saloon stopped talking by the time she was two paces inside the door. She paused for an instant—she did not think, to be sure, but her senses were in working order and she had the same instinctive gracefulness as the rest of magnificent animals. Then she moved her head slightly, as though to acknowledge the reaction, and moved toward a table. Geoffrey followed with the same foolish awkwardness as a runty handler displays in the guidance of a stakes-racing thoroughbred, simultaneously attempting to take credit for something he had nothing to do with, and trying to avoid showing his own awareness that he was hopelessly out of his class.

"Jesus," I said, from the corner of the bar where I stood frequently to talk with Miles, and I thought about the margin you need to have a girl like that, the best that money can buy. I cannot remember what Miles said, or even if he said anything. He may only have sat there, appraised her, and said nothing.

"I don't know if you can understand this or not," Barbara said that night at the airport, staring intently at the patterns she made on the shiny black table top by moving the base of her glass through the condensation that it left, then raising her eyes swiftly to convey sincerity by challenging mine, "but Miles is still a very attractive man. I suppose I know what you're thinking: King Kong would've been a bargain for me in the spot I was in. But Miles stood out in a crowd then and he still does. At least for me. Sexually he's a very attractive man. Forceful, you know? The trouble is it seems like that's all there is left, that force. He treats everything that way. It's really very frightening. Not as frightening as what you remember, maybe, not as damned . . . , well, I don't feel so helpless as I did then. But somehow I'm more afraid, more afraid of what's going to happen to me, happen to him. I *knew* what was going to happen then. I didn't know much, maybe, but I knew that at least. Now I don't know. It's worse, I really can't stand it."

What was going to happen then, in the summer of 1962, to Barbara, was not all that unusual. She was going to have a baby and she didn't have a husband. Some time during the summer she had gotten herself pregnant, with the customary assistance, to be sure, and on Labor Day night she conducted a scene at the Inn.

The gist of the plot was this: Joe Geoffrey had gotten her pregnant, and now refused to marry her. Not especially original. What made it memorable was the manner of the telling, so to speak: after a loud discussion with him, she arose from her chair and embarked upon a tour of the establishment. She interrupted each male in whatever he was doing—conversing, dancing, peaceably observing the departure of the summer by drinking too much—and explained the situation to him, quite earnestly. As may be imagined, this occasioned some stir, but Tiny and his sidemen were blowing their brains out and I was able to ignore it until she reached the end of her progress at the corner of the bar where Miles sat drinking and I had salvaged a moment for a smoke and a brief conversation with him. I was about to say that the remarks she made were pretty much as follows, but that is incorrect: I was stunned by what she said, and what followed, and the whole discussion is etched on my memory. It went exactly like this:

She said: "Excuse me. I got a little problem here, and nobody else seems to want to listen, so I thought I would tell you two gentlemen."

Miles somehow contrived to execute a courtly bow without interrupting his pouring of beer from bottle to glass. I believe my mouth
opened and remained gaping, but I am not sure.

"I been living with that rat over there all summer," she said, indi-
cating Geoffrey. I looked toward him. He was bent over the table,
doubtlessly reflecting on the colossal error of judgment that had
allowed him to bring her to the Inn. Other people were looking at him
also, some curiously, some less charitably, some enviously. Altogether,
probably one of his less comfortable experiences.

"His parents got this house down here, see? And they went to Europe
and he says, 'Come on, Barbara, let's go to the Cape.' so I came. That's
a laugh, isn't it? This isn't even the Cape. But I came all right.

"Now what it is," she said, "I got these big boobies, see?" Miles
nodded in agreement. I stared. "What's the matter," she said, "don't
you think I got big boobs?" She cupped them in her hands and lifted
them slightly, as though to call my attention to them. I gulped. I
believe I said I did think she had big boobs.

"Damn right," she said. "Now, that bastard over there, if there's
one thing he likes, it's big boobs. Which I got." She nodded.
"Absolutely. But I got something else, too. I got a nice ass and I got
the best cunt in North America." She stood back from the bar and
cupped that in her left hand. "Right here. See?"

"You certainly do," Miles said.

"I certainly do," she said, nodding again. "Know who told me that?
He did, that prick over there, him. Best cunt in North America." She
leaned over the bar and put her left arm around Miles and her right arm
around me. "Confidentially," she said, "he oughta know. He ate it a lot
of times, chewed it right up. Real hungry boy, that little bastard."

At this point Miles laughed appreciatively. She looked surprised.
Miles said: "Shouldn't wonder. Bet it was mighty tasty, too."

She was flattered by that. She stood back and rubbed it again.
"Well," she said, "I don't like to brag, of course. But I had lots of
compliments." *At* this Miles guffawed and put his arm around her.

"Oh sure," she said, brushing it away, "same as him, the little rich
shit. No candy for you, either. I come here to *talk*.

"The thing of it is," she said, confidential again, "I got this difficulty, see? See, I used to let him put something else in there, you
know? And now I'm pregnant. Just a little bit pregnant. Now, what
do I do now? Can't go home. Daddy beat the shit out of me. Can't
work—I'm gonna have a baby. So what do I do now?"

"Get married," I said stupidly.

"Right," she said, "absolutely right." She nodded again, several times. She was quite drunk, of course, and nearly hysterical. "Honest woman. Give the little bastard a name. Just what I said. But you know something? *He* won't do it. No *balls*." She pointed toward Geoffrey again, who seemed to hear her talking in the midst of the music and hung his head over his drink. "I said: No balls at all!" she said, much louder. I don't know how he stood it.

"No," she said, with combined bitterness and satisfaction, "no. *He's* not going to use a rubber. *He's* not going to miss his fun, take it out before the damage's done. Not *him*." She laughed, not prettily. "He's a big *man*. 'Hang on, kid, I'm gonna blow your ass off with this one.' But when the balloon goes up, where is he? Huh? In the bushes. hiding. *No balls at all*."

There was an interval while we all collected our breath. The rest of the louts in the Inn, give them credit, did their best to pretend not to listen. Although the men had heard most of it anyway.

"*He's* got a *career* to think of," she said. "Well, shit. He won't marry me. That's the end of that. So that's what I wanted to talk to you gentlemen about, nobody else got anything sensible to say. What do I do now? Go to a home?"

"Go to a locksmith," Miles said.

I venture to say that neither one of us, Barbara or I, had any idea of what Miles meant. When he explained, I did; I simply hadn't heard the word before. She appeared not to.

"Lockpicker?" she said. "What the hell do you mean?"

He patted her on the belly. "Get rid of it," he said. "You don't want the goddamned thing do you?"

She shook her head.

"So have an operation," he said. "Roto-rooter. Get rid of it. *Go to a fucking doctor and get rid of it.*"

She wasn't shouting any more when it got through to her. It was more of a whisper. "Abortion?" she said, as though he had recommended jumping off the world the next time it spun, "Abortion?"

"Yes, abortion," he said. "Dump it. You don't want it, do you?"

"No," she said.

"So get rid of it," he said. He lifted the glass and drank off half of a bottle of beer.

"Kill it?" she said.

"Right," he said, "or kill yourself. You're in a bind. It's either you," he squeezed her left breast twice, "or it," He patted her belly. "You kill it, or Daddy kills you. Take your choice."

"You're out of your mind," she said.

"Wrong," he said. "Is there any chance of getting a beer around this place?"

Fetching his beer positioned me so that I had to fetch several other beers, mix a couple of whiskey sours, pour a few Seven-and-Sevens, dispense some scotch, brush off the curious questions of the waitresses, and treat myself to a bourbon on the rocks. When I returned to the discussion, it was all over.

"The lady will have two shots of whiskey and four ounces of water," he said. "Make it Canadian Club." She was snuggled up against him now, and more or less smiling. I looked at her inquiringly .

"I might as well," she said, smiling as much as she could. "Why stop now?"

At the airport, she said: "It's a funny thing, isn't it? The thing that . . . the reason I married him, he was so *capable*. He always knew what to do. Now, now that's what scares me."

They had been married for about two years before I found out about it, and then I got the information by chance: the *Herald* published a picture of "Prominent Hub Businessman Miles Kendrick" attending a charity dance with his wife, Barbara. I had not understood his offer of advice, made that Labor Day night, to include marriage, so I was mildly interested in the news. But I had found better-paying jobs on the Cape for the summers between first and second, and second and third years of law school, and my closest contact with the town of Martin's Light, and the people who frequented Clay's Inn, had consisted of driving past it and them as rapidly as possible on Route Three. The picture in the paper of a calmly smiling man and a beautiful woman caused about the same reaction as those occasional brief items on the sports pages, reporting the sudden deaths of ballplayers idolized in childhood.

"I didn't go home after Miles took me to the doctor," Barbara said, that night at the airport. "I was fairly sick for a while, and it would've been hard to explain. Miles had an apartment in Providence and he let me stay there. This girl he knew—I think she was probably his mistress, or a former mistress, or something, came and stayed with me for a couple of weeks. Maybe she had had the same trouble I did, and Miles'd helped her. I don't really know. I felt so lousy I didn't really pay much attention to her.

"Anyway, Miles moved back about two weeks after I went to the doctor. School was starting. I don't know whether he expected me to move out and go home or not. Maybe he did. Maybe I just assumed that was what he had in mind. I was very upset, very depressed and all. I didn't want to leave and I didn't know where I could go. Certainly not back to Auburn. So the other girl moved out two or three days after he got there, and when he got home from school that night I was having hysterics again. He asked me what was the matter and I told him and so forth, and he just looked at me and said: 'Well, why don't you just stay here then?'

"I really couldn't believe it," she said. "He was so matter of fact about it. So I got this idea he was after the same kind of arrangement as Joe Geoffrey and I called him all kinds of names, did he think I was going to go through that again. And he said, No, he didn't mean that I *had* to stay any more than he meant I *had* to leave. I could do whatever I wanted. And if I stayed, I didn't have to go to bed with him or anything, he understood how I felt about that. Just keep things neat around the apartment, that was all, he'd appreciate that, but otherwise get back on my feet again and take as long as I needed to do it."

She smiled in the richness of hard-earned wisdom. "He's not only a very capable man," she said, "he's a very smart man. Of course the one thing nobody's ever tried on me was being kind, and halfway generous. Every other man I met used flowers and dinners and shows and big talk, but of course I wasn't in the same position with them. Anyway, Miles was smart enough to see what I really wanted, then anyway, and he gave it to me. I stayed there being sore for about two more weeks and then I stayed another week or two just enjoying not worrying or feeling sick, and I guess around the first of November or so I went out and brought home a diaphragm and started to earn my keep."

I must have permitted some expression to cross my face at this point.

"No, no," she said, "he didn't take it that way, and I didn't think of it that way myself. I *wanted* to sleep with him. I was grateful to him and he was kind to me and I wanted to do something for *him*, something he would enjoy. Well, outside of washing dishes and picking up around the place, there was really only one thing I could do, that I knew he would like. So I did it, and he did like it.

"It was his idea to get married," she said, "I never even, it didn't enter my mind, I was just so. . . . It was peaceful there. We were in bed one Saturday morning and he looked over at me and said: 'I don't see why we shouldn't get married today, do you? It's a nice day and all.'

"It wasn't a nice day," she said, smiling now in the happiness remembered. "It was a terrible day. It was cold and it was snowing and raining. But it was the nicest day I'd ever seen. I never expected to see another one as good. We drove down to Westerly and there was a justice of the peace there and we got married. I suppose it wasn't strictly legal, I don't know whether you had to have those blood tests there or not. But it was legal enough for me. I had a wedding ring and I was married to the man I was living with. He was good to me. When we were in New York last winter he took me to the Plaza to hear Lena Horne. Things were bad between us then, they have been for almost a year, and he only took me because the other men he was with were bringing their wives. It wasn't much fun. But she sang this song, 'Bill,' and I don't know why, it reminded me of that lousy day when we drove down to Westerly and go married and how happy I was then, how much I loved him, and I sat there and cried.

"He was embarrassed," she said. "He took me back to the hotel, made some kind of explanation or something, and I just hung onto him and cried. I don't think he had any idea what to think, what was wrong with me. I'm sure it didn't make things any better between us— it made him nervous about taking me places, and he doesn't like what he doesn't understand. He liked what I did for him that night, though. It's funny. That night I thought maybe we could make it work again, if I just tried hard enough and kept thinking about that Saturday back in Rhode Island. But the sun came out the next day, and it wasn't any different, just what it'd been before: rotten. He acted like nothing'd happened.

"I met Milton two weeks later in Hartford," she said. "Miles had some other business there, some investments he was promoting, and Milton was one of the people with money that came to the hotel to see what he had to say.

"You know something?" she said. "It's a funny thing. All he did for me, all the kindness, all the things he bought for me, the way he treated me in bed—I was a satisfied woman, Andy, always a satisfied woman—he never once said he loved me. I used to wonder, I used to get very affectionate and say it and say it myself, to him, to see if he would say it back, and he never did. The next day there'd be flowers, or dinner out or something. But he never said he loved me. Do you suppose he did?"

In the summer of 1966—the early part of July—I cleaned out the furnished room that had caged me through law school in Boston, packed the trunk of the weary Ford with the books I had bought second-hand with the money I had been unable to spend to replace the old clothes and the treacherous Westinghouse portable, and went back to the land on the edge of the Cape Cod Canal. I took another furnished room, this one in Martin's Light, not because of nostalgia for the place but because it was a better deal than I could find in Plymouth, where I was to practice law. Still I rejoiced to reach the Light again: the Ford had gotten sick in the course of travelling one hundred and three thousand miles, had developed a great thirst for oil, a worrisome clunk in the transmission, and several dents and much body rot in its New England winters. I was never entirely confident, when I set out, that it would get me where I was going, so there was a tendency to celebrate each time it did.

I was counting on another kind of temporal effect to rescue me from the foreseeable disaster that would arrive with the Ford's last gasp. I had agreed to practice law with an elderly pirate who collected fees in barrow-loads from probate work and the trials of auto torts. Craftiness glinting in his watery-blue eyes, glimmering in the expanded pores of his jowls, refracting in the lenses of his glasses, he told me he was getting too old to be going to court every day to contend against obvious perjury. Therefore, he said, he wanted me to take the trial work from his shoulders while he concentrated upon wills and deeds. All of this was true.

To make this offer palatable to me, he was willing to pay me thirty-five hundred dollars a year to start. If I proved to have passed the bar exam I had just taken—I would not know until the fall—and if my trial work satisfied him after a year of observing the results, he would then raise my pay to seven thousand dollars a year. He said he expected to give me a third of the practice within three years, another sixth in five years, and would continue as an equal partner until death retired him. These promises were not true, but I gauged his life expectancy, as opposed to his planned longevity, would produce the same or better effects within a comparable period. I therefore pretended a credulity which I did not have. It was, after all, the practice I was after, not an action for deceit.

Time and his cardiac insufficiency combined to justify my view. Late in 1967 both the interesting trial work and the profitable estate work passed into my hands almost entire, save for the inevitable loss of some few old ladies constitutionally unable to entrust their money for management to anyone under fifty. It was a satisfying development, and I notified the university that I would shortly commence to pay a little principal along with the interest on my debts.

I did not delude myself with the notion that I was set for life. The practice was not the bonanza Mr. Sparrow had implied. There was, to give the old rascal his due, a good deal of business. But little of it was substantial. The largest fees of dependable regularity were between one and three hundred dollars. Very seldom did a one- or two-thousand-dollar case come in. There were a lot of twenty-five-dollar time-wasters, letters and calls to be made to merchants on behalf of a number of impecunious old grouches convinced that the world was out to take advantage of them every time they bought a set of drapes or a tank of gasoline. The practice was clogged with petty collection matters. And there were a number of classic Cape Codders who spent the winters, apparently with Mr. Sparrow's encouragement, setting the law upon one another for various trespasses, violations of easements, and damages to property, real or imagined, which throttled office efficiency and brought in almost no money at all. The practice needed a good weeding.

I embarked upon this project very slowly. Inefficient as it was, Mr. Sparrow's practice was good for fourteen thousand a year, after expenses and the departure of the old. ladies. I salved my impatience by junking the Ford and buying a Riviera. It was a used Riveria, to be sure, a Sixty-five, but it was a Riviera nonetheless and it had nine years on the Ford. To the manifest dismay of Mr. Sparrow's girl, a lady of fifty-eight named Mrs. Mullens, I began a thoughtful inventory of the files, resolved to be patient, eat well, and wait for my opportunities.

In the twelve months immediately preceding that August night when I talked with Barbara at the airport, I grossed thirty-four thousand dollars, almost twenty-nine of which was mine to declare as gross income, and pay taxes upon. That amount included no more than three or four twenty-five-dollar matters: I simply refused to handle them, and sent the huffy old bastards off to see some younger tiger more needful of cash than of time. Less than five thousand dollars came from litigation fees, and two cases accounted for all of that. I farmed out the bulk of the tort work, persuaded that it no longer pays its way (because it eats up time spent fooling around in court, and nagging stupid witnesses), and partly because specializing in tort work is like aspiring to become a dinosaur: those who have battened off auto accidents have simply been too greedy, and the time is at hand when federal liability insurance, or automatic compensation, will demolish the whole hideous mare's nest and leave the vultures starving. I admit to a twinge of regret in cutting loose the trial work: it was fun, and the ham in me liked it. But I was not building a practice in which to have fun. I was building a practice in which to make money. At any rate, my pruning lost me better than three thousand dollars' worth of Mr. Sparrow's late business.

It also convinced Mrs. Mullens that I was at least improvident, certainly impertinent (to the litigous idiots who had never paid their way), and possibly insane. She came in one morning, whining, to bring up the subject of a pension which she claimed Mr. Sparrow had promised, explaining that while she disliked to bring it up, intelligent concern for her own security and an offer of a job at the courthouse—which included a pension—required her to leave unless we could reach an understanding. That was easy: Mrs. Mullens now works at the courthouse, and by her manner and helpfulness plainly indicates, each time I see her, that she harbors only pity for me.

She would entertain a different attitude if she knew about the thirty-four grand, all of which came into my hands by thorough knowledge of the files, and the lucky circumstance of meeting Miles Kendrick again.

In 1961, Edgar Sparrow had drated the Articles of Organization for the Hulsey Construction Company, Incorporated, Following normal practice, he used his office as the principal address of the corporation, thus saving Robert Hulsey and the other officers the trouble of sending legal documents which they would otherwise themselves have received from various governmental agencies.

Mrs. Mullens filed in the Hulsey folder a copy of the only statement sent to them by Mr. Sparrow, marked "paid" in the amount of one hundred and fifty dollars, dated June 11, 1961.

She also filed, obviously without interrupting Mr. Sparrow's intricate work in the protection of certain watercourses and accesses thereto, for penurious clients, a fascinating variety of later documents pertaining to the company. These were copies of writs, pleadings and suchlike, filed against Hulsey, recorded in various government agencies, and transmitted to Mr. Sparrow because he was attorney of record for the corporation. Clearly the company, shifting operations south of the Cape Cod Canal some time in 1962, had engaged other counsel, in addition to falling upon evil times. But Mrs. Mullens never knew that, and neither did Mr. Sparrow, so she kept on filing papers and no one the wiser.

In January of 1968, I went to Boston to check some pleadings in a tax case which involved an estate planned, if that is the word, by the late Mr. Sparrow. There wasn't much money in the trip, but Mrs. Sparrow had asked me to make it, as the agitated opponent of the Internal Revenue Service happened to be a cousin of hers. Grateful as I was to her, for having produced no heirs male of the practice I was then enjoying, and eager to keep her friendly to me, I made the excursion, and I met Miles Kendrick in the elevator at the federal building.

Between Labor Day night of 1962, and that sharp, wintry afternoon in 1968, Miles had completed his undergraduate studies at Brown and abandoned, halfway through, his graduate work in business administration at Boston College. He had gone into business for himself in Boston, working out of a tasteful office in a tall brown building on Milk Street and selling his services under the capacious title of Consultant. He had acquired several custom-made suits, improved his barbering by having his hair cut with a razor, and had, as I knew, achieved enough status to get touched for charity balls. He had also developed a moderate interest in the Hulsey Construction Company, Incorporated.

In the corridor outside the elevator he explained that he had come over to the courthouse to look up some papers in the office of the Trustee in Bankruptcy. He said an outfit on the Cape had petitioned for bankruptcy, and that he might be interested in bidding on some of its property. He was impressed by my knowledge of the Hulsey company.

"What it is, Andy," he said, "that group has some options I might be interested in buying for some people I have with venture capital. Now I want you to know right off the bat, I have several lawyers I do business with. I got lawyers in Maine, lawyers in New Hampshire, Vermont, Connecticut, Rhode Island. I got three lawyers I do business with in Boston alone. I got a lawyer on the Cape. But I just as soon give the business, some of the business anyway, to somebody I know. You want to represent me in this, you find a way to get me what I want, there could be some nice fat fees in it for you. I expect you to be discreet, of course."

I examined the Hulsey options which intrigued him, and I was not all that impressed. The property was mostly vacant land, situated some distance from the shorefront, inconveniently distant from existing population centers, indifferently served by secondary roads. It was hilly, uneven, and the soil, even in Cape terms, was of poor quality. The option prices were not unreasonable, but neither did they constitute bargains. I wrapped up my findings in a detailed memorandum and went up to Boston to see Miles.

"Of course you aren't going to lose money if you buy them up," I said. "Nobody loses money on Cape land. But these are recent options—the oldest was renewed only twice—and you can't bank on significant immediate appreciation. If you could, you probably would-n't have the chance to buy them: Hulsey would've sold them to keep the company afloat. They constitute most of the convertible assets of the company, because everything else is liened up. So you're going to find yourself pressed pretty hard to get a price on them even on a trustee's sale: if the options don't bring the money in, nobody's going to get anything."

"You're advising me not to buy them," Miles said.

I had the uncomfortable feeling that I was meddling in something that didn't concern me, always a disconcerting discovery when the recipient of the advice has paid you good money to give him the advice. I shaded the fact somewhat.

"Not exactly," I said. "Not at all, in fact. You told me you were interested in these options as an outlet for venture capital. I don't know who your principals are, and I'm not asking."

"Good," he said.

"But what little I know about venture capital," I said, "what little I know is that it generally consists of funds set aside for high-risk, high-gain investments. These options, in my estimation, may not qual-ify in either respect. The possibility of high gain just doesn't show. Hulsey paid a fair price for them, fairly recently, and the appreciation-inflation cycle isn't moving fast enough to've set up a potential, imme-diate, high gain. Of course the same holds true, in reverse, for the risk factor. Any money put into the options isn't likely to shrink, because no Cape land is very likely to shrink. Unless the bottom falls out of everything, in which case nothing's safe.

"But, no," I said, "I'm not telling you not to buy, or for that mat-ter, to go ahead and buy. I'm just telling you what I found out. You can make your own decision."

"I intend to," he said.

"There is one other thing," I said. "From what you told me, I gath-er you intend to acquire the options, if you do acquire them, by bid at the trustee's sale. That may not be the most attractive approach. Should I go on?"

"By all means," he said.

"This is a curious kind of a bankruptcy," I said. "There's no doubt the company's broke. It's behind on equipment rentals, purchase payments, subcontract payments, materials payments, and quite a few miscellaneous obligations: insurance, stuff like that. And there isn't any money to meet them.

"But when you add up all of the debts," I said, "you don't really come out with very much. Ten thousand dollars would put the outfit back on an even keel."

"Has it occurred to you that Hulsey knows that too?" Miles said.

"It has," I said. "But Hulsey couldn't borrow a bucket of hot coals in Hell. He's the principal stockholder. Okay. Personally he's hocked up to his jaw and than rehocked on top of that. I wouldn't be surprised if there was a personal bankruptcy around the corner for him. He'd give a lien on his wife if he could find somebody to take one. So he doesn't have any personal resources he could dump into the pot to save the company. He dumped them in a long time ago.

"As far as the corporation's concerned," I said, "that's pretty near dry too. No bank is going to advance him much on the options: there isn't enough margin. He paid about five and they aren't worth more'n eight now, if that. If the real estate market starts to skid, undeveloped land will skid the fastest. If it stays up, a rise in the prime rate could cut the conversion factor down right off. No bank is going to want that stuff bad enough to loan out American money, and even if you could find one, the deal would leave him about five grand short of even the merest solvency."

"Okay," Miles said. "You recommend?"

"At a trustee's sale," I said, "depending on what the appraisers say, you're going to pay about seven or eight thousand dollars for the right to purchase thirty-three thousand dollars' worth of land for twenty-five thousand dollars. But, if you refinance for stock and control, for, say, twelve thousand dollars, you get the options and Hulsey, who has plenty of construction know-how, never mind his financing blunders, plus whatever juice there is left in the outfit: good will, stuff like that."

"Which means the land costs me twelve thousand plus twenty-five thousand," Miles said. "It's the land. I want."

"I don't agree," I said. "The total outlay will be thirty-seven thousand, no question about that. But you'll get a fat tax loss out of the exchange, which even at capital loss rates will give you back about nine grand. Give your investors back nine grand. Which means your net outlay isn't thirty-seven, or even thirty-three: it's about twenty-nine. Now, that's a clear saving of four grand, and you get Hulsey, whatever's left of his company, and his know-how, for gratis."

"I should buy the stock," he said.

"You should at least negotiate for it," I said.

"*You* should at least negotiate," he said. "Negotiate."

In March of 1968, I made four thousand dollars for wrapping up the Hulsey deal. Similar transactions between then and August, when I talked with Barbara at the airport, brought an additional nineteen thousand dollars in fees from Miles. It was that activity which left me with twenty-nine thousand, net before taxes, when I saw her that night.

"Miles likes you," she said offhandedly. "He says you're smart."

"Thank him for me," I said, "I am." She smiled, and I did not add the rest: I am also profitable.

Detective Lieutenant Inspector Edward South of the Massachusetts State Police wore a Harris tweed sport coat, a blue and white striped button-down shirt with a moderate roll collar, a foulard tie of medium width, sharply creased charcoal-gray slacks, and highly polished black loafers. He was completely at ease in my office, sitting with his left leg crossed over his right to make a desk for his spiral notepad. He asked intelligent questions with the sort of politeness which suggests the possibility of alternative rudeness, should the politeness go unappreciated and the questions go unanswered.

Lieutenant South came to my office, by appointment, to acquire some information about Robert O. Hulsey, 41, found shot to death on January 31, 1969, in the converted house-trailer he used as a mobile construction office. The trailer was parked at the time some three and one-half miles southwest of the Mid-Cape Highway, in Barnstable.

Lieutenant South focussed the inquiry. "It looks pretty much like a suicide," he said. "The body was in the head. The feet were sticking out the door. There was a twelve-gauge shotgun on the floor, one expended round in the chamber. It appears that he stuck the barrel in his mouth and pressed the trigger."

"Jesus," I said.

"Jesus for sure," Lieutenant South said. "You were the attorney of record for the company, correct?"

"Correct," I said.

"See him recently?"

"Last week," I said. "Thursday. We had some contracts for excavation on a development in Sandwich. I took them down to see if he agreed with the terminology."

"What time was that?" the Lieutenant said.

"Middle of the afternoon," I said. "Three-thirty, four. Somewhere around in there."

"That the time you generally did business?" he asked.

"Wasn't any time, really," I said. "When I had something for him to look at, I went down. Some times it was in the morning, some times I went in the evening."

"Evening," the Lieutenant said. "How late?"

"Seven or so," I said. "Never much later'n that. He liked to get home and see his family. He lived in Wareham. It was a pretty fair ride."

"He go to work early?" the Lieutenant said.

"He could've," I said. "I don't, so I don't really know. He used to talk about it, say he was up with the sun. I really don't know."

"Was he depressed about anything when you saw him?" the Lieutenant said.

"Not in the slightest," I said. "If he was, he certainly didn't show it. Happy as a pig in shit."

"Things going pretty well in the company, were they?"

"Absolutely," I said. "This happened a year ago, I could understand it, maybe. The outfit was going bankrupt. But we got it back on its feet and then that new feeder road came through and everything was roses."

"He own most of the stock, did he?" the Lieutenant said.

"Not most of it," I said. "About a third. He sold control of the company little over a year ago. Matter of fact, I represented the buyer, fellow up in Boston named Miles Kendrick. Still do, in fact."

"Mr. Kendrick owns the rest?" the Lieutenant said.

"For investors, yes," I said. "They don't take an active part in the business."

"Just collect their profits," the Lieutenant said.

"They expect to," I said. "It's mostly paper profits at this point. When the development's finished, the shopping center, so forth, then they may collect. Of course this changes everything, Bob shooting himself to death and all."

"That's the way it looks," the Lieutenant said. "What was Hulsey's share of the company worth?"

"God," I said, "I don't know. I'd have to run a balance, get the property appraised. I really don't know."

"Roughly," the Lieutenant said.

"Don't hold me to it," I said. "I could be way off. Somewhere between ninety-five and a hundred and fifteen thousand, I suppose."

"Who gets it?" the Lieutenant asked.

"Well, that depends on what you mean," I said. "I can answer this because I drew the agreement. His widow gets the value of his share, whatever it's appraised at."

"Who pays?" the Lieutenant said.

"Insurance," I said. "The agreement's funded with insurance. Ordinary re-buy agreement, funded by insurance."

"Who gets the stock?" the Lieutenant asked.

"The company," I said. "It goes to the company."

"I'm not a lawyer," the Lieutenant said. "What does that do?"

"Nothing, really," I said. "Just prevents strangers from coming into the corporation and screwing it all up. It's a standard agreement."

"Doesn't it increase the value of everybody else's stock?" the Lieutenant asked.

"Well, sure," I said. "Yes, of course. It has to."

"Help me out here, then," he said. "The way I see it, Kendrick and his people owned two-thirds of something worth somewhere around three hundred and thirty thousand dollars, until shortly after sunrise yesterday, correct?"

"Assuming that's what an appraiser would've said, yes," I said.

"Now some insurance company's going to buy a third of that stock, the third Kendrick and his friends didn't own, and the company gets that, correct?"

"Correct," I said.

"So," the Lieutenant said, with just a suggestion of triumph, "Kendrick and his friends now own all of the stock outstanding in a business worth somewhere around three hundred and thirty thousand dollars, correct?"

" Correct," I said.

"Suicide doesn't affect the insurance," the Lieutenant said.

"No," I said. "Not at all."

Miles had been shocked when I called him to tell him about Hulsey's death. "Holy shit," he said, "you have got to be shitting me. Why the hell would he want to do a thing like that?"

Barbara Harkness Kendrick filed for divorce in the Probate Court of Suffolk County on March 3, 1969. The *Herald* ignored the matter, insofar as I was able to determine. The *Globe* printed a short squib in the first edition. The *Record* carried two short paragraphs. I called Miles on the afternoon of the fourth.

"It looks as though things are working out pretty much as we expected," I said. "I doubt anybody noticed."

"Yeah," he said. "Well, that's something. Like the doctor telling the patient the operation went beautifully but he's going to die anyway. Ah, what the hell, it's just a salvage job anyway,"

In the course of the evening we spent talking at the airport, the preceding August, I had finally gotten around to making my speech to Barbara, telling her that I couldn't represent her in the divorce because Miles was already a client.

"Couldn't you just handle the whole thing for both of us?" she asked. "I don't think Miles is going to like it very much, because he doesn't like losing any *thing* that belongs to him. But what can he do? A girl I know, I got to know her because she was married to this man in Worcester that invested some money with Miles, Ginny Samuels, her husband is a dentist and he makes a lot of money too, she got a divorce last year and it wasn't any trouble. The divorce, I mean. Sammy didn't want any publicity about it, you know? He was running around with his receptionist and she was married too. So I don't think he even had a lawyer. Couldn't you do that? I'll tell Miles I want a divorce and then you just do whatever it is you have to do to get me one, and that'll be the end of it."

I reported this to Miles and he asked me what I thought of it. "There's something in what she says," I said. "There really isn't much percentage in you fighting this thing; divorce decrees are very seldom denied anyway, and all you'll gain by opposing it is raise a lot of dust and get those stuffy bastards in the banks all tense about your credit standing. There aren't any children to worry about, so you don't have that on your mind, and I wouldn't expect her to ask for very much support or anything. Not that you couldn't come up with a decent settlement anyway, but she wants her freedom more'n anything else."

"She say anything about property?" he asked.

"No," I said. "I warned her I was your lawyer and I could use what she said, against her, but she said she didn't care, there didn't have to be any secrets. She said she's in love with another man and you're not in love with her any more and she wants to take her clothes and her jewelry and probably her car, although he sells cars and she probably wouldn't even insist on that if you pushed her, and go marry him. She said she's not mad at anybody. She just wants her life back." I saw no point in reporting what she had said about being afraid of him at the time I didn't place much credence in her fears, nor did I think them important. Relating them to Miles would only have caused him to get angry, which might have interfered with his judgment about the divorce action, and persuaded him to order me to do something that would make it messy.

"For a fucking car salesman," he said. It was one of the few conversations we had which left me with the feeling that he was not fully in control of events. "I know the son-of-a-bitch, you know. I introduced them. Stocky little cocksucker from Hartford, sells cars. Tries to make himself look taller by having a lot of hair. Not a bad guy, really, must do pretty well because he's got a lot of money, from what I hear. He put some of it into a thing I had working out in the western part of the state last spring, and then of course when I found out he was seeing Barbara I made him take it back. But he came up with fifty thousand pretty easy. He also came up with my wife pretty easy too, the easiest thing in the world to take a man's wife away from him if she feels like she's bored or something. Except I'm damned if I see how Milton Mallus could cure anybody's boredom. No imagination."

"Look, Miles," I said, "I like to think I'm your friend as well as your lawyer."

"One of my lawyers," Miles said absently.

"One of your lawyers," I said, "one of your friends. I hope I'm not the only one of those you got either. So, speaking as a friend, and I know it's easier said than done, try not to take it so hard. Isn't anything you can do about it anyway. These things happen. Who the Christ knows why a woman does something? Half the time she doesn't know herself."

"*I* know," Miles said. "There isn't any doubt in my mind. She's got a hot swamp, is all. Any brains that broad has got are right in there between her legs."

"Okay," I said, "assuming you're right, what does that leave you with? Is there any way you can change her mind? No. The only thing you can do, other than go along with the divorce, is stir up a lot of crap. And then you'll get hit with the divorce anyway. You may as well face it, if what she's got on her mind is getting loose to marry Milton Mallus, there isn't anything you can do about it."

Miles's offices are panelled and dark, filled with leather chairs and heavy mahogany desks and tables, hung with deep, soft, maroon drapes. In the late afternoon in the incipient springtime, a residual pale light came in the window behind him, and left most of his face in shadow. I remember that, now, that I couldn't see his expression when he spoke. I also recall, very clearly, what he said: "There's nothing I can do about her getting loose," he said. "I agree with that much."

At my suggestion, Barbara had retained a young lawyer named Gerry Winters to bring the divorce libel. Gerry was in practice in Plymouth also, clean-cut and hard-pressed, using an appointment as Assistant District Attorney to the same general purpose I had had in mind in going to work for Mr. Sparrow. There was a difference, of course: the office of the District Attorney doesn't die and leave you in default possession of an adequate practice. But it does give you a certain amount of exposure, not to mention trial experience, and insurance companies are fond of that combination when selecting county lawyers to defend civil accident cases. I liked Gerry. He was hardworking and unimaginative, and he gratefully accepted the referrals I sent him, representing people whose interest in conducting litigation was greater than the potential rewards of that litigation to the litigator. I explained the circumstances to him, after Barbara had retained him, and he collected an easy four hundred and fifty dollars, after expenses, for doing what everyone involved in the case wanted done. The decree came down on May 5. 1969.

July Fourth was a Friday in 1969. Milton Mallus, sometime around noon on the third, left his agency in East Hartford and drove down to his summer place at Westerly, Rhode Island. The trip took him the better part of the afternoon. He arrived just before five. Barbara's claret Thunderbird Landau—the one Miles had given her—was parked in the circular drive at the black front door of the white brick, ten-room house. She was just emerging from a long soak in the tub when she heard the tires of the gun-metal Continental Mark III crunching the white gravel drive. She wrapped a bath-towel around her body and a hand-towel around her hair. She went to the window and watched him get out of the car, close the door, look up and wave to her, and start in the direction of the trunk.

In my office at seven-thirty on the morning of July seventh, I did my best to concentrate and blearily asked her what she did next.

"I hadn't seen him for three weeks," she said. "I hurried to dry myself off. Then I put on a robe and went downstairs to meet him."

"Did anyone see this," I said.

"The housekeeper," she said, "Mrs. Hope."

"How did she feel about you being there?" I said.

"What do you mean?" she asked.

"I mean I'd like to know what she's going to say if the prosecutor turns her up as a witness," I said.

"She was very nice to me," Barbara said. "She always liked me. She knew I was divorced and that we were going to get married. She's been with Milton's family for ages."

"Of course you weren't divorced," I said. "You had several months to go before you were divorced."

"She understood that," Barbara said.

"I hope the grand jury does," I said, "if this goes to the grand jury, that is. What happened then?"

"Do you want me to tell you what we did that night?" she said.

"Not particularly," I said. "The grand jury may be interested, but I'm not. Did you hear anything that night?"

"Just fireworks," she said.

"Skip the humor," I said. "Tell me what happened."

"I'm serious," she said. "They had fireworks over the water. We could hear them exploding from the bed, and we got up and went out on the balcony. We could see the ones that went off in the air."

"Some time that night," I said, "did you go to sleep?"

"Yes," she said.

"All right," I said. "And then you woke up, some time the next morning."

"Eight-fifteen," she said.

"You remember the time," I said.

"The alarm clock went off," she said.

"Who set the alarm clock," I said.

"Milton," she said.

"Why," I said.

"Because the New York Times and the Wall Street Journal get to the drugstore at eight-thirty and he likes to read them at breakfast," she said.

"You woke up too," I said.

"Yes," she said. "It's pretty hard to sleep when there's an alarm clock sounding off in your ear."

"Then what happened?" I said.

"I was sort of half asleep," she said. "Do you want me to go through everything?"

"Everything," I said.

"He got up and went into the bathroom. I could hear him brushing his teeth. Then I heard the razor."

"You heard the razor," I said. "Gilette or what?"

"I don't know what kind," she said. "It's electric. I heard the razor,"

"The shaver," I said.

"The shaver," she said. "He came back into the room."

"Did you hear him or see him?" I asked.

"Both," she said. "I already told you, I was about half-asleep. I watched him getting dressed and then he went out of the room and I rolled over and went back to sleep."

"What was he wearing?" I said.

"Grey slacks, yellow sport shirt. I couldn't see his shoes."

"Are you sure you went back to sleep?" I said.

"No," she said. "I was drowsy. I'm not sure. I stayed in bed."

"Did he say anything?"

"He said something," she said, "I'm not sure what."

"Try to remember," I said.

"Oh for Christ's sake," she said, "he said: 'Sleep some more,' or something like that. I was half asleep. I wasn't paying attention." Then she began to sob, great racking weeping that made her bend over almost double in the chair and groan with the effort of it, weeping so severe that she sounded several times as though she would vomit, wrenching noises made when she gulped for air. " I don't remember, I don't remember," she said, "I don't remember, I don't remember. I don't know why I went down there. I don't know I don't know I don't know."

I was unable to reach Miles until late in the morning. "I know," he said, "I already heard. You want me to say I'm sorry?"

"I want you to say you don't know anything about it," I said.

"I don't know anything about it," he said. "Okay?"

"I want you to say it's all right for me to represent her if somebody decides to have a grand jury on this thing," I said.

"It's not okay," he said. "Get somebody else. Get that kid that handled the divorce for her, what's his name, Winters? He's a pretty smart kid, let him handle it."

"He's a prosecutor," I said, "He can't do that."

"He can do it in Rhode Island," Miles said.

"No he can't," I said. "He can't do it anywhere. And besides, he's not a member of the bar down there."

"Neither are you," Miles said

"I can find somebody to enter an appearance," I said.

"No," Miles said. "You're *my* lawyer. She can find her own."

"Do you expect to need a lawyer in this thing?" I said.

"I expect the unexpected," he said. "Now I got some people in here with me. Call me later if you have to."

When she had calmed down—I gave her some water and then, because she asked for something stronger, a hooker of J.W. Dant from the quart in the lower left-hand drawer of my desk—we went on.

"I'm going to have to call Miles about this, you know," I said.

"Sure," she said. "You're just my friend. You're his lawyer. I know that."

"He left the room," I said.

"He went down the stairs," she said. "I heard the front door open and shut. I heard him walking on the gravel. I heard him open the door of his car."

"You heard him open a car door," I said.

"I heard him open a car door," she said.

"Then what," I said.

"I heard the door shut," she said. "I heard, I heard what you hear when you turn on the ignition, when somebody else turns on the ignition. Just a little. Then I heard it go off."

"What the hell was it?" Miles asked, when I talked to him on the eighth. "Does anybody know?"

"Four sticks of dynamite wired to the coil," I said. "At least that much. Those Continentals are built like goddamned tanks, and it blew the thing all to shit. At least four sticks."

"He didn't feel anything then," Miles said. He waited an instant. "Well?"

"I wouldn't know" I said. "I wasn't in the car."

"Neither was I," Miles said.

"Neither was Barbara," I said. "It's just a good thing she wasn't in her car, either."

"Why is that?" Miles said.

"There were four sticks wired to the coil on her car, too," I said.

She sat there sobbing again in my office. "I went racing down the stairs," she said, "I was, I didn't have anything on and I went down there and it was awful, just *awful*. There was blood and smoke and this terrible smell, and the whole front of the house was black, and something was burning, it was terrible, and there wasn't a sound, you know? Not a sound. Just the sound of the fire burning."

"You might as well face it," I said, "Sooner or later you're going to have to. Do you have any idea who did this?"

"The police already asked me," she said dully, "I told them."

"What did you tell them?" I said.

"I told them Miles did it," she said. "Miles or somebody that was working for him. I told them Miles did It."

On the fourteenth of July, I received a call from Detective Lieutenant Inspector Edward South.

"Do you still represent Miles Kendrick?" he said.

The call did not surprise me. I knew enough about criminal law, and human nature, to know what the police would do with a statement from the ex-wife that said the ex-husband had killed the lover. And if nothing more, I was relieved that I had predicted it to Miles. "Forget it," he had said. "I had nothing to do with it. I'm not sorry, but I had nothing to do with it." I had advised him to start feeling sorry, too.

"Yeah," I said, "I represent Miles Kendrick."

"I got a warrant for him," the Lieutenant said. "Does he surrender, or do I pick him up?"

"He'll surrender," I said. "What court and what time?"

"Barnstable, of course," the Lieutenant said, "have him at the barracks at nine for prints and pictures."

"Barnstable," I said, "Barnstable? What the Christ is the charge?"

"Conspiracy to commit murder," the Lieutenant said in a weary voice. "Him and three other guys. Two of them principals, one accessory after."

"I don't understand," I said. "Are these, is this a fugitive warrant?"

"Not unless he runs," the Lieutenant said. "I'm willing to take your word he won't."

"Look," I said, "I'll have him where you say, when you say. But tell me something: how the hell did you get jurisdiction?"

There was a prolonged silence on the line. I heard Lieutenant South taking a deep breath. "Mister," he said, "I make it a rule never to give any kind of advice to anybody that I'm arresting, or that's giving advice to somebody that's going to get arrested. But in your case I'm gonna make an exception. We got jurisdiction because the job was done in Barnstable County, that's how. Robert O. Hulsey was murdered in this county. That is about the best kind of jurisdiction there is."

In my office, a week before, I had stared at Barbara for a long time without saying anything. "I hope you realize what you've done," I said. "You've just about guaranteed that your husband, your ex-husband, is going to have to stand trial for murder. What you've done, even if he's acquitted, is going to ruin him, ruin his life. No matter how It turns out, no matter what happens, Miles is going to have to stand trial now, for killing a man. And it's going to be the end of him."

She looked up from her handkerchief with an expression of disbelief on her face. "You don't like him very much," I said, "I keep trying to understand that. He grew away from you. He didn't pay enough attention to you. He wouldn't say he loved you. Okay. But you forgot some other things too. He bailed you out when you were plain down and out. He married you when he didn't have to. You told me yourself, he was always generous. And the most generous thing he could have done, the most generous thing any man could do, he did: He let you go, he consented to give you your freedom, because you wanted to marry another man. He did everything he could to make you happy. And it hurt him, hurt him as deeply as anything could ever hurt a man. Miles is not a demonstrative man. He doesn't talk about his feelings. Not even to me. But he let you go, swallowed his pride, absorbed the punishment you gave him in exchange for being kind to you. And this is the thanks you give him. I hope it makes you feel better. I hope to Christ you understand what you've done. I hope you never sleep again."

I do not have a clock in my office. I felt obliged to stare her down. Therefore I could not look at my watch, and thus I do not know how long we sat staring at each other, neither of us able to comprehend what the other believed. I have not seen her since that day, and, honestly, I am not anxious to. In the softest, most wondering voice I have ever heard, she said: "You asshole, you everlasting asshole." It was not until South called that I began to understand.

THE FIRST
OF THE YEAR

AT the intersection of Standish and Sumner Streets, a block away from Devonshire, the remains of Miles Kendrick were attended in the antiseptic chill darkness with calm professionalism by several men who knew from long experience what they were doing, and consequently did not vomit.

The trunk of the body lay on the black, perforated rubber mat on the marble floor of the entryway to Five Standish Street. The doors of the building, and the wall surrounding them, are glass. The lights of the first floor corridor had been turned on, and provided white light for the men who worked around the body. One stooped near the left shoulder; one stood erect just inside the entryway, using a putty knife to scrape the marble wall at eye level and above. He transferred the material which he scraped into a white business envelope. Behind the plate glass doors a black man, wearing grey workclothes, stood with his mouth open and watched the men outside, moving around the body.

The legs, resting on the top step, were bent at the knee as though the body had been toppled onto its right side from a position of prayer. The right foot rested on the top step, and the left foot lay on top of it. The cuffless trousers, well-creased, lay slack at the back of the knees and bulged slightly at the lower edge of the buttocks. The tails of the raincoat, dull gold, flapped in the occasional wind, exposing the seat of the pants, the faint bulge of something in the left rear pocket, and the tails of the suitcoat underneath. At the curb there was a cruiser with the motor running and the shortwave radio gabbling:

the blue dome light tinted the body and the men around it on the steps. When the radio was silent, the sound of the putty knife on the marble—harsh and now and then screeching as the detective got the wrong angle—was the dominant sound. The men around the body did not talk very much, and when they did, they murmured. The newspapermen, twelve to fifteen feet away, spoke very little.

The torso of the body was twisted slightly at the pelvis, so that it rested on the right half of the chest. The left forearm was beneath it. The right bicep emerged from the torso at a very slight angle. The forearm was at right angles to the upper arm. The right hand, clenched, touched the polished marble wall of the doorway, at the heel of the palm. The hand bent upwards, at right angles to the wrist. The second and third knuckles of each finger rested against the wall. The man with the putty knife finished his work on the outer edge of the wall; he stepped carefully over the top half of the body, and his right foot skidded slightly when he put it down. The man crouching near the left shoulder said: "Nice going shithead." He was using tweezers. He collected small objects from the upper part of the body, from the rubber mat, and from the crevice where the floor and the wall came together. He put them into a white envelope. The man with the putty knife did not answer.

A recognizable portion of the neck remained. It showed the edge of a well-tapered haircut. Above that was the red, bleeding meat. It was the shape of a genuine sponge, irregularly globular. It was striped and blotched with grey brains. It showed shattered tips of white bone. There were no ears.

In the morning Detective Lieutenant Inspector Edward South of the Massachusetts State Police arose seasonably seventy miles from Boston, and Five Standish Street, and went out in the moderate winter air of Cape Cod to treat himself to a newspaper on the morning of New Year's Day. He bought it from the machine at the door of the doughnut shop and did not open it until he had gotten inside and ordered his coffee and a cruller. Under two bylines on the third page he found the story to go with the headline: "Hub Financier 60th Gangland Victim."

"Prominent Boston financier Miles Kendrick, 31, of Weston, became the Hub's first murder victim of the year early today when, according to police, two men gunned him down as he was leaving his plush offices at Five Standish Street. Police said his head was torn off with a single blast at close range fired from a shotgun.

"Detective Lt. Maurice Shea said a passerby reported seeing a heavyset man, well over six feet tall, running from the scene. Police said the witness reported that the assailant was carrying a rifle or shotgun.

"Kendrick, instrumental in a number of large-scale land-development projects on Cape Cod, and elsewhere in New England, rose quickly to the top of his trade until he was indicted and tried last year for conspiracy to commit murder. He was charged in connection with the murder of Robert O. Hulsey, found dead last January 31 in Barnstable. Hulsey, a well-known Cape contractor, was involved with a company owned by Kendrick. Kendrick was found innocent of the crime, as were two other defendants.

"Kendrick's ex-wife, Barbara, was involved last year in a coroner's inquest in Rhode Island, probing the bombing death of Milton Mallus of East Hartford, Connecticut. Mallus was killed when his late-model luxury car exploded on the morning of July 4th outside the oceanfront house they were sharing at Westerly, Rhode Island. Early today, Rhode Island police said the Mallus investigation was still open."

Eddie South folded the paper and placed it beside his plate. He accepted a refill of coffee from the waitress.

"Looks like a nice day," she said.

"It does," he said, "it certainly does. So far it looks like a pretty good year."

SLOWLY NOW THE DANCER

SLOWLY now, the dancer began to turn in the morning light that filtered through the old thin curtains of the northern windows in the upstairs bedroom, the small white china figure in the pink tutu pirouetting atop the music box as Emerson lifted it from the dressing table. The first few notes of "Lara's Theme" from *Dr. Zhivago* were clear enough, though played too slowly, but the mechanism missed one note before it went on. Emerson supposed that dust had gotten into the strikers. Leaning on his crutches, he held the box in his left hand, and wound it with his right. He held it level for an instant, as the tempo of the music increased, and the ballerina turned more rapidly.

Then, because the crutches hurt his armpits, he put the music box back on the pale green dressing table, and turned with difficulty on the small green shag rug, the rug bunching up under the crutch tips, and left the dancer slowing down in the mirror, the music petering out under the molded tin ceiling. Still unused to the crutches, after two weeks with his left leg in a cast to the top of his thigh, he grunted with each step as he passed the brass bed with the faded pink comforter, and the nightstand with the small glass lamp, the jelly glass, decorated with small blue flowers, next to it on the doily, still half full of water. There was an empty white chamberpot under the bed. He supposed that in its way, the linoleum was more dangerous than the rug; while it did not bunch, it was slipperier, and there were fairly large cracks in it. Aloud he said, although he was alone: "Now all I need to do is sprain my ankle."

The floor at the top of the stairs was safer ground, although it was uneven. It was wide planking, painted brown, dull in the light from the thirty-watt bulb that hung from the fixture. Emerson paused, partly to rest, partly to deliberate whether to avoid wastefulness by shutting the light off, or to commit wastefulness but at the same time risk his remaining good health by descending the steep wooden stairs in the windowless dimness. There was light enough in the room where he had spent the night, the old white coverlet thrown back where he had left it when he struggled out of bed, but it was not where he needed it. "And she wouldn't approve of that, either," he said, amusedly aware that he had evidently reached the age when people started talking to themselves, "but if it's good enough reason to leave the bed unmade, it's good enough to leave the light on."

Turning to his right, he nearly lost his balance at the top of the stairs, but regained it as he pitched forward, dropping the right crutch and seizing the wall. The crutch clattered down the brown stairs, and he wobbled a bit, scared and suddenly perspiring, before he was able to decide that, on balance, it was probably safest to trust the old pipe railings. He put his weight on the left crutch and bent forward to an angle that he found awkward. Then, cautiously, he released his grip on the wall and grabbed the right railing with his right hand. Bent over, he moved the left crutch forward, and dropped it down the stairs, quickly reaching the left railing. Bent almost double now, he hoisted the left foot as high as he could, prayed fervently that the railings would bear his weight, and hopped down one step on his right foot.

"Damned railing's too low," he said. He continued to sweat.

Down in the kitchen, the telephone began to ring. He pictured it on the red linoleum counter next to the grey slate sink, shoved back just out of inconvenient reach because she had insisted upon concealing the cord behind, the red cookie coffee, and flour tins. "Shut up, you son of a bitch," Emerson said. He negotiated another step. The telephone continued to ring. In a way, he was grateful: the frustration of listening to it, helplessly, made him angry, which lessened his fear of the stairs, and thus his awareness that he was a damned fool to have climbed them in the first place. And it was a party line; whoever was calling would get someone to talk to.

Emerson had arrived at the ivory house shortly after ten o'clock the night before, his entire body stiff from the drive because it was difficult to shift his position with the cast on, the muscles of his back sore because the seats of the rented Pontiac Le Mans lacked the lateral and lower back support that he was used to, and could not be adjusted for rake. Out of habit, and recollection, he had reduced his speed to a crawl before turning off the two-lane black-top, highly crowned, into the dip created when the paving job came out higher than the old dirt road had been, at the edge of the pipe that covered the drainage ditch. Then, uncertain whether the Pontiac had better clearance than the Jaguar had had—he had nearly torn the oil pan out on that approach, thirteen years before; she had watched the performance from the screened-in porch, and had been clearly disappointed when he had gotten up from inspecting the under-carriage and announced that nothing was wrong—he crept up the steep drive in the gravel ruts, taking no chances.

Once on the level ground in the starlit darkness, Craig Emerson, thirty-six and profoundly annoyed, struggled out of the silver Pontiac. First he extricated the crutches from the back seat; he had pulled over, a few miles out of Boston, and thrown them into the back seat, after negotiating a few turns and curves in his accustomed manner and finding that the car leaned so much that the crutches on the phony bucket seat first slid to hit the passenger door, and then, on the next, slid back to hit him. He put the crutches against the open door of the car. Then, swinging himself out of the seat, he had stood up, pivoted on the heel of the cast, and clapped his hands upon the cold, wet vinyl roof of the car. He stretched luxuriously, for what seemed like three or four minutes, but must have been much less (Lenore had always said he had no concept of time) because he desperately needed to go to the bathroom.

Then, with most of his bones once again in proper alignment, he had taken the crutches, backed away from the car, and shut the door, turning off the interior lights.

He had needed some time to accustom himself to the darkness. Mrs. Shaw, from up the road, had offered, when he called his grandmother's best friend to report that Jenny Irwin had achieved her wish, to stop by the house and open it up, turn on the lights and make things comfortable for him. But he remembered that she, too, was old, had trouble getting about, and was probably as depressed as Jenny had been when she received word that another friend had died; he was also sitting at his desk when he called, and felt sufficiently in control of his life to forget that he also, for the time being, had trouble getting around. He had declined.

So, in the darkness, he hung on the crutches, allowed his eyes to adjust to the darkness, felt in his pockets for the housekeys, gazed at the dim shape of the garage and shed—he did not even consider putting the car into the garage; he remembered the trouble, years before, overcoming the resistance of the rollers rusted on the tracks of the sliding door, and the extreme disapproval Jenny Irwin had displayed at the spectacle of her grandson violating her domain by attempting to open what he had called, not realizing that she was within earshot (as she always was), the "goddamned fucking thing"—and half expected, when he turned to look at the porch where the ivy climbed on the old screens, to find her standing there, silently, looking at him.

She had been a big woman, with the ranginess and large bones of a cowpuncher, but her flesh had gone to seed. She wore flowered silk dresses, and sensible black shoes, and, late in life, she took to having her hair tinted blue, probably because she had seen other ladies, of her approximate vintage, with similar treatments, on television.

It had been a choice between watching Saturday night movies in black and white, or getting another Sony, when she visited, because, as she had explained, she had gone to considerable expense that she could not afford, to bring the cable into her own house in order to watch Lawrence Welk, and seeing his show in color was one of her favorite treats. Until the second Sony, Craig Emerson had seen a lot of ladies with blue hair on Saturday nights, and missed the first parts of several movies which had rather interested him. But he had supposed that was fair, because Jenny Irwin had invariably retired by 9:30 P.M., two hours before her regular bedtime, whenever the movie turned out to be one of his favorites: one about submarines. She had never smiled very much; only when she had gotten the best of someone, in some small matter, did the corners of her lips curve upward. She was best at suggesting that someone, acting in all innocence, and with perfect motives, had somehow sullied her earth.

He remembered, standing there suspended on the crutches, in the clear darkness, how she had reacted to Lenore, when out of duty they had stopped en route to Montreal, in 1963. The pursed lips, and behind the plain-framed glasses, the cold blue eyes of the machine-gunner. Lenore with her long legs and her short skirt had emerged from the Jag with her golden hair shining, her mouth smiling—he had failed to prepare her—and Jenny Irwin stood there looking at his new wife, the ivy curling about the warped, dull-red screen door as though to camouflage the old lady, like a gigantic, angry rabbit, determined to make up for all the tiresome foolishness reputed to the species by the Easter Bunny. "I'm very glad to meet you, my dear, of course," Jenny had said, and kissed her on the cheek. "Like Dracula," Lenore had said. We didn't horse around that night, Craig Emerson remembered. Those old beds up there creak like hell. It's a wonder she let us both sleep in the same one.

Accustomed by then to the darkness, Emerson with some concern had made his way around to the back of the car. Bracing his right hand on the trunk lid, wondering why he had permitted Molly to put his bag in there, wondering how the hell he was going to carry it, if he ever got it out.

He managed it. He got the first of the two handles of the bag in his mouth, slammed the trunk shut, got the keys out of the lock, released the bag to the surface of the trunk—very carefully, so as to leave the handle free for his teeth—and took up the crutches again. Then, lurching with the bag in his teeth, he had made his way across the slippery grass, up the short, slippery, brick walk, up the alarmingly flexible, green wooden steps, to the door.

The latch was difficult to turn, and the bag had blocked what little vision he had of it, in the dark. He had been forced to drop the bag again, then work the latch painstakingly until he coaxed it into opening. It had been difficult to get the door swung around him, wide enough to enter. He went into the porch, dropping the crutches on the dark-red planking in the dark, remembering where the tulip-shaped, green cane chairs were, the green, awning-covered daybed, locating himself by memory. Holding on to the shelf that extended around the porch at waist height, he lowered himself, the bad leg thrust out in back of him, fetched the bag in, turned, and clumsily threw it toward the house door. He had hobbled toward it, remembering the summers he had spent lying on the daybed, reading *The Adventures of Sherlock Holmes*, drinking Coca-Cola and eating Jenny's small, hard doughnuts, and the times that he had bounded up the three porch stairs, raced across the porch, and thrust open the door, to be reprimanded by her, for making too much noise.

And now, he had thought, when I'm finally forced to proceed at   a sensible rate, she's not around to congratulate me. Which also suits her.

The door lock had resisted the old key also, but capitulated at last in the darkness, and he was inside, feeling for the switch inside. The lights had come on, and leaving the bag where it lay, outside the door, he had worked his way to the bathroom. He had been still luxuriating, in the relief when Mrs. Shaw had arrived, bringing his bag in, small, bright and energetic as she had been since, he was sure, the beginning of the world.

"You should sleep in there," she had told him, meaning the sitting room, where the great brown stove stood. "Jenny did, in the winter, you know. What happened to you, Craigie, anyway?"

He had explained that he had broken his Achilles tendon, and a great deal more about the game of squash than he was interested in explaining, and still more about the adequacy of muscle power in the calf, to sever such a tendon, all by itself. He had been as patient as he possibly could be, understanding that Mrs. Shaw was as bereaved as he was not. But then she said: "How is Lenore?"

He said: "I guess she must be all right. I haven't talked to her in years." Then he was out of patience, but pleaded weariness, and contrived to get her out. He had taken the Jack Daniel's pint upstairs with him, in his jacket pocket, knowing there would be a tooth glass on the nightstand, aware that there would be no water, nor any ice, and cognizant that there was no bathroom upstairs, either. He had limited himself to two short drinks, and they had not been enough to keep the memories away.

The telephone stopped ringing well before he reached the bottom step. That was when he remembered that he had left the bag in the white bedroom, as she had always called it. Through the window above the sink, in the kitchen, he could see that it was raining. He hobbled into the bathroom to wash and shave.

There was breakfast at the Shaw house (he had conceded Libby Shaw that much, that he could not make breakfast for himself). It consisted of fried perch, fried eggs, oatmeal, and cornbread. The perch was greasy, and imperfectly boned. The eggs were greasy, and fried too soft. The oatmeal had lumps. The cornbread had been reheated, and was scorched. The coffee had been made in a battered aluminum stove-top percolator, which remained on the old wood-fired black stove, still perking, when Emerson, having made it through the mud of the driveway on his crutches, sinking in with each step, extracting first his feet and then the crutch tips, at last entered the kitchen. He was not soaked above the knees— Molly had put his raincoat in the back seat, on a perfectly sunny day in Boston, saying: "Yes, but it always rains in Vermont. At least when you go there. They ought to put you on call, for when they have droughts."

The kitchen in the pale yellow house seemed to have been done completely in blue and white oilcloth. It was everywhere: on the table, as a cloth, behind the stove as wall decoration, on the counters, and, because the curtains were blue and white gingham and the floor was blue and white squares of indoor-outdoor carpeting, everywhere else as well. Libby Shaw wore a voluminous grey dress, and a blue and white gingham apron. She presided over the stove.

"Libby Shaw," Jenny Irwin had said repeatedly, and with conviction, "is the worst cook on earth. And her house is untidy."

Libby Shaw and Jenny Irwin, at the Grange, and the Order of the Eastern Star, had been inseparable. Even as a child, Craig Emerson had perceived the intensity of their friendship, and their competition for the very occasional benignity of the pastor, Mr. Richards. Mr. Richards had expired, in 1954, of colitis, for which he had refused treatment, on the grounds that a colostomy was undignified, and the equipment, required in consequence, worse. A short, thin, sallow man, he had successfully feigned an interest in his congregation for more than twenty years, yearning all the while for a calling to Vergennes, where his family preferred to live. Still, in Fairfax, Vermont, notwithstanding his disappointment, the Reverend Mr. Richards had exacted severely those tariffs to the United Church which he deemed appropriate. From the likes of Libby Shaw, and Jenny Irwin, who were eager, the duties were commensurately heavy.

They made baked beans, and they cooked hams, and they escalloped potatoes, in veritable carload lots. When there was a bake sale, they made cakes. They also made brownies. "And Libby Shaw's used up more tuna fish and macaroni in those casseroles," Jenny Irwin said, "than Henry Shaw could sensibly afford to pay for." But Jenny Irwin conscripted her grandson, in 1949, to give a clarinet solo at the Grange Hall, and it had not gone well.

Henry Shaw, on the morning of September 29th, 1976, sat bulletheaded, silent and morose, in his own kitchen. He wore his only suit, a blue one, a white shirt, and a blue tie skewed at the neck. His face was brown from the sun. He was seventy-seven years old, and he had never, more than once, wondered why things happened to him, or cared why they went wrong. "Henry's bored," Jenny Irwin said. "Henry's been bored all his life. I believe he likes being bored, for land's sake."

When Henry had gotten old enough to sit up in a high chair, and be fed, his mother had brought him out from the front upstairs bedroom (he had now occupied it for forty-one years with Libby), down the stairs and into the kitchen. There he had been pushed up to the same table at which he sat on that September morning. The only difference, to Henry, on the day of Jenny Irwin's burial, was that he was larger, older, much more uncomfortably dressed, and eating fish instead of cereal. He did not remember the cereal. He would not remember the fish, either, by noon, even though he had caught it.

He had been the Fairfax tax collector for more than forty years, until he finally retired, at a salary ranging from four hundred and fifty dollars a year, to forty-eight hundred dollars a year. For reasons he did not entirely understand, or even care very much about understanding, he had a pension of twenty-eight hundred and eighty dollars a year. With Social Security, perch from Lake Chittenden, Medicare, an occasional legal deer, the proceeds from letting Tanner hay his property, and the help that Medicare provided, that seemed to be enough—with what they got from his garden—to get by on. Whenever someone asked Henry how he was doing, he always said that he and Libby were "gettin' by."

Henry Shaw did not respond when Craig Emerson said "Good morning," before leaning his crutches against the wall, and sitting down at Henry's table. Henry nodded, and chewed fish. Craig had not seen Henry since 1964. Henry seemed not to have noticed. Craig lowered himself into the chair nearest the door, tilting his crutches against the wall. It was shortly after 9:15 A.M.; he had traveled, with the aid of the car, about four hundred yards, and he could see Jenny Irwin's house, peeling ivory paint under the trees, in the rain, from where he sat. He began to pay his respects to the dead.

Jenny Irwin had steadfastly refused to eat anything that Libby Shaw cooked. Craig Emerson accepted only coffee from the menu that in preparation was smoking up the kitchen. He pleaded a nervous stomach, from pain-killing pills (which he was not taking). He was not completely sure that he had not made a mistake, nonetheless: the coffee had a rather meaty texture, and a very bitter taste, from the grounds that seeped through the strainer.

Jenny Irwin, so far as Emerson knew, had never, until the day that she admitted her infirmities, and moved from Fairfax, down to his house, abandoned her morning habit of walking—later, limping—up the hill to Libby's house, for coffee in the kitchen. Craig Emerson refused, that morning, an invitation, made by Libby, to sit in the living room. He had seen the living room. In addition to that, he, like

Henry, was wearing a suit, although his fit better. And while sitting in that living room was difficult, sitting, for Emerson, in any room, was imperative. His injury made it so, and his suit forbade it.

The Shaws kept cats. They had small cats, cats of intermediate size, and large cats. The cats were all orange and white; for some reason, the Shaw cats did not venture forth to seek new genes and different colors (the females, at least; it was impossible to be sure about the toms). Many of them were double-pawed, and one was triple-pawed; several had bobbed tails. They were very clean, so that the house did not stink, but notwithstanding their habits of personal hygiene, they did shed hair. There were so many of them—Jenny once alleged that there were more than thirty, but, since they had the run of the house, it was difficult to take an inventory—that there was hair on everything that had cloth on it, and much that did not. One did not, in a wool suit, venture into the Shaw living room, to sit down.

If one was prudent, one did not do so in his overalls, either. Not because of cathair, or even doghair—the Shaws kept several dogs, rather large mongrels, fat and quite contented, apparently subsisting upon rabbits and groundhogs, or squirrels and woodchucks, or stolen chickens, as the fancy moved them—but because of clutter.

Libby Shaw loved contests. She had once won a Singer slant-needle sewing-machine in a contest which required her to name the Presidents of the United States, in order, through Roosevelt—F.D.R.—and she had done it. She managed it because she had pictures of every single one of them in the living room, pasted—not hung, pasted—to the walls, and that was where the telephone was. She simply read them off, and had to be restrained from continuing with Truman, Eisenhower, Kennedy, and Johnson. Her postal card had been drawn from over twenty thousand submitted, the announcer told her. She had been on the air. She had rejected the opportunity to buy five hundred dollars' worth of sewing lessons, for three dollars and fifty cents. She refused on the air, to the considerable peevishness of the announcer. She said she already knew how to sew, and proved it, as soon as the machine was delivered, by doing a neat zig-zag stitch up the outside of her right forefinger, with blue thread (she was making another apron).

That confirmed a habit, in 1970, which had been virulent before, without encouragement. In the living room, on every available surface—particularly including the floor—were magazines; contest coupons; boxtops; discarded newspapers; catalogues; any number of cats in various conditions of liveliness; clippings from newspapers which had, for some odd reason or the other, seemed appropriate for the rubbish; soiled garments—Henry always went to bed, generally arising in the same clothes, but at least from bed, while Libby had been known to become enthralled in some challenge and live for a week or two in the living room—outdated copies of the Old *Farmer's Almanac*, unopened mail (from the County Extension Service, Sears, Montgomery Ward, Western Auto, and an insurance company in Nebraska which specialized in insurance for Old Folks, as it said on the envelope); and ashes from the stove. The stove was the same type as Jenny's, a great brown beast of a thing, but Libby was less careful, and spilled ashes on the floor. She also dropped kindling, and did not pick it up, so that there were likely to be sticks around.

Henry read *Field & Stream*, and *Outdoor Life*, and *Sports Afield*. He read them religiously. He did not talk about them, or anything else, but he read them. Then, with equal fervor, he piled them up in neat square columns, which sooner or later collapsed when one of the less experienced cats attempted to climb them, and toppled to the floor.

Henry also drank Moxie. His habit was to take a warm quart from the case in the kitchen, open it, obtain a glass, and retire to the living room. There he would make a place for himself on the couch, select one of his magazines—he reread them many times each, moving his lips to form the words, with the same rapt attention of the sixth or seventh reading that he had given to the first—and sip Moxie from mid-afternoon until dinner, at about 5:15 P.M. After dinner, he would return to his place with a new quart of Moxie, no matter whether he had finished the first, and read until bedtime at 9:45 P.M. Sometimes there were three or four Moxie bottles among the magazines. Craig Emerson did not go into the Shaws' sitting room for the same reasons of courtesy that would have prompted him to regret an invitation from two extremely large, but nonetheless hospitable, birds to profane their nest.

"Land," Jenny Irwin said, being punctilious about her own housekeepings—Craig Emerson, spending summers with her, would not have been totally surprised to return from a midnight visit to the bathroom and find his bed freshly made—"I can't see how they can stand to live in that *mess*."

"Well, Craigie," Libby said, sitting down at the table, "it's still a blessing, I suppose, she went so fast and all. When you get to her age, you know," Jenny had been at least ninety; never precise about her age, she grew even more vague about it as the years went on, to the point at which Emerson had begun to speculate that she herself was no longer quite sure of the exact figure, "you simply have to expect it."

Jenny had shared the matter-of-fact view of things that Libby Shaw expressed. Emerson supposed it grew out of an experience which demanded cold-eyed self-appraisal, but did not permit the leisure for self-development, or any other kind of self-indulgence. Jenny had been overweight, sharp tongued, ill-tempered, never—that Emerson could remember—possessed of a sense of humor, plagued all her life by straitened circumstances, and always unlucky. She complained, but she did not yield.

She was born in Scotland; Emerson had never discovered where, since she refused to talk about it. She had come to the United States through Halifax, with her mother, when she was a little girl. Emerson had deduced that when he visited her with Lenore in 1963, from the old trunks stored in the dirt cellar.

There were four of them, bulky wooden chests bound with iron straps, resting on cement blocks. He led the way, bending almost double in the four-and-a-half foot clearance to avoid cracking his head again on the wooden beams, playing the flashlight into the darkness left where the one dim bulb at the stairs cast no light. Lenore, nearly as tall as he, crouched along behind him.

"Are there snakes?" she said, in a low voice.

"I suppose so," he said. He pointed the light at the foundation of the house, where the grey stones left spaces between beams; over the years, those spaces had been used as shelves for articles that no one really intended ever to use, but could not bring themselves to discard: boxes of .22 ammunition; 12-gauge shotgun shells; the action, but no stock, of a Mauser rifle, rusted by then; an old hammer-headed hatchet, with a broken handle. "There're snakes outside, I know, and they wouldn't have much trouble coming in, if they wanted to."

"Brrr," Lenore said, touching his back. "I hope they didn't want to. I hate snakes."

He knew that. They had seen a large rattler, torpid in the desert sun in the late afternoon north of Guaymas, Sonora, that April, and although they passed him at sixty miles an hour, she had been noticeably distressed. "This damned thing better not get temperamental though," she said, when he assured her that the snake had evidently lost its wits and either stayed out too late the night before, or come out too early that day, and would in any event find it very difficult to strike them through the sheet metal of the green XKE. "All I need's a breakdown in a place where there are snakes."

In the cellar, he said:"I thought you wanted some excitement. You were the one that said she was bored."

"Can she hear us down here?" Lenore said.

"I doubt it," he said, finding the trunks in the light. "She's got trouble enough hearing what you say when you're in the same room with her."

"Good," Lenore said, "let's make it."

He had begun to laugh at that. "Snakes and all, looking on?"

"I *said* I wanted some excitement," she said. "For heaven's sakes, we're legal now."

For a long time, it had been just as much fun, legal, as it had been when, out of respect for conventions and protocols about which California motel clerks had long since ceased to care, she had carried a cheap wedding ring in her purse just as she would have done if they had been back east. Then something, which Emerson had never identified to his own satisfaction, started to go wrong. He was never exactly sure when whatever it was had started to deteriorate, partly because, he thought, days of such warmth and good feeling as those in the damp air of the cellar, even with the possibility of snakes lying in ambush, had narcotized his sense of dread.

Dread (which he escaped for a long time with Lenore, only to regain it in fuller measure when he began to see that she was going) he had learned from Jenny Irwin, directly, and indirectly from her through his mother. Lenore perceived it, and described it, when they were still in California, one morning in paradise at an old grey hotel at Half Moon Bay, where the surf sound came in and rattled off buildings that might have been the standard set for a western movie. There was a west wind off the Pacific that day. It blew the curtains away from the windows, and made her dream and talk about Tahiti. He had not joined in. She had raised herself naked on one elbow, her right breast brushing his left arm, and with her left hand caressed his right jawbone. "Got the mopes, my friend?" she said.

"After intercourse, all animals are sad," he said. "I guess."

"This animal isn't," she said. "What you've got is the wrong perspective. This is *before* intercourse."

"Did I just have a wet dream?" he said. "It was great, if I did. Best I've ever had."

"No, no," she said. "God, for an older man who's supposed to be a bad influence on me, you're awful innocent. This is before the next time, which, if you're at all cooperative, will be in about ten or so minutes."

"Oh," he said.

She rolled over onto her stomach and propped herself on her elbows, so that her nipples just touched the sheet. She held her chin in her hands, and he reached his left arm around her, and rubbed the small of her back, and her butt. Her eyes were either green or grey; in all the years that he knew her, he was never able to decide which. She frowned. "You puzzle me," she said. "One minute you can't seem to get enough of me. . . ."

"I can't," he said, loyally.

". . . and the next minute you're ten thousand miles away, and looking worried," she said. "What the hell're you worried about?"

He had thought for a while before he answered, turning a new notion over and inspecting it, as though someone had directed his attention to a large rock implanted in a yard that he had known all of his life, and informed him, with authority, that it harbored an evil spirit which came out at night. "I don't know," he said. "Doom, maybe?"

"Of what?" she said.

He had raised himself up then, so as to be able to look her in the eye without craning his neck on the thin pillows. "You want some definitions," he said. "I can't give them to you. There isn't any precision to it. My mother's folks were immigrants from Scotland. They never had a dime. She was one of those punishing, put-upon, minority Catholics, until she married him, and he was one of those punishing, putting-down Presbyterians, that convinced her that the Pope was the Devil. But he didn't *entirely* convince her, I guess."

"I'd like to meet *him*," Lenore said. She had been raised in what she called the Faith of the Westchester Catholic Church, and had no patience for it whatsoever.

"You may have some trouble," he said. "Craig Irwin's good and dead, diabetes in his fifty-ninth year. I never met him myself. But from what I hear, he fully anticipated to go to Hell, and I plan to look him up when I get there, to my surprise, myself."

"Well," Lenore said, "her, then."

"Do nearly as well," he said. "There isn't much difference between the Catholics who try to make a living out of gravel, and the Protestants who try to do the same thing. When he made her change, she just swapped one variety of gloom for another. Didn't require that much adjustment. And the life they had, confirmed it.

"They lost one son to the influenza, and another one—well, she did, he was dead by then—in World War Two, when somebody didn't make the parachute to specs, or pack it right. They had a dairy farm in Jericho that was on the way to making it, from what I hear, until all the cattle had to be destroyed. Hoof-and-mouth disease, or something. Then he was, he got a job with the County, inspecting other people's cattle, being something of an expert on the subject by then, I guess, and he only about a year and a half short of his pension when he died.

"For about three years after my mother got married," Emerson said, "her father didn't speak to her, and he was never civil to my father, not at all. Because of course my father had done the same thing to her, that Craig had done to Jenny. Only what Craig did to Jenny was okay, to Craig, because he'd saved a Papist. But what my father did was deadly wrong, because he'd damned a good Protestant by finagling her into the Church of Rome.

"I've never been completely sure of how Jenny reacted to that development," he said. "My mother told me that she didn't really mind at all, and Jenny used to go to Midnight Mass with my father, when she was visiting at Christmas. But she couldn't've just not minded. One way or the other, it has to be some kind of repudiation, or criticism, of what she'd done."

"It was the same thing," Lenore said. "Both of them did it for love."

"My mother did," Emerson said. "I swear that there are times when I've been sure she was adopted. How she came out of those genes the way she did is something I will never understand.

"Jenny didn't." He paused then, startled to hear what he had said. He said it again, to be sure that he meant it: "Yeah, that's right. Jenny didn't. Love's one of those frivolous things, to her.

"It's not that it doesn't matter. It does matter. It matters like hoof-and-mouth disease, and parachute packers who're no damned good, and Depressions, and years when it's too dry to grow a good stand of grass, when your food supply depends upon how many bales of hay Nelson Tanner can cut from your pastures. Where you haven't got any cows anymore. To feed his increasing heard of Holsteins. It matters because it's something that not only *can* get you in trouble, but most assuredly *will* get you in trouble.

"If you accused Jenny Irwin of doing something for love, she would tighten up her face, and tell you that you were being foolish. And then the next Sunday, she'd pick a small bouquet of lilacs from the bushes in the back of the house, walk down the hill about a mile, then turn left at the cemetery gate, and walk about another seven hundred yards, up another hill, to put them in that green tin vase with the spike on the bottom that she put on his grave the week after he died, twenty-three years ago. In the winter, when there aren't any flowers, she plows through the snow, to go there empty-handed.

"Maybe she's saying 'Hail Marys,'" Lenore said. "Maybe she never forgot."

"Maybe she is," he said. "Maybe she's saying 'Goddamns.' Maybe she's just going up there to give him the nagging, once a week, that he used to get every day. Jenny's hard to please, and that isn't new, from what I've been told. Maybe she does it because, if he's watching, he'll see what great pains she takes, to pay her respects, and feel guilty some more. Maybe she does it so that neighbors won't feel that she's neglecting her responsibilities. Or perhaps it's just the exercise, and the habit," he said. "I don't really know. She probably doesn't, either."

"Then it could be for love," Lenore said.

"It could be," he said. "I doubt it, but it could be."

"I think I'd like her," Lenore said.

"I'll bet you," he said, "I will bet you the performance of any unspeakable sexual act that the winner gets to name, that she will make you as uncomfortable as a scorpion in your sneaker."

In the cellar, that afternoon in 1963, Lenore had started to laugh. She had a laugh which tended to peal, and draw attention to her in a restaurant, or a bar, and there had been a time, early when he knew her, when he had wanted to speak to her about it. But, because he was learning—too slowly, but learning—he had avoided that, and put it down to her enjoyment of herself, and life, and him, and let it go. A decision, he believed, which ranked among the few good ones he had made about the two of them. "Well, there you are," she said. "You've won the bet. Wouldn't that be unspeakable, to do it in front of the snakes?"

It had taken him a while to remember the wager. He had exercised the winner's prerogative, and delayed the collection until Montreal.

Realism had never ceased to render him uncomfortable. On the morning of Jenny Irwin's funeral, he did not really know what the hell to say to Libby Shaw. To deny that somewhere in your nineties was a place where you had done well to balance your accounts against an audit: to deny that, to a woman in her late seventies, was so ridiculous it was impossible.

But to admit it was to create a large though tacit statement, that the woman had no more than ten or twelve years yet belonging to her (and probably not that much, if the truth were known, and it certainly was) before somebody looked down on her, laid out in a box, and said that she had no kick coming. And then again, it did seem, well, coarse.

Two cats, one small, one medium-sized, wandered into the kitchen, whether in search of fish or in reaction to overcrowding in the sitting room, Emerson did not know. The smaller cat advanced; the middle-sized cat sat down. The small cat approached Henry, rising up on its hind legs, placing its front paws on his leg, and raising its nose in the air. The cat moved its whiskers as it reconnoitered. Then it jumped up into Henry's lap, sat, and examined his plate. There were just a few bones on Henry's plate. The cat bent forward for a closer sniff, and established, to its own satisfaction, that Henry had been eating fish, and indeed had eaten all the fish. It tramped its feet around, turned, sniffed his face to verify that the missing fish had gone into his mouth, and expressed as much disdain as a small cat can express. Henry did not notice.

The cat got down and stalked across the floor, its tail vertical, its pace deliberate. It conferred briefly with the second cat, rubbing its neck against the larger cat, and appearing for all the world to be whispering something derogatory about Henry. The first cat sat, and the second cat stared at it. Both cats got to their feet. The second cat turned and started toward the sitting room. The first cat, respectfully, followed, turning its head at the door to look at Henry. Reproachfully.

Henry was not aware of that. He had his thousand-yard stare fixed on the sink.

"Well," Emerson said, after altogether too much silence had followed Libby's observation that Jenny ought to have expected to die, "ah, she did have a full life."

"She told me once," Libby said firmly, "that she was a little girl, when Bismark invaded France."

That would have made her, Emerson decided, about one hundred and six, on the morning that she died.

At Half Moon Bay he had told Lenore, that morning, "And there's another thing: she lies."

"Lies?" Lenore said, rolling onto her back again, and reaching down to touch him. "About what?"

"That's what makes her so tricky," he said. "She's a very tricky woman. Secretive. She lies about things that you wouldn't think would matter, and then you find out, or you figure out, that she must've been lying to you. You didn't look it up, or anything. It just occurred to you, maybe a day or so later: 'That can't be so. What the hell did she tell me that for?' She told me she remembered the day that everybody found out that President Lincoln was shot. That's ninety-nine years ago. She couldn't possibly remember something that happened in eighteen-sixty-four. She couldn't possibly have been alive. That's bullshit. But why would she lie about it?"

"Maybe she's senile," Lenore said. "Maybe she remembers hearing what her parents said, about how *they* heard that Lincoln'd been shot. And now she thinks that *she* remembers it. Hardening of the arteries. Something like that."

"I don't know," Emerson said, in the spring of 1963 in California, "I would think if you were walking around the day a President was shot, you would remember it. And if you weren't, you would have a certain dimness about it, that'd warn you that you weren't. I'll tell you what I think: I think she fantasizes. She probably really believes she was alive then. Or wants to, anyway."

To Libby Shaw, thirteen years later, Emerson presented what he hoped was an innocent expression, interrupted by a grimace as he shifted his weight on the wooden chair, and pinched the flesh of his thigh in the cast. "She couldn't've been alive then," he said.

"She *said* she was," Libby Shaw said.

Something in the exchange had attracted Henry's attention. "What?" he said. He looked at Emerson. "What'd she say?"

"She said she remembered when the Franco-Prussian War started," Emerson said.

Henry was indignant. "She ain't that old." He looked at Libby. "You won a contest thing on that once. You oughta know that. That was eighteen-and-seventy. I was right there when you was talking. It was eighteen-and-seventy- You don't remember that. You looked it up. You weren't around then. Don't tell me that."

Libby looked exasperated.

Henry lapsed back into his unfocused gaze.

Emerson, hastily taking another swig of coffee that he did not want, felt desperate. He put the cup down. "Henry," he said, feeling helpless, "not her. Jenny. Jenny said that. Jenny said she remembered that."

Libby stood with her hands on her hips. "I got to change," she said, looking furious. She began to remove her apron. She glared at Henry.

"Look," Emerson said.

"Never mind," Libby said, throwing the apron down. "Won't do no good. Never listens anyway. Just remembers things sometimes. Not all the time. Just sometimes. Don't do any good at all, talk to him."

"Henry," Emerson said, "Libby didn't. . . . "

"Recollect it very well," Henry said, nodding several times, "plain as day. Won herself a case of pineapple juice, and a chance on a trip to Hawaii. Got the pineapple juice. Remember it well."

Libby stomped out of the room.

"Well," Lenore said, in the room at Half Moon Bay, "why would she want to do that? I mean, what's the point?"

It took a long time for him to answer that, long enough so that he was ready to do something else, as soon as he did. "She thinks," he said, "that she's eternal. And maybe she is." Then he took Lenore in his arms.

The limousine pulled into the Shaws' driveway, as scheduled, at 10:45 A.M., on September 28, 1976. It was a 1972 Cadillac, and there was a good deal of cancer rusting out the rocker panels on the right hand side of the car, which Emerson could see from the Shaws' kitchen window. The rain had let up, but the skies were still dark.

Henry moved the curtain to peer out at whatever Emerson had seen. Libby was still upstairs.

"Huh," Henry said.

"I knew it," Emerson said. "I finally gave up. The bastards wear you down."

"Um," Henry said, still staring at the car.

"I should've had an inkling at the hospital," Emerson said.

"Hospital," Henry said.

"The hospital," Emerson said. "I had nothing but trouble with the hospital."

"Oh," Henry said. "Aye-uh."

"My whole problem," Emerson said, feeling rather ridiculous, "my whole problem is that I've always had the sneaking idea that nothing really mattered, and you might as well enjoy yourself. I was never really able to act on it, but that was the way I felt. Follow me?"

Henry shifted his gaze from the limousine, allowed the curtain to

fall back into place, and stared at Emerson. Henry did not say anything. The driver of the limousine blew the horn. Once. Briefly.

Henry motioned toward the window. "That's the Miller kid," he
said. "Drives for Skinner, the undertaker. Know him?"

Emerson shook his head. He did not know Skinner. He knew the
undertaker Flynn, with whom he had had sharp words, in Boston, in
connection with this event, but he did not know Skinner. He had
talked to Skinner on the telephone, and found him exceedingly dense.
He did not say that to Henry, because everyone in Fairfax, and towns
for thirty miles around, knew everyone in Fairfax, and towns for
thirty miles around.

"Look out for Skinner," Henry said, nodding furiously. "Skinner's
nimble. The Miller kid's all right. Well, he won't do nothing for you.
Works down at the milk plant. Gets off, drives for Skinner."

Henry leaned across the table. He put his elbows down, and stared
at Emerson. He tapped his left temple with his left forefinger. He
winked. He spoke very slowly. "Touched," Henry said. "Touched in
the head. He's not all there." Henry sat up, abruptly, and looked satisfied. "See?" he said.

Emerson began to be alarmed. He had not wanted the limousine in
the first place. Jenny's only other kin was Molly, and Molly, by reason
of considerable experience, had reasonably decided that the only
respects she would be able to pay, without hypocrisy, would certainly
offend the other mourners. Molly's compensation for lack of self-con-
trol was the best that she said she could manage: she stayed away
from occasions which would clearly occasion her to utter hostile
remarks (such as: "You asshole"; "Fuck you"; and the like); invented
excuses when she found herself, inadvertently, at such occasions, and
left early; and lapsed into total silence when she blundered into such
celebrations, could not escape, and preferred not to say things which
would require, the mornings after, profuse apologies.

"This one, I can't manage," she had said, helping him into the
Pontiac in the garage below the townhouse. "I simply cannot do it.
You're on your own, Kiddo." And then she shut the door.

Elaborately, Emerson had explained to Flynn, the undertaker, a
medium-sized, pale man with no noticeable hair on his head, that little was required of him. "She has no relatives here," Emerson said.

They stood in the casket selection room of Flynn & Flynn & Sons,
Undertakers, in a brownstone on Beacon Street in Boston. It was 8:00
A.M. on September 26th, 1976. Around them were bronze caskets,

brushed chrome caskets with rose-colored cushions, mahogany caskets with brass handles and blue plush interiors, and one plain oak casket, with what seemed to be a rather seedy grey fabric, filled with very little of whatever they had used to fill it.

"Her friends, then," Flynn said eagerly, nicely overlaying spurious sympathy.

Emerson had been up until 3:12 A.M., when Jenny Irwin died. He had gone home after arranging for Flynn & Flynn & Sons to pick the body up at the Massachusetts General Hospital. Molly had awakened him at 6:30 A.M., explaining it was Mr. Flynn, who needed to see him for the casket selection, and the arrangement of the services. Mr. Flynn was apprehensive that the Cathedral might not be available.

"Mr. Flynn," Emerson said, "as I explained to you last night. . . ."

Flynn looked puzzled. He had his hands clasped before him.

"I didn't talk to you last night?" Emerson said.

Flynn shook his head.

Emerson sighed. "All right, Mr. Flynn," he said, "how many Flynns are there?"

"This home was started by my grandfather," Flynn said proudly. "My great uncle, Jeremiah Flynn. . . ."

Emerson waved him off. "Mr. Flynn," he said, "how old are you? You've got to be in your forties."

"Forty-three," Flynn said, looking puzzled.

"Fine," Emerson said. "Now I am in my thirties, and next year I'll be sixty-one, at least. So I've got to hurry. When I say: 'How many Flynns are there?' I mean: right now. Today. I talked to some guy named Flynn last night, and he came and got the body. Or he sent somebody. This morning, I mean, and I am goddamned *reeling* and I don't for the life of me understand why the goddamned *fuck* it is that I have to go through a death watch and then get up early to serve *your* goddamned convenience."

Mr. Flynn looked shocked. "Our procedures," he said painfully, "are designed to insure the maximum comfort to the bereaved, and the utmost possible respect to the departed." He unclasped his hands. He took two practiced steps backward, and laid his right hand on the brushed-chrome casket, moving his fingers across the maroon crushed velvet cushion. "This model," he said, "offers. . . . "

"Oh shut up," Emerson said.

Mr. Flynn looked pained. "Mother," he said, "would certainly. . . . "

"*Which fucking goddamned Flynn are you?*" Emerson shouted. "If in fact you are a goddamned Flynn at all, and not some goddamned ghoul from Central Casting? Gimme your goddamned first name. *Right now*."

"Edmund," Flynn said.

"Good," Emerson said, hobbling and lurching toward him. He jabbed Edmund several times in the chest with his right forefinger, moving him back until he was bent over the casket. Edmund Flynn showed sudden signs of incipient goiter, his eyes bulging and his face red.

"In the first place," Emerson said, leaving his forefinger bent against Flynn's chest, because he liked the little bastard better when he was off-balance and scared, "she was not my goddamned mother. She was my goddamned grandmother. In the second place, she's *dead*, see? Don't breathe no more. Dead as a goddamned *stone*. Doesn't need any comfort. No respect, no nothing. Dead, right? Got it? *Dead*. You probably run into a lot of that, in your line of work. Which means she doesn't need no goddamned Cadillac Seville, with the vinyl roof and all the plush interior options, like the velvet upholstery, to feel comfortable, because she can't feel no more comfortable, on account of being dead, and all. She's going in the *ground*. Forget the fucking AM-FM stereo radio and the tape deck and the power windows. The woman is just as dead as she can be. Gabriel's all that she's about to hear, and probably not for a while yet, either.

"In the third place," Emerson said, beginning to acknowledge he'd begun to enjoy it, bending Flynn a little further over the silver casket, "the bereaved don't need any comfort, and genuinely don't deserve any, and will probably burst into gales of hysterical laughter if you try to give them some. Because the deceased was a miserable old bat with a filthy disposition, that somehow, Jesus Christ knows how, lived to over ninety, made everybody's life miserable, that she came in contact with, on every day of it, and somehow still lived long enough to die of natural causes. Against all odds.

"I hated the old gargoyle," Emerson said. "She didn't like me one helluva lot, either. If there was anybody else around, to put her in the ground so that she didn't spoil, I wouldn't goddamned be here. And if there wasn't anybody else, but I thought we had a competent bunch of reliable vultures on hand, to dispatch discarded remains, I wouldn't be here. And she would be on Boston Common. But there isn't anybody else, and I don't trust the goddamned seagulls. So what you do is, you give me some kind of container, cheap, that doesn't leak and you can close the cover on it. Then you rassle up one of them long black station wagons, and get some Flynn or other that can find his way to Fairfax, Vermont. Or that, if he gets lost, won't ever come back, which would be just as good, in my book. And a guy up there, to bury her.

"Edmund," Emerson said, almost losing his balance on the cast, "I had a long day and a long night, on top of it. Now you can do what I tell you, or am I gonna have to go and exhume Jeremiah?"

Flynn gulped and said: "The plain oak then, I take it?"

"How much is the oak?" Emerson said.

"Four hundred dollars," Edmund Flynn said.

"How much is the freight?"

"Five dollars a mile, one way," Flynn said.

"How about the other way?" Emerson said.

"That's for the trip," Flynn said.

"What about the gas and tolls?" Emerson said.

"Included," Flynn said.

"Put her in the oak," Emerson said. "Take her up to Fairfax, and put her in the hands of somebody who's been licensed to put dead people in the ground. You got one of them?"

Flynn swallowed, twice. "I am sure that we can find one," he said. "We have capable and experienced. . . ."

"I told you once before," Emerson said, "that I don't want to hear your goddamned spiel. You call your guy, and you give him *my* spiel. You tell him that I'm crazy, and I'm liable to run amok at any minute, and he'll probably end up with his relatives getting dignified and competent services for *him*, if I don't get my way. You got that, Edmund?"

Flynn had nodded miserably.

Emerson had less success with Skinner. He did not understand Skinner as well, or else he understood him very well indeed, but was intimidated by him.

Skinner seemed to be deaf. Comprehending, but unhearing. When, by telephone from Boston, Emerson had told him that there would be no need for a flower car at Fairfax, Skinner told him that he would have a flower car at the ready. When Emerson told him that he was the only next-of-kin, and would require no limousine, Skinner told him that the limousine would pick him up at the Shaw house. When Emerson asked Skinner why the hell anybody would want to pick him up at the Shaws', Skinner told him that the Shaws had called him, and told Skinner to have the driver meet Mr. Emerson there.

"I never met Skinner," Emerson said to Henry, as the old limousine idled in the mud outside. "I know him, I guess, but I never met him."

Henry nodded, wisely. "That's his car," Henry said.

"I figured that," Emerson said.

"He drives it," Henry said.

"Of course he drives it," Emerson said. "If it's his. . . ."

Henry shook his head rapidly. "No, no," he said. "Drives it fishing. Everything. Makes people feel bad. They know what it is. See it coming? Shouldn't do that."

"Oh," Emerson said, humbled.

"Isn't right," Henry said. He shook his head again. "Used to be worse. When he was just starting out, he drove the hearse."

"When I was in college," Emerson said, "friends of mine bought hearses second-hand, and drove them. They were cheap, and they were Cadillacs, and they didn't have much mileage on them. Furthermore, you could sleep in the back. We used to come up here skiing, in them."

Henry was plainly appalled. "That the dead people rode in?" he said.

"Henry Shaw," Jenny said, "is as close to being dead as any human being I have ever met, who's still alive. When Henry Shaw is dead, he probably won't notice the difference."

"Of course," Emerson said. "That they carried the dead people in the caskets to the cemetery in, at least," he said, wondering how the hell he had gotten into that sort of grammar. He decided that it was the cast on his leg, and the coffee grounds in his teeth. Or something. Hastily, he made another mistake. "We used to take turns driving," he said. "Two guys could sleep back in there. Couple air-mattresses, sleeping bags—it was fine."

Henry now looked horrified. "You slept," he said, "you slept where they had the dead people?"

"Henry," Emerson said, "there weren't any dead people in the hearses by the time we got them."

"They used to have dead people in them," Henry said.

"Sure," Emerson said.

"Well," Henry said.

Emerson had never known Henry to talk so much. He did not like it, either, having inspired it. "Henry," he said, "they generally didn't have more than ten or twelve thousand miles on them." That was it: waste would do it. Buying hearses was preventing waste. "They were big old Cadillacs. The undertakers couldn't use them any more, but not because they were worn out—because they were old. You could get a Cadillac about four or five years old, for less'n five hundred dollars. In

California a couple friends of mine, liked surfing, used to buy up the flower cars, and for the same reason. They'd put their boards in the back. Best pick-up truck you ever saw."

Henry was shaking his head again. "It's wrong," he said, with great emphasis. "Wrong."

"Wrong," Lenore had said, that morning in Half Moon Bay, after they had made love again. "Nobody's eternal."

"Jenny thinks she is," he said. "That doesn't make it so, but it makes it what she thinks. She can think whatever she likes."

"Wrong again," Lenore said, beginning to laugh. "That much at least, I know. There are very strict controls on what you're allowed to think. I know almost all of them by heart, and the ones that I don't know—I know enough of the other ones so that I can guess what they are."

"And what are those?" he said. "Impure thoughts?"

"Impure thoughts," she said. "Exactly. Those're well-up on the list. But first on the list is thinking some things last forever, and second is being sure that nothing will."

"You're very Delphic today," he said, rubbing her butt again, absently.

"That feels nice," she said. "No," she said, putting her head on the pillow, closing her eyes and smiling, moving a little under his hand, "I've just got a sure sense that some things, that are also nice, do last forever, I think that I can pick them out from the ones that aren't nice, or are, but won't last."

Henry was becoming more agitated as he talked. Emerson had never seen him so agitated. He was moving his chair back and forth, and shaking his hands in the air. He clearly wanted to stamp his feet. Age had slackened the skin of his neck, and it shook in his excitement. "I'll tell you what it is," Henry said, "I know what it is. People don't have any respect for anything, anymore." He was pleased with that. He nodded some more, vigorously. "I've seen enough of it," Henry said. "I've seen it on television."

Henry and Libby Shaw did not own a television. On Mondays, Fridays, Saturdays and Sundays, they abandoned the contests and the outdoor magazines, and walked down the hill to Jenny's house. There they watched, until 10:00 each of those evenings, whatever programs she had selected for the evening.

"You remind me of Henry Shaw," she had told Emerson when he woke up bleary-eyed and mildly hungover, the morning after Carlton

Fisk's sixth-game, twelfth-inning homer had confounded but not dispatched the Cincinnati Reds in the 1975 World Series. "He'd spend every night of the week, if I'd let him, planked down in front of my television set, drinking my port and watching baseball games."

Jenny's doctor had prescribed port as a general toner for her system. She preferred heavy, sweet, tawny port, and drank two large tumblers of it each night. On arising, she took a good slug of dark rum before her orange juice, Rice Crispies, and strong black tea. But Jenny also believed firmly in strict discipline, and was particularly insistent upon it in others. She allowed Henry one small glass of port each night, and did not offer him more when she got up to replenish her own glass. To Libby she was somewhat more generous. "Henry knows which glass is his," she said, grimly. "There's no complaint from him.

"I declare," she said, "I do believe that man is probably in my house every night while I'm away, staying up 'till all hours, watching baseball games." The Shaws kept the extra key to Jenny's house, and watched it for her when she was away.

"I doubt that Henry would go in when you're not there," Emerson said to her, being actually convinced totally that Henry would not go in.

"I know it," Jenny said. "I don't believe he's got the initiative. But he'd like to," she said. "If he ever thought of it, he'd like to. Too much television isn't good for you, you know."

"Jenny," he said at the breakfast table, aware that he had brought it upon himself by choosing to have too much to drink while she was visiting, because she went from crustiness to outright aggressiveness when she caught a regular victim in an unusually weakened condition, "you watch television more than any other human being that I know."

"That's different," she said. "Doctor Cookson says my eyes are perfect."

Jenny squinted most of the time, and invariably wore her glasses on the cord around her neck; Doctor Cookson was a general practitioner in Fairfax, quite possibly educated as a veterinarian, who wore glasses himself, the lenses as thick as the top of Craig's glass cocktail table. Emerson's mother had suspected Jenny of designs upon the Doctor, for several years; when nothing happened, she decided that the Doctor had been too lethargic to notice what Jenny Irwin had in mind. Doctor Cookson, Emerson knew, had probably never said anything at all about Jenny's vision, or that, if he had, what he had said was not to be trusted. "I watch television to keep up with things. A body needs something to do, you know."

"Why?" Henry Shaw said, although Emerson had not said anything. "Why, it's because there's too many people minding everybody else's business. Now you look at Senator McCarthy."

"Oh, Henry," Emerson said, as the limousine idled in the grey day outside the window, "Eugene McCarthy hasn't got a chance. He's running for President out of habit. He'll probably do it every four years now, now that Stassen's semi-retired. It doesn't mean anything."

The smaller of the two cats, which had inspected the remains of breakfast on Henry's plate, now reappeared at the door to the living room. It peered around the corner as Henry's voice rose.

"President?" he said. "I didn't know he was running for President." An expression of delight came over his face. Emerson had never seen such an expression on Henry Shaw's face. The cat withdrew its head.

"Sure," Emerson said. "As an Independent."

"Land," Henry said. "I thought he was dead and gone, all these years. Imagine that. *Libby*," he shouted.

The smaller cat came to the door again, entered the kitchen and sat down near the refrigerator. Close behind it was the medium-sized cat, followed by two more small cats, another medium size cat, and one very large cat. Two more small cats came through the door after the big cat.

They all sat near the small cat, except for the smallest of the last two cats, which evidently felt kittenish, and rolled on its back in front of the rest.

"Yes, Henry?" Libby called.

"Senator McCarthy's running for President," Henry said. He looked sharply at Emerson. "You mean President of the *United States*," he said.

Emerson nodded. One of the medium-sized cats batted the small playful cat with a paw, and the small cat, quickly abashed, got up and moved to the end of the line. All eight cats were now looking on with dignity, scratching their ears with their hind feet from time to time, the large cat yawning every so often, but otherwise fidgeting very little.

"*No*," Libby said from upstairs.

"He *is*," Henry said, looking at Emerson, who nodded confirmation. Henry nodded again. "Craigie says so."

Jenny Irwin had always called him *Craigie*, and had thus habituated all her friends to the same form of address. Emerson hated it, and his distaste was not recent; he had hated the diminutive as a boy. He had told his mother, who began his practical education around age six by explaining: "Yes, I know you don't. I didn't like it when she decided that my name should be Mamie instead of Mary. James could have endured *Jim*, but he hated *Jamie*. Robert sort of liked being called *Rob*, and she always called him *Bobby*. Dad had a perfectly good name, and she always called him *Daddy*. He'd say: 'Goddamnit, Jenny, I'm not your father, you know.' Then he'd take the newspaper and go out to the barn and read by himself. After we named you after him, I was a little bit afraid she'd call you *Daddy* too. So count your blessings."

Libby Shaw came into the kitchen with much less gracefulness than the cats had shown. She wore a grey dress that was all but indistinguishable from the one she had been wearing when Emerson had entered the kitchen. Her grey hair hung down to her shoulders, and she was brushing it vigorously, turning her head from side to side. The cats looked up at her with mild interest, then returned their attention to the table where Henry and Emerson sat. "*No*," Libby said.

"Yes," Henry said. Emerson nodded. "Really," Emerson said. "He hasn't got any money, and they won't let him into the debates, and I doubt if he'll carry a single state. Except maybe this one. But he's a fighter. . . ."

"And he's a real good talker," Libby said. "Goodness but that man can talk."

"Well," Emerson said, "he was a teacher, and he was in the Senate, and all. He could screw it up pretty well for Carter, if he's lucky."

That morning in Half Moon Bay, Emerson had said to Lenore: "That sounds to me like an unreasonable reliance upon luck, expecting things to last forever just because you've got some second sight that tells you which ones to pick. Isn't the Pope supposed to be the only one with that?"

"That," Lenore said, "is certainly the Pope's view, at least until this Pope, from all I've heard. My own opinion happens to be somewhat different. And, in addition, it's perfectly all right if your explanation turns out to be the one that's correct. Because I *am* lucky. That's another thing I've always known. If I pick the thing, it's one of the things that's going to last. Just because I am the one that picked it. If you picked it, it might be the same thing, but it probably wouldn't last, or else it wouldn't be nice. Because you're convinced that nice things end, and bad things happen, and that means just that you've got bad luck, but you're fortunate enough to know it. Which is a *little* good luck, at least." She reached down and touched him again. "Stick with me, Kid," she said, "and you'll wear diamonds."

"I don't know," Libby said, bringing her hair up into a bun again. She had two large hairpins in her mouth. "I was planning to vote for President Ford."

"Keep still, woman," Henry said, showing more animation, still, than Emerson had ever seen. "You'll do no such thing." Libby paid no attention at all. "You just hurry yourself along there. Fellow's been waiting while you dawdle. Look at the time." It was 11:05 A.M., on the morning of September 28th, 1976. To Emerson, Henry said, some vague foreboding showing on his face, "You're sure, now."

"Of course I'm sure," Emerson said.

"Sure," Emerson had said to Lenore in the California morning thirteen years before, "that's what you tell all the boys, I'll bet. But then you won't respect me in the morning, if I do."

"The fellow," Henry said, faltering.

"The guy from Minnesota," Emerson said.

"Wisconsin," Libby said, automatically. The cats took in that contribution, and returned their gaze to Henry.

"*Joe* McCarthy?" Emerson said.

" Yuh, " Henry said, "Senator McCarthy."

Oh my God, Emerson thought. "Oh," he said, unable to account for the embarrassing feeling that he was the one who had been extremely stupid, and had caused pain as a result. "No, uh, well," he said, "ah, I was, I was talking about *Eugene* McCarthy. The, ah, the other one."

"The one that was against the war," Libby said.

Henry's face had collapsed. On the morning of Jenny Irwin's funeral, he had at last become sad. "Well," he said slowly, "then the real one is dead."

"Senator Joseph McCarthy is dead," Emerson said. "

"Oh," Henry said. He looked out the window. One by one, the cats stood up and filed out of the kitchen.

Emerson injured himself, getting into the old limousine.

In consequence of playing college intramural basketball in an overheated gym, Craig Emerson at the age of twenty had developed a major-league case of jock itch, or crotch rot, as it was then known at Brown. After several days of torment, during which he squirmed and writhed and clawed at himself, and was gleefully accused of having crabs, he walked down Waterman Street and up to the drugstore in Angell Square, and confided his problem to the pharmacist.

The pharmacist recommended an ointment, liberal use of powder, frequent showers, careful application of the towel, and a new jock-strap. He was a compassionate man, and a realistic one: "The trouble with that stuff," he said, "is that when you get it once, you got a pretty good chance of getting it again, you know? I don't know why that is, but if I had it to do over again, I would be a dermatologist, because nothing that them guys treat, anybody ever gets over, and they don't die of it, either. So you get yourself one of those skin practices, boy, and it's like you had yourself an annuity."

It was a warm day in September of 1960 and the druggist mused for a moment, staring into the bright afternoon. "What it is," he said, "you got to get yourself ventilation. At least that's what I think it is. You got to dry yourself off, you got to make sure you get all the soap off and then you dry yourself off real good and put on the ointment until it stops itching. Then, when it goes away, make sure you use the powder. If that's what you got, of course."

He stared at Emerson penetratingly. "You're sure that's what you got, I guess."

Emerson said he was sure.

"Because if it's the other thing," the pharmacist said, "none of the stuff I'm talking about's gonna help you, see? For that you need penicillin, and I can't give you none of that—you got to see the doctor, you know?" Emerson said he knew, and that he was confident that he did not have anything that would require a prescription.

"In a way," the pharmacist said, "what I'm telling you to do'd make it worse, if it was that, because instead of taking care of it, if it was the other thing, you'd just be letting the other thing get worse."

Emerson said he realized that.

"You haven't got any pain, or any burning sensation, things like that, when you go to the bathroom, or anything?" the pharmacist said.

Emerson, unable to resist any longer, scratched furiously and said he did not. The pharmacist seemed content, and sold him eight dollars' worth of ointments, powder and jockstraps.

On the following Wednesday, Emerson received an alarming telephone call from a young lady named Evelyn, with whom he was acquainted, at Wheaton College, in Norton, Massachusetts. Evelyn reported certain disagreeable sensations attending urination, and inquired of Emerson as to whether there was some information that he had irresponsibly withheld from her during their reunion, after the summer, at the Colgate weekend. He assured her that there was not, despite a rush of rage, and the foreboding that a young lady named Donna, from Marymount College in Tarrytown, New York—she said it as though it had all been one word: MarymountCollegeinTarrytown-NewYork—had failed to be entirely candid with him, when, in August, they had agreed it would be sensible to reduce living expenses by sharing quarters in a small, unfinished house in Dennisport. But Evelyn telephoned again on Friday, her voice much more cordial than it had been forty-eight hours before, to tell him that her gynecologist had diagnosed her problem as a common yeast infection; by Saturday evening he was on much better terms with Evelyn, and feeling far less hostile toward Donna.

"There's one other thing," the pharmacist had said. "Like I say, these things're recurring things, you know? So, you wear Jockey shorts?"

Emerson said he did.

"Don't, anymore," the pharmacist said. "You got a problem like that, you're gonna have to go to the boxer shorts, and get them a little big, if you do anything. What you got to do is, you got to let the air get in there and circulate." By then Emerson was itching so badly that he would have agreed to wear nothing but a loose-fitting trench coat, if it would stop the agony, and he would carry the memory of that discomfort for the rest of his life.

Emerson, therefore, on the morning of September 28, 1976, was wearing light-green cotton boxer shorts under his glen-plaid suit. After the cast had been placed on his leg, Emerson had reviewed his wardrobe and found that he possessed only two suits cut full enough in the trouser legs to allow him to put the pants on over his cast. One of them was a brown cheviot, which was far too heavy for late September, and would have given him a heat rash on his good leg. The other was the plaid. "You're not going to the track for the afternoon," Molly said, when she saw him packing it, "you're going to a funeral.

"I know what I'm going to," Emerson had said, "and I'm sore enough as it is just about doing it. I'll be damned if I'll ruin a good suit in the bargain."

The truth was that the plaid suit was part of his fat wardrobe, which he maintained for use in the holiday season when his weight went up. He had had it made when he was about eighteen pounds heavier than he was on the day of the funeral. It was therefore very full in the seat and waist, as well as in the legs, and it allowed his genitals, unconstricted in the pale green boxer shorts, to move about freely in his clothing.

The cast came to the very top of his hip, and the inside edge of it was surprisingly rough. There had been some confusion at the Shaw house, when Libby at last was ready, at 11:15; the driver, who looked normal enough, had sprung out of the car in the commencement of a fine mist, and opened the right rear door as Emerson negotiated the two wooden steps, and then moved through the soggy ground, toward the car. Emerson had his head down, being careful where he placed the crutches. He also had the forgetfulness of the recently, and temporarily, handicapped: since he was required to be conscious of his injury whenever he was moving, he tended to assume that everyone else was conscious of it also, and of precisely what he had to do to compensate for it. On the gluey surface of the Shaws' wet yard, he looked up, astonished, when the Miller kid interrupted his concentration: "Get in here," the kid said, looking embarrassed because he did not wish to be peremptory, understood that he was not authorized to give orders, but did not know how to make sure that things were done right without seeming to give orders.

Emerson looked down again. "No," he said, because he thought it should be apparent to any fool that it was easier for him to get his body into cars on the left, and then swing his leg in.

Aware that he was being rude as well as stubborn, he worked his way around the back of the car. He came up to the left rear door and stopped. He stared across the roof of the car at the Miller kid, who remained, miserably, where he had been, holding the door as the Shaws, in old coats and hats, came out of the house. Emerson shook his head and got the door open. He braced himself with his left hand and went through the drill of putting his crutches into the back seat. Then he put all of his weight on the left leg, bent at the waist, pivoted slowly, eased his butt into the car, bent his right leg, began to turn his trunk slightly, lifted his right leg to bring it into the car, and moved just so that his scrotum slipped in between the top of the cast and his thigh. Immediately understanding that he had made a mistake, he tried to correct it, shifted his weight and position, in precisely the wrong direction, and severely pinched his scrotum inside the cast.

"*Fuck*," Emerson said.

Libby Shaw had just begun to settle herself in the back seat. The blush that flooded her face would last, in full color, until the limousine was more than halfway to the Skinner funeral home. Henry heard him also, but did not quite believe what he had heard, and thus merely stopped in mid-motion, his hand suspended in mid-air, reaching for the door handle.

Emerson, caught between sitting and standing, unable to remain in that position, and at a loss to decide which was the right way to move to stop the pain which he had caused himself, said: "God*damned* fuck. Will one of you bastards get over here and gimme a hand before I castrate myself, for the luvva Christ?"

The Miller kid by then had come around the back of the car, and stood in front of Emerson, looking at him.

"Take my left hand and pull me up," Emerson said. He endured a good deal more chafing, which he did not enjoy, as the Miller kid pulled him upright, out of the car. With his back to the Shaws, Emerson reached inside his pants and shorts, gingerly moved his left leg slightly further to the left, and extricated his scrotum from the cast. "Ahh," he said.

On his second attempt, Emerson made it into the limousine without incident. The Shaws were staring straight ahead. Oh, Jesus, Emerson thought. The car was well out of the muddy yard before he decided that his display had been fully warranted by the occasion, and therefore determined to allow the Shaws to be as stupefied as they wished. Absently, Emerson began to whistle "Another opening, another show." He had gotten as far as the part which goes with the words, "In Philly, Boston, and Baltimo'" when he caught the Miller kid watching him in the rearview mirror.

"Look," Emerson said, "this road's got curves in it, and I've seen cows crossing it from time to time." The road swung down through the foothills of Fairfax, toward the town, greasy and, he supposed, slippery in the light mist. "Watch it, not me, okay?"

Emerson had never had good luck in limousines. Along with accordions, their appearance at any occasion put him on guard, convinced that something disagreeable would certainly occur before he escaped. He had been delighted to discover that Molly shared his view that certain people had been best advised to avoid certain inanimate objects. She had never been subjected to an evening's entertainment featuring a fat kid who played "Lady of Spain" for a full fifteen minutes on the accordion in a hot Legion hall, as Emerson bad been when his sales manager chose for a second wife an impressively vacuous twenty-year-old girl with long blonde hair and big blue eyes from Polish family in Broclton—"I can explain it easily enough," he said to Molly. "All you need to do is look at that body, and you've got the explanation. But Jesus Christ, all you've got to do is look at her mother and her father, and you can see the Pats'll be drafting her in the third round in a year or so. She'll look just like her stock, and they look just like blocking backs."—but Molly had had similar experiences with silver-plated punchbowls, and Polaroid cameras.

Those experiences she had suffered at the hands of patients grateful for her services as a psychiatrist. She was affiliated with the Peter Bent Brigham Hospital, but she conducted most of her practice from her office in Newton, specializing in the treatment of troubled adolescents. Many of them were junkies, A good many of them came to her because a District court judge had seen enough of them on previous occasions, and had decided to see if counseling might possibly achieve a civilizing effect theretofore denied the best efforts of parents— "which are usually pretty halfhearted, when they weren't downright stupid," Molly said. "It's no wonder the kids aren't housebroken, considering the damned fool way they were raised."—police, and probation officers.

Now and then, by the implementation of some brilliant insight that a kid from a wealthy family in Brookline was stealing Corvettes in understandable vengefulness toward a father who ignored him, or a mother who disliked him, she met with success which startled pretty matrons and prosperous orthodontists, who had begun to fear their weekend golf and tennis would be regularly interrupted by the obligation to visit their offspring in the Massachusetts Correctional Institution at Concord.

It was an indication of her devotion to medical ethics, and her dedication to the welfare of her patients above even her own, that Molly persisted in committing such successes whenever she could. "Because, when you do," Molly said, "the bastards always try to get even."

Frequently the bastards invited her to parties. "You get a whole lot of advice, not to do that," she said, "and the people who give it to you are right. But the only friends I had, when I got here, were in Chicago and New York, and other places that are a hell of a long goddamned weekend commute. Especially when you're on call on the weekend." Molly had graduated from Johns Hopkins, and from the University of Chicago Medical School. "All I ever saw was nurses, and doctors, and other crazy people. So if somebody invited me, and I thought there was the remotest chance I might run into a geologist, maybe, or a reporter or a construction engineer, *something*, I'd go.

"That was a mistake," she said. "In the first place, I thought they were asking me because they liked me. Shows you why shrinks need experience before they get turned loose upon mankind—we don't know anything, any more than anybody else does. Those parents looked at me and saw someone who'd done something in a little while they hadn't been able to manage in a good many years, and it really pissed them off. What they wanted to do was pull me down to their level.

"They didn't think of it that way," she said. "Probably they thought they were pulling me up out of the gutter, giving me a little class and polish, that sort of thing. Introducing me around like some prize pig,"—which in fact, Emerson had informed her, might be just a coarse way of saying that she was very special and extremely good in bed; "Oh, shut up," she said—"to all their blazing asshole friends, and being smug about it.

"Now that I've got some sense," she said, "I should've seen the tip-off was the silver-plated punchbowls. The ones that look like great big flowers, with those ladles which force you to spill at least as much of that terrible red punch as you get into those wretched little glass cups with the handles that are too small for your index finger, but just big enough to stop from just holding the glass in your hand. And the red stuff that you spilled is on the side of the glass, after some of it's dripped down on your clothes, of course, so your hand gets all sticky. You stand there under the damned tent—they always have yellow and white stripes—in the blazing hot sun, and your feet sink into the ground because it always rained two days before, and they always have the party on the part of the lawn where the run-off settles in, and you talk to some jerk who manipulates the securities market, or pretends he does, at least, and thinks he'd like to settle down some day, 'find a woman to take care of me.' Jesus."

Molly's first husband was Jonathan "Tinker" Mallory, of the Chevy Chase Mallory family. "As opposed," she said, "to the Long Island Mallorys, the Tiburon Mallorys, the Palm Beach Mallorys and the Oyster Bay Mallorys. Boy, has that family deteriorated since whoever that first Mallory was, who ran around the country, coast to coast, knocking up women." Tinker Mallory alternated between the management of the family businesses—South American petroleum development; apartment complex construction; purchase of distressed cargoes of commodities; "a whole mess of other scuff he didn't bother to tell me about, because, he told me, I wouldn't understand it"—and advisory positions with Republican administrations. He dressed well, drove a Mercedes 450SLC, kept in shape with paddle tennis, socialized with current movie stars and people who owned franchises in the major leagues, skied at Sundance and fished off Cozumel.

After Craig and Molly had started fooling around, they met Tinker one evening at the Cafe Budapest in Boston. His party included a former ambassador from Argentina; Tinker was with a woman who had just won a quarter-final match from Rosemary Casals at Longwood, before losing to Evonne Goolagong in the semi-finals. After they had gone to different tables, Molly said to Craig, *sotto voce*, looking at the woman: "You get one more chance, Honey, and you better make the most of it. Lose at Forest Lawn, and you won't see Tink again."

Molly said she had gotten up one morning and gone into her bathroom in the house in Palm Springs, and started to think. "I turned on the gold fixture that made the hot water come out of the swan's mouth," she said. "I put my hands on the black marble vanity and I looked in the mirror. Face fine, no wrinkles, boobs pretty firm, no noticeable stretch marks; I decided I was taking pretty good care of myself. 'So,' I thought, 'brains enough to practice medicine, don't look like Ma Barker yet, how come you married an asshole? Is it because you're an asshole yourself?'

"Then," she said, "I went out to the Bolton, and I fiddled with it until I was pretty sure I had the speakers on in the bedroom, and I put on 'You're So Vain,' and hit the volume switch and ran back in there.

"Waking Tink up," she said, "is like having root canals—it takes a long time, and there isn't any discernible progress. But he made it, and he sat up in bed. 'What's going on?' he said.

"'I like music while I'm packing,' I said," Molly said. "I never went back."

That night in the Budapest, Tinker was cordial. "What's your line, Craig?" he said.

"He's a car salesman," Molly said, before Emerson could answer.

"What kind?" Tinker said.

"Second-hand," she said. "Craig's very big in secondhand stuff with low-mileage on it."

"I don't know," Emerson had said, after they sat down. "I'm not sure but that I haven't been a little more flattered by some of the other ways I've heard my business described."

"Nope," Molly said, "wouldn't do any good at all. Tink's never heard of Juan Manuel Fangio, or Mike Hawthorne, the Marquis de Portago, any of them,"

Fairfax village consisted of a cinder-block milk-processing plant, its parking lot crowded with stainless-steel tank trucks silver in the grey mist; a general store painted ivory; one gas station; one white church that was Protestant, and one low, cinder-block building that was more or less flesh-colored, and served as a Roman Catholic Church. There were three white houses, and the two-story, white, wooden-frame building with a gravel drive and a black sign that said in white: *Skinner*, *Mortician*, and in smaller print: *Notary Public*. Surreptitiously, as the Miller kid brought the car up to the open porch where Skinner stood, Emerson put his left hand in his pocket and tried to adjust his shorts so as to create a little pouch that would prevent another injury.

"Of course," Molly had said reflectively one night, "you're not exactly right off the assembly line yourself."

"Just broken in," he had said. "Not broken down."

"We'll see," she said.

The undertaker, Rufus Skinner, was much more robust than Emerson had expected. He was in his early thirties, a large, peaceful-looking fellow with fairly long black hair, and he was big in the chest. About two or three inches over six feet, somewhere over two hundred pounds, he wore a well-tailored black suit, and stood carefully away from the white four-by-eights that flanked the steps of the funeral home, and supported the roof of the open porch.

The Shaws, without having said anything since entering the car, got out as quickly as they could, and went hurriedly into the home. Emerson rearranged his clothing after he had emerged from the car, somewhat regretful that he had unnerved them, but mostly resigned to the fact that he had in common with them nothing but a dead Senator and a dead woman to discuss.

Skinner misunderstood. He came down the three steps and approached Emerson. "I'm sorry," he said, "you must be Mr. Emerson." Emerson nodded. "Can I give you a hand?" Skinner said.

"With the steps, maybe," Emerson said. "I broke my god-damned Achilles tendon, pretending I was eighteen years old again, and it's like to drive me out of my goddamned mind."

Skinner nodded, guiding Emerson by the left elbow. "I know," he said. "Broke my ankle on a boot-top spiral fracture down at Mad River last winter. I was in a cast for nine weeks, and I almost went crazy."

"I can imagine," Emerson said. They had reached the steps.

"Could not understand it," Skinner said. "I've been in Cervinia. Down to Bromley. Innsbruck. Three years ago we went to the Andes. Never so much as turned an ankle, let alone break anything. But they had a little ice that day at Mad River, and they got it without telling anybody. Lord did that hurt. You want to hand me the crutches and lean on me?"

That seemed like a good idea. Emerson negotiated the steps on Skinner.

"Funny thing is," Skinner said, "it'd never really crossed my mind, what a hell of a thing it'd be, in this business, if you couldn't stand for very long. My father used to worry when I was on the ski team at Middlebury. I never gave it a second thought. Sure, I could get hurt. But I'd heal, I'd mend, right? Right. Trouble is, I never did get hurt, until I was the fellow that ran the business."

They were on the porch now. Emerson accepted the crutches from Skinner, and got them under his arms.

"It was just a good thing for me," Skinner said, "that I made Terry learn to fly, too, and get her embalming license." He opened the door. Emerson glanced up at him. "My wife," Skinner said. "Maybe you heard of her. Terry Kaplan?"

Emerson, confused and busy, confessed that he had not. The fibre welcome mat at the door occupied his attention. It looked like a treacherous inanimate object to him, and he hesitated to put the crutch tips on it.

"The U.S. ski team, nineteen-sixty-four," Skinner said.

"I didn't follow it," Emerson said.

"Lot of people didn't," Skinner said. He opened the door. "Funny business," Skinner said, as Emerson crabbed his way into the funeral parlor, glad to see that the maroon carpeting in the hallway was nailed down.

"Very funny," Emerson said.

"Unless you know about it," Skinner said, ignoring him, "you never stop to think about it. But you are literally on your feet all the time."

To Emerson's right there was a parlor. In the parlor there were perhaps six or seven people. They were sitting on folding chairs. Emerson recognized the oak casket. He started to pivot on the right crutch.

Skinner took his left arm again. "Not right away," he said. "Let's go down to my office." He guided Emerson down the hallway, past the dark maple banister rising along the narrow stairs to the second floor, under the wrought-iron chandelier, to the stained oak door on the left. Skinner opened the door, stood aside, and waited for Emerson to move inside.

The office was small. It had the same maroon carpeting, a small grey steel desk, a four-drawer, grey steel file cabinet, a maroon vinyl chair, a calendar which gave the month, and the message: ". . . *Service*, in time of *Need*."

Skinner sat down in the grey steel chair behind the desk. He put his hands on the arms, and tilted back. "I don't know what you want," he said.

"Well," Emerson said, "you came to the right fellow. I can tell you, exactly."

Skinner leaned forward. He put his elbows on the desk and grinned. "Understanding, of course," he said, "that I may have some suggestions of my own."

"Understanding too," Emerson said, "that I may be in a mood to reject your suggestions."

"You made," Skinner said, "a big mistake in the Can-Am Series."

"Now look," Emerson said.

"You did," Skinner said. "All you had to do was hang in there. They would've let the RSR Carrera compete, if you'd played your cards a little differently. Monzas and Firebirds, for Christ sake. Shit."

"They ended up doing it anyway," Emerson said.

"After you pulled your team out," Skinner said.

"Factory orders," Emerson said.

"Afraid of BMW?" Skinner said.

"Bee Em Vey," Emerson said. "No, I drive one myself, as a matter of fact. Nice car. Factory orders."

"Same question," Skinner said.

"Same answer," Emerson said.

Skinner laughed. "Okay," he said, "here's the next thing: the boys in Boston did a lousy job."

"Now I *don't* understand," Emerson said.

"Flynn and Flynn?" Skinner said.

"Oh," Emerson said.

"Were you very close to her?" Skinner said.

"Several times," Emerson said. "A hell of a lot closer'n I wanted to be, at least."

"I can speak frankly, then," Skinner said.

"I plan to," Emerson said.

"All right," Skinner said. "They really did a lousy job. She looks, you should pardon the expression, like death warmed over, and not very well, either."

"She didn't look that hot when she was alive," Emerson said. "Not when she was mad, anyway. Which was most of the time. At somebody. She had this awful way of grimacing."

"She's still got it, but this is a little more serious," Skinner said. "I can shoo everybody out of there, and let you have a look, if you want."

"I'll take your word for it," Emerson said, shrugging.

"It's not that simple," Skinner said. "Not up here, anyway. There has to be some explanation."

"For what?" Emerson said. "There's a box in there. Looks to me like the same box I bought from Flynn and Flynn. Is there a body in it?"

"Certainly is," Skinner said.

"Is it, did it used to be, Jenny Irwin?" Emerson said.

"Near as I can tell," Skinner said. "I didn't know her very well, which brings up a problem with the minister that I'll get to, in a minute, but as near as I can tell, yeah."

"I'll take them in sequence," Emerson said. "One problem at a time. You got any booze?"

Skinner reached down with his left hand. He opened the bottom drawer of the desk and brought out a bottle of Old Forester. He reached in again and produced a stack of small plastic glasses. "This is going to be Problem Number Three," he said.

"Still in sequence," Emerson said. "Just pour me a reasonable one."

"We've got some kind of a custom here," Skinner said, "that my father explained to me several times, and I never really understood that well myself." He finished pouring, and shoved the glass across the desk. Emerson accepted it. "Sorry there's no water or ice," Skinner said.

"God'll punish you," Emerson said, drinking.

"The idea is that the close friends and relatives come to the home, and the casket is open, and they view it. The body. Then the casket is closed, and we go to the church, and then to the cemetery."

Emerson put the glass down. "Seems fair to me."

"Not to me," Skinner said. "Understand, now, that I don't give a shit. Twenty minutes after you leave, everybody around here'll know that embalming job wasn't my work. It won't do my business any harm. Shit, I did better work when I was crippled and had to hurry the job."

Emerson said nothing.

"It's really a wipe-out, no-good, shit job," Skinner said.

"That bad," Emerson said.

"Yup," Skinner said. "She really looks like hell."

"Tell me something," Emerson said. "In the normal course of things, all right? You guys embalm before you sell the casket, or afterwards?"

"Depends," Skinner said.

"Uh huh," Emerson said.

"What does that mean?" Skinner said.

Emerson shrugged. "Means: Uh huh."

"Okay," Skinner said. He looked at his watch. "We've got to hurry, here. Due at the church at noon."

"What happens at twelve-thirty?" Emerson said. "The President coming in for a speech or something?"

"Look," Skinner said, "I have to work here, okay?"

"Okay," Emerson said.

"Now," Skinner said, "this is my recommendation: I go in there, and thank everyone for coming."

"Shouldn't take very long," Emerson said, drinking again.

"She was old," Skinner said, unperturbed. "Then I'll hustle them all out, and we'll take her to the church."

"Fine," Emerson said. He finished his drink.

"Problem Number Two," Skinner said.

"Go," Emerson said.

"The pastor is a callow youth named Scott," Skinner said. "From Jenny Irwin, he knew not at all."

"A fortunate man," Emerson said.

"He doesn't know that," Skinner said. "And I couldn't do much to enlighten him."

"I could," Emerson said. "Christian charity forbids it, or I would."

"That probably resolves the second problem," Skinner said. "You'd just like him to run through the regular service, and some platitudes about how wonderful the deceased was?"

Emerson said: "Might as well."

"Neighbors aren't really going to like it," Skinner said.

"The fuck do I care?" Emerson said.

"Look," Skinner said, leaning forward, "you're leaving here."

"Without question," Emerson said.

"We're not," Skinner said.

"Again," Emerson, "without question."

"What matters to you," Skinner said, "doesn't matter to us."

"If I didn't know that was true," Emerson said, "I'd take it on faith."

"And *vice versa*," Skinner said.

"Us?" Emerson said.

"Them," Skinner said, nodding his head toward the parlor.

"Um," Emerson said.

"Do you suppose," Skinner said, "you could give me a few little things that you liked about her, so the Reverend Mr. Scott wouldn't have to be faced with explaining to her friends, for the next two years, why he was such a rotten son of a bitch to Jenny Irwin, at her funeral? He really is a kid. That'll be hard for him to do, and he won't do it very well."

"I see," Emerson said.

"That's encouraging," Skinner said, "since you don't even live here."

"She made good doughnuts," Emerson said. "That's a lie, but I won't stand up and holler, if he says it."

"Let's try a little harder for some truth, that's good," Skinner said. "There's liable to be somebody in the congregation who had one or two of her doughnuts. We don't want any muffled laughter, particularly since the casket's going to stay closed."

"I'll have to think," Emerson said.

"That might not do you any harm," Skinner said, and Emerson began to laugh.

Forced by the lack of headroom in the cellar to work from a stooping position, Craig, that day in 1963, had labored to lift the top trunks from the ones below, to put them on the floor where they could be opened.

"My God," Lenore said. "How the hell did those things get up on those blocks?"

Grunting, Craig set the first trunk down. Then he knelt on the floor, to straighten his back. The dirt was dry under his Levi's. "Well," he said, "she's got a sometime-handyman. Wiry old bastard named Felix. Spends most of his time riding around the state on an old black bicycle, passing out Bible texts. Calls it his preaching, but he doesn't really preach—just gives the stuff to people and tells them that the Lord is coming. When he runs out of money, he comes back here, and she gives him enough work to keep him busy. He could've done it."

To Skinner, thirteen years later, Emerson said: "But I never knew his last name, I don't think. If she ever mentioned it, I've forgotten it. She let him sleep in the barn, and she gave him enough money for what he did, to get by on. He had some kind of a little pension, I guess, and that was the way he lived, doing painting and fixing-up, pruning the bushes, picking berries. He must be dead now, I should think. He was older than she was. But I don't know where he came from, and I don't know where he went to, and what he did in the winter. I never asked and she never told me. But it was still generosity on her part, to give him what she did."

"For working for her?" Skinner said.

"She didn't have much herself," Emerson said. "She wasn't indigent, by any means, but she was very far from being well-off. And as for the work, the work that he did, at least, well, it wasn't that heavy and there wasn't that much of it. She could have done most of it herself, and probably would've, if he hadn't shown up when he did. She was a very strong woman."

To Lenore he had continued: "But I doubt she had Felix store them—she doesn't like people messing around with her things."

"Is she going to be mad at us, for doing it?" Lenore said.

"Probably," Emerson said, "but there's no net loss in that, because she'll be mad at us for something, no matter what we do. Might as well be something that's at least interesting."

The first trunk contained linens: sheets made of coarse, ivory cloth that had been worn down to an uneven roughness.

"Now what the hell do you suppose she's saving those for?" Lenore said.

"She makes curtains out of them," Emerson said. "The curtains in the bedrooms upstairs are all made of this stuff. I was here one summer, visiting, when she made the ones that're up there now. I must've been about nine, ten, I don't know. It was the summer that my little sister . . . there was a polio epidemic that year, and it got Linda. My father was really broken up over it, and my mother told him I had to come up here so that the damned thing wouldn't get me, too. But I think it was really to get me out of her hair, so she could concentrate on him, and pull him through it.

"Jenny spent the better part of a week making those curtains," he said, "and I just sat there and watched. There really wasn't much of anything for me to do, except go across the street to get drinking water from the Coopers' well, and Jenny really didn't have much notion of how to entertain a kid. So I sat there and watched her cut up sheets and make them into curtains. These sheets came with her from Scotland."

To Skinner, in the office at the funeral home, Emerson said: "she was a very careful woman, too."

Skinner laughed. "If that's supposed to mean *stingy*, we all are, at least when you foreigners are looking on. Everyone'd be broken-hearted if a Vermonter got caught picking up a check. Have to live up to your expectations, you know."

"Yeah," Emerson said, "but wouldn't that please them, that she did it?"

"I suppose so," Skinner said.

"I don't think she ever had much opportunity to waste anything," Emerson said. "But if she ever saw one, and took advantage of it, I wasn't around to watch. When she moved in with us, down in Boston—we all pretended she was just waiting out the winter a little longer, and we all knew damned right well that what she was really doing was waiting out death a little longer—she almost drove us nuts with it, conserving things.

"My wife and I are kind of casual about a lot of things that used to matter more when Jenny was young, I guess," Emerson said. "Our habits annoyed her. When things started to click for Molly and me, we got ourselves a townhouse on the Hill and tore the guts out of it. Molly's kids are away at school most of the time. Nine rooms for the two of us: Jenny thought it was scandalous.

"Molly has early patients—at least three mornings a week she'll be out of the house by six-thirty—and I have late customers and conferences, so most nights I don't get home much before nine-thirty, ten o'clock. That left Jenny rattling around all day with no company except for the maid, who's Jamaican, black, and, I think, crazy. I swear she's practicing voodoo or something, when she shuts the door to her room.

"Now Jenny, first of all, didn't mind being alone very much, I guess," he said. "Whenever I came up to stay with her, she seemed kind of uncomfortable, having somebody else in the house. She'd lived alone for, what, close to twenty years or so.

"But she'd lived alone in *her* house," Emerson said, "and that was different. It was her dining room table, and it was made of honest oak, not chrome and glass. It was her kitchen, and her black stove, and if there wasn't enough hot water to take an honest shower, let alone a bath—and there wasn't, because when she had the electric hot water heater installed, she got the smallest one she could because it had to stand in the kitchen, next to the stove—it was her bathtub that didn't have enough hot water in it. The draughts that forced you to wear a sweater unless you sat right next to the living room stove in the early part of October, those were her draughts, and she wore her sweater.

"At our place," Emerson said, "well, first of all, there was that company I mentioned, the maid. Jenny thoroughly disapproved of paying somebody to do *housework*, to clean up after you, and wash your-socks. She also disapproved of Melinda personally, on the grounds of her color. She called the woman a *nigger* several times, and Melinda heard her at least twice. It cost me a five buck raise to get her to stay, to keep Melinda, because even though she's crazy, she's very industrious. She stays out of the way. She does her job and she doesn't steal, and we wanted to keep her. Now I don't know as the Reverend Mr. Scott would want to mention that the dear departed could easily have passed muster in the Ku Klux Klan, but Jenny *was* a bigot, a genuine, unreconstructed racist."

"Well," Skinner said, "I don't really know. Yes, Scott would be horrified, you're right about that. But some of the congregation might feel that was a point in her favor, actually. They don't want blacks up here, you know. The Underground Railway was one thing, because they just kept right on going, passing through on the way to Canada. But there's no determined campaign to recruit them to settle in these parts."

"That's too bad," Emerson said. "I could give you the names of several notables in Boston who'd be happy to assist you, if you were scouting around.

"But that was just part of it, too, that saving business. Jenny used to ask us why we didn't think it necessary to sit down to a meal together, at home. Well, part of the reason was that we didn't want to. Molly never has time for more than coffee in the morning, and one of the first acts of self-discipline that I ever committed was to start to get a handle on my weight problem by cutting out breakfasts. There isn't any lunch for us unless it's business, because we're both busy. Molly usually grabs something from the freezer when she gets home, tosses it to Melinda, dashes upstairs to change, and comes back down before the microwave can finish cooking it, so she can eat before she goes out to a meeting. If I haven't stopped for a beer and a cheeseburger with some of the guys, I do the same thing when I get home.

"Then Molly and I sit there and watch the late news, and if there's a good movie on, we watch that, or else she reads something that interests her and I get on the telephone if we've got a race coming up that weekend. Neither one of us needs a hell of a lot of sleep, so we don't make time for it, and that annoyed Jenny, too. 'Staying up half the night, the way you folks do, I shouldn't wonder,' she'd say to Molly: 'I should think you'd want to stay home and take care of your house sometimes, instead of being out gadding around all the time.'

"Now Molly," Emerson said, "is probably one of the best children's psychiatrists in the country. She's Board Certified; she's a Fellow of this and a Director of that; she's on the faculty at Harvard and BU both; and she delivers at least one paper each year. I mean, Molly White Mallory has an international reputation, every bit of which she has earned. In addition to which, she's got a good back hand, a mean forehand, and a serve that hooks away from you when it hits, but it doesn't really matter because she hits the thing so hard there's no fur left on it when it comes up anyway. We play two nights a week, and she usually beats me.

"I met Molly," Emerson said, "when I had my team down at Watkins Glen, and she was running her Nine-Eleven in an auto-cross. She's got her license from the Sports Car Club of America, and she drove a couple times for Bob Tullius' Triumph group. She took up sailing when I started seeing her," Emerson said. "Now guess who's completed the Advanced Navigation course with the U.S. Power Squadron—which she calls a lot of hard names because they won't let women join as full members—and who hasn't.

"Now," Emerson said, "Jenny was a formidable woman, no question about it. She maybe didn't terrorize my mother, but that was only because my mother had a lot of experience with her tricks, and was willing to use every ounce of energy she had, in stopping them from working. But when she started trying to get Molly out of her Porsche and into embroidery, she took on more than any human being could manage."

"They didn't get along," Skinner said.

"You could say that," Emerson said.

"My own mother," Skinner said, "thought it was a great idea when Terry soloed. Ma's always worried about me taking a heart attack in

the plane, and it made her feel much better. But Terry's *father* was fit
to be tied."

"Well, Jenny didn't stop trying," Emerson said, "and Molly, naturally, showed no signs of surrendering. So for the past four winters,
and a good part of this summer—whenever we were at home—I
kept my head down while they used siege guns on each other. It was
no fun, I can tell you."

When Craig and Lenore opened the second trunk and shone the
flashlight into it, they found books. There were several copies of the
New Testament, and a full dozen of the Old. There was a full set of
the Waverly novels.

To Skinner, Emerson said: "She wasn't an educated woman. She
wasn't a cultivated one. Which. . . ."

". . . isn't surprising," Skinner said. "Terry says the Commanche,
and the airport at White Plains, are the only things that keep her sane.
We've had some pretty hairy trips in weather that should've kept us
on the ground, just because I figured it'd be even hairier *on* the ground
if I didn't get that lady out of this town and into Manhattan for a
weekend."

"But it is surprising," Emerson said. "She never said much about
her people in Scotland, but some of them must have done some reading. I never saw her read anything but the newspaper, no matter how
much time she had on her hands, and then the only one she really paid
attention to was the *Burlington Free Press*.

"She didn't have a sense of humor," Emerson said, reflecting. "I
don't really think the woman ever really had any fun in her whole life,
ever really enjoyed anything." Then he remembered the third trunk.
When he and Lenore had opened it, in 1963, they had found it filled
with wooden toys: small horses; small dolls, made of wood and
dressed in gingham; a set of wooden fish in graduated sizes; and a
small wooden Locomotive with a tender and three cars.

"Look at that," Lenore had said. "Were those yours?"

"I've never seen them before," Craig had said. He mentioned them,
later, to his mother, and she had never seen them either.

"Maybe," he said to Skinner on the day of Jenny's funeral, "may
be she did have fun once, as a child. I really don't know."

Craig and Lenore never opened the fourth trunk, in the fall of:
1963; Jenny had called to them from the top of the stairs, while they
were still inspecting the toys. "I've got fresh custard pie." she said,
"right from the refrigerator."

"For God's sake," Lenore had said, "we just had lunch. What the hell's she feeding us for now?"

"To get us out of her cellar," Craig had said. "She suspects we're taking pleasure in something."

"Well," Skinner said, when Emerson had finished, "I guess Scott'll have to do the best he can, with what there is."

Nelson Tanner, with the face of a fifty-year-old ferret and a compact body to match, sat without moving in his dark blue suit, alone in the front row of folding chairs before the casket. Before Emerson even thought to notice the other ten mourners, scattered among the other two rows of chairs, he remembered Tanner's dogs.

Nelson owned the property at the top of the hill. His pastures abutted Jenny's, surrounded them, really, because he had steadily increased the farm he had inherited from his father.

When he was small, Craig had often gone down the road two hundred yards or so from Jenny's house, to knock on the door of Marlow Spence's place and see if Marlow might have time to play. Marlow was about sixty, then. He drove the school bus, which he kept in his barn, and used in the summer for his private transportation, a practice which was perfectly acceptable to the school department because Marlow owned the bus. It also suited Marlow, because he could not otherwise have afforded motorized transportation for himself and Mildred, without going to work, and the county decision to pave most of the roads had made his horses, Sam and Bill, footsore. The horses, which themselves were pretty old, stayed in their stalls in the barn with the bus until Marlow released them in the early morning, disturbing the barn swallows who slept beneath the eaves of the brown-shingled building, to graze in the mist that remained over the grass, to drink from the wide place in the brook that divided the pasture, and to whicker in the fields of praise. They were dapple-grey geldings, and Marlow spoke with fondness of the sight they had made, pulling him and Mildred in the two-wheeled carriage with red seats, by then covered with a tarpaulin, and stored out of the way of the bus at the rear of the barn. "Durin' the war," Marlow said, "Sam and Bill was considerable better than a car. Couldn't get any gas."

Jenny had spoken with feeling about Marlow. She believed that something had happened to Marlow, when he had his heart attack while still in his early forties. "Gave him an excuse," she said. "All he ever did was sit around and drink anyway. And fish."

When Craig had first met Marlow, Marlow still had his oxen, Buddy and Joe. They were great, grey, stupid-looking animals, and Marlow kept them in a pit that was ten feet deep, and had a fence around it, because they were also very mean, and had enormous horns with which to do something about it. "They were better when they were working," Marlow said.

He had used the oxen, before and during the war, the same way that he used the school bus when Craig came to know him: he rented himself, and Buddy and Joe, to farmers who had land under cultivation, and could not afford to buy tractors for plowing. "I was better when I was working, too," Marlow said, "but I didn't start off as mean as they did."

Marlow was a thoughtful sort, who assumed that anyone whom he addressed was as thoughtful, and as experienced, as he. "Of course," he said, "when I was a young bull, nobody came around and cut my balls off. I suppose that might have something to do with it."

"Marlow's sense of security was false," Craig told Lenore, the morning in 1963 when, after easing the green Jaguar out of Jenny's yard, they had started down the road, back toward what Lenore called civilization. "About four or five years ago, Mildred finally got up in the middle of the night, and caught him in the bathroom, pissing blood. First it was the prostate. Then it was the colon. Then it was his testicles, and finally it was Marlow. Though, knowing him, I'd have to guess that Marlow pretty much lost interest in the proceedings, after the nuts got cut off."

"It was really ironic," Craig said, "that Marlow and the Reverend went the same way. The same thing, at least. That was probably the only thing they ever agreed on."

Marlow was a Freethinker; at least he described himself as one. "The whole of the wickedness in this world," he said one day when they were fishing Lake Champlain, "the whole of it, is because of the priests."

Craig had just received the Sacrament of Confirmation. He had spent several months of Wednesdays, memorizing books that showed empty milk bottles, which were souls without Sanctifying Grace, and full milk bottles, which were souls that were filled with Sanctifying Grace, in order that an auxiliary bishop, having arranged to have a large group of prepubescents attired in red robes with white collars and herded before him by nuns, might push the replay button and get the answers he desired before anointing them with certain oils, and softly slapping them across the face. Craig had received a Brownie Hawkeye camera from his parents, for that accomplishment, and he cherished it because it had enabled him to take a very good picture of his dog.

It made him uncomfortable to listen to Marlow, in the middle of a green rowboat on Lake Champlain, without rising in Defense of the Faith, because he understood that Confirmation had made him one of Its Soldiers, and he was apprehensive that malingering might, if discovered, constitute grounds for forfeiture of the Hawkeye.

He was also unnerved when Marlow, on such fishing trips, announced that it was "time to make water," and, fishing an old coffee can out of the bilge, stood up and urinated carefully into it. Then he emptied it over the side. Craig always returned from such excursions with a bladder strained to the point of explosion. He did not know what to make of being required to watch another male voiding his urine; he was equally perplexed by Marlow's practice of using the can instead of delivering the product directly to the water; and he knew if he sought out any advice from anyone that he might find at Jenny's house, he would not be allowed to go on any more excursions with Marlow.

The barn, the bus, the horses and the house, low and grey-shingled, were all gone in 1963, when Craig drove Lenore past the old Spence property on the way to Montreal. "Nelson Tanner bought the place when Marlow died," Craig said. "Tore down the buildings, filled in the oxen pit, put his herd out to graze there."

"Nelson's got me cornered now," Jenny said, when Mildred capitulated to the nursing home's demands that she sell her property, to pay for her care, "it'll be just a matter of time before he gets this piece, and then he'll have all the land on this side of the road. I know what he's after. Well, he'll just have to wait."

"Nelson Tanner's got three dogs," Craig had told Lenore that sunny morning as the XKE, apparently in a good mood, rumbled along, the chains of the double overhead cams singing faintly under the long, graceful hood, "three beagles. Purebred, I'm sure. Nelson looks like a farmer, until you look real close, and then you realize that Nelson's an entrepreneur, dressed up like a farmer. He does it pretty well. It's a good disguise, good enough to fool a visitor, almost good enough to fool me, but nowhere near good enough to mislead a real farmer.

"The dogs help to give it away," Craig had said. "I always thought a beagle was a fairly companionable sort of dog, chase a rabbit now and then, but otherwise wag its tail and come around to have its ears scratched. Not Nelson's beagles. Nelson's beagles are downright calculating. They remind me of Siamese cats. When he stops to talk to you, they're always with him, two beagles sit next to his right leg, and one beagle sits next to his left leg, and they *study* you. Cock their heads, peer at you, sizing you up, all the time.

"The next thing you notice," Craig said, "is that Nelson's doing the same thing. The dogs must've learned it from him. He doesn't talk much. He's like a Boston pol: he won't write a letter if it's something he can say; he won't say anything if he can whisper; he won't whisper if he can get by with nodding; and you've got to be offering something that he really wants, before you can got him to do that."

"Nelson *will* wait, of course," Jenny said. "He's very patient, and he knows he's young enough to get the better of me. Then, some day, he'll get this property. He'll probably be the only one that wants it, since he owns every thing around it, and he won't sell, and it's not enough, by itself, to keep a herd big enough to make any money, so he'll get it. He's all but got it, right now. He's got the haying, and he needs hay anyway. He'll probably leave it in hay, after he gets it, for the winter silage. When he tears the house down, and the garage and the barn, he'll get even more hay."

"Maybe she'll outlast him," Lenore had said, that day. "Now that I've seen her, maybe she's right, and she's eternal after all."

"I don't think so," Craig said. "If she's not eternal, anymore, she's still infallible. If she says Nelson'll get the better of her, the question's not whether, but when.

"Nelson is shrewd," Craig said. "Jenny recognizes shrewdness. She never had much to be shrewd about, so it never attracted any worldwide attention that she was so good at it. Now, if she'd been Howard Hughes, or John Paul Getty, then she'd have a reputation that Barnum would've envied, because nobody ever bamboozled Jenny Irwin, I don't think. But since she didn't have very much, it went unnoticed.

"That still doesn't change it. If Jenny thinks she's got old Nelson pegged as a scrofulous Shylock," Emerson said, "he is probably a scrofulous Shylock. Jenny can be difficult, but she's very seldom wrong.

"It's a funny thing," Emerson had mused, as the Jaguar ate up the road, "the way things work. I liked old Marlow. He took me fishing at Huntington Gorge, and he showed me how to kill a northern pike, so the bastard wouldn't bite you when you got him in the boat. Marlow took the back five rows of seats out of his bus every summer, when school ended, and we'd hoist the boat in there, and go fishing. He was full of shit, of course, blaming the churches for every calamity that ever happened, from the Gold Rush forward to Pearl Harbor, and back to the Black Plague, but he was somehow *nice* about it. He wasn't haranguing you. He was just telling you some things that he'd noticed, that weren't generally known, because he thought you might be interested. It might help you to know them. And if you weren't interested, well, that was all right. It wouldn't bother him. He was just as ready to talk to a kid as he was to an adult—Mildred, I suppose, had already been completely filled in on all the terrible things that Cardinals and Archbishops were trying to do, so there was no point talking to her anymore—and we'd go wading into Big Otter River and fish for brown trout while he went on.

"Also the Jews," Craig said. "Marlow was also very suspicious of the Jews. He thought they wanted all the money, and had most of it, and they were going to buy up all the land with it as soon as they got it, and throw everybody else out.

"That one," Craig said, "I discussed with Jenny. A couple of kids that I played basket ball with, in school, were Jews, and I certainly didn't want to stay friends with them if they were going to drive my grandmother out. So I asked Jenny about the Jews, and she started talking about Nelson Tanner."

The wrong ones die, Emerson thought, as he moved slowly into the room where the casket was. The mourners, for some reason, stood up. He was puzzled for a moment, until he remembered that they expected to have a final there-but-for-the-grace-of-God look at Jenny. He felt a surge of protectiveness toward her, which rather startled him, and a sense of satisfaction that he had, with Skinner's help, deprived them of their mean sport.

Skinner came into the room behind Emerson, and eased past him. "You folks can sit down," Skinner said. Emerson remained on the crutches. The people looked at him expectantly. All of them, including Skinner, seemed to want, him to do something.

"Oh," Emerson said, catching on, "I, uh, I'm not going to sit down. Those chairs, these things, it'd be too difficult for me to manage. Easier for me to stay the way I am."

"Certainly," Skinner said. He rubbed his hands together. "Uh, Folks," he said, "ah, well, Mr. Emerson and I have discussed this, and we think, under the circumstances and all, knowing that you folks are Jenny's oldest friends, that, well, it would be better if you were to go on remembering her the way she was when you last saw her. Alive," Skinner said. "She had," he said, looking at Emerson for confirmation, "she had a rather rough time of it. Lost a good deal of weight, that kind of thing. And we've decided, while we understand that you came here to pay your final respects before we go to the church and the cemetery, that she probably wouldn't, that she would want it this way, too.

"We're sure you understand."

The mourners continued to sit.

"All right." Skinner said, briskly, "now, if you'll just go out to your cars, if you want to drive to the church and so forth, well, we'll be there" he looked at his Omega Speedmaster Chronograph, "in just about fifteen minutes. All right?"

It was clearly not all right, but Tanner and the Shaws and the others, whom Emerson did not recognize, got to their feet and started to put on their raincoats. Emerson saw that he should say something. "I'm sorry," he said. "I'd like to thank you also, on behalf of my grandmother, and I really do feel this is the best way. For her. I'd also like to invite you to come back to the house, after the services, but I'm afraid, with my foot and all, I can't manage very much, and I'm sorry. Thank you for coming."

After they had filed out, Emerson said to Skinner: "I'm sure you noticed this long before I did, but doesn't it usually turn out that the people who supposedly come to offer sympathy, really expect to get it?"

"Absolutely," Skinner said, turning toward the office. "I tell you what," he said, "if you want to, go to the bathroom."

"I don't need to," Emerson said.

"There's some Lavoris in there," Skinner said. "Use a couple rinses, so people don't think you've been drinking."

"I have been drinking," Emerson said.

"I know you have," Skinner said. "*I* don't mind. But if they can smell it, and they'll be able to when you're shaking hands, they're liable to think that you've been celebrating. Her friends are old," Skinner said. "They're very suspicious of people two generations younger, when they see them at funerals of their contemporaries. They don't like to see the next of kin looking too relieved, or like they seem to be enjoying themselves. Makes them nervous.

"And you go out to the car, after that," Skinner said.

"Why?" Emerson said. "Am I making you nervous?"

"I've got things to do," Skinner said. "I've got to call and brief Scott, and I've got to do it right now, or he'll throw a gasket. And I've got to get Granny out of here and into the hearse, and some of my farm boys've been know to drop one. So get the hell out of here, and do the best you can to look gloomy."

On his way to the bathroom, Emerson braced himself on the crutches, and patted what he hoped was the head of the casket.

The United Church, in 1976, looked no more menacing from the outside than it had in the summer of 1949, when Craig Emerson had entered it for the first time, to play his clarinet for some appreciative ladies and their largely tone-deaf husbands. If the church had been situated on a knoll, and flanked by a few sugar maples, it would have been suitable for depiction on the *October* page of any calendar published by an insurance company with offices in New England. It was small, but it had a nice steeple, and the light through the tall windows gave it a feeling of spaciousness.

Generally willing to perform what was expected of him, if the consequent pain was no more than he felt acceptable, Emerson went all the way down to the front pew, got in and sat down. The Reverend Mr. Scott, entering stage left from the vestry, came up to the pew and offered his hand. He was a rather pudgy fellow, with red hair and a cavalry officer's red moustache; Emerson thought he was probably in his late twenties; he was likely to be extremely earnest.

"Considering your infirmity," the minister said, after they had reached agreement on each other's identity, "I think no one will be particularly offended if you do not rise during the singing."

Emerson reflected quickly. He was right: in the two weeks that he'd been in the cast, that was the first actual benefit he had received. He accepted it gratefully.

Among numerous annoyances he had experienced in four years as a divorced Catholic was the periodic and acute embarrassment of not knowing what the hell to do, when the liturgy of ceremonial occasions requiring his attendance called for the congregation to move. He sat down when he should have kneeled, and stood before anyone else. The process begun after Vatican II—condemned by his father, Walter Emerson, as transforming Mass into "a goddamned Rotary Club meeting, stand up, sit down, fight team, fight"—had proceeded apace without Emerson, once he decided that the exasperation which curdled his Sundays was so great and so unrewarding that it justified his non-attendance at the Holy Sacrifice; he was irremediably vulnerable to some new wrinkle laid on since he dropped out. He was unprepared when people shook hands with each other at one place, and then, at the next wedding, all ready to shake hands when the folks started kissing each other.

There was a program in his brain which caused him to mutter "et cum spiritu tuo," when the celebrant of the Mass intoned "Peace be with you"; when the faithful started chanting "Lord, I am not worthy, that you should come under my roof," Emerson got funny looks from those nearby, for saying, automatically: "Domine non sum dignis, ut intre sub tecturm mea, sed tantum dic verbo. . . ," before he caught himself, short of *et sanabitur anima mea.*

Ashamed of such lapses, he had speculated, on the drive up from Boston, on the nature of what even greater foolishness he would certainly commit, when propelled into a Protestant lash-up; to be excused from movement was therefore a substantial relief, and left him to guard only his tongue.

Which would, he thought, give him quite enough to do anyway. It was that damned indoctrination that the altar boys had gotten. The words to "Tantum Ergo" were properly in Latin, and the hymn did not sound right to him in English. It did not particularly offend him, when sung in the vernacular; he simply felt, when it was over, that while the melody had been played, as required by Benediction, the recitation of the praises yet remained to be done. He found that feeling discomforting.

He had alluded to it, on a warm day in April of 1973, while dickering with the Right Reverend Monsignor Lawrence F. X. Jowett, about arrangements for his mother's funeral.

Encountering Monsignor Jowett, Emerson had told Molly later, was something like stumbling upon a dinosaur, or perhaps a brontosaurus.

"I guess I thought those fellows were extinct," he said. "That they went the way of the whooping crane when Monsignor Canavan was called away to straighten up some procedures in paradise, and had to give somebody else the hopeless chore of restraining us from our animal habits.

"Not so," he said. Maybe it's Saint Barbara's Church, the rectory and the school. Or maybe they've got a secret lab someplace, where they clone a few of the ones with the mossier backs, or get them to lay eggs, like the dwindling race of peregrine falcons that they saved by incubating. So they'll always have a supply of screamers to make sure that if you simply won't spend your useful life civilizing twelve new monthly contributors, to run the goddamned paper drives when this generation gets too old, well then, by God, if you won't do it, you're damned right well at least going to feel miserable about it. If they've got anything to say about it. And by God, they've got plenty to say."

"Did you have a fight with him?" Molly said. Molly had been raised a Unitarian, but had given it up because, she said, "golf lessons, and folk singing, and spending Sunday mornings ruminating on better ways to disrupt life in small Mississippi towns didn't interest me that much." She was permanently mystified by Emerson's ability to work himself into a rage, merely by reading a newspaper article which quoted some auxiliary bishop inveighing against homosexuality, heterosexuality, birth control, divorce, or the terrible erosion of American life demonstrable from the open sale of *Playboy*, and the incidence of dirty movies. "You can go to a dirty movie, if you want," she said.

"I know I can go if I want," Emerson said. "If I want to go and sit next to guys who've got hats in their laps in the dark, I can do it. And if I ever get simple, I probably will. That's not the goddamned point."

"No," he had said, "I didn't have a fight with him. That's because I didn't have anything to fight *with*. Monsignor Jowett keeps a ledger. Canavan put the envelope system in, years ago, so he could fix his beady eye on the poor bastards making fifty-six hundred dollars a year, and trying to raise six kids on it—like he said they were supposed to—and make them squirm because they weren't also dropping a five in the basket before the Offertory, and another buck or two after the Offertory, plus the quarter a seal for those over, I think it was six, plus at least twenty-five bucks at Christmas, and ten for the coal collection, and a generous sum at Easter, too. Bill Canavan used to listen carefully when that basket went around; he didn't like to hear any clinking at all—just rustling.

"So Jowett knows that Mamie managed to restrain her impulse to beggar herself toward the divine purpose of buying him a new Lincoln every year, when he held the Grand Annual Collection," Emerson said. "And he knows why, too, because she told him."

Monsignor Canavan, by then close to eighty, had cornered Mamie at the newsstand one day in 1972, and conveyed, in his bullhorn voice, his sympathetic intention to beseech heaven in his prayers, that she might be comforted in the terrible burden that she had to bear. Then Canavan's assistant pastor, Monsignor Jowett, had been with him.

Mamie had been fairly puzzled; she had stopped at the newsstand for a copy of *Sleeping Murder*, because she was flying to Bermuda for ten days, and dosed herself with Agatha Christie before plane flights the way that others used scotch. She said that she did not understand.

Monsignor Canavan, Jowett as supportively mournful as a bloodhound at his side, had complimented her upon her courage in suffering the fact that her son had "gone bad." After much more eloquence, she perceived that Canavan had received confidential information from the Throne of Heaven, establishing that her son had been declared *persona non grata* in those precincts, for having entered, by way of a civil ceremony, into an adulterous relationship with a pagan woman.

That had failed to console her. According to one account that Craig had received, from the owner of the newsstand, who was one of his customers, Mamie had emitted billowing flames and clouds of smoke from her nostrils and mouth, severely scorching the reverend clergy. "Goddamned old gossips," was reported as one observation she had made, preliminary to comparison of the good Monsignori to Pharisees and hypocrites, ending with his nomination as a member in good standing in the company of meddlesome old damned fools.

Emerson had chided her sternly for this, when she returned. He reported her misconduct in detail to Molly, who had made the initial suggestion that Mamie, perhaps, might enjoy the mink jacket which Molly had seen in the window at Kakas on Newbury Street, that day. As Mamie did, particularly at the 10:30 Mass which Jowett celebrated every Sunday.

"The bastard's a throwback." Emerson had said of Jowett, "but he's also got a bit more style to him, than Canavan had. Canavan, well, he may have had some intelligence, but it wasn't a hell of a lot; he thought Father Coughlin was a hell of a guy, from what my father told me. And he had no education whatsoever. He was the kind of priest that was the only educated man in the parish because nobody else'd gone beyond grade school. So he would tend to use a bludgeon, when the rapier would have been the more artistic weapon.

"When I was a kid," he told Molly, "my mother and I were up seeing Jenny in Fairfax, and the old lady got it into her head that everybody else from the Canadian border down to Brattleboro would be paralyzed with envy if I played the clarinet at the Grange. In other words, if she could inveigle me into making a damned fool of myself—because I was not a very good clarinet player, which explains why I'm not ruining my liver these days, touring the country in a Greyhound bus with Woody Herman and the Thirty-Fifth Herd—she could strike all her friends a mortal blow.

"It seemed harmless enough to Mamie," Emerson said, "so of course it seemed harmless to me. I didn't want to do it, because I knew I was a lousy clarinet player, but I was vain enough to think I was probably the best clarinet player in Fairfax that summer, under the age of thirty, at least, so I let my mother try to slick down my cowlick, and I put on my little tweed sport coat, which was hotter'n hell in the summer, and I did the best I could, at nine, to teach the lady who played the organ how to keep in tempo with me on the piano, and then I went down to the United Church one night and I got up on the stage and played "Beautiful Dreamer" and "The Flight of the Bumblebee." I fluffed a few on the "Bumblebee," but nobody cared, if anyone noticed. That was perfunctory applause, which was enough to make me play an encore that I was going to play anyway, and then I was given many thanks and some lemonade. It was in the paper in the local news, the next day.

"My father was very seldom reckless," Emerson said, "but he was also in the Holy Name, which meant he spent a lot of time with Canavan, choosing speakers for the Communion Breakfasts and thinking up ways to make Lent even more dreary than it was to start with. So my mother sent him the clipping, and it was just the sort of thing that made him lose his judgment. He showed it to Canavan, how I was wowing the rustics up in Vermont, and would surely have Benny Goodman looking over his shoulder in a week or so.

"That was a very, *very* bad error of judgment," Emerson said. "The clipping not only mentioned the Grange, which Canavan strongly suspected of being a subversive organization—to wit: Protestant—but also the United Church, which Canavan knew at once to be subversive: not Catholic. So, in the midst of wondering whether anybody at Saint Barbara's knew Frank Leahy well enough to get him for the annual Fathers' and Sons' Communion Breakfast, Canavan leaps right out of his skin and demands to know if there was any praying done at this anti-Catholic festival where they were probably immolating virgins, up there in Vermont, and my father said he didn't know. Not that it would've mattered, what with me rubbing elbows with the handmaidens of the Devil as it was.

"Dad called up," Emerson said. "Just by way of no harm, he asked my mother if there was any praying going on. Now Mamie never saw any harm in praying. Did quite a lot of it, in fact. Good deal of it right in the United Church, with her own mother. Good deal more in Saint Barbara's. And there *had* been a fellow who stood up at the beginning and talked at quite some length about the beauty of the woods and the fields, and the streams and the brooks, and he probably said something about the birds of the air, too. Maybe mentioned the One Who created all this. I don't know. 'Yes,' she said, 'the Master of the Grange opened the meeting, and he said something at the end, too.'

"When we got back," Emerson said, "there was merry hell to pay.

"Let me tell you something about Saint Barbara's," he said, "and do the level best that you can do, to believe it, because it really happened. I was not allowed to join the Boy Scouts of America? Can you imagine why it is that to this very day, I have no idea whatsoever why the Cub Scout follows Akela? Why I cannot tell, a bowline from a half-hitch even when there's somebody trying to tie me into one? Why, when I tackle that fireplace, everybody in the joint starts thinking about turning up the thermostat, to take the chill off?

"I will tell you why," he said. "It's because the Boy Scout Troop was operated out of the Congregational Church. Some of the fellows in the Men's Club decided it'd be a nice idea if there was a Boy Scout Troop in Meredith, Massachusetts, so they got together and got a charter, and formed one. I guess the minister probably approved of it. So far as I know, he never did anything to arrange for those who joined to be funneled into the Andover Theological Seminary as soon as they made Eagle Scouts, but he certainly didn't oppose the idea of the Troop.

"For Canavan," Emerson said, "that creased it. The Boy Scouts were a Protestant front organization. Any good Catholic boy found in open and gross association with such an underground would be promptly dealt with, and harshly, too. It was bad enough that I was going to public school. Almost all of the other altar boys went to Saint Barbara's, and it was only because of the conspicuous piety of my father that he made an exception in my case. But if I took to hanging out with them Protestants, hunting for arrowheads and studying tracks and memorizing Indian lore. I would be summarily unfrocked, and ever after deprived of the privilege of getting up at five-thirty in the morning to serve Mass for Father Canavan, and wonder why the hell it was that you could smell wine on his breath *before* he went out of the vestry.

"Well," Emerson said, "the dire fate I'd avoided, by renouncing the Devil and all his works, including the insidious Tenderfoot badge, I very nearly blundered into by playing "Beautiful Dreamer," to a bunch of farmers who thought it was okay when somebody said he thought it was pretty nice that God created squirrels, and other living things. They let me stay on as an altar boy, but only grudgingly, and now they knew that I'd bear watching.

"So there I was, with a background as a suspicious person," Emerson said, "sneaking into the Rectory this morning, in broad daylight, trying to con the pastor into letting his parishoner, Mamie Irwin Emerson, who's dead and all, be buried the way that she wanted.

"Now Jowett is the kind of Monsignor that you can absolutely infuriate by calling him *Father*. Which I surmised at once, and therefore didn't do it until he'd completely infuriated me. But then I did.

"He sat there, pretending to be Richelieu," Emerson said, "and never once did he tell me that he hates my guts, and had some reservations about Mamie's. No, what he did, instead, was act on it. It was not, I thought, anything near an earthquake that I had in mind to stage. I just wanted the organ lady to play "Mother Dear, Oh Pray For Me," and have it sung, because Mamie liked that song.

"Could I have it?" Emerson said. "Not on your life. It wasn't approved, by some other domestic prelate or something that apparently took it upon himself to decide what songs the dead people liked, and made the decision retroactive."

"Did you win?" Molly had said.

"I called him a rotten son of a bitch, to his face," Emerson said, "if that's what you mean. No, he won. Maybe it was when I did that, that he won. I don't know. I get in more trouble with songs."

In the United Church, on the afternoon of September 28th, 1976, a woman with the voice of a crow began to pound on the organ, at the same time hollering the words of "A Mighty Fortress Is Our God." The Reverend Mr. Scott, now in his robe, emerged on the plain stage, behind the Communion Table, and clasped his hands before him. He cast his eyes down. Outside the. skies darkened, and the rain became heavy.

The Reverend Mr. Scott was actually quite good, Emerson decided. He had a Maryland accent, which Emerson recognized because it did the same thing to vowels that Molly's did, but he had filed most of the edges from it. And he had a nice diffidence toward his subject, a decent respect for the opinions of mankind, and no noticeable incli-

nation to claim a personal acquaintance with Jesus, formed during
their years in the Alumni Association.

Mr. Scott began with the Twenty-third Psalm, causing Emerson to
be thankful that this was a Protestant service. He greatly preferred the
King James version to the abomination that he had heard at his last
Catholic funeral. "You don't understand," he had said to Molly. "I
like the part where my cup runneth over. I don't like it when the cup
is filled to overflowing."

The skies grew progressively darker, and the Reverend Mr. Scott
stood with his head bowed, while the crow in the choir loft demolished "Faith of Our Fathers." She sounded like somebody sharpening
a lawnmower. Emerson kept his head bowed also, in order to conceal
his grin. He supposed the racket that she made was no worse than the
profanation of the temple he had committed with a clarinet, twenty-
seven years before.

"Man," the Reverend Mr. Scott said, when the crow had left the
hymn for dead, as well, "is born to sorrow, as the sparks fly upward."
He lifted his eyes to heaven. "So it was with your servant, Our Father,
Genevieve Irwin, whose spirit we commend to you, today."

Genevieve, Emerson thought. Never in my whole life did I ever hear
a mortal soul call her *Genevieve*. Of course, nobody ever called her
Jennifer, either. I wonder what the hell her name was?

"He that increaseth wisdom," the Reverend Mr. Scott said,
"increaseth sorrow. But Jenny Irwin was fearless, and at the peril of
increasing sorrow, daily increased her wisdom. And that is why, in
exercise of selfishness, we mourn her today. Because she loved us all
so much, and we accordingly miss her."

In a minute or so, Emerson thought, I am going to throw up.

"Her hallmark was charity," the Reverend Mr. Scott said.

It may not take a minute, Emerson thought.

"She had compassion upon the multitude, which she manifested by
compassion upon the individual. To the preachers of the Gospel, the
harbingers of the Lord's Word, she extended hospitality, surcease and
support. She welcomed them, and housed them. Whosoever giveth a
cup of water in My Name, he hath given it to Me.

"She had," the Reverend Mr. Scott said, "the courage of her own
convictions, the strength to bear adversity without complaint, the
fibre to endure the loss of her two sons, and, late in life, her beloved
daughter, neither kicking against the goad, nor turning away from the
burdens that life presented her, but, always, trusting in the Lord.

"'I am the Way,'" the Reverend Mr. Scott said, warming to his subject. "'I am the Way, the Truth and the Light. He that believeth in Me shall have Life eternal, though he shall die.'"

Shall *live*, Emerson thought. Walter Emerson, in 1965, going home in his dark blue Cadillac convertible from a meeting of the Board of Directors of the Meredith Trust Company, suffered a cardiovascular accident which knocked him unconscious, and fetched the Cadillac up against a utility pole. Eleven hours later, in the early September morning, he was dead, never having regained consciousness. And just as well, too, if the doctors were right about the massiveness of what had happened to him.

"I'll tell you what went wrong," Molly said. "Well, not exactly what went wrong, but when we should've known that something had gone wrong. Badly wrong. We should've been prepared. It was when they started to stop making convertibles."

She said that in March of 1976, after he had shown her a story in the *Globe* detailing the elaborate measures taken by Cadillac to insure that no one would be able to claim with certainty that he owned the last American convertible (the final 200 were painted white, striped on the outside and upholstered on the inside, in the same way). "Bull*shit*," he said. "The only thing the bastards ever did right was make the top go up and down, when somebody pushed the right button."

He had said something like that, to the same general effect, in 1963, when he and Lenore had brought the Jag crosscountry, before they were married at the Church of Our Lady of Good Hope in Mamaroneck that September ("Which prompted a good deal of 'Notice my tight lips, how I'm not saying anything about something that I really find annoying,'" he had said to Molly). The tan top fitted well, and looked trim when it was up, but it was enough to require three men and a boy to raise, and it leaked like a bastard at the top of the windshield. East of Tulsa, in a downpour, he had gotten drenched, and mad, and pledged that he would never drop the goddamned thing again. "Well," she had said, practically, "I *told* Daddy what I wanted was a Cadillac, and he told me I should've chosen Daddies more carefully, because he didn't sell Cadillacs—he just sold Jags."

"And Rovers," Emerson would say to Skinner, on the morning of September 29th, 1976. "Triumphs, MGs, Austins, an occasional Rolls, and your odd Alfa Romeo." They were in the air, by then.

"Lenore's father was a very bad influence on me," he said. "I was expecting some dumb son-of-a-bitch that played golf all the time, and was really pissed that Nixon lost, and I was going to have a whole bunch of trouble getting along with him because I was some kind of a grad school dropout that was probably on hard drugs, and didn't know what the hell I was doing. Instead I run into a guy that's more radical, in his own sweet way, than I was.

"The first full day I knew the guy," Emerson said, "was a Wednesday. Which I can pinpoint because we were supposed to arrive on Sunday night, but I spent the whole of Sunday and a good part of Monday, fiddling with the condenser and the points on that goddamned thing.

"'I know it,' he says. 'You buy one of them, and you think you're getting a car, and what you're getting's a bag of spare parts. It's a nice-looking bag, prettiest thing around, but Jesus, what a pain in the ass. I've told them and I've told them and I've told them. Doesn't matter. They don't do anything. We can't get parts, ourselves. I got a new system, now. What I do is give the customer the number of the parts division in New York, which is unlisted, and let those bastards listen to the guy, and let them tell him why it is they can't send him his grille that some jerk took out, backing up a Pontiac in the lot next to the liquor store, for another four months. You'd be surprised how much air freight comes in the next day. Works wonders for them, letting them listen to all the mad guys and the pissed-off folks, instead of us listening, and then calling them.'

"The next day," Emerson said, "we're at Aqueduct, because he's got a friend with a few horses on the card. Of which my first wife also disapproved. She wanted me to go play tennis at the club, and then get displayed to several of her mother's friends. When I had a chance to go down to the garage in the morning, and watch somebody who knew what the devil he was doing, fix that goddamned car so you didn't have to idle it at seventeen hundred, if you didn't want to let it stall. I learned a lot about cars from the Jag and Lee's father," Emerson said. "I didn't mind learning it, either. The old man was a rowdy. Too bad his daughter wasn't."

"Jesus Christ," Emerson had said to Molly, "it wasn't when they *stopped* making convertibles, that things started going wrong. It was when they started."

"Nuts," she said.

"So," he said, "so, and so, and so. 'Somewhere west of Laramie. . . .'"

"I never bought that," she said.

"You maybe didn't think you did," he said. "You went for that whole horseshit thing, the romance of the automobile."

"They were pretty nice cars," Molly said. "I went with a guy in college that had a metallic blue Starfire, a Nineteen-sixty-two, and that was a very nice car. White leather upholstery."

"How was the back seat?" Emerson said.

"Also white leather," Molly said. "Didn't show. . . ."

"Ah, shut up," Emerson said.

Walter Emerson's obsequies were the beginning of Craig Emerson's instruction in the holy art of burying people according to the strictures of the Church of Rome.

"I was still kosher with Father Canavan, then," he told Molly, on the day of his quarrel with Monsignor Jowett. "True, I hadn't gone to Boston College, but my father had, and had been a loyal alumnus, and Father Canavan was disposed to grant to the deceased what he would have withheld from the surviving infidel. Except one thing: I could not have "For Boston" as a recessional. I simply could not have it.

"Now," he said, "I knew very goddamned right well, it was not because Father Canavan disapproved of that particular anthem. Because the old walrus, when his tusks were a good bit shorter, had gone there himself. For two years. Before the Seminary. Therefore, why the hell not?"

"'Because,' he said, 'it's not churchly.'

"Now there," Emerson said, "is your basic, oh-for-Christ-sake, what-the devil're-you-talking-like-that for, type of challenge. Which is about what I said. I settled for "Holy God, We Praise Thy Name." I hadda fight for that."

He remembered it all, then, as the Reverend Mr. Scott spoke. As it was promised to Abraham, and his seed. And may the angels welcome you into paradise. Emerson had his head down, still, and he kept it down.

"And so," the Reverend Mr. Scott said, "Jenny's friends are confident, today, that she is now with God the Father, in the peace that passes understanding, among the Blessed."

There was a tremendous thunderclap, and a sheet of lightning momentarily illuminated the entire church.

He's right, Emerson thought. She's there. And she doesn't like it.

Rufus Skinner, heedless of his own vulnerability to upper respiratory infection, commanded all of the thirty mourners to wait patiently in the vestibule of the United Church, while he charged out into the rain, wrestled in the downpour with the trunk lock of the limousine, and returned, drenched, with six umbrellas. Marshalling the people into columns of twos, Skinner distributed five of the umbrellas, retained one for himself, ushered Emerson to the limousine, saw the Shaws into it, retrieved umbrellas and began again, until everyone was out of the church and into cars, with no more damage than wet feet. Emerson sat silently in the limousine with the Shaws as the lightning leaped down the sky, and the thunder rolled through the valley town.

He was not accustomed to rain at funerals, although he considered it appropriate. His previous experiences had occurred in incongruous sunlight, which had perversely annoyed him because, for both his father and his mother, he had shelled out seventy-five dollars extra, for the rental of canopies at the graveside. Skinner had not suggested such a luxury; at the time, Emerson had felt a certain mean satisfaction, but on the afternoon of September 28th, he was properly remorseful, as though suffering from a hangover which he richly deserved.

Molly did not believe in remorse, for any reason. For the morning which followed excesses, she prescribed whatever medicine the sufferer found effective: in her case, two Bloody Marys, and in his, three cans of beer.

Emerson initially resisted such therapy, on the theory that a self-inflicted wound must be endured.

"By you," she said. "If you were the only one that had to endure it, I wouldn't mind at all. You could moan and whimper, and vomit and shake as much as your little heart desired."

"Propitiation," he said.

"Right," she said. "But I haven't got anything to propitiate today, my darling, and since I've got to live in the same barn as you, that means I'm in for almost as much secondary misery as you, primary. I wouldn't do it to you, and you're not going to do it to me. Now sit right up and drink your Bud like a good little boy, and try not to get the dry heaves anymore—it's bad for your mucous membranes and stuff."

Angelic Lenore had extended less mercy. Molly's curiosity about her was minimal (she admitted to bouts of furious jealousy, whenever she thought about him in bed with another woman. "Goddamnit," he said, "I didn't know you then; I haven't been, since we started fooling around; and I'm reasonably certain that a careful physical examination would show you weren't exactly virginal when you got me drunk and seduced me one night in Connecticut, when I was minding my own business." "That," Molly said, "has nothing to do with it."—but when Molly became pensive, she sometimes inquired about what had happened. Emerson at once became wary; Molly had a tendency to deny herself tantrums, and she refused to sulk, considering that demeaning; she chose the middle ground of seething. It never lasted more than one evening, but Emerson dreaded those evenings.

"Look," he would say, "I know you've had a hard day. But I've had a hard day, too, and my resistance is down. I'm liable to say something perfectly reasonable, in a perfectly stupid way, and then you'll sit there and glare at me until I can think up some plausible excuse to go to bed early. Which I don't want to do, on account of Moose's got a couple engines all in bits down at the shop, and if I don't call him around twelve-thirty, the bastard'll decide I've gone to bed early, and quit. Whyn't you tell me what's hacking at you, because I just made a quick examination of conscience, and I think, I'm pretty sure, I'm in the clear."

"I suppose you had lunch with some broad today," Molly said.

"I suppose you had lunch with some stud too," Emerson said.

"What I do is *my* business," she said. "Did you?"

"What I do is *my* business," he said.

"Oh no, it's not, Buster," she said. "What you do is my business."

"I don't follow that," he said.

"All men," she said, "are dogs. You're just like dogs with hydrants, with women. You're nothing, you're just as bad as the rest of them. Look what a push over you were for me."

"So," he said, "you admit it."

"Fickle," she said. "Fickle, fickle, fickle."

Several times, two or three days after such an evening, Emerson had sneaked as best he could around the periphery of the mood swings that she experienced. The difficulty was that he was not very good at sneaking around the periphery of things, and tended clumsily to trespass at once upon the subject that actually concerned him. "Oh no you don't," she said, "you chauvinist pig. The next thing, you'll be asking me if I want you to run down to the drugstore for Midol."

"Now look," he said.

"Tink was the same way," she said. "Come to think of it, every man I know is the same way. The first thing that happens when you get grouchy, is that you blame the whole world because you're grouchy. When we get grouchy, it's hormones."

"I've just never understood it," he said. "This undifferentiated hostility," he said, "as many times as I've seen it. . . ."

"Ah hah," Molly said, "you've been paying attention, you little sneak. I think I'm going to make a deal with you. Tomorrow, you go to the office and try to figure out why this perfectly charming young lad has got a police record from stealing things, and no septum left from snorting the coke he bought with the money he got, from selling the things he stole. Instead of being on the sophomore Dean's List at Dartmouth. And I'll go down and find out why the hell Moose is having so much trouble getting Number Thirty-One to run right."

"It's still pretty ragged," Emerson said.

"Unless," she said, "you tell me where it was, who it was, that showed you whatever it was you think it is, that you've seen so many times."

At the time, he had attributed his first perception—he was not at all sure, later, that it was his first experience, but it was the first that he acknowledged—to the pressure of surroundings and events upon Lenore.

She was inescapably golden. Transplanted from New York to California, she had, in two years, obtained, if she had not brought them with her, all of the qualities which California girls acquired at birth, and New York girls never had. She was as loose as ashes on the Coast. But then, when she came East, she tightened up noticeably.

At the time, he was not concerned. A stevedore would have tightened up in the round of dull parties, stuffy luncheons, country club dances, yacht club cocktail hours, and, what Lenore called other Catholic versions of Jewish *kitsch*, that preceded, attended, and would certainly follow, their wedding. The parties were buffets, served and thronged by her relatives, their children, and the parents of her friends.

The older generation was composed of women who wore tailored clothes, and strings of pearls, and whose hair had been painstakingly teased into arrangements so natural as to have been seen, theretofore, only upon corpses. The men wore blue blazers; they had beefy red complexions, and iron-grey hair. They spoke knowingly of yachts, and disparagingly of certain specific holes on famous golf courses. Emerson could not stand them.

The younger generation was worse. The males were disinclined to serve in Viet Nam, which Emerson found sensible enough, but they were equally disinclined to do much of anything else. They talked about preparing for careers in finance, and administration, and marketing, as though the subjects had been metaphysical, and they were French philosophers. The females were appallingly well-versed in the Post-Impressionist period, and seemed, as well, to know a great deal about French Provincial furniture.

"It wouldn't hurt you to try to talk to them, at least," Lenore said, after one dance at the country club which had left him bored just short of coma.

"Jesus Christ, Lenore," he had said. "I read a book once myself. I've been in a museum. I even saw a play. I'm sorry, but those things just don't strike me as grounds for boasting. The broad in the furry red wool dress there. . . ."

"Francie is boring," Lenore said.

"Boring?" he said. "I thought she was dead. I was going to take her pulse. And the guy with her is worse."

"There were some other people there, as I recall," Lenore said.

"Mannequins," Emerson said.

"Well, these are the people I grew up with," Lenore said. "My parents have to live in the same town with their parents, and my father has to do business here, after we've left. If those people think you're a stinker, my parents will soon hear about it, and when you get to know Mother a little better, you'll understand that when Mother hears about something, *I* hear about it."

Mother had taken an active part in the wedding arrangements. So active that Emerson had speculated that they planned a last-minute switch on him, so that he would end up married to her instead of Lenore. Mother had chosen the orchestra for the reception, and specified several melodies to be played, because they were favorites of hers. Mother had responded briskly to his declaration that there was to be none of that folderol about the bride cutting the cake and throwing the goddamned garter and feeding cake to her new husband. "Nonsense," she had said, "everyone does that."

"Nonsense, nothing," Emerson had said, aware that he was getting off on the wrong foot, and not giving a shit. The orchestra leader, a small Italian man who looked worried even when things were going well, shifted his eyes back and forth as each of them spoke, as though he had been watching a tennis match. "Mr. Coppola," he said, "let me give you some information. My best man was known as the Animal in our dorm. He weighs about two hundred pounds, and he drinks, and he sometimes becomes combative, which is a very impressive sight, I can assure you. Also, when Tommy is drinking, and looking for something to be combative about, he will often look to me for suggestions, *and he will do anything I say*. Now hear this: if you start that whoop-de-doop stuff, or any other recklessness that will make me look like a goddamned fool, I will instruct Tommy to go over and clean your clock for you. Do I make myself clear?"

"This is *Lenore's* wedding," Mother said, in a severe voice.

"Well," Emerson said, noting that Lenore was displeased, and becoming angry about that as well, "forgive me, but I fancy myself an indispensable guest for the ceremonies. Like the Thanksgiving turkey, only with more rights. I came back here to get married. Not to submit to treatment that would get any sensible man to have me certified as a simpleton, and put away to prevent me from harming myself or others."

"Mr. Coppola," Mother said, looking to Mr. Coppola for confirmation, which she immediately received in a series of frantic nods, "is *very* popular here. Everyone says that he runs a *very* nice wedding. Don't they, Mr. Coppola?" Mr. Coppola agreed so energetically that Emerson feared he would injure himself. "Mr. Coppola," Mother said, "provided the music for every one of Lenore's friends that has gotten married. He always does a very good job."

"Good," Emerson had said. "In that case, I'm glad we understand each other so well. We *do* understand each other, don't we, Mr. Coppola?"

Mr. Coppola was now helpless. He looked pleadingly at Mother. Mother was plainly angry. Mr. Coppola was afraid that Mother was upset at him. He Looked pleadingly at Emerson. Lenore got up swiftly from the ivory brocade couch. "Mother," Lenore said, " I'm afraid Craig has certain qualities that we will have to put up with. For one thing, he can be very obstinate. I suggest you give him his way on this."

Mother did so, with a lack of grace so pronounced that Emerson became smug. It was not until the reception that he discovered that Mr. Coppola's five-piece combo consisted of a piano, a drum, a bass, a saxophone, and to Emerson's horror, a very large accordion.

Mr. Coppola played his accordion like a man involved in a struggle with a large, angry alligator. He played with great swoops of his arms, and bending of his knees, flinging his head this way and that, stamping his right foot, singing to himself, perspiration blossoming on his face. He played "Lady of Spain" and "Moonlight and Roses" and

"Tea For Two." To the general, delight of the older guests, he played "The Mexican Hat Dance" and "The Bunny Hop" and "The Hokey Pokey." All of the fat people, by then flushed with drink at the Tottenham Country Club, responded as directed with their ample backsides, shouting and singing with gusto, bellowing demands that the happy couple join them in their disgusting display.

The wedding night was accordingly chilly, because Emerson had refused. In the room at the Plaza (Mother and Dad's wedding present was to have been a honeymoon in San Juan; he and Lenore flying out of Idlewild the next day. "But goddamnit, Lenore, I don't want to go to San Juan." "Mother and Dad go every winter." "That's another reason. And besides, the place is crawling with Puerto Ricans." "They want us to have it." "Lenore, what they want, and the way we can afford to live, are just not the same thing. Try to remember, they gave you that Jaguar. I didn't buy it, and you didn't buy it. Your father gave it to you. We can't afford trips to San Juan, any more than we can afford Jaguars, and I'll be damned if we're going to start off pretending that we can. They'll end up owning us, if we do." They had compromised by accepting a weekend at the Plaza, which in turn required Emerson and Daddy to fend off Mother, to her ostentatious hurt, when she proposed that they all meet for brunch on Sunday. Lenore was silent.

Emerson, being unfamiliar with that side of her personality, had not learned to leave well enough alone. "Well, I don't know," he said. "What is it, that you want an annulment, and you think you can't consummate a marriage in advance? It doesn't count, or something?"

"Look, you son of a bitch," she said, at once permanently convincing him that it was a serious mistake to try to jolly her out of a bad mood, "the way you were acting today, I just might go for one."

"Hey," he said.

"I mean it," she said. "I know what they are. I grew up in the big white house with the columns on the porch. I was the gardener's pet, and the maid's little treasure. I thought public schools were where they sent wards of the State. I went to Bermuda every spring vacation, and I had my own charges at Bonwit's and Bloomie's when I was twelve years old.

"I was a princess," she said. "Hell, I was *the* princess, and nobody crossed me without getting into deep trouble."

"Well," she said, "I know what I was, and I know what they are. But *they* don't. And you might as well just've come right out and told them, the way you were acting, the expression on your face, everything. Where the hell do you come off, judging people like that? This was supposed to be a nice day for them. It wasn't just ours, it was theirs, too. And you couldn't even summon up the decency to let them enjoy it, and have fun, and be glad that their daughter was getting married. Just sat there with a goddamned sneer on your face, looking like you just smelled cat shit. You spoiled everything for everybody."

"Your father seemed to find me acceptable, "he said, very lamely.

"My father is a cheerful old slob," Lenore said. "If Daddy were a dog, he'd be a big, happy, Irish setter, and you'd dread to see him living in the same house with you, because he'd be trying to get into your lap all the time. If I brought home Jack the Ripper, and Daddy was convinced I loved him, he'd buy the guy a new switchblade and take an interest in the best places around Mamaroneck to locate whores to stab. You could have hair growing all over your face, and great big white fangs, and work nights because there's no moon to bay at in the daytime, but if I liked you, by God, Daddy would like you.

"Tonight," Lenore said, "Daddy's getting his feet held to the fire about you, because Mother doesn't believe in getting mad at the people she's got a perfect right to be mad at—she gets mad at Daddy, instead. She's raging around up there, chewing him out for drinking, nagging him for laughing too loud, criticizing him for buying too many drinks for everybody else, so that they got drunk, and also inviting him to lambaste Tommy for the way *he* behaved. You *are* a team, aren't you, you and that pisshead, Tommy? He's got all the manners and class of a wharf rat, and you pal around with him and then have the goddamned common gall to sneer at my parents and my friends. Jesus. But Daddy, of course, won't do it, because Tommy's a friend of yours, and you're my husband. Which means that after a while, Mother'll get as tacked off at Daddy, without any right to be, as she is at you and Tommy right now, and Daddy'll get all the shit that you and Tommy really deserve."

Tommy Swenson, having discharged his official duties as best man, had abandoned the delicate champagne glass which he had used for the toast, and found several larger ones, along with a bartender who understood what was meant by each of four or five orders for a double Old Crow on the rocks "with some ice," as Tommy preferred to put it, taking no chances. Then he returned to the champagne, using the highball glass. Then he surveyed the bridesmaids.

Tommy Swenson believed that there were more than enough people, in any gathering, willing to do the expected thing. He therefore specialized in doing what no one else had considered. At considerable expense, and after a great deal of persuasion, he had had his body decorated in a tattoo parlor in Newport, late one Saturday evening: clouds of black smoke ascended in billows expanding around his spine, to his shoulder blades. On his right buttock, the Devil stood, shovelling coal from a large pile stenciled on his left buttock into Tommy Swenson's ass, the flames visible at the edges of his cheeks. Tommy Swenson had been known to display his artwork to people at cocktail parties.

Tommy Swenson did not do that at what Emerson, without even thinking about it, had always referred to as "Lenore's wedding." At the reception, instead, he selected the ugliest bridesmaid as his particular amour, and fell upon her as though she had been a tethered goat, and he a tiger.

Lenore did not especially like Naomi Billings, but Naomi's parents and Lenore's parents were best friends, and spent their summers together in the Hamptons. It was a convention that Lenore and Naomi, who had graduated from Marymount College, and thus made Emerson uneasy by her very presence, were best friends. Naomi was an actuary with Mutual of New York. "And as far as I know, at least," Lenore said, "she's never had a date in her life."

Emerson found that understandable. Naomi was of average height. She had the face of a chipmunk, and her mousey hair was cut in a manner which did not flatter her. She had a lousy figure, no personality, and extremely thick ankles. "Naomi can't do anything, except math," Lenore said.

During the luncheon, Naomi, returning from the ladies' room to the head table, showed the poor judgment to walk to her seat by the route which took her behind Tommy Swenson's seat. Tommy grabbed her ass. Naomi did not entirely conceal her pleasure, by her scream. That was additional poor judgment, and Emerson believed it was in turn the cause of Tommy's decision to pull her dress down while they were dancing. She reacted in the same fashion to that outrage, perhaps because Tommy had been introducing her to the rewards of Old Crow on the rocks with some ice. Friends and family, solicitous that Naomi not miss the opportunity to vie for Lenore's bouquet, found Naomi unconscious in the cloakroom, with Tommy Swenson working hard, though unsuccessfully, to remove her Playtex panty girdle. Infuriated by the interruption, Tommy had abused two of the other bridesmaids in colorful, language. One of them summoned her boyfriend, a large young man named Theodore who had graduated from Columbia and rode to hounds. Tommy knocked him cold. Emerson had had to quiet Tommy down.

"From which I gather," Emerson said that night at the Plaza, "that you've got a headache."

"I've got my goddamned period," she said.

"If that was it," Emerson said to Molly, when she asked, "it was the longest period on record. Oh, there were times when we had fun. Lots of them. But something went haywire, and for the longest goddamned time, I didn't even notice."

Molly did not know what he meant. "I know you don't," he said. "Look, I really don't, myself. There were times, lots of times, when she had me pretty good, because of something I did, or put one of my friends up to doing. When she really had a right to be goddamned mad. She hated Swenson, and I would have to say that I probably couldn't blame her. He gave us this massive martini pitcher for a wedding present, and every time we saw him, he had a couple of quarts of Beefeater's in his paws. So we would have contests involving first the filling of the pitcher, and then the emptying of it. Which generally led to Swenson staying over, and we didn't have a hell of a lot of room in that apartment, either. He had to sleep on the couch, which was in the living room, and you had to go through the living room to get to the bathroom. She was never sure he wouldn't wake up, or what he'd do if he did, so she had to wear a nightgown, and she didn't like to do that, either.

"On the other hand," Emerson said, "there were lots of times, when she was really pissed off at me, and it had to be for what I was, not for something that I'done.

"Lenore was good," he said. "She was really good. She just sailed through all the bullshit in graduate school, the language exams, the obstacles that the bastards leave up just because they had to get over them, so everybody that comes along after them will be sure to suffer in the same way. She got into Simmons with that Master's and just ripped the place up. In the meantime, she was carrying a full load at Harvard, for the PH of D."

"I was sort of a hangover, I think," he said. "The residue of the year she felt rebellious. When she was, when she didn't know that she was really good. That year, she was uncertain. Just come out of a small school for women, wasn't too sure she had any ability, feeling,

her way. I was the fail-safe. If she blew it, well, at Least she had some
no-good son-of-a-bitch that was just as much of a bungler as she was,
and therefore wouldn't mind. And she was so goddamned sure that
she was going to blow it, she never even thought about what it'd be
like, to have a no-good son-of-a-bitch around that was just a bungler,
if she made it. I was the Bohemian Period of Lenore Marie Moriarty.
The trouble was that when that Period ended, I was still there."

On the day after the funeral, Skinner was tolerant. He satisfied the
demands of the control tower at Burlington and levelled the
Commanche off around 4,500 feet, heading southeast. It was a clear
day, and the undertaker wore the expression of a man doing something he enjoyed.

"In the first place," he said, "we don't run things the way we do,
just for our convenience. Most of the people we run into are pretty
upset. They're all at loose ends. They don't know what the hell to do
with themselves, and they really need something to do, and somebody
to tell them what it is. That's all we do: we give the survivors a fairly
tight schedule of mostly harmless chores and keep them occupied until
a pretty bad business is over with."

Emerson was aware that he was being cranky, and considered that
he had every justification. He did not like small planes, which
bounced and yawed even more than big planes, and made him franti-
cally nervous. With his right foot elevated, and an ice pack in place on
his ankle the night before, at Jenny's house, he had described in detail
his distaste to Skinner. The Jack Daniel's was gone, but Skinner kept
an adequate supply of Old Forester, as Nelson Tanner and Henry
Shaw had been pleased to note. Henry drank his with ginger ale.
Nelson drank his neat. Neither said a great deal, and both went home
early, leaving Skinner and Emerson in the frontroom with the bottle.
Terry was at the funeral parlor.

"You'd be surprised," Skinner said, "how many people want Terry
to do the work, when the case is a woman. She travels all over the
state. Damnedest thing. That's really what made her decide to get her
license, her pilot's license. We pick up a tremendous amount of business from that."

"You'll be burying her some day pretty soon," Emerson said, "flying around in those little puddle jumpers. I hate'em. I'll test out
Number Thirty-one at a buck-and-a-quarter, a buck-thirty, right on
the goddamned highway, with state troopers hiding in the bushes, and
it doesn't bother me at all. But you get me into one of those little

things with wings on it, and it scares the bloody blue bejesus out of me. You make me do it and you'll have to wrap me in a wet sheet to keep me from grabbing you."

"Look," Skinner said. "you haven't got any choice. It's that simple. You can't drive."

"It'll go down by morning," Emerson said.

"It will not go down by morning," Skinner said. "It will go *up* by morning. It will hurt and it will turn a tasteful shade of blue, with some green and black highlights, and it will be about the size of, oh, a young cocker spaniel. And you will *not* be able to bear weight on it; you will *not* be able to press the accelerator with it; and if I were a pedestrian, crossing the street in front of the Middlebury Inn tomorrow, against the light, when you come down the road, I would be very worried about how hard you'd be able to step on the brake, so as not to hit me and break several of my bones. If you drive with that thing, you aren't being brave at all—you're just being stupid."

"*Brave* I do not claim to be," Emerson said. "I'm just being realistic. Right now I'm just an outpatient. You get me into a light plane, and I'll come out a basket case."

"I'll have Miller drive the damned thing down for you," Skinner said. "Get your wife to meet us at Butler Aviation, and you and I can both sleep late while the kid goes storming down the highways in the morning."

"I don't want to," Emerson said.

"No dessert, then," Skinner said.

"Ah, shit," Emerson said, moving in the large, threadbare brown chair, the crocheted antimacassar bunching up under his neck, "why the hell do I do these things to myself? No, you're right, I have to. But you can let the kid sleep, too. It's a rental."

"Why the hell," Skinner said, "is a car dealer renting a car? You ought to have a yard full of them."

"I do," Emerson said. "Thing of it is, there's damned few automatics among them, and the ones that are there, I might very well have a customer for, while I'm on this little excursion into the verdant countryside.

"Now, " he said, " if I rent the damned thing, I spend eighty bucks or so. If I don't sell one of the things I've got on my lot, I don't make about three hundred bucks. Maybe I don't make it anyway, because nobody who wants what I've got happens around. But then again, maybe I do. I'm Jenny's executor, after all, and my lawyer tells me that anything I spend for such things as selling her property is deductible from her estate. So, if it's a choice between maybe losing some money, and Jenny paying some that I don't think she's gonna get a chance to spend anyway, I figure Jenny ought to foot the bill."

"You're selling the place to him, then," Skinner said.

"Of course I'm selling it to him," Emerson said. "He wants it, for one thing, and for another thing, he's got the money."

"What's he offering?" Skinner said.

"*Say,*" Emerson said.

"Well," Skinner said, "it's not as though it was the kind of thing that was a secret, you know. For one thing, Nelson'll tell. He'll *lie*, but he'll tell, and since we've all got a pretty good idea of how much Nelson adds and subtracts, when he lies, we'll be able to come pretty close. And, for another thing, I've got a pretty good idea of what it's worth, and I was wondering if you were getting it."

"All right," Emerson said, "what's it worth?"

"I'd say: forty to forty-three," Skinner said.

"Jenny said it should bring at least thirty," Emerson said.

"She was old," Skinner said. "The old folks've got no idea how property varies. The acreage and the buildings, down the road a mile, would be worth just about thirty. But you've got the hill, and you're right in the middle of what Tanner owns now, and Nelson found out about all the folks who like cross-country skiing. My guess is that he'll turn this place, *and* the barn, into a dormitory. He'll hay the land in the summer, and he'll fill it with New Yorkers in the winter. Squire Tanner. He'd pay forty grand for that alone.

"I don't know about the amount," Emerson said, "but that's exactly what he plans to do with it."

"Uh huh," Skinner said. "That should be good."

"Why?" Emerson said.

"Selectmen," Skinner said. "Sewerage. Fill this place up with people, you're going to need more bathrooms. Cesspools won't handle it."

"Gee," Emerson said, "I didn't realize there was so much environmental concern in these parts."

"Well," Skinner said, "it all depends, on who's doing what, to whose environment. There's a bitch of a lot of jealousy around here for Nelson Tanner. People don't like him."

"Strange," Emerson said. "He seems like such a cheerful fellow."

"Yeah," Skinner said. "I've had cases that were more laughs'n Nelson."

"He *is* a grasping son of a bitch, isn't he?" Emerson said.

"Something fierce," Skinner said. "He's got easily enough to keep himself and his family in luxury until the end of all their days. Does he do it? He does not. They all live just above the poverty line, and he scrapes away now the same way he did a hundred years ago, as though they didn't have a dime. I can't figure Nelson, and I never really could. Of course, Nelson can't figure me, either."

"Does he want to?" Emerson said. "Is he interested?"

"Oh," Skinner said, "extremely interested. What the hell do you think we rubes do in the winter, spend our time cheating each other?"

"Sure," Emerson said.

"Yeah," Skinner said, "well, that's true, of course, Got to keep in practice. But we also like to keep tabs on each other. It's very important, to everybody in Fairfax, what everybody else is doing. I tell you, boy, when I married Terry it was the biggest growth industry in town for a month or six weeks.

"Why?" Emerson said.

"She's *Jewish*," Skinner said. "Good heavens, man, the only thing that could've made it worse was if she had one leg."

"She'd be better off than I am, now," Skinner said.

"When I brought her back here," Skinner said, "it was like a geek show. Curtains moved in every window that we passed."

"Great," Emerson said.

"Actually," Skinner said, "I enjoyed it. My father was an old fraud. He dressed up like an undertaker, and he did business as an undertaker, so he kept himself looking like a Vermont undertaker. But he had something else going for him: he had a telephone.

"My father," Skinner said, "ran the undertaking business as a hobby. And he didn't tell people it was a hobby. The way he explained it to the postman, *The Wall Street Journal* was a hobby, and *Barron's* was a hobby, and he had one of the few private lines in town, so nobody overheard what he was telling his broker.

"Ben spent his mornings on the phone," Skinner said. "Now and then one of our ten Catholics died, and he was torn away, but mostly he buried Protestants in the afternoon, and spent the morning on the phone.

"Stocks?" Emerson said.

"Uh huh," Skinner said. "And commodities. And options. And even currency markets." He produced a thin cigar from his inside jacket pocket, lit it, slid down in his chair, and smiled around the smoke. He removed the cigar from his mouth and inspected it. "I am very glad to say," he said, "that he taught me all he knew. In addition to which, I picked up a couple moves on my own, when I was working for Bache and Company, out of college.

"It's a useful skill," Emerson said. "1 never had it, but I knew guys who did, and it beats the hell out of working."

"It beats the hell out of having no money," Skinner said. "It *is* working."

"I suppose you have to pay attention," Emerson said.

"Perfect attention," Skinner said. "It's all a matter of avoiding distractions. If you don't have your own ticker, you've got to make the morning calls, and the afternoon calls, faithfully. Never mind if you're on a vacation. Never mind if you're in the air. Plan your schedule differently, but be next to a phone at quarter of four, and sitting at one in the morning."

"I always had trouble, paying attention," Emerson said.

Lenore alleged that Craig was the most inadvertent man she ever knew. "Things are always happening to you," she said. "You never plan for anything."

"Yes, I do," he said. "It's just that nothing ever works out the way I planned it, and I have to do something else."

Craig Emerson quit Boston University Graduate School one year short of completing course requirements for the degree of Doctor of Philosophy in English Literature. "But why," Lenore had said.

"I don't want to teach full time," he said. "There must be something in this world to do, besides sit around all day, drinking coffee and wondering what the hell the Modern Language Association's going to do next. Who gives a shit, anyway?"

"And that wasn't so, either," Craig had told Molly, one night when she had taken to the hemp hammock suspended over the stairwell in the townhouse. She went there to reflect, her body swinging over thirty-five feet of space, and a flagstone floor in the foyer, scaring the shit out of him. "I wish to hell you'd get the fuck out of that thing."

"It's perfectly safe," she said.

"So's almost everything," he said. "I admit to being irrational. Will you get the hell out of it, please? Not that I want to watch."

When Molly got into the hammock, she climbed up on the couch, which was upholstered in a coarse white tweed, and reached out over the void. She grabbed the hammock by its edge and swung it in over the couch. Then she got into it, and it swung out over the stairwell. When she wished to return to earth, she swung the hammock back and forth until it reached the back of the couch, held on with her right hand and flipped herself onto the cushions.

"It's like watching the Flying Wallendas," Emerson said. "And I don't like that, either."

"It's my hammock," she said. "It's also my house, too, as much as it's yours. Goddamnit. If I want to lie in my hammock, in my house, I think I can do it. I like it here. Nobody can get at me."

"And when they scrape you off the floor downstairs," he said, "you'll be a quadriplegic, and nobody will want to."

"Ahh," she said.

"What I really wanted to do," Craig had told Molly, "was exactly what I was doing. I was teaching nine hours a week, and making almost nothing, and that was the excuse for me moonlighting down at Constable Foreign Motors."

On the evening of September 28th, 1976, Emerson described it to Skinner.

"What I was doing," he said, "was dull. It was unremittingly dull. I was teaching two sections of freshman comp, and one of contemporary American lit, and it was like house-breaking a dog. Every day I did the same thing. Every lunch I spent being bored by people who never talked about anything but John Milton and tenure. There were nice people there, and there were absolutely intolerable people there, and they were all dull.

"Lenore and I had this little apartment in Allston," he said. "Walk up four flights. Get used to the neighbors heaving the crockery at each other, and playing the hi-fi too loud. By the time you got a couple cases of beer up those stairs, you were so thirsty you drank one of them on the spot. Hot water in the toilet, but almost none in the shower. Except when there was a hell of a lot of it, all of a sudden, and it blistered your ass for you.

"There was a guy next door who used to fight with his wife. He weighed about three hundred pounds, and she weighed about ninety, but she was a match for him until she got him pissed off enough to get physical with her, and then the shrieking stopped and he started throwing her against the walls.

"On the other side there was a couple living in sin. Now and then.

He evidently had an old girlfriend down in Florida, who still liked him. Or else she hated him. I never could decide which. They went away a lot. Her timing was perfect. Whenever they went away for a week, she saw to it that the postman delivered one of those caymen to him, the little alligators? And the bastard'd die out there in the hall, and stink the place up.

"The disposal only worked when you didn't have any garbage and they were all rigged the same, so the neighbors' garbage was out in the hall at the same time you had to put yours out. In the summer it was ripe. There was no other word for it. It was ripe. With the alligators, it was damned near purgatory.

"We parked the Jaguar on the street," Emerson said. "I want to tell you, you've got your mind on other things, when you're at home in Allston late in the evening, and you've got seven thousand, eight thousand dollars' worth of metal unprotected on a curb on Commonwealth Avenue. The bastards come howling through the curves, losing Cadillacs and old Buicks left and right. In the winter it wouldn't start, and in the summer the vandals and the thieves were out with package knives, slitting tops and looking to steal radios when they didn't have an order for the whole car. Every time I heard a siren, I was out of bed, and looking around the shade. When there was a crash, I was practically out of the window. Like I will be tomorrow, when you get me into that plane."

"I can get you sedated, if you want," Skinner said.

"Somehow, I don't think so," Emerson said. "I'll never quite get over the idea that you guys're drumming up business."

The cemetery in Fairfax, Vermont, is set well back from the road, on a fairly steep slope. The main driveway is gravel, and it crosses the slope in gentle zigzags. On the afternoon of September 28, 1976, it was covered at regular intervals by the runoff of the storm, broad streams of water coursing over it on more direct paths down the slope among the old grey stone markers and the small, weatherbeaten metal flagholders on the graves of those who had served in the Grand Army of the Republic. There was a small waterfall over a tomb built into the hillside, all but its small iron door overgrown with grass. The grass, Emerson noted from the steamy window of the limousine, was very much in need of cutting, and stood almost hay-high around the bases of stones which marked the graves of those whose descendants lacked the interest to attend them, or had themselves perished since the stones were last marked with new names.

"When she went to the cemetery," Emerson told Lenore on the way to Montreal in 1963, "she put a pair of old scissors in her pocket. To trim the grass around the headstone. Now keep in mind that Jenny's been arthritic at least since I can remember. Look at her hands, all gnarled up. It's always surprised me that she just wolfed aspirin for that. It must have hurt her something fierce. Would've been a legitimate subject for complaint, I should think, but I never heard any. Jenny was a professional: actual pain was too easy a subject, maybe. Any amateur could bitch about something that hurt. Her art was more refined. Also, maybe that would've been a sign of weakness, to say something that'd be admitting that there was some power that could get to you."

"Not so strange," Lenore had said. "Most people don't complain about the obvious."

"She certainly didn't," Emerson said of Lenore to Molly. "At least, that was her explanation. I really didn't see it coming, or her going, until just before she finally came right out and said that she was moving on."

"I would've thrown you out, instead," Molly said. Her curiosity was considerable, so that Craig felt obliged to answer when she inquired. But it did not block the jealousy which she experienced when he replied.

"There wasn't a hell of a lot to throw me out of." Emerson said. "It was a nice one-bedroom apartment, but it was still just a one-bedroom apartment. And we'd done a lot with the stuff we had, but it was still just stuff that we had. The bookcases held all the books, but the fact that we painted the boards and the bricks white didn't make them opulent. We had slipcovers made for the chairs that we cadged from her family and mine, but those chairs were, still twenty or thirty years old, and not exactly the most comfortable things you ever sat on in your life. I thought Design Research'd done a damned nice job on the coffee table that we bought for fifty bucks, but it was still a fifty-dollar cocktail table. And it was a good thing for us that Tony was a good baby, because he had to sleep in our bedroom.

"She did a lot with plants," he said. "She also took the plants with her, when she left."

He remembered, clearly, the disoriented feeling that he had on the morning after the first night that he had spent alone in the apartment. It was a clear Tuesday, June 13th, 1967. "We were very civilized about the whole thing," he told Molly. "None of that tiresome business and showing-off that you pulled. We weren't smart enough to show that, that we were mad as hell at each other."

"Maybe you weren't," Molly said. "Maybe that's why it was necessary."

"I don't think so," he said, remembering the almost palpable aura of Lenore, which seemed, that first morning, still to surround the things that she had touched. The imprint of her body on the canvas sling chair that she had preferred. The chromed gooseneck lamp in the bookcase over the chair, still at the angle which she had found, after multiple adjustments, to be best for her. The faint white marks on the window ledges and the coffee table, and the indentations in the rug, where plants had stood.

The last of her Viceroy stubs was in the clay ashtray on the end table at her chair. The fourth Brandenberg Concerto—the Von Kariajan, Berlin Philharmonic version—remained where she had left it on the KLH turntable. There were three or four *Vogues* in the magazine rack, but the sterling silver Ronson table lighter, that she had gotten from her favorite—thought impoverished—aunt when they were married ("Yes, I know it's hideous. Moira has hideous taste. But Moira also has damned little money. The only time we'll see her up here will be when Jake consents to drive her up, and she'll have to bunk in on the couch. She'll look for it."), was gone.

Stark naked, still particularly stunned by the discovery, upon awakening, that Tony's crib, missing when he'd gone to bed, was still missing, he had stood in the hallway and inspected all of the familiar objects, for a clue to what was wrong. After a while he walked into the kitchen and rummaged through the cabinets when he could not find the coffee-pot where it belonged, adjusting to reality by becoming angry with her for taking the damned thing without telling him. Then it had occurred to him to open the dishwasher, where she had left it.

The pot working, Emerson, with some vague idea of showering and shaving, had detoured back into the living room, his balls swinging against his legs. He chose Lenore's chair, removing at least the most recent of her impressions on the cloth by substituting his own. Stupidly, with his hands folded over his genitals, he sat blinking in the sunlight from the fourteenth floor of Tremont on the Common, the balcony before him vacant of the standing plants she had moved to it as soon as weather improved the previous year. The Folies Bergere poster, in its black frame, was gone, but it had not been there long enough to leave a cleaner wall area behind it, and it was a while before he had remembered that it had been there at all.

"The only things I want," Lenore said, the Sunday before that, "are the things that're obviously mine. And Tony, of course." She had explained that she had not intended to tell him that night. "I don't really know when I did plan to tell you," she said.

They had been busy all weekend, a cocktail party, Saturday night, with some friends of hers from graduate school, now teaching in various places around Boston; he had confessedly behaved badly, using a three-sale day at Turnpike Porsche as justification for doubling the six drinks he had had after work, when he commenced his celebration. Then he allowed the effects of the twelve drinks, around two, Sunday morning, to inspire him to candor in a conversation with a Chaucer specialist who taught freshman composition at Wellesley, looked like a halibut, and regarded himself as an expert on foreign policy.

"You know something?" Craig had said, interrupting a long catalogue of calumnies against Dean Rusk, with each of which Craig completely agreed. "I've seen you before."

He had seen the man before, at several other gatherings in Cambridge, Martha's Vineyard (when Lenore's parents had given them two weeks in a cottage at Menemsha, the previous summer) and Wellesley. The man had paused, and was about to remind him.

"In the window down at Anthony's Pier Four," Craig had said. "Fourth one on the right, next to the lobster, right above the squid. Lying on the ice. Are those halibut or mackerel? Which are they?"

"I *know* he looks like a fish," Lenore said.

"You're the one that told me he looked like a fish," Craig said, having a devil of a time unbuttoning his shirt, and an even harder job of speaking clearly; he had to speak very slowly, to manage it at all. They undressed in the living room, when they came home late and relieved the babysitter, because Lenore believed that lights in the bedroom would awaken Tony. "You're the one. It's your fault. You put the idea in my head in the first place."

"I also put it into your head," she said, "several times, that he's a brilliant scholar. He'll have his doctorate before he's twenty-three, and to be honest with you, my friend, he is not the kind of guy I want mad at me for the next forty years of my career. I'm not asking you to go on peace marches with him, or even to be nice to him. Just leave him alone. Stay away from him. Stay away from all my friends."

"Don't drag me to their parties, then," he had said.

"That," she said, "was an announcement I was thinking about making in the morning. But if you want me to make it now, I'll make it now. From now on, I'll go to my social occasions by myself."

"Good," he said.

"No," she said, "it's not good. It's damned annoying. But I'd rather go and say that you're working late, than have to face those people the next time I see them, and tell them that I regret your boorishness, and listen while they speculate that you may have a problem with alcohol."

"When I'm with them," he said, "I do. Concede it. No matter how much I drink, I can't seem to pass out. I can still hear them, and see them, and I have to listen while they reform the world between eight and midnight. They're not making booze like they used to."

"There was this one blazing asshole," he told Molly, "some woman who looked like a man and talked like a dictionary and probably wore leather underwear. She was a vegetarian, which was one of the things that you hoped to Jesus nobody'd give her an outside chance to talk about, and you knew at the same time it wasn't going to make a goddamned bit of difference, because no matter what she talked about, she knew every thing in the world there was to know about it. Interrupting her was like trying to outshout Niagara. But if you didn't interrupt her, she'd go on all night. She must've had the lungs of a Filipino pearl diver; you'd never catch her pausing for breath.

"There was a man," he said, "who taught the Romantics and looked like John Wayne, except that he was about Peter Lorre's height and had the same damned voice. It was like finding yourself face to face with somebody you'd been watching on a twelve-inch television, and all of a sudden he got out of it and there he was, right in front of you, the same size. he'd been when you were watching, him, the face from one movie and the voice from another one, he talked about bridge, and chess, and organic gardening."

"Jesus," Molly said.

"Ahh," Emerson said, "I could've endured it. But the whole goddamned bunch of them were so goddamned pontifical."

On the Sunday morning after the party, Emerson had consumed two Bloody Marys between 11:15 and noon, wearing his bathrobe and a noticeable stubble, sitting on the corduroy-covered couch in the living room while Lenore nursed Tony, wincing as she turned the pages of the *Globe*. "Does your head hurt, Darling?" she said. "Does the sound of paper cause you pain?"

"Must be," he said. "I haven't noticed any other sound in this place."

She turned another page. "Good," she said. "You deserve it."

Talking to Molly, and aware that he was making a mistake, he said, "She had a genius for negative timing. Something like Jack Benny, only what she said, after the long pause, didn't make you laugh. It made you mad." He remembered Lenore sitting there, her breasts exposed, and edited his reaction out of what he told Molly. "I was pretty meek that morning," he said. " I would've groveled for forgiveness."

"For a piece of ass, you mean," Molly said.

"I would've settled for a kind word," he said, lying. "I didn't want combat. I wasn't up to it. it wasn't as though I even wanted amnesty. I would've cheerfully accepted the some of civility that strange dogs give each other, when neither one of them particularly wants to fight, or be friends.

"Did I get it?" he said. "Nope. What I got was, 'I suppose you're not going to be up to going to the Geigers' this afternoon.'

"Noah Geiger," he had told Molly, when she met the old man on the third day that he knew her, in Connecticut, "is a genius."

"I believe it," she said. "He looks like General Rommel. No one could look like that, and be stupid."

"Look," he said to Lenore, "I've got to go to Noah's." She sighed. Immediately there boiled up through his nausea, his headache, and the dry and furry residue (left in his mouth by the bear who had slept in it the previous night) an anger so hot that he was simultaneously aware that it must, at all costs, be contained, and that at no cost could it be.

He decided to enjoy it by himself. He derricked himself from the couch and went into the kitchen, where he made another drink and poured a cup of coffee. Then he went into the bedroom. He propped both of the pillows behind himself, and sat on the bed, alternating gulps of Bloody Mary, and sips of coffee. When he had finished the Bloody Mary, and half of the coffee, he went into the bathroom and showered. He shaved, and used Visine to good effect. He returned to the bedroom and dressed in a sportcoat and slacks. Then he went into the living room, where the baby crawled on the floor, and Lenore sat, her white turtleneck sweater on, reading a book, without looking, up. He picked up his clothes from the night before, and returned to the bedroom, where he hung them up.

"Then," he said to Molly, "I went to the Geigers'. I did not utter Syllable One to her, and she did not speak to me. All things considered, I thought it was a net gain. When I got back, she was in bed. That was reasonable enough. It was two A.M. It was also what I had in mind. Exactly what I had in mind."

"While you were getting laid," Molly said.

"That," Emerson said, " is a coarse way of putting it."

"Noah Geiger," he told Skinner on the night of Jenny's funeral, "is one of those unflappable people, who always seem to know exactly what they're doing, and precisely how to do it. I envy those people more'n anyone else I know."

"Why?" Skinner said.

"My life's so fucking *random*," Emerson said. "Look, all right? Noah was an engineer. He worked for Doctor Ferdinand Porsche at Stuttgart. Then he worked for Doctor Ferry Porsche. He worked on design. He worked on distribution. He worked on international trade problems. When they finally decided they had to do something about the screw-ups in North America, he came over here and did something about the screw-ups. Then they asked him what he wanted, and he said: 'My own dealership.' Which he got. You take a problem to Noah, and he starts dialing Social Security numbers. Pretty soon he's talking in German to somebody named Hans, who's sitting there as startled as hell, in Zuffenhausen, and the part arrives, Air Express, the next day.

"What do I do?" Emerson said. "I'll tell you what I do: I blunder into things. Some of them work, and most of them don't. So far, I've been lucky. In American dollars, the ones that did work outnumber the ones that didn't. I got one thing that did work, and about five things that didn't, and the one that did work, gave me a living. I was plain, damned-fool lucky."

"Coarse, it may be," Molly said. "It's also correct."

"As a matter of fact," Emerson said, "it's not correct. I blush to admit it, but I didn't do a goddamned thing that was sexually out of line that night."

"You wanted to, though," Molly said.

"Sweetie," Emerson said, "when I stop wanting to, I'll go down to the Southern Mortuary, and check myself in."

Vaguely, as he showered that morning in June, he had wondered where the note was. It was not that they had agreed upon a note. "We agreed upon two vacations," he told Molly."We agreed on two vacations, at three o'clock in the morning. A Monday morning. I would vacate the place when I got up, and stay the hell out of it until at least eleven o'clock that night. She would vacate the place between nine in the morning, and eleven that night."

"Now," Lenore said, "stinking of drink and other women as you do. . . .

"Drink, yes," he.said. "Other women, no."

"Not for lack of trying," she said.

"Not for lack of need, either, "he said.

They sat up in bed, and they fought in the dark. "You could've fooled me, Jack," Lenore said. "I think I'll cash it in tomorrow."

" Okay, " he said.

"I don't want you around," she said. "While I'm doing it."

"Or anything else, for that matter," he said.

To Molly he said: "Can you imagine that? And then, when we finished that, we both rolled over peacefully, and went to sleep, in the same bed, with our son sleeping across the room. Jesus, civilized folks are weird. "

"Or anything else, for that matter," Lenore said. "I can get a couple kids and a U-Haul, I think."

"Meaning, of course," he said in the darkness, "that you know very goddamned right well you've got two kids and a U-Haul arriving at the freight elevator at some specific time this morning."

"Nine-fifteen, as a matter of fact," she said.

To Molly, he said: "I slept on it, until seven-forty-five, and decided if it was not the best deal I could imagine, it was the best deal I was liable to get. And I got the hell out of there. By eight-ten.

"It was the damnedest three or four days I ever had," he said. "I sold two more Nine-Elevens on Monday, went out and got roaring drunk, got home in a cab about one in the morning, went to bed, got up, confused, staggered around for a while, and sold two more on Tuesday. Reran Monday night, on Tuesday, and sold another one. That was when Noah called me into his office," he said, "and asked me if I had any money.

"'Of course I do," I said. 'I got enough in commissions alone, since Friday, to retire on.'

"'That's what I meant,' Noah said. And that was how I got the

Porsche One Two Eight franchise. With what he owed me, what Dad left me, and what I was able to borrow."

Skinner nodded.

"There *was* a note," Emerson told Molly. "There was in *fact* a goddamned note. It was in the kitchen. It was in the refrigerator. It was under the Bloody Mary mix. I didn't find it until the following weekend."

"Served you right," Molly said.

"It certainly did," Emerson said. "It said: 'I hope it rains on your parade. Here's my key. I figured you'd be sure to find it here.'"

"By then," he told Molly, "I knew where to find the coffeepot, because it was just where I'd put it. I didn't have any trouble with the furniture, because I'd seen it all before. I knew where they were, because I'd called her at her parents, and talked to her. And they were all right. She and Tony. It was not an all-right thing, but it was better, I guess, than the other thing. It was the best I could do."

The procession for Jenny's funeral paused for a while on the slope, while the hearse went on ahead, and the casket was unloaded onto the white canvas slings. Then the limousine and the cars that followed, went forward in the rain. The limousine stopped at the plot, the grey stone—IRWIN—wet and ominous in the rain, the passenger side door on the uphill slope. Craig allowed the bearers to open the left rear door. He got out slowly, wearing his raincoat, tucking it in around his crutches as it blew in the wind. He worked his way around the back of the car, the crutches sliding in the gravel. Then he came to the grass of the adjoining graves, lurched his crutches forward, felt them give way, and fell forward and to the right. He felt his right ankle buckle as he toppled into the mud. He heard the other mourners sigh.

Craig Emerson said "Fuck" at his grandmother's funeral. For the second or third time.

With small, sidling steps, the mourners adjusted the spaces around them at the graveside, until they felt as comfortable as possible in the rain. Rufus Skinner attended the Reverend Mr. Scott with an umbrella, and Miller used the second one from the trunk of the limousine to protect the chief mourner, already soaked and muddied, from the rain.

Moisture falling on others, but not upon him, seemed to lubricate the Reverend's disposition into an unctuous eloquence that he had not displayed indoors. Emerson, his ankle throbbing dully, his right trouser leg plastered to him, his pride damaged and his ass bruised from his fall, diverted himself from the interminable recitation of favorite Psalms as best he could, thinking of whiskey and women, open roads and fast cars, lobsters Thermidor, strong coffee, warm beds and hot showers. In his line of vision there was a lady whom he did not know, a fat-faced, heavy-bodied, bovine creature with large jowls and enormous breasts, short, dressed in a flowered skirt and a green cardigan and a knitted red wool hat pulled down over her ears. She held a fat infant in the cradle of her left arm, the baby dressed in a pink knitted suit with a hood, its head turned upward, asleep in the rain. One half-pace behind them, to her left, a gaunt, seedy-looking fellow at least twenty years older than the woman stood with an expression of guilt on his face. Emerson speculated idly for quite a while as to whether he was the woman's husband or father, before he noticed that, the woman was silently and copiously crying.

"At least there was somebody there, who was sad," Emerson said to Skinner that night.

"Dolly's sort of a lost soul," Skinner said. "Not entirely a lost soul—she cooks reasonably good lunches for the kids in the school cafeteria, and she works hard. But people here tend to look at her funny. She's from Arkansas. Fort Smith, I think. Some place.

"Married Donald Fisher," Skinner said. "Donald was a local boy. Bit of a hellion. Knocked up the Pratt kid, when they were in high school. She went to Florida, to visit her aunt of course, and the baby got put up for adoption. He joined the Air Force. Went down to Lackland, in Texas. Dolly apparently was in the process of getting out of Arkansas, and she'd gotten as far as a root-beer stand, which is where Donald found her, and knocked her up, too. She lost that one, after they were married. Which must've pissed Donald off.

"I don't know," Skinner said, "but I've heard she used to be a fairly good looker."

"Hard to believe," Emerson said.

"She's only about thirty," Skinner said.

"Harder still to believe," Emerson said.

"People go to hell fast," Skinner said. "Doesn't take any time at all, when they're really getting rapped around. Donald, the Pratt kid was a striking looking girl. She ended up dancing bare-ass in Boston, and living with a guy who killed her. *That* caused some stir around here, I can tell you.

"Dolly," Skinner said, "came up here looking a little forlorn, but she was a tiny little thing, and all she was doing was waiting out

Donald's tour in Viet Nam. Then Donald turned up MIA, three, four years ago, and she started to gain weight.

"Skinny Fisher lost his wife about twelve years ago," Skinner said. "He doesn't do much, and what he does, he does badly. He's shiftless. He's sneaky. And I suspect that Dolly started gaining weight because he raped her, and she was trying to buy time."

"For what?" Emerson said.

"For anything," Skinner said. "To hide it. So she wouldn't have to think about what she had to do. So she wouldn't have to do anything. Think about it. Face it. What the hell *could* she do? Go someplace? Where? Tell somebody else? Who? Two thousand miles from home, no money, I don't know who got Donald's GI policy, if he had one, or if they paid it. What the hell could she do?"

"What did she do?" Emerson said.

"She married Skinny," Skinner said.

"What about Donald?" Emerson said.

"Still missing, far as I know," Skinner said.

"She have him declared legally dead?" Emerson said.

"Not as far as I know," Skinner said. "And I probably would've, if there'd been any legal papers involved. Those people can't afford lawyers anyway. Probably never even occurred to her. She was pregnant, and hiding it didn't stop it, so she got married. If Donald rolls in from Singapore some day, that'll be another problem. If he doesn't, it won't be, and she won't ever have to do anything about it."

"What he could not explain to me," Emerson said to Molly, on the evening of the 29th, "was what the hell she was doing at Jenny's funeral. He tried, but he didn't come close."

"What did he say?" Molly said.

"He said he thought probably the ladies of the Eastern Star did something for her," Emerson said, "and Jenny was the one that delivered the layette, or something."

"Dolly," Skinner said, " is not particularly bright, as you might imagine. It wouldn't take very much to impress her, because nobody pays any attention to her, except to gossip about her. Maybe your grandmother said hello to her, or something, or just treated her like a human being."

At home in Boston, the next night, Emerson said: "So we got her up there this morning, to the house, and I told her to take the dishes and the bedding and the tablecloths and towels, anything else that she could use."

"Good," Molly said. "I was wondering what we were going to do with all that junk."

"You know what threw her?" Emerson said. "I thought she was going into some kind of a swoon. It was, Jenny had this whole trunk full of little wooden toys, and she saw those and practically tossed a fit. 'They'd be so nice for Ralphie.'" "Did you give them to her?" Molly said. "I did not," Emerson said. "Skinner's having them shipped down. Those people, including Dolly, would steal your ears if you'd let them."

On the morning after Jenny's funeral, Nelson Tanner, without removing his black overcoat or his grey hat, crouched, on a chair at the cherry veneer table in the kitchen and, like a somewhat animated cadaver, watched Craig Emerson move toward it. Emerson winced each time he put weight on his right ankle. At last he reached the rush-bottom chair at the opposite end, and sat down.

Tanner leaned forward and rested his elbows on the surface. He clasped his hands. Leaning his crutches against the wall, Emerson from the corner of his right eye saw Tanner's lower lip move ferally. To Molly, that night in Boston, he said: "Until he did that, I was prepared to go along quietly. But for Tanner to do that was like a slum kid swinging a set of brass knuckles on one hand and a bicycle chain in the other. Brought out the worst in me. I think I would've let the place sit idle for the rest of my life before I would've let him get the best of me.

"Well," Emerson said to Tanner, "what am I offered?" "Well," Tanner said, "of course you might get more, if you wanted to wait. Little strapped for cash, this time of year."

"Now look," Emerson said, "it hurts when I walk, and it's not so goddamned comfortable when I'm sitting down, if you want the truth. So I want to get this over with." Tanner pursed his lips.

"One way or the other," Emerson said. "*One way or the other.* Ordinarily I don't mind horsing around all day with a guy that wants to buy something from me, if I haven't got anything else to do. But today I have. So let me give you some important information, and you kind of ponder it before you say anything.

"First of all," Emerson said, "I don't need the money. I assume you know what that means." Tanner stared at him. "It means," Emerson said, "that I am in a position to do as I damned right well please, with this place. I can sell it, or I can keep it."

"Upkeep," Tanner said. "Hayin' won't cover it." "Who said I decided to sell the haying this year?" Emerson said.

"Well," Tanner said, "Jenny. . . . "

To Molly, Emerson said: "You've got no idea how it upsets a bird like that when you won't let him finish a sentence. He prides himself on saying damned little, and when you don't even seem to be interested in hearing that, it throws him off-balance."

"Jenny needed the money," Emerson said to Tanner. "I don't. See? That's the kind of thing I meant. I can rent this place and have somebody else operate it, and never come near it. . . ."

"Lose your shirt," Tanner said, reflectively. ". . . and write off whatever I lose and save money on my taxes," Emerson said. "Furthermore, I never knew of country property that decreased in value. It may not go up much, but it very seldom goes down, and anything I make when I finally sell it is capital gains, a hell of a lot lower'n my regular income bracket.

"Which gets us to the second thing," Emerson said, "and that is that I'm not going to sit here and dicker with you. Give me your best offer first. If it's good enough, I'll take it, and if it isn't, I'll turn it down, and we can both go about our business.

"Don't know how much you want," Tanner said.

"Give it your best guess," Emerson said.

"House, land and furnishin's?" Tanner said.

"Except for the television and the personal stuff that I want to keep."

"Other stuff's not worth much," Tanner said. "Have to pay a man, cart most of away. Whatcha doin' with the television? "

"Gave it away," Emerson said.

The Shaws, on the afternoon of Jenny's funeral, received the wet mourners in their house at the top of the hill, Libby shooing cats from their perches in the living room, and placing sodden coats on top of the magazine stacks as the cats vacated them. Exhausted, sore and wet, Emerson had no choice but to sit on the furry couch, considering that no further harm could come to his suit anyway.

"Nobody talked to each other," he told Molly the next night. "They stood around, drinking bad coffee and staring, like a bunch of cows waiting to be milked. It was the strangest goddamned sensation. It was like they'd formed up at the Shaws' for a parade, and at orderly intervals, in groups of up to three, they put down their cups and put on their coats and went out into the rain. I don't know what they were doing there. I don't know what they thought they were doing there. I guess if there was a funeral, and you went to it, then after the funeral you had to go to somebody's house and have a cup of coffee. Nobody seemed particularly alarmed that Jenny was dead and buried. If anyone was, I didn't hear about it. They looked at me the same way that kids look at llamas in the zoo: a little curious, sort of a funny-looking animal there, but the legs are on the expected corners and it's about the shape you'd expect a llama to be. 'So that's a llama, huh? What the hell good is it?'

"Of course I didn't know what the hell to say to them, either," Emerson said. "Most of them were total strangers, and the ones that weren't, might as well have been. You know something? We don't know what the hell to do, how the devil to handle things. Important things. When something ends. What do you do when your marriage collapses? Generally you stand around. If you're the one that leaves, you go out and buy pots and pillows and blankets and spoons, for the second time, feeling like a goddamned fool, and then you stand around some more. You haven't got any place mats. You go out and get some. You get home at night and you can't find a dish towel. You lop a couple minutes off your lunch hour the next day and go buy a dish towel.

"I had it easy," Emerson said. "Lenore only took most of the linens, so I didn't run out of sheets for about a month, when it occurred to me to change the bed—it was kind of rank—and I discovered I only had two sheets and two pillow cases. I was always improvising. I had canned soup because I forgot I ran out of frozen lamb chops the last time I ate at home, which was ten days ago.

"I didn't have any cream for my coffee. I drank black coffee for almost a month after the cream went sour, because I kept forgetting to stop and get some of that sawdust that tastes rotten, but makes the coffee look like it's got cream in it, and besides, it doesn't spoil. I learned to sew buttons on my shirts when the button-smasher at the laundry got them. What I didn't learn was to stop and *buy* buttons, so I would have them when the smasher got them, and it was almost a year before it dawned on me that maybe what I really needed was, a new laundry. Have you got any idea of the joy you experience when you get a new laundry and discover with the first load of fluff-dry that they went and mated your socks? Ecstasy. The rapture of the gods. And they folded your hankies and stacked your undies, too. Remarkable. For such a laundry, you would kill, and do it cheerfully.

"It's the same thing with funerals," Emerson said. "Skinner's right. There isn't any purpose to what people do at funerals. The people who go to them, not the people who run them. The people who run them are engaged in getting the perishable goods into the ground, which is reasonable enough because otherwise they'll rot and offend everybody. But the people who go don't really have anything to do, and that's just as well, since they probably couldn't do it anyway. So they just stand around a lot, and then after a while, they go home. And wait their turn."

After all of the other mourners had left the Shaw house, and Skinner had returned with the limousine to see if there was anything that he could do, Emerson, in pain, arose from the couch, covered with cat hair, and spoke to Henry Shaw. "Tomorrow morning," he said, "I'd bring it up, but I can't manage it, tomorrow morning, come and get the television."

"What do I do with it?" Henry said, ready to be obedient. "Well," Emerson said, "maybe you could watch it. Do anything you want with it."

"I can't afford it," Henry said. Henry appeared to have suffered a sudden attack of goiter.

It costs about a nickel a day," Emerson said. "To buy it, I mean," Henry said.

"Henry," Emerson said, "you're not buying it. I'm giving it away. It's mine, now. I don't want it."

On the morning after the funeral, Emerson listened patiently for three minutes, while Nelson Tanner talked longer than he ever had before in his life. Tanner talked about tax rates and labor costs, vandalism and maintenance. "And another thing." Nelson Tanner said, "there's going to be a unified school district, and that's going to cost."

"Fifty-three thousand," Emerson said.

"Huh?" Tanner said.

"Fifty-three thousand," Emerson said.

"I got him," Emerson told Molly that night, "for fifty-one. It cost, the man eleven grand to piss me off." Then, wounded as he was, he managed to go to bed with her.

Rufus Skinner was obliging. He climbed the brown stairs and fetched Emerson's bag. When he returned to the kitchen, he had the dancer on the music box in his hand. "I didn't know," he said. "I thought may be you might want Dolly to have this. "

Lenore's Aunt Moira, in addition to her penury and lousy taste, has a broad streak of sentiment. "Cheap sentiment," Emerson had said in 1965, when the Christmas packages were opened. That had not helped either.

"It isn't mine," Emerson said to Skinner.

Jenny had openly coveted the music box. Lenore had given it to her. "Take it," she said, in the apartment in Boston, with something more than contempt in her voice. And Jenny, without seeming to notice, had taken it.

Skinner held it now, turning it slightly, and the dancer began to turn as the first notes faltered through. "I thought it might be something personal," he said.

"It is," Emerson said, relaxing and beginning to smile. "It used to be. It isn't anymore. And that's why I don't want it."

THE HABITS
OF THE ANIMALS:
THE PROGRESS
OF THE SEASONS

RIGHT after I got back from Korea—I had a certain amount of money—I took every nickel I had and bought a piece of land up in New Hampshire, south of Center Ossipee. That was in nineteen-fifty-four. The chrome on most cars was about a whisper thick and there was some kind of clear lacquer on it that had a tendency to peel and whiten when you washed it. But you could buy woodlots in New Hampshire for about twenty-five dollars an acre; I bought fifty-three acres, more or less, on a pond, and it cost me sixteen hundred dollars. It was all you could do to buy a halfway decent Chevrolet for sixteen hundred dollars then, and I got an apple orchard all gone to seed, some fine oak trees and pines, and several meadows full of tall grass and sloping very gradually down to the pond. There were beavers in the pond, and in the evenings it was still.

My wife was fit to be tied. It was not that she wanted, really, the Chevrolet. What she wanted was a house in, say, Framingham or Braintree or maybe Swampscott, Massachusetts. Definitely not any apartment in Quincy, which was what she had had during the war, and what we had had before the war. To do her justice, it wasn't much of an apartment. It was about the kind of an apartment that a police officer could expect to be able to afford in those days, which is about the same as saying it was the kind of apartment a police officer could expect to afford these days: not much of an apartment.

I tried to convince her that the kind of house we could afford to replace the apartment wouldn't be much of a house either, but that didn't work. If I had gone out and gotten the house she wanted, she wouldn't have liked it, once she lived in it for a while. But it wasn't the house itself—the house we could have swung with the down-payment I used for the land, instead—that I was fighting: it was the idea of a house. That was a lot harder, because it included cosy evenings by the fireside and prize-winning roses and gin-and-tonics on the porch in the summer evenings with the fireflies going on and off. It was not just a lot harder. It was a losing proposition.

I lost as graciously as I could. That was not very graciously. I was kind of annoyed that she seemed to be glad to have me back chiefly because she thought it meant I would now do what she wanted me to do, and that was to buy some rattletrap house that'd fall down if she snapped the shades. But I did my best to avoid talking about that. and I took a lot of grief. I figured that when the flak was over, I would still have the land in New Hampshire, and I wanted that land badly enough to put up with the abuse.

It took me a very long time to understand that there was more involved than the abuse. I tended to assume that when the noise died down, the matter was over. I neglected the lingering resentment. For ten or twelve years that neglect was all right: the resentment was still there, and it cropped up in most arguments (there will be a few when you spend the better part of your life away from a crummy apartment, at the barracks or on patrol), but I didn't understand that the fury I caught from time to time was really the continuing reaction to the New Hampshire land. I honestly thought that was over. So, where I would have gotten mad if I had understood that she was still flogging me for buying the land, ten or twelve years after I thought the matter was settled, I did my best to shrug off the complaints because she stated them as something else. Such as: Why the hell don't you get out of police work and into something that pays enough so I don't have to work all the time?

I didn't get out of police work for two reasons. First, because I couldn't; I was too old. When I got back from Korea it was my second hitch—I was thirty-two years old. I had six years in, which left fourteen for a pension, and I was just too old to start in all over again, going to school and selling storm windows nights. Second, because I didn't want to. I liked police work. I still do. I was perfectly satisfied to spend my time working on murder cases to make a living, and doing the living that I made on the land I bought on the pond.

There wasn't much to the property but the natural advantages I have already described. The man who sold it to me was an old swamp Yankee that farmed it on and off when he felt like it, and didn't when he didn't. Meantempered old son of a bitch, I gather; if he ever had a wife he didn't have her when I got there, he didn't mention ever having one, and there wasn't any evidence of a woman ever having been around the house. The day I arrived to look the property over he was wearing one of those dark grey shirts and a pair of pants that'd gone out at the knees several times, and he nodded toward the house and said: "I lived here since I was a boy, forty years or so, and I'm sick of it. Going up to Maine. Not going to haggle. Sixteen hundred dollars, cash. Take it or leave it." To go with the house—three rooms: kitchen and sitting-room down, one large bedroom up, cramped bathroom that'd obviously been converted from a pantry—there was a small barn getting ready to fall down and a fruit cellar dug out of the side of a slope, with a leaky root made of tarpaper and the door all choked in with brush. There was a stone wall that marked off the easterly boundary of the land, and the remains of a wooden fence leading away from the barn toward the orchard that never quite made it, but fell away into the tall grass before it reached the trees. I took it all.

Buying it was like joining a church, because it committed me to spending every weekend I could get, at least in the summers, working on the place. I started with the house. I jacked up the foundation and ripped out the plumbing. I replaced every pipe in that house with copper, and then I repaired the walls and painted them light colors, white and yellow. Most of the windows needed new sashcords and I had to reglaze every light of glass in the house. I stripped the floors downstairs, sanded and varnished them, and upstairs I covered the naked beams with wallboard and painted it light blue. I did all the wiring I could—most of it—and spent two weekends working paid details on the highways to get enough extra cash to pay an electrician to do the rest. I took out the rusty black stove in the sitting room and put in a Franklin stove that I got from Sears; when the doors were open, it was just as good as a fireplace and it threw a lot of heat. There was a massive iron stove in the kitchen that burned wood for heat and range oil for cooking. I left that where it was, but I gave it the first polishing it'd had in at least twenty years. I put in a used refrigerator and I ripped out the old slate sink—it leaked—and put in a porcelain one. Then I built up a cabinet around it, and I did the same thing in the bathroom and put in a shower, too. It took me almost six years to do all those things, and when I finished I decided I wasn't content with the heat. So I went back and put in radiators and a gas burner in the cellar—I had to make a concrete platform for it on the dirt floor—and I built a small shelter to conceal the propane tanks outside the kitchen window. I put a bird feeder on the corner of that shelter and on Thanksgiving morning in 1960 I got up early and went downstairs and watched several sparrows doing their best to frustrate a bluejay after the suet and grain. There was a heavy frost on the meadow that sloped down to the pond and there was ice at least ten feet out from shore that reflected the sunlight in the frozen weeds. My wife slept late. She generally did on such days. She said holidays depressed her because we had no children and holidays were meant for children, so she slept away as much of the day as she could.

With the house repaired, painted white on the clapboards with dark green trim and the roof reshingled, I became better acquainted with the land itself. I set out to prune the apple trees and clear away the brush that was stunting them, having it in mind to bring in a crop every year. The idea appealed to me. The few dwarf Macks that I rescued from the local deer tasted good. But I consulted some people who actually knew what they were doing and they told me that spraying and cultivating an apple orchard probably wasn't the way I wanted to spend the rest of my life, and they said it would take about all of that. So I lowered my sights a little. I just cleared out the orchard, removed the brambles, and burned over the deep grass. Even that small attention seemed to make a considerable difference: the trees seemed to straighten them-selves up, and the apples the next year were noticeably larger. The real improvement, though, was the way the orchard began to attract animals. Particularly in the early spring, and from the middle of September on to about the first snow, deer came in groups of two or three to browse in the morning and again in the late afternoon and evening. There was a knoll about fifty yards away, and by sitting below the crest, to avoid frightening them with my silhouette, I got a good two or three hours' entertainment every week or two, watching the deer. I posted the property.

I left the stone wall alone. It had been constructed well—from which I concluded it was probably at least a hundred years old, because the previous owner never would have done anything that well. Anything that has lasted a century deserves to be let alone. But I brought in new poles and rails for the fence and I painted the barn the appropriate red and used it to store my tools. I chopped up the wood from the old fence and burned it, along with the usable pieces of wood I had saved when I tore out the fruit cellar, in the Franklin stove.

In the spring of 1964—I believe it was May—I discovered a family of squirrels in the barn loft, apparently getting along nicely with the barn swallows, and a noticeable increase in the number of pheasant around the property. There had always been a lot of rabbit tracks around the place in the snow, but now I began to see them often. In April I had disturbed a fox hunting in the field south of the house, and during the summer I saw the vixen herding her cubs along the edge of the pond. There were groundhog holes in the field, of course, but I found tracks around the barn that I matched in a book with raccoon prints. From time to time I heard an owl.

These things gave me pleasure, and did not offend my wife. Perhaps she was so completely annoyed at spending all of our leisure time at the place that it took a complete catastrophe to upset her. At least that was what I concluded later, after the skunks.

I found the skunks the next year, keeping house in the darkest corner of the old fruit cellar. Fortunately I saw them going home, and was able to watch from a safe distance to see where they went. I had no interest in exciting them. At the time there were two, fully-grown. I suspected that there might be offspring around, but I did not investigate.

My wife's ability to contain her enthusiasm for my wildlife observations had long before gotten me into the habit of saying nothing about what I had seen. In that instance, having some premonition of her likely reaction, I said nothing. On the Fourth of July she saw a small grass snake crawling away from the propane tanks, and nearly lapsed into hysterics, and I reflected on the wisdom of my silence about the skunks.

I saw the skunks again, from time to time, but I never saw them with any young. Occasionally I would see one skunk, and more often the pair, but I never saw anything to indicate that more than two of them were holed up in the fruit cellar. Always I saw them at the northerly end of the place, out of sight of the house, and in a careless sort of way I rather hoped that they would confine themselves to those precincts. For three years they obeyed my silent wishes.

On Easter morning of 1968, my wife, doing dishes at the sink, looked beyond the bird-feeder and saw the skunks peacefully mincing across the front of the barn, heading back to where they lived, I suppose. She was very concerned, and directed me to shoot them at once. I refused. I can summarize what happened next a lot more comfortably than I can report everything that was said. She permitted herself the hysterics she had narrowly avoided when she saw the snake, and to me, at least at the time, seemed perfectly incoherent. The substance of what she said was that I preferred the skunks to her, because I would not kill them as she wished. I told her about Wicklow.

In 1948 I made corporal in the State Police and was assigned to Holderness barracks. There was a rule that you were not supposed to drink in the barracks, any barracks, and there was a longstanding custom of drinking in all of the barracks. Particularly at Holderness, which was away the hell out in the woods ten miles from God, but centrally located, as far as geography was concerned, on Route 81. In the Holderness barracks in 1948 there was also a big stupid trooper from Worcester named Wicklow.

Along with everyone else, except Sergeant Fitzmaurice, who had stomach trouble, Wicklow drank in the barracks. Perhaps the rule against it was declared to prevent the kind of things that happened when Wicklow drank: he wasn't a bad fellow, really, but he couldn't drink and he did. He did not become belligerent, or anything like that. It was simply that he was stupid when he was sober, and alcohol did not help him to be smarter.

The procedure of forbidden drinking at the Holderness barracks was as follows: prohibited beverages were consumed from their original containers in the two unoccupied bedrooms at the rear of the second floor. When the container was empty, the consumer raised the bedroom window and, using an underhand delivery with a lot of snap in the wrist, flipped the dead soldier out over the cruisers in the parking lot below and into the gully beyond them. The gully was full of underbrush, and in the course of time it also acquired a lot of empty pints and beer bottles. Two years ago, I understand, they burned over the gully in the process of enlarging the parking lot, and when the fire went out they found they had to go and get a dump truck to cart the empties away. Headquarters was furious, and for several weeks afterward, I am told, nobody drank in any of the barracks.

Wicklow and the rest of us deserved, although we did not, of course, receive it, a substantial measure of that anger. There were prodigious drinkers in the Holderness barracks in 1948, and we kept the gully rustling just about every night.

The local animals kept it rustling after we had gone to bed. There were rats and mice and rabbits and squirrels—and foxes and owls and hawks that came to hunt them—and skunks. Rats and mice and squirrels and skunks congregate at convenient trash piles. Partly they came looking for the sandwich wrappers and so forth. Partly they came because there is nothing a scavenger likes better than the nice starchy dregs of an empty beer bottle.

One night in July. Wicklow came back from patrol and pulled the cruiser into the parking lot just in time to see a skunk on the early shift heading for the gully. Wicklow was not completely stupid: he knew enough to stay in that cruiser until the skunk got well out of range. Then he came into the barracks with his bag of beer and he was all upset. He was outraged. "There's a skunk out there," he said as though there'd never been a skunk anywhere before. "Right out there under the goddamned *windows*."

No one paid much attention to him. He went upstairs and joined up with some other gentlemen, also having a cold glass on a warm night. He sat there drinking his beer and going on about the skunk and getting thicker and thicker about the whole thing. When he finished the last bottle, he raised the screen, and when he did that he saw a skunk coming up out of the gully, going home. Little unsteady on his feet, too, weaving out of that dark gully, full of beer, halfway dazzled by the light in the parking lot.

"There's the bastard now," Wicklow said. "I'm going to shoot him."

Wicklow was a pretty good shot, drunk or sober, but no one was interested enough in his announcement to think about the possibility that he might hit the skunk. He got out his service pistol and he shot that skunk, a nice clean shot that look its head off. And that headless skunk went ass over teakettle and started spinning around just like a pinwheel, except that what was coming out of his back end wasn't sparks. Wicklow hit the skunk fat, and the skunk hit the cruisers—one had the windows open, not that it mattered—and the back floor of the barracks and the nice, porous brick walls and the curtains in the mess, someone had left the windows up after dinner. It was six weeks and more before the place was fit to live in, and the smell got into the uniforms and the bedding. We woke up with it and we carried it with us on patrol and speeders grinned at us when they handed over their licenses and registrations, and our wives claimed we brought it home with us.

I reminded my wife of the summer of 1948 when she said I preferred the skunks to her. She was not persuaded. She said that if I didn't start doing something to make the place livable, beginning with shooting the skunks, she was never coming back to the property. The skunks proceeded delicately into the grass in the sunlight on the anniversary of the Resurrection of Our Lord and Savior Jesus Christ and I stood there staring at that woman I had married twenty-two years before. Considering Korea and the other hours I spent away from her on other obligations, I figure we had spent the better part of those twenty-two years away from each other, learning things separately that were so different that we ended up never further apart than when we were together. Last November we were up there for the first snowfall, and in the early morning I saw three deer feeding on the tender branches of the apple trees. I made no effort to report this to her. I did not shoot the skunks, and she each week comes more than close enough to keeping her promise, though she is there in the still evenings when we do not speak.

OLD EARL DIED PULLING TRAPS

TIM Borland viewed the crowd around the Bristol County Courthouse in Oldfield, Massachusetts, with reluctant satisfaction. There were out-of-town reporters looking shabby in tan raincoats, television anchor people ducking in and out of vans to keep their coiffures perfect, and television technicians slouching in quilted jackets, looking bored. There was a ragged picket line of perhaps a dozen young men carrying printed placards tacked to sticks—the signs said: *Equal Justice Under Law*. Tim squinted as he read the signs aloud. He nodded firmly. "Yup," he said, "that's just about the speed of things we ought to have down here, with that damned building there. This is the first time since I've been on this earth that we had anything going on inside that courthouse that seemed grand enough to justify it.

"I always said that," Borland said. "When I was saying it, I've got to say, I didn't mean that what I had in mind was that I ought to be the one that'd finally start a fight that would be big enough, if you know what I mean. Let alone the fight'd be with Desmond Carey's kid that nobody including Desmond ever thought he'd ever get around to having the first place. And now, goddamnit, I wished we'd all been right.

"You know what this whole circus proves?" Tim Borland said. "It proves what's gonna happen when your goddamned employees get to telling you they've done a job you know damned well they don't like doing, and you don't like checking on them so you don't. And as soon as those young bastards see you don't like checking on the jobs they don't like doing, they quit doing them. And the next thing that is bound to happen is some guy you barely even know except by name comes back to you and says he's got this case of athlete's foot and he knows he got it in your shop. And he did, too, because those goddamned kids didn't like to go around and disinfect the shower stalls like they're supposed to and you told them that they had to do, every night before they quit and left the premises, because you just quit checking on them and they knew it. Jesus Christ. That's all that's really going on in there, inside that goddamned courthouse that looks like some king's fort or something—nothing but a goddamned case of athlete's foot.

"The thing of it is," Tim Borland said, "that isn't what it looks like. Just like the goddamned courthouse there. There she sits, right in the middle of the goddamned green there, and you'd figure, looking at it, anything that big should have a fair-sized city all around it. Few buildings, at least, there were more'n three floors each, one or two with actual elevators on account of there'd be top-floor offices that a man of decent dignity'd feel he oughta ride to, 'stead of getting there all sweaty on the eighth floor or the tenth and out of breath before he even tried to make his million-dollar deal. And we don't have none of that. You look around that square there and all you're gonna see no matter how hard you should look's a church that's got those silly animals on every corner, got their bodies all stretched out there and their pointed ears laid back like they spent the whole of every day and night just fighting off the devil every time he showed up. And the devil never had no business here. There's just not enough that's going on in Oldfield that he'd think was worth the trouble of attending it. They put that big stone church up there, they might just as well hired on Phil Spitalne and his All Girl Band to pose for any kind of statues they were putting on those eaves there, for all the devils ever came around this place they'd ever have the chance to frighten off, and the same damned thing applies right down the line, it comes to that old courthouse there. We always took complete charge of our troubles in this town, made 'em up and settled 'em ourselves.

"That goddamned thing," Tim Borland said, "you know why that damned thing is here? Because somebody had some big ideas and a good grip at the same time on the county's money, and he was looking all around to see if maybe there was something he could do with it that'd be a lot of fun and make a lot of friends around here for him and they wouldn't come around a few years later and decide he ought to go to jail for doing it. And that was what he did. He built that goddamned courthouse, and there she sits today, as useless as two tits on a bull. It costs a goddamned fortune when we heat her in the winter, which we do because we have to keep it nice and warm for all the god-damned fools that work in her and never did a goddamned bit of work that wasn't foolishness in all their days on earth, and nobody dares to do a thing about her. If you start to thinking some day that human nature and the government've changed since people gave up using horses when they had to get somewhere, you just take yourself a walk to Oldfield Square and take a good look at that courthouse, and you'll see they haven't changed a particle, neither one of them.

"The problem that they had in those days was the Wops," Tim Borland said. "At least they had the Wops and they thought the Wops was problems, so that made them Wops a problem. Myself, I would've been inclined to doubt that if I'd been around then, but I wasn't and it wouldn't've made one bit of difference if I had've been. For some rea-son or the other, there was Italians coming to this country then like they was running out of meatballs back in Italy where they come from in the first place, and some white men that was here first decided they was problems and that was just about the end of it. Just like them fairies there today, carrying their signs. I understand that there's been queers around since people first got started writing down the things that happened to them, but now they say they're different and they got some kind of rights, and here we all are now, making goddamned fools ourselves and using the old courthouse for a circus tent to do it in.

"Those Wops," Tim Borland said, "you call them *Wops* today and you'd better be damned careful you choose yourself a small one that can't fight before you call him that where he can hear it. *Wop* is an insult now. It wasn't, then. It just meant that they first come to this country Without Papers, and some lazy immigration fellow didn't want to write the whole thing out so he wrote W.O.P. and people called them *Wops*. As far as anybody knew then they were just as good as anybody that was here already and first got here with his papers for that matter, but for some reason or the other they decided that they had to do some damned thing with them. And nobody knew what in Jesus that might be.

"See," Tim Borland said, "they didn't speak much English and they didn't see no market then for pizzas and spaghetti like they do now, and they couldn't run you up a good suit in a jiffy like a Jew could then, so what in Jesus name was anybody going to do with them? They were all over the place, jabbering and doing this and that, and people started getting nervous. Didn't find them something they could do, first thing you knew they'd all turn out like Sacco and Vanzetti there we had to put in the electric chair, plotting with the Communists to overthrow the goddamned government. Which the more I think about it now I'm not so sure it might not've been the best idea, the long run, but at the time nobody seemed to like it much.

"Well," Tim Borland said, "what they come up with that the Wops could do besides start a revolution, they could work with stone, by God, and they could really do that. You gave a Wop a chisel there and a good-sized slab of rock, and you told him what you wanted done in words so he could understand you, and by God he would do it. My grandfather—his name was also Tim—he used to say when he was running this boatyard he started here that's got me in this heap of shit I'm in today, he used to say if you could make a boat from stone, all you would need was three able-bodied Wops and then just go and pick out the color rock you wanted your new boat to be, and in a month or so you'd be out looking for an engine that could make her go. And it would look right and everything'd fit right when you launched her, too, if you could figure out some way to make her float. Which now with this new ferrocement some folks're using to make boats, I guess somebody finally did figure out, now that I think of it. Although by now of course it's 'way too late to do them poor Wops any good. They're all in real estate these days, and being lawyers now and sitting on the bench. And wood, too, as far as that goes. There was some of them around then that were just as good with wood as the others were with stone, and all they wanted then was jobs.

"Well," Tim said, "they got the jobs and that courthouse's the result of it. That, and we had a whole population of nice quiet law-abiding ghinnies for those several years while she was being built here, and then went on to building something else and didn't ever make no trouble anybody had to go and get himself worked up about. Which I suppose if you was to go and look at it from that point of view, the building's a success. She's the finest granite on the outside there, you know, and you'll still have people tell you that she's even more impressive when it rains and the fine stone they built her of gets wet. Which is something you might want to keep in mind, I guess, if you got nothing else to think about more pressing than'll let you stand around for ten days or two weeks until it rains enough to change the colors for you. You're not going to make what I'd call a good living if that's what you're gonna spend your time on, if you ask me, but there she is if that is what you want to do.

"Then," Tim said, "when you get tired of that, the next thing I suppose that you could do is go inside the thing. If I was you I would not make it on the same rainy day that you stood out there in the square to see the color of the outside change when she got wet, because the floor inside the place is marble. You should wait for a dry day to go inside and see the marble floor. Because if you should ever want to do something that will make you start to thinking seriously about how it might affect your brains if you happened to take a spill and fall down on your head, that courthouse is the best place that I ever saw for bringing it to mind when you walk into it with some moisture on the soles your shoes. Liable, feet go right out from under you, slicker'n a baby's arse, and there you are, flat on your back in the middle of things and feeling the results a damned good crack on the head you gave yourself the same time. What you can do while you are lying there and waiting for your senses to come back, you can look up at all them curlicues and furbelows and I don't know what the shit're all the technical names that they have got for all that goddamned fancy work and decorations that don't do a goddamned thing except cost a pretty penny for the county to keep looking like they should, in case some poor bastard such as you falls down on his head on the wet rose marble floor and wants something to look at while he's lying there and waiting for the ambulance to come.

"Anyway," Tim Borland said, "the goddamned place looks dignified as hell. It looks a damned sight more dignified and proper than anything that ever happened in it up 'till now, at least that I was told about and I lived here all my life. Except for the Magnuson property case, of course, which even that did not exactly measure up to it, the way that things turned out. Although Des Carey liked it well enough, I guess, and he's dead now so it doesn't make no difference to old Desmond how it finally turns out for me that didn't have no interest in it anyway, goddamnit, and probably—hell, *for certain*—still would not if I had a choice about it. Which I don't.

"Them Magnusons was funny ducks," Tim Borland said. "Judging by everything I heard, at least, and all of it was told to me since most of them was dead by the time I started paying any sort attention to the things that was going on around me. The thing about this town that they seem to've been the only rich people to ever really notice was that by rights she ought to be on Cape Cod, if you follow me. You look around here and you'll see we got all the same sort things that make everybody crazy if they live someplace that hasn't got them, so they

will spend every dime they got and some more they haven't got to get
to Cape Cod where they got them. And what it is the Cape's got is the
beaches and the sailing and all the rest that stuff, which we have also
got, plus all the people that're going broke to get them, which we
haven't got and most of us're damned glad of it. Because when you
have got all of those people that're after that stuff, you have got one
hell of a lot of goddamned rigamarole that you have got to go through
before you can get at them in the summertime when all those other
people start to come around to get them too.

"Now," Tim Borland said, "as far as I'm concerned, it's just as well
nobody but the Magnusons ever noticed this, because you are welcome to my share the Cape, last summer, next summer or any other
summer that you'd care to name. That goddamned place. I'm usually
obliged a couple times each year, go over there and make arrangements to bring back some boat one my regular customers' managed
to disable, bring her back to Oldfield here and fix her up so he'll be
satisfied she's running right before he takes her out again, and I am
here to tell you that I learned from that I want no part of old Cape
Cod when everybody else in this world does. There isn't anybody
there in summer, hasn't got himself at least three kids, every one of
which is screaming, and the whole lot of them riding around the goddamned place in some goddamned Volvo station wagon so a man
can't get around and do his ordinary business. Especially if his business is down beside the water, which is ordinarily where you will go
to find the boats, and it is a sunny day when they all take their brats
the beach. It's awful, and I admit that I'm surprised nobody but the
Magnusons as far as rich people are concerned ever seemed to notice
we had pretty much the same sort thing right here in Oldfield, and
you didn't have to get yourself involved with crossing them damned
bridges the Canal they're always fixing so the traffic's got a man tied
up for several hours every night when all he's out to do is get himself
to home at night so he can have his dinner. Until now, of course, that
Walter Carey and his friends come in.

"But that's the way it always was, that I knew about," Tim Borland
said. "Then Magnusons made themselves one great big shitload full of
money there with textile mills in Lawrence, and for some reason or
the other they come down here instead of heading north to Maine and
putting up their houses there. They bought up all that property there
on Pigeon Point, put in the riprap and docks, cut a nice beach out the
rock they had there and set her up so's they could truck sand in and

it wouldn't wash away the first time that the tide was high and then went out again, and then they started building things. I swear, the time they got through building more things and hitching them to things that they'd already built, that old yellow main house there must have forty rooms or so in her, you come right down to it, and that still leaves the boathouse and the stables and the garages for the cars and carriages and all that damned equipment that they had to run the place. Them Magnusons, I tell you, they must have had the money up the gump-stump there, even when you take in account the fact that the old dollar was worth damned near a dollar, you spent one of them in those days. They put together one fine place themselves, they did, the Magnusons.

"But they was it," Tim Borland said, "as far as wealthy people and this town were concerned. If there was anyone around here that expected they would draw a lot of their rich friends and see them putting up big spreads their own, it never seemed to happen. The Magnusons from what I heard was always pretty private sort of people that kept to themselves, rode their horses in their woods and did their swimming off their beach.

"My grandfather," Tim Borland said, "did all the work their boats required. It was natural that he would, them being right across the harbor there from us. They moored their boats with us and had us haul the larger vessels in the winter, commission them when springtime came around, and we found them to be good customers. Kept their boats in topnotch shape and paid cash, too. Good parties to do business with. They was a large part of the business that he had to build the place up to the size it is today. And they had a lot to do with several of the other large accounts he had, too, because they talked us up right fine when they went sailing up and down the coast here, and that is quite important when you're talking about boatyards. Advertising don't do much for boatyards. What people want to get when they go out to choose themselves a boatyard is good people they can trust to do good work, and most of them, you'll find, make their selection based on word of mouth. You get one bastard bad-mouthing you from Stonington to Eastport and it'll play the devil with your trade in no time, I can tell you. And the opposite is also true, which was why my grandfather was grateful for the Magnusons even if they didn't otherwise attract much trade to Oldfield and they had the reputation they were cheap.

"Now my father," Tim said, "my father was a different article from what his father was. My father's name was Earl and he inherited the boatyard from his father just like I ended up inheriting the place from him. Earl passed away there about, well, it was November eighth of Nineteen-fifty-four there, and I remember it pretty well because I was out there with him on the workboat very much against my will, helping him pull those goddamned lobster traps he kept putting out long after it'd gotten too damned cold for any man that had his right mind to be working traps unless he made his living at it. Earl was like that. He'd get something in his head and there was no way on this earth you could get it out. And he had the heart attack. I tell you, I was baiting this pot here and he was pulling in another one behind me off the stern there, and I heard this noise behind me like you'd hear if somebody fell nearby where it happened that you couldn't see him, and I turned around there in that workboat and there he was, his head hanging down there on the gunwale, and I thought he must've slipped and hit his chin on her that way and knocked himself unconscious, but it turned out it was a little bit more serious'n that and he was dead. There wasn't no way me nor anybody else was gonna bring old Earl around that day, like you could when he was drunk and just passed out but you could still revive him some. He was deader'n a haddock there, by Jesus, and that was pretty much the end of him as far as anybody doing anything to help him was concerned. The doctor told me there, I brought him in, he said old Earl was probably dead before he hit the deck and made the noise I heard. 'Wasn't nothing that you could've done for him, my friend,' he told me. 'You can just set your mind to ease on that point.' Which I done and I inherited the boatyard then, just like Earl'd done from his father, Tim, that he'd named me after. And just like I'd expect my son would do from me when I up and die some day, if I'd've ever had one, but I didn't and there's no use talking about that, either.

"My father Earl's best friend was Desmond Carey," Tim said. "Des was the best goddamned lawyer that we had practicing in Oldfield. 'And also the only lawyer that is practicing in Oldfield,' Des'd say if someone said that so he heard it, and a damned good man Des was, too. Old Desmond run a string of pots out there from Patriot's Day to Thanksgiving, every year that I knew him, at least, and he did all right with those pots, too. Des was the reason, him and his pots staying in the water 'till Thanksgiving Day, my father Earl and I was out there tending ours November eighth when a man his age that didn't make his living from it had no business doing that. Des was about six, seven years older'n Earl, and if Des wasn't going to bring in all his pots until Thanksgiving, Earl wouldn't bring his in until Pearl Harbor Day, by God. My father always swore some Christmas when old Desmond came to dinner he was going to serve him up a nice fat lobster we pulled in that morning, and I was scared to death some day he'd really try to do that, keep his pots in until Christmas Day was over, but he didn't. Probably because he didn't get around to it while he was living, and he didn't manage to live long enough to get around to it. Earl and me and Des always had the holidays together, the three of us being just about the only people that any one of us had to be with on the holidays, my mother being dead and Des not having any family to be with. My father Earl was close with him, although I can't say I was ever sure that Des was quite as close to Earl as Earl thought he was with Des. Des always had a tendency I noticed to keep most of his thoughts chiefly to himself. I suppose that was because he was a lawyer and he was used to keeping other people's business private when they told it to him. Old Earl was never like that. You got a few drinks into Earl there and he would tell you absolutely everything that he had in his mind, if you asked him the right question, and sometimes even if you didn't. But Des'd stop by at the office in the mornings, he got back from pulling in his pots 'fore he went home and got his suit and tie on for when he was a lawyer during the day there, and he'd have his boots on there and smelling of the fish that he'd been cutting up to bait his traps, and have a cup of coffee. And my father Earl'd give him a good ration shit, now and then, tell him he was getting soft, no lobstering between Thanksgiving, Opening Day, and say that he was probably something of a sissy. Sissy didn't mean then what I guess it means now. And Des'd just laugh there and say he didn't always have to have some reason he could use, pretend that he was doing in the harbor when he went out there to keep an eye on what my father Earl was doing to the boats that Desmond's clients owned, in case Earl messed them up so they would decide they might want Des to come around and sue us for the damage. Actually, of course, that would not have happened because Desmond was our lawyer that did all our work for us the few times that we actually found we had to have a lawyer. Things was different then and people didn't sue each other every time the goddamned sun decided it would go behind a cloud or something like they do these days. Damned good lawyer, Des was, too. Done what needed doing and he didn't charge too much.

"Well," Tim said, "like I said, Des married late in life and it came as some surprise to most of us. Him and my father'd gotten to be pretty close chums after my mother died when I was ten. In a way I guess that was a good thing for my father, when you think about it, because Desmond wasn't much for raising hell like Earl always thought he was. I don't know's Earl ever raised the kind of hell that he always talked about, and if he did he sure did damned well keeping it from me, but I think he would've liked to and he probably would've tried it if it hadn't've been for Des to keep him pretty much in line. They used to joke around a lot, when I got old enough, pretend I wasn't listening or I didn't understand what they were saying. 'Well, Des,' old Earl'd say, if I happened to be out in back the office there or something, maybe working on accounts or seeing if there was something I could do to straighten out some goddamned outboard that we put there for winter when we'd have some time to take them all apart and see if we could figure the hell it was that wouldn't let them start. 'Well, Des,' old Earl'd say, 'you know young Tim there's getting old enough to be in a position there before long to be going with us there, we go to visit all them whorehouses over there in Providence.' And Des'd laugh and say: 'Well, hell, Earl, you know the price of things and all, I was kind of hoping maybe Tim'd help us out a little closer here to home, find out where we could do a little better and get the same kind of service here for free.' And then they'd both laugh, like there was actually some truth to what they said.

"The trouble is, there wasn't," Tim said. "There wasn't one damned atom truth to any of it. The girls around here then that I knew was all saving it for marriage, like I guess they don't do any more, and there wasn't any of them that seemed interested in wasting it on me, you know what I mean. Let alone two old goats like Desmond and old Earl. We didn't have them divorcees around here then like we got now, which from all I hear I guess're pretty easy, though that's another one of them things that you sure can't prove by me. And as for them, old Earl and Des, their actual idea of one good old high time was they'd go out to dinner now and then and I'd go home by myself and fix my own right there, and they'd drive off down to Jim Deacon's Tidewater there and have themselves some lobsters and some steamers and a little whiskey, get to telling lies in general and reminding each other what great guys they were and what a shame it was they didn't have no wives. And then they'd laugh and tell each other they were probably better off. Although I remember one night, as a matter fact, I was older and once or twice they invited me to go with them and I did until I just decided that I didn't have much fun just sitting there and watching two old guys get shitfaced, my father puts his arm around me so I knew that he was pretty drunk because he had to be to do something like that, and told old Desmond there at least he did have me, and Desmond started crying. Old Des said that he didn't have, he was gonna die without a son. Desmond was about six sheets the wind himself that night, they started talking all that foolishness. Come to think of it, I think that might've been the last time that I went with them. I didn't mind if they wanted to go off and get themselves in that kind of condition, it was perfectly all right by me, but I was damned if I wanted to go along myself and see them like that, so I didn't go again.

"Well," Tim said, "time went along the way she will there, and the way things turned out finally old Desmond did go and get himself a wife, although I'm not a bit sure that he meant to when he did it. Because the way that happened was the boatyard there.

"Now," Tim said, "me and my old man, and his father that he named me after, we got ourselves a damned good reputation in our business and we worked damned hard to get it. Get it and then keep it. We're not in one your fancy towns there, Newport or Hyannis, all them Kennedys around, but we do damned good work here and we don't come around after we have done it and tell you that you got to go and hock your house to pay for it. And furthermore, by Jesus, when we tell you that we checked your seacocks and they didn't look quite sound to us so we went ahead and put in two, three new ones, that's exactly what we did. We did that work and we used them new parts that we charged you for. You want to, you still got a perfect right to get yourself a flashlight and go ahead and ruin a good pair of pants that's still got a lot of wear in them, crawling around there in your bilge to see if we have done that work and that the work we said we done was in fact the work we did, and you will find we did. There'll be two, three new bronze seacocks in there, whatever that we told you that we did, and if you've got to pay six hundred bucks a copy for them, well, that's what good materials cost these days, but you got exactly what we're asking you to pay for. You're not gonna get in there and find out that we put in goddamned gatevalves that're made out of white metal there and you'd better not look at them crosseyed or the goddamned handles'll shear off on you, no sir. We didn't cheat you and we never will.

"Well," Tim Borland said, "that sort of thing gets out by word of mouth, and that's what I was telling you about them Magnusons. That in addition to being pretty decent customers themselves, they sent us a good amount of further trade from other people that they talked to and said we was reliable. Boaters're a gabby lot, especially they get a few drinks in them which quite a few of them seem to like to do quite regular, and we gradually over the years built up one damned fine reputation up and down the coast here. There is one shit-load of rich people between Port Jefferson, down there on Long Island, and the Maritimes up north there, and there's a lot of them got boats. Those people haven't got time to tend their money and their boats, so what they like to do is concentrate their time upon the money and leave other people take the time to look after what needs lookin' after on their pride and joy, the boats. So you start talking to those people there and if they ask you where you put your boat up for the winter and get your work done on her, and you say you get it down in Oldfield, the first thing they will say is: 'Oh yeah, Tim Borland's Boat Yard there.' If they're old they'll mean my grandfather, and if they're middleaged they'll mean my father because most people thought his name was Tim just like his father's was and mine is—they just assume the Borland the owns the yard's named Tim, and there never seemed to be much point in telling them the contrary. Although come to think of it my grandfather's been dead nearly forty years and there can't be very many of his old customers still around, so it's either Earl or me they mean when they say Tim. And most of them'll probably mean me. My father didn't manage to outlast his old man by much, the way I've done. I never could get Earl to take a reasonable amount of look-out for his health. It seemed like every time Doc Barney told him to do something for his health it was pretty near the surest way on earth to make him do the opposite. Doc Barney knew that. He got so he would call me after old Earl finally got to some point where he had to go and see him, and Doc'd tell me what was wrong with Earl and what he had to do to make sure that he lived a little longer, and see if I could manage to convince him that he ought to do it, but I never could. But anyway, those people that turn out to know us, they'll say something like: 'Ain't cheap, those Borlands, but they are reliable.' And that's exactly what the truth the matter is.

"Now," Tim Borland said, "one of the customers we got as a result that reputation was Mister Malcolm Larch. There wasn't any other reason on this face the earth for Malcolm Larch to come to us, except for what somebody must've said to him. And when he started coming here, old Earl was still in charge but I was gradually taking over handling most the daily contact with the customers because old Earl never did like doing that and he had a tendency when there was something that he didn't like to do, he wouldn't do it. He was drinking pretty heavy even then. Drinking was one thing that Earl did not mind doing one small bit. Old Earl was very good at drinking, but that did not bring in the customers or keep them coming back. So when Malcolm Larch brought *Temptress* in here for the first time, I was the one that did the dealing with him.

"I was just a kid then," Tim said. "I didn't know a damned thing about Mister Malcolm Larch or any of the prominence I guess he probably had. The only thing I knew about him was she was his boat and he wanted all the billing done his office in New York, and that wasn't anything much different'n the sort of thing I'd grown accustomed to with people bringing their boats in that lived some other place, so that was it. See, in this line of work you never worry too much about where you find the customer, because the customer is always crazy and your main problem with him's probably going to be how the hell you stay away from talking to him. And the other thing is that you've got his boat, so if he's a little slow in paying up or he don't pay at all, you're gonna sell the boat and get your money out of it. We got security for our money in this line of work. So we don't make many inquiries, and I didn't when the Larch boat came for the first time. There wasn't any reason to.

"He didn't look like anything out of the ordinary at all," Tim Borland said. "He was about five-ten and he had the sort of brownish hair that was getting kind of thin on top like most of us've got to face sooner or later, and his eyes were kind of weak as well. When he wanted to read a chart or something, he had to take out this pair of spectacles that'd be okay for safety glasses, you had a little spot-weld that you had to make right off. But he was a damned good sailor and he was also one smart bastard at the same time, I guess, even though he didn't act like he expected to be treated like one. International finance, I guess it was, one of them big Wall Street outfits nobody ever heard of until somebody found out how he could make a lightbulb or some damned thing like that and it turned out somebody such as Malcolm Larch'd bought up all the tungsten in the world the previous Wednesday 'cause he didn't have much else on his mind that day and he thought he might just as well corner the damned market in some stuff that nobody 'till then'd figured out a damned thing it was good for. Understand, I'm not saying that was one the things he'd done, but it was the kind of thing I guess he spent his time in doing, and he made a lot of money doing things like that. And he decided he was going to keep his boat here, which he did.

"Now," Tim Borland said, "when Malcolm started doing business with us, he transferred from where he had been doing business somewhere down there on the Connecticut Shore, I think it was, and he arrived without no wife or woman. This didn't cause no comment. We had a lot of men like that for customers. Men that didn't seem to have no women anywhere in sight attached to them, and in those days you didn't think a thing about it, that it might mean something more than that. We just assumed that most of them had women, one description or the other, but there's a lot of women that want nothing whatsoever to have anything to do with boats, and their men do. I think lots of times the reason that the men like boats so much is because the women don't want anything to do with boats, but that's speculation. All I know's we've got, we had, a lot of customers that were men that we'd never see any women with, and damned few women customers that come in here with no men around, so it did not impress us Malcolm Larch didn't have a woman with him. And it was during that time Malcolm got the athlete's foot.

"The fact the matter is," Tim Borland said, "when you got public showers, things being what they are, sooner or later somebody that's got athlete's foot is going to use them, and that will leave the fungus in there for the next guy. That was true back then before Earl decided that he'd have his heart attack and leave me obviously the only one in charge the place, and I was doing just about the best I could to run the place while Earl spent all his time just doing what he liked. And one the things I guess I must've overlooked was making sure the boys put the disinfectant in the showers. Because the fungus likes a shower better than it likes any other place on earth except the goddamned jungle. It's nice and wet in there and the water's almost always nice and warm, so your fungus there can get itself off one foot and aboard another foot without the slightest inconvenience, even. You get yourself a busy time of day, like the evening of a Saturday when everybody on the moorings's been out on the water the whole day, got themselves all crusty with the salt, and that shower's going to be in just about continuous use for a good two, three hours. And the same thing with the real peak of the season, when we get those real hot days when there hasn't been much wind but everybody's been out there sweating all day long, drifting around and hoping that there'd be some. Lots of showers taken those nights, too. A fellow gets real dirty, he's not gonna satisfy himself with no drippy little pressure shower that he might have right there on his boat and the water's going to be most likely lukewarm if it's warm at all, no sir. He wants the regular high-pressure and the good hot water and lots of soap that he can lather up and then rinse off", and that ride in on the launch to get it at the yard doesn't seem like it's too much trouble for him then.

"Now," Tim Borland said, "we know this. We know our customers that stay on their boats all weekend long, they're going to want a place where they can wash up. They come in, they're maybe going out that night ashore to tie the feedbag on, and we provide them with those showering facilities. Got three stall showers for the ladies, on account of women for some reason don't like to get undressed in front of other people even if the other people happen to be women that you'd think'd be built just about the same as them. And we got this one big gang shower room for men that's got nine nozzles in it, but actually about the most men that can use it at one time is six unless they don't mind getting a lot friendlier with each other than the majority of our men customers claim's their usual practices to do.

"With a shower like that," Tim said, "there's only two ways you can stop people from getting athlete's foot, and you've got to use them both without fail if you're going to have any hope at all of succeeding. One of them's that you've got to disinfect that shower faithfully, and hose her down when you get finished with the pine oil. And the other is that since you can't do that every five minutes, soon's one guy comes out you go in there and hose her down real good before the next guy can go in, you've got to make sure everybody using it's got on those thong things that they've got there for people's feet. And you can't do that, either. The hell you going to do, hire somebody that will sit there and keep everybody out that isn't wearing them? So Malcolm Larch and I'd imagine a good number other people got themselves infected that first summer I was really running things but doing all I could to do it without people noticing that old Earl wasn't running things no more even though it looked like that he was because he was still here and all.

"The thing of it was," Tim Borland said, "Malcolm was the only one of them that brought the matter my attention. He wasn't nasty about it or anything. Just made sure we knew about it, by way of no harm. Come in the office one Thursday afternoon—used to come up here on Thursdays in the summer, stay the weekend and leave Monday nights—for some damned thing or other, just let it drop in passing he'd picked up one real fine case of athlete's foot in our shower room and it was playing just about the devil with his social life. Now, I don't mean to say he wasn't all right about it. He was. He treated it like something he'd expect to run into, using that kind of facilities, just another one those goddamned things that happens to you when all's you're doing's minding your own business and doing something that you've got a perfect right to do. 'I'm getting married next week,' he says, 'and I'm going to look damned funny doing it when I show up there wearing white socks like my doctor says I've got to, when I've got my dress suit on. People're going to look at me and think that I'm some kind of hick or something.' His doctor, see, his doctor told him that he had to wear white cotton socks with no dye in them until it went away. And we had ourselves sort of a laugh over it, thanked him for telling us and then went down and give the kid hell that was supposed to hose that goddamned shower down, even though of course we knew damned well that wasn't going to put a stop to it. Especially since by then a good number of our regular customers had to have it, if Malcolm Larch'd caught it. But except for that, the only thing that we paid much attention to was him telling us that he was getting married. We were kind of curious about that.

"The reason was," Tim Borland said, "we had a certain amount excitement around the yard with men getting married for the second time. It wasn't nearly then quite as common as it's now, when there's hardly a week that goes by without us getting letters from some lawyers telling us we got to get a boat appraised or sell one because the owner of it's getting a divorce. We're used to it today, but back in those days we were not.

"As far's a boat's concerned," Tim Borland said, "a man don't change much when he gets one or when he decides it's time get rid the old one and get himself a new one. Season to season, year to year, if a fellow comes into the yard the first time with his boat and he's a decent sort of fellow that a fellow can do business with, that's almost always the sort of decent fellow he will be until the day he dies. And the same thing if he's a goddamned lunatic when you first meet him—the chances are he won't improve much no matter how long you do business with him. It seems like when a man gets himself a boat he thinks about that thing as representing something that he had it on his mind to get all settled, and he did it and that should be the end of it. Oh, he may decide he wants a new boat, maybe something bigger if he's making more'n he was when he got the first one, maybe something smaller if his family moved away, but that won't change him much.

"A woman is a different thing entirely," Tim said. "A man that always was a good egg can go out and get himself a woman and the next thing that you know he'll be acting like he was a perfect asshole. And the other way around, too—you'll get a man you couldn't have much hope he'd ever get some sense, and one day he'll tell you that he's found himself a new wife and after that it's like dealing with a fellow that you'd wish you'd known your whole life. So when it's a new woman that the fellow says he's got, we kind of look at her up close. Some of the women they bring in can really screw the boatyard up.

"You get some of these women that come down here to go sailing in the summer now," Tim said, "and we didn't used to have this problem in our line of work that's mostly sailboats although I understand it's always been a problem around yards that serve a lot of power boats, they've got their little shorts and bathing suits they wear that don't even come close to covering their cheeks, and that is when they're standing up. Those women take it into their heads they're going to stretch or they might just as well bend over so's to reach something, you can see clear to California if you want. It's pretty nearly all that we can do when that happens, keep the boys' attention on the work that they supposed to be doing. We had one guy in here that was the quietest timid little bastard that you ever saw, had himself a little twenty-two-foot catboat and never made a minute's trouble for a soul. And then he went and got himself a whole shitload of money and went out and bought himself a fifty-five-foot yawl that he didn't have no more idea of how to handle'n he would've had if he'd made himself ten shitloads and used the whole of it to buy himself the *Queen Elizabeth the Second*. And I'll be goddamned if he didn't take to coming down here in the spring before he took her out and damned near rammed and sank every other goddamned boat that we happened to have moored here in the harbor, and that bastard had more women than a man could shake a stick at. And from the way they dressed it would've a wonder if a stick was all was ever shook at them, although the way they acted I don't think they would've minded much if it was something else you showed to them. *Tramps* is what I would've called them, but I guess that I'm old-fashioned. Jesus Christ though, if it didn't look like some damned girlie show that he had floating in this harbor here when he had them aboard, I guess I never saw one then. Or felt the lack of it, as far as that's concerned. Whores don't belong on sailboats.

"Well," Tim Borland said, "that's the sort of thing that we was on the lookout for, when Malcolm Larch said he was getting married. We all assumed she had to be his second wife, and sometimes you will find a man that's otherwise pretty reasonable in most things will come up with some strange article when he gets himself a second wife. But Malcolm Larch's second wife was not like that. She was nice and quiet and polite, which you will find a lot of women with rich husbands won't be, get to thinking that the boys around the yard're just a bunch of servants they can order up and order down any time it suits them, generally making quite a bit of trouble for someone in my position and even more for their dear husbands if they only knew it when the skipper gets his boat out on the water and can't figure out why somebody around the yard appears to have gone and wired his bilge pump backwards, so she pumps in instead of out. Malcolm Larch's wife from the first day that she got here treated everybody in the yard as though they had as much right on this earth as she did, and even though a damned fool could've seen she was one fine-looking woman, she was always dressed the way a decent woman should be. The only thing you'd notice looking at her clothes was that what she had on obviously cost a lot of money, which was all right because her husband had a lot of money and how the hell else should she dress with all the money Malcolm had? So since she fitted in so well it was a pretty long time 'fore it occurred to any of us that she was at least twenty, twenty-five years younger than he was. And we didn't notice that until he started bringing his kids down here from his first marriage and they obviously could not be her kids. They were his kids and they were damned near just about as old as she was. They were nice enough, two girls and a boy, but I guess they didn't care for sailing or they didn't care for her, one thing or the other, because we only saw them a few times and then we didn't see them any more.

"She and Malcolm, they did, though," Tim Borland said. "Barbara and Malcolm came here every spring and summer and they kept coming in the fall, for six or seven years it must have been. And then one morning in October here, nice day, trees turning along the edges of the marshes out there in the back, I was sitting in the office with a cup of coffee and the paper, seeing if they drew the deer permits for Nantucket yet. I generally try to get myself a deer over on Nantucket every year, like to hunt there because there's not a lot of goddamned brush you got to hack your way through if you're going to have a chance of seeing one, and I had pretty decent luck over the years getting one the permits that they draw for in that lottery they have. Although I guess that just about everyone that asks for one is liable get one. And I happened to be glancing at the death notices there, and I see where Malcolm Larch dropped dead. And that apparently was some big deal in the banking world on Wall Street there.

"Well," Tim said, "this business is like any other business, I guess, except the undertaking business probably, where you don't really get your customer until he's dead. You're in it long enough and you build up your trade, you're going to lose a certain number of your customers each year. Some of them you'll be sorry to see go, because they always were the kind of people you could have a cup of coffee with and shoot the shit and so forth, and some of them you'd just as soon you never saw them in the first place and you figure that the devil's probably got himself a more or less bad day ahead of him when he checks that bastard in, because nothing that the bastard ever had on earth'd ever seemed to suit him. And Malcolm was pretty much right in the middle there, I guess, although if I'd've had to pick one category for him, I'd've put him closer to the kind of guys I didn't like to see die, I never got to know him very well, which was just as well with me, but what I did know I never had no real complaint about. So I just thought: 'Well, shit, there goes the Larch account.' Because since I'd noticed that his kids didn't go that hot and heavy for the sailing and I never yet seen more than one or two widows in all the years that I've been running things that kept the boats their husbands had when they died, I just assumed the next person that I heard from about *Temptress*'d be the lawyer for the estate that calls you up and tells you to go ahead and put the dead man's boat in brokerage and have her appraised for sale. I often advise people that I talk to that find themselves in that position, especially if it happens they didn't know the boat themselves or know much about all boats in general, most sensible thing to do as far as everybody is concerned is probably have us keep her here and appraise and broker her. Saves the estate a good amount on transportation and that sort of thing, and then there's the fact we generally know the boat in question better than just about anyone there is that took a look at her, what kind of care she's had and all that sort of thing. Generally we know the boat better than the owner did, it comes right down to it, and where you've got an owner that is dead, well, it don't matter much if he did do most the work himself, him being dead and everything.

"Now," Tim Borland said, "I don't mean to pretend that we don't make an honest dollar off of this when that is what the estate people decide they want to do, because we do, and there is nothing wrong with that. That's what we're in business for, just like they are. What'll often happen is we end up selling that boat there to somebody that took a liking to her when the dead man was still alive and sailing her, and we'll sell her to that fellow and he'll have us broker his old boat as well, and we make two commissions and the dead man's boat ends up staying right where she was when he died in the first place. We got three, four vessels in here, we've been several owners with them. I got this one lawyer up in Boston there that represents a lot of these rich families, or at least his firm does, and he's got this one estate that the boat in question has gone in and out of three times here and she ain't never left my boatyard. And he says to me one day that it's begun to look to him as though it's actually our boat and we just let his clients use it as they come along, one guy has it 'till he kicks the bucket and then the next one has her. Which is the way that things worked out with that particular boat. So, I read there Malcolm Larch was dead, it happened Desmond Carey come in shortly after that and I naturally made some mention of it to him. Says to him I hoped I'd get to handle the sale and that sort of thing. Because I was assuming that *Temptress*'d be sold.

"'Well,' Desmond said to me, he wouldn't want to be too sure of that. 'I was talking to Barbara yesterday,' he says, and this's the first inkling I got that Desmond there'd had some dealing with the Larches, 'and she was more or less prepared for him to go. And she told me, she said one thing to be sure and do was tell you that the boat was staying here and there wasn't going to be no plan to sell her. In case anybody should come around and ask when it came out in the papers that Malcolm'd checked out.'

"So," Tim said, "in the first place this was the first time that I ever heard anybody that was usually around the place refer to Mrs. Malcolm Larch as Barbara, and here it is it's Desmond that turns out to be the one that's doing it. And why the hell with her husband lying there was she on the phone to Desmond? And he tells me, smooth as silk, he talks regularly to all his clients, especially the ones he likes along with them asking him to do their business for them, and Malcolm Larch and Barbara were that kind of clients. And he told me he just finished, he'd spent the past six weeks or so handling the Magnuson property for them, which I didn't even know'd been for sale, let alone that they had gone and bought it. 'Well, shit, Desmond,' I said, 'I didn't know a damned thing about that, them buying up the Magnuson property.' And he said to me he didn't see no need to go around and tell his clients' business to everybody else, even to his other clients, unless it was also business that concerned the other clients, which the Larches buying up the Magnuson estate was not. Not mine, at least. And he was right about that.

"Well," Tim said, "Malcolm Larch may've gone out quick there from the shock he had there, and it was probably just as well. From what Barbara told me later, he wouldn't've been no better'n a vegetable if he'd've gone and survived it. But that did not mean it was going to be no slick thing getting matters straightened out after he was dead, which I knew just from what I was going through about then with the mess that Earl'd left things in when he dropped dead in the lobster boat. It took me almost two years, get his affairs in order, and the only thing old Earl owned was the boatyard and the house we lived in, actually. So Barbara made it clear there were a lot of things that she and Malcolm's kids did not see what you'd call eye to eye on, and when there was something that they could fight about, they would. And she said that now that he was dead, she imagined there'd be quite a few things they could fight about. What they did was they would side with Malcolm's first wife. Barbara was his secretary that he married after he divorced the wife. Which after I got to know Barbara, not that I ever knew the wife, I could see where he might have decided he would do that. She was one goddamned right fine looking woman when you started to look close at her, and I tell you, my friend, even if she was a few years older'n I was at the time, we didn't have rules against fooling around the customers in this place, if she'd've given me the high sign I would've gone for her in no less than a jiffy. And those kids of his, they didn't like her one bit.

"Well," Tim said, "one the things they had to fight about with her was that Magnuson real estate there, and the first thing Barbara did when that come up was get ahold of Desmond there to be her lawyer. Which was reasonable enough, of course, since he'd already been both of their lawyers when Barbara and Malcolm first set out to buy the property. And one thing led to another and there was this big court case there, over in that very courthouse where I'm suing Desmond's kid today.

"What those kids had it in mind that they were going to do," Tim Borland said, "was they were going to get that property away from

Barbara. And they brought in these slippery sharpies from New York to handle the thing from their point of view. And of course they also had another smooth-talking SOB from Boston that came down and tried to make it look as though he was the one that actually was their lawyer. And that whole thing come up before Judge Whiting there from over there in Middleboro, and all that Barbara had on her side was old Desmond, sitting there all by himself. It didn't take too much in the way of brains to figure out which way that that case was going to go if Judge Whiting could possibly make it come out in Desmond's favor, but I guess those kids and their high-powered lawyers couldn't see that.

"The thing of it was," Tim Borland said, "for quite a while, it didn't look as though old Desmond fully understood that. Those kids' expensive lawyers in their custom suits quite obviously come in here thinking it'd be nice if they went and tried the divorce matter all over once again, and get Judge Whiting there convinced that Barbara wasn't nothing better'n a hooker that'd turned old Malcolm's head to get his money, which I guess was the position that their mother'd tried to take when her and Malcolm got divorced, and that should mean that they should get the real estate.

"I can see why they might've thought that it would work," Tim Borland said. "This here is a small town, and Judge Whiting didn't look like anybody that would be likely to go around believing that adultery was perfectly all right. But what they overlooked was that Barbara was the only Mrs. Larch we'd ever seen, and she always treated us exactly like she should've. So naturally that stuff that made it seem as though she wasn't always quite so shy and modest as she acted, well, we were all interested in it and I began to think I probably knew what made Malcolm name the boat the way he did, but it didn't really change the way we thought about her.

"What bothered us," Tim Borland said, "was how Desmond sat there smiling and let them throw all of that shit at her. Here was this woman who's his client there, and keep in mind that this was close to thirty years ago and people weren't as broadminded about things as they seem to be today, and her step-kids were making out that she was something like Delilah there, and Desmond's letting all of it sail right into court there, all of these reporters sitting there and taking notes about what kind of hot-pants little number that she was there, and he's not doing one damned thing about it. And it's not like he didn't know how to do something when he wanted to in court, either.

Desmond was a country boy, but he was one smart country boy and this was his part of the country. There wasn't much that happened in a case that he was trying without him having something in his mind that he thought he would gain by letting it, but for the life of us in that case we couldn't figure out just what the hell it was.

"So," Tim Borland said, "there they all were, proving that she did this thing with Malcolm, down in the Bahamas, and they bought a piece of land there with a house on it. And then she got him down to Mexico and he decided that it might be nice to have a place in Mexico as well, so he went and bought one there. And they took some trips to Europe where they bought some real estate, and apparently old Malcolm had a fine time for himself when the two of them flew over the Pacific all the way to Hong Kong there, because it came out that they also had a small apartment there they owned. Now, I don't know what Barbara did to Malcolm when she got him into bed, but it didn't take a great deal of imagination for a man to figure out he must've liked it.

"Well," Tim Borland said, "finally those kids and all their high-priced lawyers run out of things that they could say that Barbara must've done to Malcolm to make his brain turn soft so they should get the Magnuson property that her and Malcolm'd bought down here in Oldfield for themselves, so they said that that was all they could come up with and they sat down. And Desmond there stood up and said that since they brought in all the stuff that Barbara'd done with Malcolm everywhere from here to Africa, it oughta save the courts a whole bunch of time, the long run, if the court that heard it all already was to decide once and for all who was to get the stuff the two of them'd bought in every place they visited. And that's when everybody figured out why Desmond'd let all that stuff come in to evidence, so he could just sit there and spike the plans those kids and their big-city lawyers had to sue their stepmother in every other town the goddamned world, most likely, until she had enough and just give up.

"Judge Whiting was just tickled pink," Tim Borland said. "He looked like he must've looked when somebody first told him what was perfectly all right a man to do with his own wife if they was alone together in their own bedroom, and he agreed with Desmond. Then Desmond went and brought in both the lawyers and all the Magnusons there was left that had anything to do with selling Pigeon Point there to the Larches, and they all testified that Barbara didn't have no part whatsoever in Malcolm buying it. They said that it was Malcolm that handled the whole thing and all that he could talk about was how he was buying it as a present for his lovely wife, and how he just went on about her 'till they thought she must be some kind of combination of a saint and holy queen. And Judge Whiting there heard all of that and he agreed with Desmond on that argument as well, that Barbara obviously didn't skin old Malcolm out the money that he spent on Pigeon Point because she didn't even know that he was buying it until he'd bought it, so Judge Whiting gave the Magnuson to her. And then, as long as he was at it, he gave her every other piece of property that they had mentioned Malcolm buying while him and Barbara was married to each other, and those kids and their high-powered lawyers just sat there with their mouths all hanging open like they'd been fishes and Desmond'd just gone and reeled them in.

"Well naturally," Tim Borland said, "they didn't find that nowhere near as funny as Desmond and the rest of us that watched them getting it, and they made it clear it wasn't going to stop them just because Des Carey'd fixed their wagons for them here. They said that just the same they planned to go and see what they could do to make that woman's life just miserable in all those other places, too, and she could just wait and see what some judges in Manhattan thought of Whiting and the things he had to say. But they could also see of course there was a chance that they would lose in a fair number of those other places, because some judges'd decide what Whiting said was good enough for them as well, so that the sensible thing to do from everybody's point of view was be reasonable with Desmond and just cut the whole deal up as close to fair and square as they could make it and quit all of that goddamned expensive wrangling. Which they did, and Barbara ended up with about six million bucks as well as Pigeon Point, which wasn't bad, a lady didn't know but one thing besides how to type and shorthand when she first met Malcolm Larch.

"Well," Tim Borland said, "when everything in that case was all over, or at least we thought so at the time, we got the next surprise. Which was that Desmond who was pushing fifty-five or so'd finally gotten himself married, to Barbara Larch. And goddamned if that news'd just come along, it seemed like, when the next thing that we hear is that she's going to have his kid as well. Which she did and that was Walter, and Walter was the son that Desmond always said he wanted."

Tim Borland frowned and cleared his throat. "I think," he said, "I think that Desmond until Walter was about fifteen or so was just about the happiest fellow that I ever saw in Borland's Boat Yard on anything approaching what you'd call a regular basis. He was so proud that kid it like to make you sick to listen to him. But then all of a sudden Walter went away to school, and after that we never saw a great deal of him, and we heard even less. At least from Desmond. Oh, he'd stop by for his coffee in the morning, and he'd admit that Walter was at Yale and then doing pretty well in Harvard Law if the question happened to come up directly, but he didn't brag the way he used to and he looked kind of mournful for a man who looked like he'd got everything he ever wanted. The only thing that Desmond bragged about when he come in from pulling traps was the size of any lobsters that was in them."

Tim Borland sighed and gazed at the reporters and the picket lines in front of the county courthouse in the morning mist. "I know the reason now," he said, "I know it now real good. It was because, old Desmond acted that way, kind of hangdog and down in the mouth with Walter's name came up, because he'd found out Walter was a homosexual, and that was more'n Desmond could find it in his heart to come to grips with, that his kid was queer. I know's I blame him, or that it'd do much good if I was to do that, him being dead and all now, and Barbara along with him now. What difference would it make? Walter's habits never caused me any trouble, or anybody else around here. What difference does it make to Borland's Boat Yard if Des Carey's son's a queer? Don't make any difference whatsoever, least that I can see. And if Walter and his friends decided that that they're going to use the property on Pigeon Point to put up condominiums where them and all their fairy pals can come for their vacations in the summertime, what the hell on earth do I care, huh? What difference does it make to me, Tim Borland?

"Well," Tim Borland said, "quite a lot, it turns out. My boatyard customers've told me in no uncertain terms they don't like the notion all their friends in Boothbay Harbor and up in Marblehead'll think they're queer themselves if they say they keep their boats in Oldfield, Massachusetts, and they think that's what their friends'll think if Walter's plans go through. The trouble is my customers don't own land here that's next to Pigeon Point—it's boats they own, and boats ain't property of the sort you've got to have to fight a condo project. It's land you need abutting those to put up any fuss, and I'm the one that's got the land.

"Therefore," Tim Borland said, "I got to fight with Walter. Because that land is all I got, that the boatyard's occupying, and if I lose my customers because they don't want other folks to laugh at them for having boats in Oldfield, that land the boatyard's on ain't going to be worth one pisshole in the snow. What the hell's an old man such as me about to do with a boatyard that hasn't got no boats in it, I ask you? Starve, is what I'm going to do, and I don't relish that.

"So," Tim Borland said, "I am suing Walter to prevent him and his friends from doing what they want to do with his land, and he is suing me right back for suing him, and all his friends hate me and all my customers hate him. And this is all because some folks that haven't been alive for some time now just went ahead and did the things they wanted without meaning any harm anyone."

Tim Borland shook his head. "I tell you what I wished," he said. "I wished to God I understood about a third the things that go on in this world and end up getting everybody in big trouble that they never had no notion they were getting into when they did it. The older that I get, the less it seems as though I understand, except for just one thing, and that I think I finally have got figured out. I think now I know why old Earl gave up everything but drinking everything he could and pulling lobster traps. I think he figured those were the only two things that he even halfway enjoyed himself while he was doing them, so he decided those were the only things that he would do and goddamn all the other stuff. I'll tell you something about old Earl, my friend, and that is this: I think the least the old bastard might've done was tell me what it was that he was up to, when he decided he would do that. My father Earl was not what you would call the best pal that a fellow ever had."

WARM FOR SEPTEMBER

DONNELLY always called Carolyn Busby at the paper when he was in Boston, and they always met for drinks downstairs at the Parker House.

"I know I don't," she said, when the waiter brought the second round.

"You ought to do something about it," Donnelly said.

"*You're* getting fat," she said. "You ought to do something about that."

"There's only one thing I can do about getting fat, and I'm already doing that," Donnelly said. "The trouble is that it isn't working, and it won't work either, because my problem isn't what I eat."

"It's what you drink," she said.

"Not that, either," Donnelly said. "My problem is that I'm getting old, and therefore getting soft. My weight's actually about the same as it was the last time I saw you. When was that, in the spring?"

"Uhh," she said, "let me think. It was before I went to St. Louis for him, wasn't it? Did I tell you about St. Louis?"

"No," he said.

"Then it was before I went to St. Louis," she said, "because I know I would've told you about that if it'd been after. Must've been the first part of May."

"Then I'm right," Donnelly said. "My weight's been the same since I moved to Silver Spring and finally got myself a bathroom scale again after five years. One-eighty-six."

"You look fatter," she said.

"What I am is softer," he said. "Out of shape."

"Better watch it," she said. "The young stuff'll lose interest if you're not careful. A dirty old man's one thing, but a paunchy dirty old man, I don't know. You're liable to wind up having to pay for it."

"Nope," Donnelly said, "it doesn't do any good. The only thing you can do is look on, helplessly. The only cure for what I've got is youth, and that's not available on my salary. When I was thirty I had the body of a thirty-year-old, and I wasn't surprised that it sagged a little more than the one they were letting me use when I was twenty and playing basketball. Now I'm forty-two, and it doesn't surprise me at all that I've got a forty-two-year-old's body. Oh, I'll tighten it up some when I get back down there and start playing handball three times a week again, but it's a losing proposition. Now, your thing's something you could do something about, if it interested you. With you it's just inertia."

"It's more'n that," she said. "I don't do anything about it because I honestly can't think of anything to do. It isn't that I haven't thought about it, because I have. I think about it when I get up in the morning, and then for some reason, when I get to work and see him there in his usual place, I don't think about it. If I have to go out on something, I don't think about it, and as a matter of fact, I don't think about it until after I leave. If I'm not seeing him. If I'm seeing him, I don't think about it until after he leaves. But I go to sleep thinking about it, and I wake up thinking about it, about what I could do to make it better, and there isn't a single, solitary thing. Nothing. Must be love, I guess."

"I thought love was supposed to have beneficial effects," Donnelly said. "Firms up the step, brightens the eye and gives you a shiny coat. You just look tired."

"I am tired," she said. "It just wears you out, being in this kind of situation. No, it's not love. I haven't been in love, if that's how you tell, since I was twenty-four."

"Oh dear," Donnelly said, "and I was all set to receive a compliment."

"And that only lasted about, oh, I guess it was a little over two months," she said. "I fell in love with Michael because I thought he was the nicest guy I ever met in my life, ever would meet, and I guess he was, but my *God*, he was boring. He was good-looking, he was successful, he worked for Cyrus Vance and he was always dashing off to Washington again after two days of a three-day weekend that he had to postpone four times before he finally made it, and he introduced me to Robert McNamara and got me the special tour of the White House. I smoked twice as much for a month afterwards, so I could show off all hundred and fifty packs of matches I stole from the White House Mess. But when I was alone with him, and I thought at that stage of my development that he was good in bed too, when I was alone with him I was so bored I was just about paralyzed. God, if I'd ever married him I would've been catatonic in a year. I don't see how he did it, all the things he did and the people he knew, and still be the most boring man in the world. Now you can say what you want about Marshall, and that hanging around with him's making me look like hell, as you so pleasantly put it, but one thing he isn't is boring. She had a detective on him last week."

Donnelly laughed. "What hell's she doing that for?" he said. "I thought part of the problem was that she didn't want a divorce."

"She doesn't know what she wants," Carolyn said. "But he doesn't seem to know what he wants, either, although there are times when I'm quite sure he does, and that he just doesn't find it convenient to share his little secret with me. I think she'd just like to get something on him, because it might be useful."

"If he knows what he wants, and he's not telling," Donnelly said, "that means he's got what he wants and he's afraid telling'd spoil it. And that means you're in even more trouble than I thought when I started in on you."

"When you started in on me," Carolyn Busby said, "I was in minimum trouble."

"Oh come off it," Donnelly said.

"I *was*, Deke," she said. "I could handle the shit I was getting then, and I could handle us. I don't mean you screwed me up. You didn't screw me up at all. I'm simply saying that I could handle the problems I had then, without very much trouble. They were smaller problems. But now I've got big problems, and what I learned in peaceful combat with you, and not-so-courteous treatment from others, just doesn't help me very much in what I'm in now. And to be very honest with you, since you were rude enough to bring it up in the first place, I could use some help."

"Do you want to get married again?" Donnelly said.

"That'd be something, wouldn't it?" she said. "I can just hear all the crap I'd have to take, after the stuff I've written. Jesus, it'd have to be to a woman if I did, some bitch with a leather dildo, or I'd never hear the end of it. I guess I'm not really sure," she said. "Do you?"

"Nope," Donnelly said, "I'm too old to get married again. Of course I'm also too old to be single again too. It's been very hard, trying to get used to it. But I'm getting used to it, and I've got all that time and energy invested in it, four years, after all, and I'm not sure I've got the stamina to turn around and get used to being married again. Besides, I'm reasonably satisfied with things the way they are."

"Sam's okay?" she said.

"If you and I," Donnelly said, "were doing as well as Sam is, we'd have God in His Heaven and the lark on the wing. Gail's second litter, Tom's kids, think Sam's, I don't know, that Sam's wonderful, and he takes care of them and he gets a big bang out of it. Makes him feel good. Gail's done a marvelous job with him."

"You're lucky to be able to say that," Carolyn said. "When I was going with Ed, there were quite a few nights when he came back to the apartment literally in tears about the way his ex-wife was manhandling the kids. And making them hate him, incidentally, of course. A little kick in the balls for Daddy, for walking out. Now that was exhausting, too, the pity's-love bit. I'm not going to do that again, either. There're quite a few things I'm not going to do again, and that's very solid on the list. Along with duty's-love, horniness-is-love, and we've-got-the-same-politics-so-we-must-be-in-love. Well, maybe I'll do horniness-is-love again. But not the others. It depends."

"Good God, I should hope so," Donnelly said.

"Well," she said, "I'm not so sure. I might, but then again, I might not. The simplicity of it is nice. Nobody expects anything from anybody, except frequent and relaxing orgasms, and nobody gets in anybody's way. But then there's nobody in the world that cares about you. And pretty soon, when you get the blues and under the rules of no burdens, you can't talk about them, or you're not supposed to, anyway, you have to keep them, and that means the other party doesn't get what he's entitled to in the bargain. Which is really a series of one-night stands that just happen to be with the same person every night. I don't like going to bed with strangers, even with a stranger I've been living with for six months or so. You get your cookies, but that's all you get, and after a while you're not getting your cookies anymore, as a result."

"Someone to take care of you?" Donnelly said.

"Only when I'm very tired," she said, "and very insecure, and lonely and worried and lonesome, and feeling little."

"That, for me," Donnelly said, "happens about three times a week, and I get up and put on that Sinatra record that's got 'Someone To Watch Over Me' on it, and then 'The Wee Small Hours Of The Morning,' and I get fairly maudlin."

"Then what do you do?" she said. "This may be useful information. I've been using the FM for that."

"It won't work," Donnelly said. "When you need 'Yesterday,' all you can get is a bunch of mazurkas. And when you need some genuine treacle, some Andy Williams stuff, to make your mood so sad you can even begin to laugh at it yourself, they give you Mozart piano and you just collapse. You've got to be able to tailor it, control what you're getting, learn your own tolerances and cater to your weaknesses. That's the trick."

"Isn't that what I've been doing, that gets me into trouble?" she said. "Catering to my weaknesses?"

"Sometimes it does and sometimes it doesn't," Donnelly said. "Now those disgustingly youthful types at the bar, who'd scorn me, and the boys that'd grab you . . . . "

"Yeah," she said.

"True," Donnelly said. "They've been watching you."

"Sure," she said, "wondering if I'm a quick lay, and if I am, never mind how I look. 'All cats're black in the dark.' Didn't I hear somebody say that once?"

"You did a number or two on me, too," Donnelly said. "What I was going to say, I had to fight back with something, you know, for Christ sake. Twelve years was it, you said? That was nice of you. Let's we just try and keep in mind what happened five years ago, and how come that ended."

"You had something to do with that, you know," Carolyn said .

"Never said I didn't," Donnelly said. "Another thing I didn't do, and I haven't done it since, was start blaming you for what I did."

"There were too many problems there," she said.

"There were," Donnelly said, "and most of them were mine, and I didn't handle them very well. I wasn't handling them very well. But I didn't say they were your fault, and I didn't go around pretending they weren't doing damage, and I didn't go out of my way to be nasty when you couldn't take the damage anymore, which happens to be the reason we ended up the way we did, and you know it."

"I don't happen to think so," she said. "The way I remember it, you were getting divorced or separated or some other damned thing, and the more I saw of the way you were acting, the more I was damned sure you didn't mean it, and you'd go back to her in a minute if she looked at you cross-eyed, and I figured the next thing that was going to happen was that she would, and you would, and then you'd move out again, and then you'd move back again, and then you'd move out again, and I just couldn't face it."

"That's what I said," Donnelly said.

"What you said didn't sound like that was what you were saying," she said.

"Well," Donnelly said, "that's what I said."

"That's what you said, then," she said. "It doesn't matter to me."

"It matters to me," Donnelly said. "It matters more to me because it sure-God ought to matter to you. What the hell's the matter with you?"

She sighed. She looked down at the table when she answered. "It's been a hot day," she said. "It was close to ninety. I've been up at the State House all day, trying to get a straight answer in an election year from some politician who's so scared he'll lose if he tells the truth that he won't say it for attribution, that the people who wouldn't let Kennedy speak about busing, and tried to beat up on him and threw fruit at him, are a bunch of goddamned animals and the best reason anybody in the world could think of to write laws that do exactly what they don't want done. It's warm for September. I can't stand humidity. You know that. It makes me sticky and mad."

"Uh huh," Donnelly said.

"That St. Louis trip was a bummer," she said. She clenched her teeth and started talking through them. "It was nothing more'n a sweetheart piece. Marshall got a letter from somebody who was in Porcellian with him, and this fellow was making a film, a television film for the Bicentennial celebration, and Marshall decided he was going to give the kid a freebie on the feature page. Marshall also decided that the freebie was going to be done by me. A nice trip out of town for Star Writer. Also, something else. I think her name's Mary Lou. She works at the *Globe*.

"So I did it," she said. "Now, I was underwhelmed. St. Louis late in May. Like a steam bath. But I went. And I met this asshole, this absolute asshole, who's thirty-two years old and there is absolutely no shape to his face at all. It's just flesh, just pink, round, unmarked flesh. I bet he doesn't shave twice a month. And he works in a bank. He's an executive vice-president in this big bank. 'I'm in Finance,' he says, and there's only, oh, maybe sixty other jerks like him making fifteen thousand a year kissing the real boss's ass, all executive vice-presidents, of course, because their families've got money and they haven't got any brains and they don't need any. The boss's got brains; his name is Horace Royce, and he's an old pirate who uses those guys to wipe his feet on, and they *revere* him for it. 'Gawd,' they say, 'marvelous old man.' He could've run Buchenwald, and they'd help him and say the same thing.

"Well," she said, "Marshall's friend had another friend in town for the week. His name was Peter and he was about twenty, and his connection was that Marshall's friend and Peter went to Exeter, but not at the same time, and Peter'd just gotten into Porcellian, and Peter came from Louisville, and Peter was going into *Finance*, and he wanted to locate in the mid-*South*, and somebody at Porcellian'd given his name to Marshall's friend, and Marshall's friend was introducing him to his contacts. Now Marshall's friend was *sure* that I'd adore Peter, or maybe I was supposed to adore him, it wasn't very clear, and also Mister Royce, and this pear-shaped woman that Marshall and Marshall's friend had known for ages, ever since she was at Miss Porter's. So before I could see this extraordinary movie—'Very talented fellow,' Marshall told me, 'not just that he's a friend of mine, but a very talented fellow, absolute banking genius,' but Mister Royce doesn't think so; Mister Royce wouldn't trust Marshall's friend with the stamp money—I had to have lunch with these twerps, and then drinks with these twerps, and then dinner with these twerps and this dull, dull woman, who does weaving and they all talked about how they were going to 'summer' on Martha's Vineyard, and perhaps I could join them there for a drink. Oh yeah, I could just see that. And cheap? The bill for cocktails came to eight-oh-five, and Marshall's friend and Peter divided it up, and Peter had more beers than we had drinks, so he owed four-twenty, but then there was the tip, and Marshall's friend was being *very* nice, and wasn't going to ask me for my share—I had two J and B's, and when they started that, I wished they'd been doubles—and Peter started off wanting sixty cents change, and Marshall's friend worked him down to fifty, he had a five-dollar bill, and then to forty. Now these guys knew the pedigree of every family between Charleston and Kansas City, the 'good families,' at least, and Peter's best girl's mother owned the horse that won the Kentucky Derby, and Peter's second-best girl's daddy owned a 'very nice place at Grosse Point,' and Peter's little brother, Chris got an

MGB for his sixteenth birthday and was up visiting his girl, Sally, in Chestnut Hill—'You must know Chestnut Hill, Carolyn,' Marshall's friend said, and then he started telling me about every Wasp family that ever had dinner at The Country Club, or played at Longwood— and they also knew who owned all the good houses between the ocean and the Rocky Mountains, between the end of the Civil War and the present. And they were negotiating the tip, which Marshall's friend said was never going over fifteen percent while he was living .

"I got so pissed off," Carolyn said. "I got so pissed off that when Marshall's friend got Peter down to twenty-five cents' change, I grabbed the goddamned thing and said: 'Look, I'm a woman of the world. Gimme the fucking thing and I'll ride it on the fucking expense account. Now I'm goddamned starving. Let's get this goddamned show on the road.'

"It was a very strained evening," Carolyn said. "We met Tubby at Tony's and we had to wait a long time. In the bar. Marshall's friend talked about how, when he got married, he was going to invite all his old girl friends, whom he clearly wished us to believe he'd screwed, as, well, a series of acts of noble charity, so that he could see the 'scraggly types they married.' Peter thought that was mighty hilarious. Tubby said nothing. I got two dimes out of my wallet and gave them to Marshall's friend and said I'd spring for the whole project and throw in an extra dime in case the girl's mother answered the first time and she was out. 'I'm no virgin,' he said through his lockjaw. 'Yes, you are,' I said through my lockjaw, 'but you don't know it.'

"Then we had dinner," Carolyn said, "and Tubby and I talked about Women's Lib, which infuriated Marshall's friend and puzzled Peter and fairly well baffled Tubby, too, if you want the truth, but she didn't want to be baffled. And Marshall's friend and Peter talked about more families, and more houses, and money management, and then the check came and they sort of looked at it, and I took it and paid it, and we got up and started out, but I looked back, and there was Marshall's friend handing the tip I'd left to the waiter. I know why that bastard's in Finance. He's cheap.

"From there we went to a little place where they had two maybe-genuine Irishmen who sang about the rising of the moon." Carolyn said. "Marshall's friend asked them to sing 'Shenandoah' and they refused. Then he talked all the time while they were introducing their songs, and when they started 'Wild Colonial Boy,' he said: 'I don't see whey they won't sing any *American* songs.'

"I saw the movie the next day," she said. "'It traces the history of a composite American family, read: those of the people he knows, from Sixteen-thirty-nine to the present." Right. I asked him what kind of camera he used—this was before I saw it, after which I didn't need to ask, and he said, well, I expected him to say 'Arriflex,' or at least 'Bolex,' and he said: 'Super Eight. But it has sound.'—and that whole damned film took forty-five minutes. Forty-five minutes. I saw it and I went out to the airport and got on the plane and came home.

"'Great guy, huh?' Marshall said," she said, "and I didn't say anything. 'Very creative,' Marshall said, and I didn't say anything then, either. But I wrote the story, all right, and I was very specific when I filed my expenses, and Marshall got just as pissed off as I'd been, twice, once for the story and once for the expenses of entertaining his measly friends, and since then, if the truth be told it's been less than blissful around my digs, on those nights when he chooses to appear."

"Three months ago?" Donnelly said. "Stroking my beard, I'd say you better, ah, terminate with extreme prejudice."

"Are you saying that," she said, "because that's what you think, or because you know I only go to bed with one guy at a time?"

"Because that's what I think," Donnelly said. "An hour ago, for the other reason. Now, for that one."

"Okay," she said, "I asked for that."

"You always do," Donnelly said. "You always did."

A PLACE OF
COMFORT, LIGHT
AND HOPE

LATE in the afternoon, in northeastern Connecticut, the train went through the trailing edge of the storm. When it pulled into the station in Providence there were only a few flakes in the air. At the Massachusetts line there was only cold and accumulating darkness.

Lane and Donnelly sat in the lounge car on the blue tweed seats. They drank bourbon and water, and, deprived of the patterns of snow against the windows, without anxiety permitted long periods of silence. There were brooks full of dark water along the roadbed, and the snow covered the discarded tires and paper boxes and bottles on the banks. In the Attleboros (by then it was nearly dark) there were warehouses and factories with sharply peaked roofs against the darkening sky, and the outside floodlights shone on the grey, dry shingles and the dry, dull, red clapboards, and the snow that had drifted in around the buildings in the wind. At a grade crossing, a large black dog stood patiently in the flashing red light as the train went through. Behind the dog was a Buick with one headlight out

"You want to know when the trouble starts?" Lane said. "I can tell you when the trouble starts."

"When you decide to go to work for a newspaper in the first place," Donnelly said.

"Nah," Lane said. "That's no different'n deciding to go to work for the railroad. You think the people that're supposed to keep this car up, so all the Amtrak advertising turns out to be true, you think they feel any different about the things they do?"

" I can tell they don't," Donnelly said, rubbing the fingers of his right hand through the grit on the window-sill.

" Well," Lane said, "what the hell can you expect? Neither one of us . . . , I bet, this train's almost full, and I bet there's not fifty people on it that'd be on it if LaGuardia wasn't socked in. Nobody takes the train except when he has to. You're in New York, and you've got to get to Boston, you fly. You can't fly, you've still got to be there, okay, down to Penn Station. And they all know it. They're running a god-damned fall-back, and they know it. I think working a second-class job can take a second-class man and make him third class. It gets to you. And that's when the trouble starts: the day you figure out, it all of a sudden dawns on you, that maybe you're working for a first-class operation, but what they've got you doing really isn't very important to anybody. It's just something that needs to be done, that nobody with any sense of self-importance'd want to do himself, so he's got you doing it, and that tells you what he thinks of you, boy. And then you think: well, I'm doing it, I've been doing it all along. So he must be right about me."

"And thinking that," Donnelly said, "thinking that . . . . "

". . . makes him right," Lane said, "Exactly. They ought to start you off honest, tell you right at the beginning: 'Actually, Mister Lane, we're not sure you've got the talent to write a column, or the brains to run a bureau, or the intelligence and drive to be a correspondent. And from your clips, well, you don't write very well, either. So if you think you're coming aboard to do some heavy hitting, forget it. You're too limited. But that doesn't mean we haven't got a place for you. There's a certain amount of donkey work in every operation, and this paper's no exception. Somebody's got to read copy, somebody's got to cover religion, somebody's got to watch high school track meets and rewrite the garden club news releases, because the people we put this thing out for . . . . "

"'The advertisers,' " Donnelly said.

"Right," Lane said, "'the people who sell things, sell most of the things to the people who want to read more about the sports their kid-s're playing in high school'n they do about Sadat of Egypt or Kitchener of Khartoum. Roving correspondents and Washington bureau chiefs are for the people who put out the paper to brandish at people who put out other papers when they all get together at The Greenbrier to talk about the Role of a Free and Responsible Press in a Time of Crisis and elect each other to various things that they can publish in their own papers and show what great fellows they are. There's donkey work in this business because we're in the business of talking to donkeys, and we think, we're *convinced*, that you can bray with the best of them. '"

"Gawd," Donnelly said.

"Damned right," Lane said, "Awful. But a hell of a lot better'n bringing the kid in from the Athol *Daily News* and putting a lot of stars in his eyes, so that six years later, when he gets home from the three-to-eleven on the desk, his wife's looking at him the way a chicken farmer looks at a hen that's quit laying, so he doesn't go right home after a while: he waits until she's in bed. 'I thought you were going to be Walter fucking Lippman,' she says, only she never says it. She doesn't need to. Thinking it's enough. 'I'm a limited man, my dear,' you say, but you don't need to say it, 'I lacked his brains and his natural advantages to boot. I'm a singles hitter. They don't drive Cadillacs, maybe, but they can keep up the payments on a two-year-old Impala, and you do the best you can in this world.' Thinking it's more'n enough. 'You gave me to understand you were a home-run hitter,' she thinks. You did, too. That's the hell of it. And the worse hell of it is that it matters to her. It really does matter. It matters like a bastard. Oh boy, can a man have a drink or two on that discovery."

"You straightened it out, though," Donnelly said. "That's more'n I can say."

"I got through it," Lane said. "I didn't correct anything. I got through it. I survived it. I didn't get dismarried to Jean. I didn't get prostrate from the booze, although I came good and close. I didn't fuck out to the point where you couldn't carry me anymore, although I came pretty close."

"Close enough to suit me," Donnelly said. "Some time when you're buying flowers, get a bunch for Ernie Clark. There's a man who can hold back a question when the answer'd force him and the rest of them to do something they really don't want to do."

"I know it," Lane said, "Ernie's decent. He's a decent man. If he can throw you a rope, he will, and if he can't, if he just doesn't have a rope to throw, at least he won't drive the boat over while you're thrashing around. I'll light a candle for him if he wants."

"Don't tell him, if you do," Donnelly said. "It'd embarrass him if he thought you really appreciated something he did. He wouldn't know how to act around you. You'd make him uncomfortable. Make him uncomfortable long enough, and sooner or later he'd do to you, healthy, what he prevented happening to you when you were in trouble, and he wouldn't even know why he was doing it. Just to get you out of his sight. Ernie's got a very low gratitude threshold. He doesn't want any, none at all. Scares the living bejesus out of him. Call Ernie a stubborn son of a bitch, and he'll reason with you and try to get you to see why he has to tell you to do what he's telling you to do, even though you don't like it. Tell him you think he's wrong, and he wants to hear all about it, and five times out of ten, he'll end up agreeing with you. Say 'Thank you' to Ernie and he starts shuffling papers on his desk and coughing and moving back and forth in his chair. You know what Ernie does? He goes to Mass and Communion, every day."

"I know it," Lane said, "I caught him coming out of Arch Street one day, when I was drinking while I was supposed to be interviewing somebody, well, I'd done the interview, actually, but I wasn't in any hurry to get back, and out he came. 'Son of a bitch, ' I thought, 'lousy goddamned luck, ' And then it dawned on me, he was more rattled than I was. I've seen guys, coming out of motels, didn't look as sheepish as he did, coming out of the Shrine. It's a funny business, when you get right down to it, "

The train went through swamps where stunted oaks and maples, bare of leaves, stood dark grey in black water around the bases of their trunks, and snow piled up on small russet hummocks,

"It's something fierce, when you get right down to it," Donnelly said. "When the trouble starts, that is. I don't know what the hell you do about it. I never have. That's the only progress I've made. Now I know I don't know, what the hell you do about it. I've been puzzled for years, and I just found out I was puzzled, and it's all I can do to keep from bragging about it."

"You feel like you're repeating Columbus," Lane said,

"Always," Donnelly said. "That's exactly what it is. You figure out something, and you feel like Lindbergh. Nobody ever figured this out before. 'The earth ain't flat, fellas. I got documentary proof. It's as round as a fuckin' bowling ball, no way you can sail off the edge. ' And everybody stands around looking at you, as though you'd just taken leave of your senses. Which, of course, you did."

"I was different," Lane said.

"Sure," Donnelly said.

"I was," Lane said. "I was craftier. I didn't tell anybody, when I figured everything out."

"Which time?" Donnelly said.

"Every time," Lane said, "All of them. All hundred of them. I kept it to myself, that's what I did. I made a fool out of myself too many times, all by myself. I'm not looking for help, to do it again. I almost lost my job, I almost lost my wife, I was, the only reason I didn't go around babbling foolishness to people was that I was babbling foolishness to myself, and I was such a good listener, I didn't need anybody else. I'm a hell of a fellow, you know that?"

"I do," Donnelly said.

"Sure," Lane said. "What're you doing tonight, assuming we get there by tonight?"

"Seeing the kid," Donnelly said. "Me and Bob Cratchit. No holding us, around Christmas."

"Rough?" Lane said.

"Actually," Donnelly said, "no. Much better. What came before, with Gail, it was a lot worse. You were lucky."

"Yeah," Lane said.

"You were," Donnelly said. "I'm not minimizing anything. I don't do that. It's like this. I had a car at Logan, The planes aren't flying. Okay, I call ahead, and I take the train, and if everything works right, which it never does, I'll get into South Station and find a goddamned cab and get over to the Avis office and they'll have a car for me. With snow tires. And if something goes wrong, they won't, and I'll have to get another cab, and go over to the airport, and when I get there, they'll have my car, or else they won't, and I'll have wet feet, and when the whole thing's over, I'll either be where I'm supposed to be, to see my kid tomorrow, or else I won't be, but luck hasn't got anything to do with it, and now he's old enough to know that. For you, it did. You never got into anything deep enough so that luck wasn't any good anymore. I did."

"Wrong," Lane said. "It wasn't luck that did it. It was resignation."

"Yeah," Donnelly said.

"Yeah," Lane said, "it really was. You know what it was, that really got to me? She wouldn't lie. And she wouldn't keep her goddamned mouth shut, either. The result was, I knew everything she was doing.

"Now, I didn't *want* to know everything she was doing," Lane said.

"'He that increaseth wisdom,'" Donnelly said, "'increaseth sorrow.'"

"Damned right," Lane said. "I didn't want to know what she was doing, For Christ sake, I knew she was disappointed with me. That was bad enough. What she was doing about it, revenge or anything else, what the hell did I need that for?

"I got it," Lane said. "I didn't want to know, she knew I didn't want to know, she was damned and determined I was going to know, and so she told me. Bullshit, Without being asked, I actually discouraged it. Didn't do any good.

"You know something I'll never know?" Lane said, "I'll never know why they can't leave a man alone, I will just never know that. It was none of my business, I didn't want to mind it. I didn't even want to have it forced on me. Is that such a hard thing to do, to leave a man alone when he's minding his own business and not making any trouble for anybody? Why the hell should I have to make amends for knowing something, that she did, that I didn't want to know about in the first place? I never told her anything I did. Big fucking deal: she's getting laid, to get back at me. What'd I need that for? Why the hell did I have to hear about it? "

"For revenge," Donnelly said.

"Sure," Lane said, "and that's where luck drops out, as a factor. Then, when you've got something like that, the only thing you can do is choke it down."

"Did you?" Donnelly said.

"I must've," Lane said. "I'm still with her, I didn't beat her up yet. She didn't get me between the third and fourth ribs with the pinking shears. We must've."

"Well," Donnelly said, "it's better'n a poke in the eye with a sharp stick, I suppose."

"Hey," Lane said, "I'm just back from New York, I was interviewing somebody whose name I forget, and I'm gonna have one hell of a story for the features on it, and, hell, what if I never do see Lhasa, huh? It's a living. My dear wife picks me up at One-twenty-eight, and the sitter'll have a fire going when we get home, and I'll have a little Lancer's white and hear about how the septic tank overflowed again. Is that so bad? "

The train began to slow into the One-twenty-eight station. The platform was deserted. Beyond it, cars with parking lights on sat amber in the cold gloom.

"You tell me," Donnelly said.

"It's the best I can do," Lane said. "After all of this, we made some progress. We don't tell each other, anymore,"

THE DEVIL
IS REAL

DAN Flynn went out on the road in the hot morning to finish interviewing people for his presentencing report on James F. Teal. He started at Runciman Wire & Cable in the Taunton Industrial Park, where he had a 9:15 appointment with Teal's former supervisor.

Amelio Marino was a middleaged man with a barrel chest and iron-colored hair. He looked at Flynn appraisingly and said that Teal had been a satisfactory employee for his whole eleven years with the company: "steady, reliable, honest." He said all of Teal's colleagues on the sales force had been "shocked" by Teal's arrest and subsequent conviction.

"We all think it sucks, too," he said, "if that makes any difference."

Flynn wrote in his field notebook: "Spvsr. cites sympath. for Def. w/coworkers." Aloud he said: "It doesn't. It won't to the court at least."

Marino snorted. "That's what I figured," he said, "but all the guys asked me to tell you that, and I said I would, so I did."

"Mister Teal was well-liked?" Flynn said.

"Of course he was," Marino said. "Hell, we all knew he was having trouble. The past couple years, naturally, we knew the guy was under some kind of pressure at home. Said his wife'd gone batty over religion. But it didn't seem like anything that couldn't be worked out. Everybody gets divorced, for God's sake. Over half the people in this plant've been divorced. I'm not saying it's fun, but it's done. He should've been all right."

"Our understanding," Flynn said, "is that his wife didn't want a divorce."

Marino gazed thoughtfully at Flynn. "She sure didn't," he said. "If what I read in the papers was true, what she wanted was his goddamned head. Got it, too, looks like."

"It's true," Flynn said. "That's how they found out. When he came to visit his kids, he took them out on the porch, where she couldn't hear them talk. Left his coat in the living room, samples in the pockets. She went through the pockets. She looked at the bills. All the numbers were the same. Then she made the call. After that it was simple. All they had to do was have an undercover guy approach him and make the buy."

Marino had let out one rough laugh. "That's Jimmy for you," he said. "Natural born salesman. Day or night, he's always ready, case there's a customer. How she'd know, though, to look? You wanna tell me that?"

Flynn snapped his notebook shut. "Would if I could," he said. "I don't know myself."

Marino snorted again. "Bullshit," he said.

"Think what you like," Flynn said, standing up. "Thanks for your trouble and time."

Flynn's second stop was Teal's former home in a development enclosed by tall pines east of Route 24 in Randolph. There he met Teal's estranged wife, Carol. She was petite and had short blonde hair. She had dark eyes and she wore a divided denim skirt and a flowered cotton blouse and white sneakers with sockies that had little pom-poms at the counters. She smelled of Ivory soap. With tight lips she introduced him to the two daughters, ages fourteen and twelve. To them she said: "Mister Flynn is here from the Federal Probation to talk to me about Dad." To Flynn she said: "Do you want to talk to Molly and Jennifer, or is it just me?"

"Ah, just you, I think," he said to her. To the two girls he said awkwardly: "Nice meeting you." They did not answer but fled immediately to the second floor of the eight-room ranch.

"We can talk in the kitchen," Carol Teal said. She gave him instant coffee and assured him his visit was no trouble. She volunteered her explanation for Teal's problems. "James," she said regretfully, "is not a moral man. We were married very young. I was only nineteen. He had just turned twenty-one. We were very much in love—perhaps I should say infatuated—the way you are at that age, and we didn't

think very much about how we should serve the Lord." She said she
had counseled several times with her pastor and prayed with him and
alone for guidance about how to bring her husband to the Way.

"What did you decide to do?" Flynn said.

She looked at him pityingly. "Mister Flynn," she said, "the wife is
as much the helpmeet of the Lord as she is of her husband before the
Lord. And she must first, as the Lord's handmaiden, be His servant in
enlightening her husband to the Way.

"When her husband will not hear the Lord," she said, "she must
gain his attention. And you are a mature man. You know there is but
one means to turn his eyes to Zion, when he will not heed."

"I'm not sure I do," Flynn said.

She became severe. "The conjugal act, Mister Flynn," she said.
"The conjugal act between husband and wife is a sacred one and is
the measure whereby he may be brought to the Lord."

"I'm still not sure," Flynn said.

She looked exasperated. "I told him I had counseled and that I had
prayed. I told him that until he embraced the Lord, he would not
again embrace me."

"I see," Flynn said.

"His neck remained unbent," she said. "I had fellowship and counseled and we prayed together, and James remained stiff-necked. He
left me, Mister Flynn," she said. "He left his family." She paused. She
looked sorrowful. "I heard what he was doing. Stories reached my
ears. I pondered those things in my heart.

"And I became sure," she said, "sure in my heart, and with Reverend
May, that it was the Lord's will that James must bow to the secular arm
before he would be reborn." She paused and nodded. "James is in the
grip of Satan." She said it calmly, but her eyes glittered. "Satan in the
form of the harlot that he keeps. Satan's whore where he resorted after
rejecting the Lord and me. The Lord told me what to do."

Flynn wrote in his notebook: "Wf. v. relig." He cleared his throat
and said: "Uh, when you say 'the Lord,' Mrs. Teal, did you talk to
anyone else?"

She gazed at him suspiciously. "What do you mean?" she said.

"Well," he said, "you told me you counseled with your pastor, and
you prayed and so forth. But what exactly was it that prompted you
to search his coat?"

"The money," she said. "I said that at the trial. He was trying to
buy the loyalty of the children from me and the way of the Lord.

Those big radios he bought them—awful things. And the music tapes they played. All about drugs and sex. That was Satan at work, Mister Flynn. I knew that in my heart."

"Well, ah, yes," he said, "but what made you search his coat? How'd you happen to do that?"

She sighed and spoke slowly, as though addressing a limited child. "I testified at the trial, Mister Flynn," she said. "I counseled with Reverend May and sought guidance through prayer. And I became sure that James was in the bond of sin. And I called the FBI."

"You called the FBI," Flynn said.

"Yes, I did," she said. "I told them that my husband was spending far beyond his means, that he was secretive with me, and that he was consorting with a whore of Satan. And they asked me what evidence I had of these things. And I said I was sure in my heart. I knew he had been in Acapulco with the harlot, but I did not tell them that. And they told me they would need something more. And I said he no longer lived here. And they said without evidence, they could do nothing.

"So the next time he came," she said, "I went through his pockets, and I found nine fifty-dollar bills which I knew he could not have gotten honestly. And I called the FBI. And they said that was not enough. And I believed, well, I was unsure. I believed that they might be laughing at me. And I asked them what would be enough, because I knew James was locked in sin, and they said that the next time he came, I might do it again, and write down the serial numbers and they would check to see if the bills were stolen. And I did that. And there were six of the bills that time, and each of them had the same number. And they told me to wait for the Secret Service to get in touch with me, and that is what I did. They called that same morning." She took a deep breath. "It was God's will, the first step in his rebirth. I was the instrument. They were his instruments as well, the FBI men and the Secret Service. The devil is real, Mister Flynn. He roams the earth seeking whom he may devour. But God is not mocked. God is not mocked. We serve Him even when we know not, in our daily lives."

Flynn rewarded himself for enduring his morning with lunch at the Eire Pub on Gallivan Boulevard in Dorchester. By the time he got back to his office, late at 1:50, he was already regretting his decisions to have onions on his hot dogs and a second Bally Ale.

There were four people seated in the reception area when he checked in at the desk. Two of them were men in their middle sixties. They sat stiffly and ostentatiously apart from each other on the green vinyl couch, neither wishing nor needing to inquire of each other about their common shames. They would be in to confer about sons who would be middle aged and therefore career offenders who had first embarrassed them many years before and taught them the routine.

Two women uncomfortably occupied wooden armchairs opposite the couch. One of them was extremely attractive, about twenty; she looked teary and was chewing on her lip. Flynn figured her to be Veronica Richards, in to see him about Teal, but when the reception- ist handed him his pink phone message slips and said: "Miss Richards has been waiting for you," she nodded toward the other woman, who stood up at once.

She was in her early thirties. She had dark hair cut short and feath- ered at her temples. She wore small diamond stud earrings and slight- ly too much blush makeup and a black silk dress with a scoop neck- line which Flynn would like to have seen his wife wear to a dinner dance, and which June would not have worn because she said she knew what she had and he knew what she had and there wasn't any need to go around in public showing them to everybody else. The woman took a hesitant step toward Flynn and offered her right hand which he took. "Ronica Richards," she said, as though he and not she had been kept waiting. She had a small brown leather purse in her left hand. She wore black sandals with high heels. She weighed a little bit more than she had when she had bought the dress and the slightly overloaded bra underneath it.

Flynn accepted her hand and shook it and said as he ushered her to the door to the offices behind the counter: "Dan Flynn. I was held up in traffic." His stomach punished him for that half-truth by rolling audibly. He pretended that had not happened and when the buzzer announced the door was unlocked, took her down the marble hall to his cubicle. He asked her to sit down in the visitors' chair while he put his maroon blazer on the wire hanger on the hook behind the door.

He sat down at his desk and positioned a block of white, lined paper and three sharpened pencils precisely in front of him. He frowned. He picked up one of the pencils. He looked up at her. "It's all right," she said anxiously. "That you were late, I mean. The expressway, I mean. The construction? Half the people that I work with, and the ones that come in to see them, half of them're late all the time now, too. Nobody can get anywhere these days."

"Yes," he said. "Well, since I did keep you waiting, and away from your job and all. . . ."

"I didn't mind," she said quickly. "If it'll, you know, if this's something that'll help James, you know, it's all right."

"Because," Flynn said, "that's the reason generally we try to go around and talk to the people that know the defendant where they work, you know? Or see them at home, after they get through work. Because, you know, we don't like to impose on anybody any more'n absolutely necessary, and we know these delays'll occur. We can't help them. There's nothing you can do."

"I know," she said. "It's just that, well, you know, I mean I'd rather come over here and see you, like I said on the phone, because it's just a short walk from where I work, really, and this way, the other people in the office, well, they know about Jimmy, you know, and me and him seeing each other, but I just didn't want them listening, you know? It's like, well, they all know about James, of course, and what happened to him, and I know they're all sorry for me. But still, you know, it's like they're too interested, you know? In what's going on, and everything. Like they're sort of enjoying this, you know? And there really isn't any place there that we could talk, without them doing that."

"I would've come to your home," Flynn said. "I told you I'd do that. We often, we make lots of visits to people's homes, after they get through work, like I said. I would've done that."

She shook her head. "That wouldn't work either," she said. "I got neighbors, you know? In my building. Where I live. And they're really nosey, like the only thing they've ever got to think about's who I'm seeing, or if he's staying over and like that. When I first started seeing Jimmy, well, it's been like that with anyone I had over, you know? Like even for dinner, or maybe when they come to pick me up to go out someplace and I have them in for a drink. Or when we come back and they come in. The neighbors always, the next day they're giving me these looks, and the same with the guys I'm seeing, give them the looks too. And it's, well, I don't like it, that's all. So I would rather come here."

"That's understandable," Flynn said. "Like I say, we know we're imposing anyway, on people that just happened to know the defendant and really didn't have any part in what brought him to our attention, so we try to make it as painless for them as possible, and if coming here'll do that for you, well, we're flexible."

She opened her eyes wide and gave a short, incredulous laugh. "Did I say something?" Flynn said.

"Well, yeah," she said, still looking startled. "Yeah. I mean, you saying 'painless' and all. It isn't like that, like it was painless. I can tell you that for sure."

Flynn felt very awkward. He rearranged his block of paper and sele-cted a different pencil. "Well," he said, frowning as his stomach rolled again, forcing a cough to cover the sound, "it's not as though. . . , nothing we can do is going to make this whole thing into, you know, something that the people we talk to in most cases're ordinarily going to actually *enjoy*. Or anything like that."

He looked up at her again. She had lots of small freckles on the tops of her breasts. June freckled like that when she sun-bathed. He had been married to her for nine years before that summer, when he noticed that freckles had begun to cover her breasts. He did not say anything but became watchful, and when the next Saturday night came when each of the three kids was staying overnight at a friend's house, he didn't turn off the light as she preferred before she came out of the bathroom. He discovered she had freckles on her rear end, too, and well below the line where the top of her bikini would have shielded her abdomen. He did not tell her what he had seen. He did not tell her he had deduced why she had insisted that their backyard swimming pool be installed above the ground, with an eight-foot fence of woven redwood slats surrounding it. He did tell her, as usual, after they had finished making love, that their only problem with sex was its infrequency, and she told him, as usual, that when the kids were in the house sex made her uncomfortable because he made too much noise. "And they would know, honey, and we would have to tell them something, and they're still too young for that." He could feel himself getting an erection. He squirmed in his chair and surreptitiously dropped his left hand off the top of the desk to adjust his shorts.

The woman sighed heavily. "Well," she said, "that's good. Because I can tell you right now, you know, that it isn't. 'Painless,' I mean." She exhaled. "It isn't that at all. This's the worst thing I ever had to go through, and I thought I'd been around. This is just *awful*" She worked her facial muscles and her eyes were very wet. "This's just about the worst thing that's ever happened to me, the absolute worst thing."

"You cared deeply about Mister Teal?" Flynn said solicitously.

"Not that," she said. "He isn't dead, you know, even if this did-happen to him. He's still going to come out some day, isn't he? Even though this happened? It's not like he's never coming back."

"You still care about him then," Flynn said. He made a note: "GF. obvious sincere aff. for Def."

"A lot," the woman said. "I care more about Jimmy'n anyone I ever knew before in my whole life. He was the best thing, ever happened to me. I thought, like, you know, like I loved other guys I went with before I met Jimmy. And that was two years ago, almost, when he come in the office one day and just luck, really, that he got assigned me, that I hadda straighten out what his problem was at the time, and it was like, you know, ka-boom, right? It was like the, from the minute he comes in and sits down at my station and I start taking his history, I couldn't keep my eyes off him, you know? And I'm sitting there and I'm asking him questions, and I'm praying, just *praying*, that this guy isn't married, and if he is, it isn't going to matter, and I know that already, because it don't matter to me when he's sitting there if he's married or not, or he really loves his wife, or he's already going with somebody, or *anything*, you know? Anything. It just isn't going to matter."

She took a deep breath and shook her head. "It was like, I don't know, like somebody'd just hit me on the head or something. Like I was out of my mind. That never happened to me before."

Flynn had to clear his throat. "Yes," he said. He wrote: "GF strng sxul attra. to Def." He said: "And did he tell you he was in fact married at that time?"

"Oh, sure," she said. "He told me all that stuff. Well, I mean, he hadda, didn't he? If he wanted us to process his claims, like when his wife or his kids went the doctor or something, he hadda tell us the truth. And he told me that. That he was thirty-six at the time, and he'd been married to his wife almost fifteen years, and they had two kids, and they weren't getting along for about a year or so before that and he was, he'd moved out and they're, they were probably gonna get a divorce but they weren't in no hurry about it and besides, the way things were going for him right then and everything, he couldn't afford it right then anyway. But he told me. He told me everything."

"And what he told you was the truth," Flynn said.

"Oh, yeah," she said. "I mean, as far as I know, it was. It all checked out and everything. The stuff we checked, at least. Yeah, it was all the truth. He didn't lie to me that I know. That I found out, at least." She paused and managed a small, sad smile. "I might've fibbed to *him* a few times," she said. "I might've told him some things that weren't, you know, absolutely true. But if he ever lied to *me*, I didn't catch him at it. I never found out, if he did."

"Like what did you fib to him?" Flynn said absently. He wrote: "GF spks v. hi Def.'s verac."

"Oh," she said, "I don't mean I ever actually, you know, *lied* to Jimmy. But like that first day, when I met him, you know? I took all his history and said all the stuff you're supposed to say, when he'd be getting his card, and we'd send the bills to his place, his apartment where he was living since he got separated, and all that stuff, you know? And then I said to him, I said: 'Look, all right? I mean, we're not supposed to do this, you know? And if you're some kind of one of them spotters we're always hearing rumors they've got going around and checking on us, you know, if we're following the rules and stuff, I'm going to be getting myself in a jam here. So I really hope you're not, because we're not supposed to get too friendly with the customers, you know? But if maybe you might be, you know, free for drinks after work, well, I never did this before and I'd like to see you someplace.' And that was *sort* of a whopper, you know, because, well, because it just was."

"How was it a 'whopper?' " Flynn said.

"Well," she said, twisting the small leather purse in her hands and looking down at her lap, "well, I mean, because it just was, that's all." She looked up defiantly. "I mean, like, I'd done it before. Tried to pick up customers. Not very much, maybe only two or three times. At the most. But I'd done it. And, you know something? It's really a wonder, I did it again. Because the guys I did it before, I picked up like that before from a new membership or an adjustment or something like that, they turned out to be such *jerks*? And I made a promise to myself, I wouldn't do that again. And then, well, I did it again."

"I take it he was just as interested?" Flynn said.

"Oh, yeah," she said. She grinned. "He was *very* interested. I mean, I never been married or anything, you know? Me and Jimmy, before all this stuff went down, we're going to get married or something some day pretty soon, but I mean, like he wasn't the first guy I ever went out with, all right? He wasn't the first guy I knew. I was twenny-nine years old, and I'd been out with a few guys, and sometimes, with a few of them it got pretty serious and I thought. . . , well, you know. But that never happened. But I could still tell, I knew when a guy was interested. It's not that hard to tell." She giggled. "Soon's he stood up again, I knew he was interested. I knew that right off."

"So you started going out together," Flynn said. He underlined "strng sxul attra." on his notepad.

"Yeah," she said. "After work that same night, I met him down the Ninety-Nine, and we had a few drinks, and we talked, and we had something to eat, like a burger or something, and after a while I just said to him: 'I hope you don't think I'm always like this, but I been doing all right with it so far today, so, you know, we go to your place or is it mine? Because I don't really care which one it is, so long's it's one of them and it's pretty soon, because I don't think I can stand it much longer.' And that was the truth, I can tell you, because it was, you know? And geez, we went back his place and I practically attacked the guy. Which, lucky for me, it didn't bother him. Me acting like some kind of rapist or something. Said it turned him on." Her eyes teared up and she looked down at her purse again. She shook her head. "He said it. . . , he said I turned him on."

Flynn wrote: "GF obv. feels v. strngly abt. Def." He said: "Did Mister Teal, ah, did he ever tell you about what he was doing, this, that it might lead to the kind of problem he's got now?"

She looked up. Her eyes were full. "What do you mean?" she said. She snuffled. She opened her purse and took out a wad of Kleenex. She wiped her eyes and blew her nose.

"Did he ever mention to you," Flynn said, "what he might be doing?"

She put the Kleenex back in her purse. She shook her head. She snuffled again. "No," she said, "he didn't. I mean, it wasn't the kind of thing that somebody'd put down on a claim form, you know? Or to get benefits. That not only was he, did he have his regular job at Runciman, you know, wire and cable rep and all, but that he was also selling fake money."

She paused. She looked very worried. "Besides," she said, "I don't think, I don't think he was doing it then. Messed up in that stuff. Because he didn't have any money, you know? When I first started seeing him. The first thing I knew about that, the first time I was really sure, I mean, knew there hadda be something going on, was when all of a sudden he started having a lot more money and we're flying to Acapulco and he's buying me stuff, and things. And I was, well, you know, I was afraid for a while it might be dope or something. But then I thought about it. And, like, I knew him, you know? And Jimmy wouldn't get involved in dope, not with his kids the way he's got. So I thought, well, maybe he's just on a hot streak at his job. And I believed that. Which actually, well, I knew things didn't get that much better selling cable, not that fast at least, but I didn't want to think

about it. Where the dough was coming from. But the first thing I actually knew for sure what it was he'd been doing, it was when the Secret
Service showed up and they arrested him." She paused. "I didn't
know the Secret Service did that stuff," she said. "Counterfeiting. I
thought all they did was be bodyguards, you know? For the President
and them."

"Did you ever actually see any of the bills?" Flynn said. "Did he
show them to you, or anything?"

"Well," she said, "you know, that's funny. Because naturally, when
this happened, I figured I must've, you know? Fifties? But then I start
to think back, like: When did I ever see him using fifties? And I could-
n't think of one single time I ever did. When we went away, like to
Acapulco there, he always got traveler's checks. Or his Mastercard, he
would use that to pay. I don't think I ever did, is what I'm telling you.
I don't think I ever did."

Flynn wrote: "GF cnfrms Def.'s sty GF nvr persnly pssd bogus." He
said: "Did you, have you ever asked him since the Secret Service came,
whether he kept any of the bills himself and used them to finance
things?"

She stared at him. "No," she said.

"Would you tell me if you had?" Flynn said, staring right back. Her
breasts heaved. He tried to keep his eyes on her face.

"No," she said.

"That's what I thought," he said. He wrote: "GF obvsly trthfl."

"Can I ask you some things?" she said. She twisted the leather
purse.

"Sure," Flynn said, "fire away."

"What's going to happen to him?" she said. "I mean, I know he's
probably going to jail, but. . . . "

"Almost certainly," Flynn said, looking up. "The US Attorney's
office waits until it gets our reports before it decides on its recommendation for sentencing, so I can't tell you precisely what that'll be
just yet. And then, of course, his lawyer makes a recommendation—
or asks for the street, more accurately. And the judge decides then
what it'll be. But in Mister Teal's case, him getting himself involved
with at least one operation where the undercover agents purchased
four hundred thousand dollars in counterfeit fifties, the likelihood of
him hitting the street, well, it isn't very good. Not very good at all."

"But his first offense and everything?" she said wistfully. "Won't
that help a little?"

"Oh, sure," Flynn said, "it'll help a little. But not very much, I'm afraid, for your sake. From your point of view, I mean. Or his."

"Like, what, then?" she said. "What's going to happen to him? Can you tell me that?"

He sighed. He shook his head. "Miss Richards," he said, "I hope you believe me when I tell you this is the part of my job, maybe the only part of my job, that I hate the most. Answering questions like that, from people like you. Because the only thing I can tell you, pretty much for sure, is that James Teal is going to go to jail. For how long, I don't know. Mister Teal refused to cooperate with the grand jury about where he got the bills. The US Attorney usually doesn't like it when defendants, when that's the decision a defendant makes."

"But he was *afraid*," she said, almost wailing. "He was afraid if he talked. They know that's why he did."

"They do," Flynn said. "And they don't like it. They want people in his position to be more afraid of them than they are of other people, and when people in that position aren't more afraid, show that they're not more afraid of the US Attorney than they are of somebody else, then the US Attorney asks the judge to show them they made a mistake. Which in this case will most likely mean they'll ask for seven years."

She gasped. "Seven years?" she said.

He nodded. "They probably won't get it," he said. "The case's before Judge Goodman. She's no pushover for defendants, but she's not a rubber stamp for the prosecutors, either. My guess is she'll hit him with about five years. Which he'll probably end up doing about two years, maybe two and a half. If he's lucky, in Danbury. If he's not, in Leavenworth."

"Oh my God," she said.

"I know it," Flynn said. "But it's a serious offense, even if it is his first. And he was obviously one part of a fairly sophisticated operation, which he refuses to testify about. I can't lie to you, Miss Richards. He's going to go away."

"And I'm going to go insane," she said. "He did this, I know part of the reason that he got involved with this, was because of me. He used to tell me, he used to say that I meant so much to him, you know? That he'd do anything for me. And I would tell him, I would say: 'Jimmy, all I want is you. Can't you understand that? That all I want is you? You don't have to give me things, take me places, stuff like that. All you ever have to do is tell me that you want me, and show me in the bedroom, just like you've been doing, and that's all I'll ever need. You like to see me walking around naked? You don't think I don't feel the exact same way about you? You think, you think when you get in the shower with me, that all I'm doing, that the only thing that's going on is I am pleasing you?'"

Flynn had to drop his left hand and adjust his shorts again. He cleared his throat. "Uh, Miss Richards," he said, "did you, ah, did you ever tell this sort of thing to anybody else?"

"Somebody else?" she said.

"Yes," Flynn said. "Did you ever say to anybody else what you've just said to me?"

"I don't think so," she said. "That was just, you know, what I would say to him. I would tell him, you know," she said, "because sometimes he'd get worried, you know, he was asking for too much? Because, like, we would do it every night, at least. And when we woke up in the morning, if he spent the night, we'd do it again. And I would say to him: 'Originally, James,' which is how he gave his name the day he came into my office, 'originally James, I thought you were the best thing I ever saw. And I still think so, and you're everything I ever wanted. Nothing else. Just you.' And he didn't believe me."

"And you never," Flynn said, "you never said this to anybody else? Never told anybody else, how you felt about Mister Teal?"

"Uh, uh," she said. "Nobody." She paused and looked worried. "Unless you mean, like, well, I told his wife."

"His wife," Flynn said.

"Yeah," she said. "She called me one day at the office, you know? And I didn't know who this was. Like I thought it was somebody had a problem with a claim. Because that is what I do. And she asked me, you know, she was very nice and everything, was I the woman that was seeing James. And I said: Yes, I was. And she just started in on me. Did I know that he was married? And of course I said, 'Sure I did,' because he told me. And if I realized, you know, that this was against God's will, what James and I were doing? It was a sin against God? Stuff like that."

"And what did you say?" Flynn said.

"Well," she said, remembered resentment showing on her face, "I naturally told her: 'No, it's not. Nothing that makes two people feel the way we feel, nothing that does that is wrong. We belong to each other. Don't tell me that's wrong.' "

"And what did she say?" Flynn said.

"Nothing," she said. "She didn't say a thing. She just hung up on me."

"And did you tell Mister Teal about this, this call you had from her?" Flynn said. "So he might be on his guard, when he visited the house?"

She looked down in her lap and shook her head. "No," she said. "I didn't. I was, you know, afraid, that he'd get all upset. Besides," she said, looking up, "I didn't think it mattered much, that she had called me up. She knew we were together, I mean. It wasn't a secret. And I don't think that she believed me, any more than he did. Neither one of them believed me. Neither one of them."

"Oh, she believed you all right," Flynn said, thinking of June lying naked on the deck of the swimming pool at home, sun-bathing the body she did not want him to see, "and she had a pretty good idea of what God's will was, too."

A PRINCIPLE
OF DOMINANT
TRANSIENCE

"I'M ashamed of myself," Donnelly said to Ernie Clark in Clark's office at the *Globe*, "man of my age, acting like that."

"Ah, forget it," Clark said. He had a very lean face and his grey hair was crew-cut. "You know as well as I do, we never run that stuff unless you kill somebody, and then we don't do it because we want to. I think it's a lot of foolishness anyway, charging somebody with a crime because of that, if he didn't hurt anybody or break anything. Put him in a cab and send him home. He'll be all right in the morning."

"Well," Donnelly said, "most of them'll do that, if they can. But they couldn't, with me. I was passed out. If they'd left me there, I would've frozen to death by morning, and if they were going to take me in where I'd be warm, they had to book me. I haven't got any complaint against the cops. I wasn't a whole lot of help to them."

"They took the precaution of offering you the Breathalyzer, though, I notice," Clark said.

"Well," Donnelly said, "if they're going to treat you like they treat everybody else, they've got to treat you the same way they treat everybody else. Point-fourteen? Well, that's pretty good. Maybe I wouldn't've frozen to death after all, with that much antifreeze in my system. God did I have a headache. I've had some experiences before, but waking up in a cell with a hangover's got to be one I could've done without."

"You have had some fun for yourself, haven't you, the past year," Clark said.

"Ernie," Donnelly said, "the past *five* years. I've had a disorderly life. Drunk, seldom, but disorderly, quite a bit."

"What the hell happened to you?" Clark said.

"Well," Donnelly said, "a glimmer of conscious wisdom survived to me, in my inebriated state. When the white, broken lines in the middle of the road became double, white broken lines, I was perplexed. Double, solid yellow lines, those I have seen. But double, white, broken lines were unfamiliar to me. Now, when you're in that condition, unfamiliar things are frightening. You look around you for reassurance, because after all, it's hard enough to drive when you're drunk without having to deal with strange things at the same time. It's a damned imposition, in fact, and you get angry about it. So, when I saw a car ahead of me, I looked at it very carefully. *Very* carefully. It was a car with two sets of taillights. The cars coming toward me, on low beam, had four headlights: the ones on high beam had eight. I'm not a Gemini, Ernie. I'm a Leo or something. Maybe I'm a Taurus, I dunno. But I'm only used to one of a thing at a time. So I got nervous, and when I came to two signs that said *Rest Area*, I pulled into the two rest areas and shut the thing down and closed my eyes and commenced to meditate about what a cruel thing the gods were doing to me, to show me two of everything. The next thing I knew, the cops were rapping on the glass, and inquiring after my health."

"There's nothing like a few cops to liven up a dull evening, I should think," Clark said.

"The evening," Donnelly said, "had not been dull. In my lucid state, I can acknowledge that. It seemed dull, but it wasn't.

"It started in the afternoon," Donnelly said. "Actually, it probably started in the morning, maybe even the day before. Gail and her husband've got a condominium up at Waterville Valley, and they haven't been able to use it for about three years, very much."

"No snow," Clark said. "My son, the society doctor, got one of those things at Stowe back in Nineteen-Seventy, and I told him he was crazy at the time. 'Rent a place,' I said to him. 'When you want one, rent one. Let somebody else take care of it.' Nothing doing. Can't get what you want, when you want it, he said. Well, I'm not used to his standards, I guess. I'll take what I can get, when I can get it. So he took a nice bath on it the next year, and the year after that, and then again last year. Knows everything, that kid. I can't understand how a kid that bright could get sired by a man as dumb as I am. "

"You're proud of him, though," Donnelly said.

"Um," Clark said, "yeah. Yes, I am. But he thinks he knows so much, and there're times when I kind of think he doesn't remember how he found it out. Sally and Regina are the same way, of course, and their husbands're worse'n Skipper is. Goodness, there isn't anything they don't know. But I'm not responsible for their foolishness. I didn't put Sally's husband through the Cross, and Regina's husband was invented long before I met him, and if they can come up with the Caribbean vacations and the French restaurants that it seems to take, on what they do, well, I'm responsible for what it seems to take, I guess, but I sure couldn't come up with it and I don't know how they can, either. I worked hard all my life, just like you did, and as far as I can see, they never did, and they probably never will, and still they can go flying around as though they didn't have a care in the world. I couldn't do that. I wonder how they can."

"You could do it if you wanted to," Donnelly said.

"I can't, because I can't want to," Clark said. "I'm not built that way. There isn't much between Margaret and me, and the abyss. A good long illness . . . , when my mother got sick, it wiped my father out. That was before Blue Cross. It was also before I finished Boston College, and so I never finished BC, and BC didn't cost very much then, either. I could've gotten my degree, two more years of tuition and books and carfare, for what those kids spend on one toot to San Juan. But I didn't have it. Now I have got Blue Cross, and a pension, and you know something? If I get something that's a good long illness, it'll wipe Margaret out, and she'll have to depend on them to help her. Which they'll do. But it'll kill her. What are there, two sets of rules? One for people under forty, one for the rest of us? Where are those rules? Who wrote them? Why wasn't I consulted?"

"You would've disapproved," Donnelly said.

"I don't like it, if that's what you mean," Clark said. "I surely do not."

"That's why you weren't consulted," Donnelly said. "Now you take me: I am consulted. And I don't like it. But I'm different from you: I go along with it."

"How old is Sam?" Clark said.

"Okay," Donnelly said, "he's eleven."

"You haven't had the full effect of it, then," Clark said. "The dim kind of apprehension you can feel, when something's probably going wrong, is nothing like the reaction you get when it's gone wrong and you have to sit there and look at it, day after day, year after year, people that you tried the best you could for, to do something for, and you did it and they turned around and came out rotten."

"People that you love," Donnelly said.

"Loved," Clark said. "They're like strange creatures that I cannot understand. They talk about things, and I look at them, and I have to keep reminding myself that—if they're all there, all six of them, with their kids—that I raised three of these people, had them right in my house, in their formative years. Fed them, clothed them, talked to them, listened to them, all the rest of that stuff. Astounding. They look just like everybody else that they hang around with, facile and well-dressed and superficial and infuriating. They're absolutely infuriating people.

"You know something, Deke?" Clark said. "You want to know something? They don't know *anything*. Nothing. That's what it really is. They just don't *know* anything."

"After what I did," Donnelly said, "I'm in no position to comment on anything anybody else knows, or doesn't."

"You overlooked something," Clark said. "When a man knows something, and there's other people that know he does, well, look, what'd you do when you got in the can? "

"Did as I was goddamned right well told," Donnelly said. "Got in the cell, lay down on the bunk, kept my mouth shut and went back to sleep. Damned right."

"Got up in the morning," Clark said, "feeling like hell . . . . "

"Went to court and said: Yessir and Nossir a lot," Donnelly said.

"As a result of which," Clark said, "for some reason or other, somebody forgot to prove something when you got tried."

"It was more subtle than that," Donnelly said. "According to what I could see, anyway. What they did was charge me with drunk, which I was, and operating under the influence, which I was doing, but that was before they caught up with me, and all the kid had to do was move for acquittal on the operating because all the evidence they had on that was that I was sleeping, and then the judge threw out *drunk* and told me to go home. So I did.

"Regina's husband," Clark said, "the famous broker and all, too good for Church anymore, got himself a fine skinful one night down in Scituate, a year ago. He was driving home and he took out a whole mess of arrow signs and stop signs and reflectors on a traffic island in Weymouth. He was wearing his Coupe de Ville at the time, tore the oil pan out of it and they had to have it towed. So he gave the boys in blue a good deal of vulgar advice, and they threw him in the jug but they didn't take his lighter off him, and sometime around dawn, he woke up, pissed off. Set the blanket on fire. Then they came around and told him to quit it, and he put it out. By pissing on it. Lovely smell in the stationhouse. You know something?"

"He got convicted," Donnelly said.

"Certainly did," Clark said. " 'Oh, Daddy, keep it out of the paper,' she said. He was sentenced to jail, for the luvva Mike, six months in the House of Correction. She loves him dearly. Never mind he's gonna entertain a few fellows without really wanting to. His sphincter'll heal. Keep it out of the paper. 'Take it up on appeal,' I said, 'and have him get a good lawyer, and make him go down to the stationhouse and apologize, and do it right now.'"

"Did he make it?" Donnelly said.

"He didn't go to the can, if that's what you mean," Clark said. "He did lose his license for a year. He had to pay for having his car fixed— I didn't ask about that. He still doesn't know anything. He never will."

"Neither will I, I guess," Donnelly said.

"Not much more'n you do now," Clark said. "Few of us ever will. But enough to keep you out of serious trouble, and to get you out of it when you're close to it anyway.

"I get depressed," Donnelly said. "I always operated on the idea that if today wasn't enough to do something, I'd take care of it tomorrow. There was always an endless succession of tomorrows. There wasn't, of course, but it seemed like there would be. It was something you didn't have to think about. Then I got into this situation, gradually, and I ended up where I am. And now it's something I have to think about.

"What happens," Donnelly said, "is that time becomes a factor. Your whole life's the Two Minute Drill. There isn't any leisure. The pressure's always on. It's not like it used to be, that if the kid doesn't finish the conversation tonight, you'll be home again tomorrow night, and you can start again. Because you won't be. Tomorrow night, you'll be some place, and he'll be at Waterville Valley, because his step-father's got a condominium there, so it's got to be finished tonight.

"Well, as a matter of fact," Donnelly said, "two nights ago was no night to finish anything. Too bad, but that was the way it was. And he went to bed, with nothing finished, as a result. Kids get cranky too, I notice. And so do I. But the trouble was that he was going away the next afternoon, and what with one thing and another, well, not so hot."

"What was bothering him?" Clark said.

"Basically," Donnelly said, "he wants to come and live with me. Well, he doesn't want to come and live with me, and that's a good thing, because I'm not about to bring a kid down there. But he thinks he wants to come and live with me, and it tacks him off, because he can't do it. *I* can't do it. Not that he really wants to do it. But when you get into that kind of situation, you're playing as though there was an endless succession of tomorrows, and in fact you're dealing with the principle of dominant transience: 'Whatever it is we've got going, whoever the hell it is we are, doesn't matter whether we're related, not related, bound by affection or annoyed with each other, it's all the same thing. Get it over with, right now, because if we don't die tomorrow, we're still not going to be around here. ' Pop, pop, pop.

"Some things," Donnelly said, "you can't rush like that. They take a bit longer, a little brooding, a few trips, some poetry, it doesn't matter. Ripeness is all. But when you're in that kind of situation, you haven't got time. The court said you've got this much time, and that's all the time you've got. You can insist on the time you're entitled to— what the hell is a reasonable time, anyway—or else you can let the kid go to Waterville, which you end up doing. Either way. There isn't any time. Every single goddamned second counts, and when you get a series of bad ones, it hurts your head. Everything's too important. Things, time, shouldn't be too important. You should have a few throw-aways. You don't.

"Then," Donnelly said, "I went up to my brother's house in Stoughton. I left my kid with his mother, and I took my Avis car and went up to Stoughton, and it was awful. He's got his grandchildren— he was married, he's nine years older'n I am—living with him, and he doesn't want to talk about it, which is all right with me, but his wife's one of those women that doesn't know anything, and she verbalizes everything. Everything. The weather report. What happened to the neighbors. The price of broccoli. Hog futures, if she knew them. She's got an untidy mind. Nothing that happens to her is real until she says it to someone else. A nice woman. A fine woman. But noisy as hell.

"Now," Donnelly said, "I didn't feel very good, when I got there, and the more I was there, listening to her, the more I had to drink, and the more I had to drink, the drunker I got, and I ended up in the two rest areas, like I said. But I had to get out of there, and I didn't insult anybody, and somebody along the line remembered me, and apparently, when you leave the tumult and the shouting, there's still some of them that remember you."

"Nobody I talked to," Clark said, "had any trouble."

"Ernie," Donnelly said, "that's about what I figured."

"I didn't do anything for you," Clark said. "Don't think that."

"Not for an instant," Donnelly said.

AN END
TO REVELS

"THERE were two Castles," John Hastings said, on the night I remember him best, "the uncle and the nephew. The nephew was worse, although the uncle was a liberal education in his own right. I hated both of them," he said thoughtfully, "contemptible little bastards that they were. But I only underestimated one of them. The nephew. I guess it was a natural enough mistake—I never dreamed a man like Bernie Castle could exist. You couldn't, not believe in a merciful God at the same time."

That night John Hastings had a little more than two years to live. He thought he had about twenty months. He had committed suicide in the civilized manner, with cigarettes, and he was waiting around for the returns to come in on his work. He had been a newspaperman for twenty-three years; he liked that, and he liked drinking beer and talking. He disliked being a newspaperman on the Boston *Patriot*. He believed he had been gypped.

I was twenty-four when I got to the *Patriot* and ran into John Hastings. I had worked at two newspapers before that, first the Waterbury *Republican* and then the Hartford *Times*.

"When I started with the *Courier*," John said, "Faneuil Norris Castle the First was Great and Respectable Ruler of the Lower Nile, or something vaguely powerful like that. You were supposed to be terrified of him because his mother owned the paper and nobody who had any sense wanted to lose his job in the Depression. So most of us were. Anyway, I was new, and he was anything but new. He had nothing particular on his mind, so he appointed himself to break me in."

When I arrived at the *Patriot*, John was well broken-in. He hadn't yet screwed up the courage to go to the company doctor and find out exactly what was hurting him, but like most people who have what he had, he didn't really need to be told. He was wearing then a shabby brown suit and a bedraggled grey hat and a greyish-brown tie that was all out of shape. He changed his shirt in the middle of the week. His complexion was greyish also. He looked as though the world was scrubbing all the color out of him, turning his life and his body into monochrome. He couldn't do anything about it.

"I learned hatred under that man," John said, "he was a rat. He'd give you instructions and send you out, and you'd follow them and come back and he'd go up the back and down the front because you'd been silly enough to do what he told you. This racket's changed some, Gingerman. You guys come in with your bachelor's degrees now and they give you a beat and make you an expert. But when F. N. Castle was nailing the flag and your ass to the mast, respect was earned, not donated. You guys more or less expect decent treatment, and I'm glad to say you get it, but when I started they dipped your parts in printer's ink and acted surprised when you didn't like it."

We sat in the Pilgrim Tap on Washington Street while he told me these things. It was a newspaperman's bar—the beer was cheap and cold, there weren't any women around, although there was no rule or anything that kept them out, and you could cash a check there or buy three bottles of beer illegally after the package stores closed at eleven. John did most of his drinking there because it was handy to the *Patriot* offices. He had started drinking there because it was also handy to the *Courier*, the doors of which had been closed for twelve years by the time I got to Boston.

"Anyway," he said, "I got broken in. And finally I was sufficiently trained to know I was going to be pretty good at this job. This is the only business I've ever known, so I can't say how it is in other things. But I kind of think it's the same way— you more or less graduate yourself, so that when you start to show a little confidence they take the hint and give you some real work to do. I think the break came for me when F. N. Castle came up with a bum ticker and took off for Florida. He was maybe fifty-one or -two. The Castles don't have the habit of dying in harness. But I had outlasted him. I was at least proud of that."

John had a memorable face. I can see it now as clearly as I could when I sat across the battered table near the rear of the Pilgrim. His hair, grey and shiny from the oil he used on it, lay combed down low on his forehead. His eyes were a rather pale blue, and it was hard to look at them by the time I arrived because he was ashamed of a great many things and the guilt showed as misery. His nose was heavily and noticeably veined. His cheeks were puffy, and no matter how often he shaved there remained a remnant of a grizzled beard in the folds of his skin. Years of work on the night shift, of eating principally sandwiches washed down with beer, had given him a false chin, soft and somehow embarrassing, and he perspired visibly on his face and neck. When he said he was proud of something I always felt he was defying me to say that whatever it was was not really very much to treasure.

"I had nine fat years after that," he said. "I did pretty well. Like you are now. I knew my job and I worked at it. On a given day in Boston there might have been a better police reporter working but day in and day out there wasn't anyone better.

"It was too good to last," he said. "I should've known it. Bernard Faneuil Castle came to work one day, and that was the end of it. See, old F. N. was probably a little unbalanced along with being stupid. But that was all right, in a way, because it put you on your guard. You didn't trifle with him. Bernie had all his uncle's bad habits—shiftless, crafty, all the rest of it—and he was also as sane as an angel. It was a mean combination. I should've known well enough to leave well enough alone.

"But I didn't. I was young and things were going good. I might even have been a little vain. I was still under thirty-five, I could stay up all night tonight and all day tomorrow and still drink three cops under the table tomorrow night, and here was this misfit about forty-five years old coming in to begin his adult life and try honest work for the first time. I didn't know enough to be impressed by a man who didn't have to work unless he wanted to.

"You see, Gingerman, the clan Castle is an old and worthy line in Boston. WASP in the loftiest traditions of the breed. But it lacks the vigor it once had. Like most of us. I don't know what bled the brains out of the family; maybe too many cousins taking the marriage vows. Anyway, it turns out one functional idiot per generation. There's a certain class of people in this town which takes malicious amusement from a thing like that, so that it's very difficult to have much respect for the victims, even though they are rich and could buy and sell you and ten more like you this afternoon out of petty cash.

"The majority of the Castles aren't stupid," John said. "It's the smart ones who kept the *Courier* stock. It made a nice plaything and it gave them a convenient place to farm out the ones who couldn't master the balance sheet. After all, Gingerman, as any small-business-man can tell you, and will, if you're not careful, any fool can be a reporter. I don't know whether that's generally true or not, but if the fool happened to be a Castle it was right on the mark.

"So Bernie Castle came to the *Courier*. And that brought him into contact with me. And I made him miserable enough to drive him out of the business, and with him, his family. And with his family, *The Boston Courier*, mornings, evenings, and Sundays. I wish I knew some Latin I could say that'd make sense of it."

I have a couple of friends who drank too much one night and came to in a boot barracks at Camp Pendleton. They survived the Marine Corps training, but they told me afterward they very nearly washed out on purpose to get away from the stories the sergeants told about Iwo Jima and Guadal and the Chosin Reservoir. Another friend of mine teaches political science in a small liberal arts college and rants continually about economics professors discussing John Maynard Keynes. A whole generation of mystery fans wonders about the fate of Judge Crater, and lawyers I know can talk endlessly of the Rule in Shelley's Case. In the newspaper business, part of the deposit is having a theory on what killed *The Boston Courier*.

"A lot of people think the *Courier* expired because nobody read it," John told me. "There's a whole legion of reporters and other rascals in the sinkholes of this town who think it died because it had a spineless editorial page, no sports coverage worth reading, and a crippling inability to perceive that any one of these champions of the English language and general clean living deserved four hundred a week in cold cash for representing it. Which is about par for the course for the Boston press: common knowledge, widely believed, fiercely defended, totally wrong. Everybody's sure he's got the truth by the short hairs and nobody but the Castles and I know enough to teach them otherwise. The Castles have other things on their minds and I don't give a damn.

"But just because you're a nice guy," John said, "and also because this is your beer I'm drinking, I'll tell you how it really was. The facts are right enough. But they don't have any relevance to the case. You can dump them together and make a plausible-enough explanation, but it's wrong.

"It was a *lousy* paper. No one ever read it. At least I never saw any-one reading it. And I never heard anyone quoting it. We had letters to the editor, but you can write those in the toilet. Who the hell ever checks a letter to the editor? We used to print a lot of them signed 'Lucretius' and 'K.J.P.,' that sort of thing. There's a distinct possibili-ty that whole editions, except for the comps to the wire services and the other papers, got used for ballast to freight down the remains of Italian gangsters slain in Roxbury. Maybe the trucks went out on reg-ular schedules to get beer for the composing room. The Castles are capable of maintaining something like that for a toy. Or were, at least. Now they don't need to, not anymore.

"But that wasn't the reason the *Courier* shut down, even if it was true. The *Courier* died one October night when Bernie Castle told the family's high privy council he had had it and wasn't going to soil his hands anymore. So they gave him an allowance and sent him off to idleness in Palm Beach. Maybe he was going to write books or some-thing. I forget. He must've had some noble purpose.

"The council thereupon adjourned. A special session of the high tribunal was summoned. Before this bench, the *Courier*, poor hapless bedraggled thing that it was, was arraigned *in absentia* and without representation on charges of high treason. Specifically, of having will-fully and with malice aforethought squandered, dissipated, lavished and laid waste to an annual three millions or so of traditional, respectable Castle dollars, made a good many years ago in the slave trade. It was adjudged probably guilty and bound over to the auc-tioneers. Sentence first, trial later.

"Which put the staff out on the streets, just like that," John said, snapping his fingers. "The next afternoon. We got a week and a half of severance pay and the best wishes and regrets of the Castle family. They put out a mimeographed sheet describing their sorrow.

"There was quite a bit of bitching. Some of the boys were a little peeved, especially the ones who'd put in twenty or thirty years for the rag. But I didn't say anything. I got my ass in gear and hustled over to the *Patriot*, and I got the only job they ever handed out to show their pity for the men of the loyal opposition. Because I was first. Of course I got put on the lobster again, after nine years of civilized hours, but I had a job to support my wife and kids and it wasn't selling suits or creeping around from weekly to weekly, trying to find five or six of them to pay for stringing out of Boston. I suppose it was good enough for me, maybe too good."

John didn't see much of that family of his while he was working for the *Patriot*. Working from midnight to 8:30 in the morning, with Thursdays and Fridays off, it's rather difficult to maintain a normal relationship. He and his wife had two children. She and the children had that same helpless look he had, as though silently blaming him for running out and dying on them. John was a little better off. He had Lobster's Personal Miracle.

The substance of the miracle was a pint of Carstairs in a brown paper bag. He kept it in the typewriter bin of his desk. No one ever saw him replace it, but it was never empty when he needed it. He needed it often. He was generally two or three sheets to the wind on the job, coming off that murderous shift in the morning sun as thoroughly embalmed as a dead Pharoah, and reason and logic would tell you that bottle had to be empty. But he would come to work the next night with never a telltale bulge in his coat, spend the wee hours shoving pencils into the bin, cursing to pretend he had dropped them, sneaking drinks and coming up looking angrily ashamed for the indignity and weakness he suffered. People, including the administration— as much of it as there was around at that hour—carefully left him alone at those times.

"Good enough for me," he said, "because the *Courier* had gone down for lack of a Castle to buoy it up. It was a clear case of hot air being valuable. It was also a fairly serious mistake on my part; I never dreamed the son of a bitch was worth a damn, and here I was forced to conclude that his hobby had been keeping men in jobs.

"He wasn't very big," John said, "five and a half feet tall, a hundred and thirty or forty pounds, no more than that. He didn't look any age, really, unless you were satisfied to say somewhere between thirty and fifty. His face looked young, you know? Soft, and pampered, like he had facials, regularly. He had this silver hair, and I don't mean it was grey. It was silver the way a new watch is silver. It looked as though it might tarnish if it wasn't polished regularly. He was fussy. He had this dainty way of walking—he minced. And he dressed like that too, spent lots of money and still somehow managed to look as though he shaved in some goddamn boudoir.

"He was vain, Mike, vain and pretentious and about as irritating as a woman in menopause. And about as irritable. And," John said, sighing, "he was all of these things because he was frightened. Scared blind.

"He was a critic for the *Courier*. He went to everything that honked, howled or hooted in the city. He wasn't very good at it. He had this carping tone, and he somehow managed to be timid at the same time. I never heard of anyone paying the slightest attention to what he said. He wrote in a vacuum, and that, of course, was precisely what the family had in mind. "The brass, of course, loved him. They knew what was good for them, naturally, but they also felt sorry for him. And they had good reason to. The cruder types called him Fanny.

"Like I say, I never liked Bernie Castle," John said, an expression of distaste on his face. "I thought he was a mean little sneak. But a thing like that is a hell of a thing to endure. It was especially tough on Bernie because he'd lived kind of a sheltered life and I don't think he'd ever run up against real, brutal ridicule before. He didn't understand why men should hate him just because he was Family and doing well because of that and not because he was a good newsman, or even a competent one. And particularly he didn't understand why they thought he was a fairy, because he wasn't, and, more to the point, why they clearly enjoyed believing a thing like that.

"He got kind of desperate. Inside of six months at the paper he'd caught on to what they thought of him and he didn't know what to do about it. He tried being one of the boys. He used more bad language— real vile stuff—than anyone this side of Camp Lejeune. He hated using it; he wasn't bright, but he wasn't insensitive either, and it hurt him to pretend to be something he wasn't to prove he wasn't something else. Of course it didn't help. You could see he was uncomfortable trying to get comfortable, and the mob scourged him the more. He had this little, thin, high voice, and he went around accusing people of incest never them milder forms—and sounding like the Vienna Boys' Choir. It was awful. It was worse than that, it was pitiable. He may not have been King Kong—as far as I know he never had a woman or a wife, or didn't *seem* to feel the lack of one—but he was a thoroughly natural man and he never dawdled in the men's room.

"I didn't ride him," John said. "I hated him, but I felt sorry for him too, simultaneously. I would've let him alone if it hadn't been for the desk. And I didn't even plan that. I just got itchy one night and decided to make some trouble and one thing led to another and . . . oh, hell, I don't know. Why the hell do you do anything anyway? Impulse.

"The editors felt sorry for him, like I said. They couldn't stop the razzing—every time they tried, the bully boys figured it was on orders from the Castles and just went to prove what they'd been saying all along—but they tried to make things more tolerable. Never let a deskman try to help you, Gingerman. He's generally an unimaginative cuss and he'll make things worse before he's through.

"But they were caught just like everybody else. They couldn't fire Bernie and they couldn't fire all the reporters who hated him, although one or the other was what they really would've liked to do, since it was the first thing that occurred to them and they don't like to worry any more than the rest of us. So what they did was single him out even more than he was singled out already.

"They gave him stuff the managing editor would've been in tears of joy to get. The rest of us, merely keeping the paper going, had beaten-up old metal desks with sprung drawers that wouldn't open all the way and wouldn't close either. Bernie had a kidney-shaped thing that looked suspiciously like mahogany. We had those creaky old metal chairs with no cushioning and small gaps in the seats that pinched the more sensitive parts of the body if not treated with care. Bernie had a satin-metal, swiveling, tilting, black leather armchair. We had those old upright phones and used them for business and Bernie had a little switchboard all his own that he used to make personal calls. It had an intercom on it. If we wanted something in the morgue, we walked for it, but Bernie called Miss MacKitchen and had her look it up for him. For forty-odd reporters there were three dictionaries and pretty battered ones at that, but Bernie had a whole shelf of reference works and a little radio to soothe him too. Bernie Castle had it good.

"That was what was so hard for me to bear. I didn't object to feeling sympathy for him—I think he deserved some of that. But he was a punk newspaperman and he didn't care who knew it. He didn't even pretend to work very hard. Half the time he didn't even show up for work, just went to whatever it was he was reviewing and called in his foolishness. He was pitiable, sure, but that didn't make him any less of a little bastard.

"I had this typewriter at the *Courier*," John said, as though he still found it difficult to believe what he had gone through, "which I firmly believed was used to type the Magna Carta. And later dragged across the Atlantic on a rope behind the *Mayflower* and left out in the rain for a hundred years until some German invented it. I guess I've probably used twenty typewriters in the course of my career, and most of them jammed and stuck and wouldn't shift right or reverse the ribbon. I don't think I've ever had a decent typewriter. But this one took the cake. It not only thwarted every attempt you made to write on it but somehow pinched your fingers to boot. I think there was something wrong with the space bar, something sharp in it.

"And I had this desk. There was something in it that vibrated, nice and soft, whenever you tried to run the typewriter that was trying to bite your fingers off, and it liked to drive me out of my mind. So I was sitting there one night in the chair that grabbed my ass every time I got careless and tried to start a new blister, and I was nervous because I didn't have anything to do. That was bad because if someone saw you it meant you'd be doing obits or rewriting Cub Scout news or weddings for the rest of the night.

"It was one of the nights that Bernie hadn't deigned to come in. So just about the time the chair made another snatch at me and the typewriter nipped me for the fourth time I happened to glance over into the high-rent district and see Bernie's sanctuary, soft and comfortable and genteel and empty, and I guess something snapped.

"I started thinking what he was getting away with, and things got mixed up and I didn't feel sorry for him anymore. All I could think of was that he was making a very good thing out of being incompetent and lazy and stupid and picked on, doing no work and getting coddled for it, and I was doing the work of ten men and getting roasted. He was like a little kid, a little goddamned spoiled brat who likes his mommy petting him so much he doesn't even mind that the big boys are picking on him—not only doesn't mind but doesn't want them to stop because it'll mean he'll have to start working and earning some of what he's getting.

"So I got up from my desk and walked across the city room and planked myself down in Bernie's chair. And I want to tell you, Gingerman, it was one hell of a lovely chair. Then I put my feet up on the desk. It had a glass top and my heels left marks. I moved them around some so as to make real good marks that'd take a while to get off. I could see everybody watching me and no one was seeing a thing and they all loved it. I could see they loved it. You get one guy acting like a schoolkid in a place like the old *Courier* and almost everybody'll join right in, like they were all twelve years old.

"I just sat there for a while, wallowing in it. Then, after a while it wasn't so much fun. There was going to be trouble next time Bernie came in, and I don't care how good a man is, he doesn't want trouble on the job. Old Bernie was going to come in there and find someone'd been at his porridge, and he was going to get all wrathy and indignant and go and find at least three sizeable bears and complain. And they, to keep their jobs, were going to have to do something about it. That something was going to be me.

"But I'd gotten myself into it," John said, "and I had to get myself out. I couldn't very well weasel out of it then, not with the whole city room watching, and anyway, I'd already done more'n enough to foul things up anyway. So I was stuck. It was as much out of not knowing what else to do as anything else that I started going through his desk.

"I hauled open the bottom right drawer and I put my foot in it and lit a cigarette very calmly to show I wasn't scared, and I opened the top center drawer. I hope to heaven nobody ever goes through my desk—it's like ripping open a man's soul, all his weaknesses right there in front of you.

"Bernie had three rulers, six refills for Papermate pens, a small metal box with a hinged lid—it had aspirin in it—a teaspoon and a small hammer with a brass handle. The handle was hollow and there was a little brass screwdriver inside, and inside *that* there was another little screwdriver that had a hollow handle, and I guess you know what was in that: a very small screwdriver indeed. And anyway, who the hell buys *six* pen refills at once?

"There was a brown, Morocco-grained, leatherbound appointment book at the back of the drawer. It was stamped in gold as the gift of Emmett Bond Wheeler to Bernard Faneuil Castle. It was dated 1943. All the pages were blank.

"I opened up the left-hand side of the desk and found a typewriter on a swingaway table. And what a typewriter, Gingerman. It could do everything but croon to you, and the oil wasn't even off the carriage.

"The top drawer on the right was partitioned off with those slanted metal plates to make compartments to store things. Bernie Castle stored such valuables as three calendars from the Merchants' National Bank, one from the First National, and one from the Shawmut. They were all for the same year, 1942. There was a Christmas catalog from a clothing store he would never have visited, a pamphlet describing a fund-raising drive for the Boston Symphony in such terms as to make it more an offer of stock than a piece of begging, a book of poems by David McCord lauding the Boston that buys books of poems by David McCord, a prospectus from Merrill Lynch that sounded more like begging than the Boston Symphony letter, and a statement envelope from the High Street Bank and Trust. Which Bernie's family owns.

"The second drawer was full of carbon and copy paper. The third drawer had my foot in it. I took that out. There was a plastic raincoat underneath, in case we had a tidal wave or something on the fourth floor, and a pair of folding rubbers. Rolled up inside one of the folding rubbers was a folding plastic cover for your hat. There were three different kinds of patent nose drops and a fourth bottle with a prescription label that looked to be the same thing. There was a black leather portfolio of selections from his columns. A few letters with Palm Beach postmarks obviously came from members of his family and I put them aside. I didn't mind ransacking his desk but I was a little squeamish about reading his mail.

"Underneath all that junk there were eleven girlie magazines. I have to admit I was startled. Nowadays you've got people who read *Playboy* and go to Cinerama and finally get so they think all the good things of life come in three sections. Well, it's always been like that, but in those days the flesh-mags didn't even *look* respectable, and now at least they're expensive. I don't think there was much question but that these were dirty books.

"Well, I still didn't have a way to protect myself against old Bernie," John said, "so I succumbed to my baser instincts and started looking through the skin books. And that's where I found the way—there was writing in them, handwriting. On the pictures.

"There wasn't much doubt about whose it was. It was black ink and it was Bernie's spidery script, and Mike, it was the filthiest stuff you ever read in your life. What an imagination. It made the stuff on the walls in the public toilets look like the Girl Scout's Pledge.

"So I had him. I just left the magazines all jumbled around in the drawer and tore one of the juicier shots rather roughly out of the top one, folded it and put it in my pocket. So he'd know I had it. Like I say, Bernie was fairly sensitive. He wasn't bright, but he was shrewd enough. I was as sure as could be he'd know right off that if he bitched I'd expose him, and if he was miserable when falsely accused of being a queer, he wasn't going to be exactly comfortable when the boys found out for sure that he was in fact an adolescent sexually. I was as safe as if I'd been in church.

"The hell of it was, I was right. He came in the next night and almost immediately saw that someone had invaded his domain. And he started to get mad. He hit the desk with his fist and everything, and he started right off to find somebody big enough to do something about it. But then he stopped and went back to the desk. He went right to that bottom drawer and opened it and bent over it, leafing through the magazines, and then he shut the drawer and rested his elbows on the desk and just sat there with his face in his hands for a while.

"Finally he looked up, and he caught me watching him. And right then, without needing anybody to tell him, he knew who'd done it, gotten the goods on him. He looked like a puppy that's been caught peeing on the floor. Trapped. I don't say I was proud of what I'd done. I wasn't. But I took a certain amount of satisfaction in what I'd accomplished in preventing his taking any revenge. I didn't feel noble, Mike, but I did feel smart.

LIFE WAS
ABSOLUTELY SWELL

BRIAN Maher brought the agents into his private office and shut the door. He offered them the two chairs in front of his desk and sat down behind it. The agents were young, well-groomed and polite. They opened the jackets of their poplin suits, put their attache cases on the floor beside their chairs, opened them, and took out yellow legal pads, and like synchronized dancers poised their ballpoints, ready to take notes.

Maher said he wasn't sure whether he knew anything that would help them, but would do the best he could. He said he had known Donald Lewis for a long time, "but mostly socially, not well. I don't mean I didn't like him," he said, "because I did. I had some high old times with Donald. Donald was the type of guy that when you met him the first time, you knew him all your life. Just that kind of guy, you know? Really easy to be with. But when this whole thing surfaced, you know, I started thinking: 'Geez, I know this guy. I've known him a long time. Been a while since I've seen him, but this is a friend of mine.' But then I start to think: 'Yeah, but how well do I know him? Just what do I know?'"

"So," he said, "I start to think: 'When did I meet Donald?' I moved into the neighborhood, let's see, in Sixty-five, and Donsie comes in two years later. Would've made it Sixty-seven. Maybe late in Sixty-six." He had a thick thatch of greying black hair and he wore a red and white striped shirt with white collar and french cuffs with oblong gold links. His tie was dark blue silk patterned with the Mercedes

Benz three-pointed star in silver. His watch was a Porsche design analog chronometer with a black matte finish band. His suit was a two-button dark grey worsted. The pants were beltless and he wore black loafers with tassels.

"You know the kind of neighborhood," he said somewhat anxiously. "Everybody was the same age, within ten years or so. The ones that'd made it early were maybe twenty-eight, and the ones that made it a little later, or maybe inherited some money or something and that was how they got there, were in their middle thirties. Everybody had kids, right? But not too many kids. I think probably Dave and Judy Reilly down the end of the street had the most kids of anybody there, and they only had four. But everybody had kids, two kids at least—Eileen and I had three—and all the kids were so that the youngest ones were two or three and there weren't more'n a couple that were over ten or twelve. And you had the dogs, and you had the jungle gyms, and you had the, everyone had problems with their septic tanks, all right? Because when you've got kids like that, that age, you're going to do a lot of laundry and this is before everybody gets all jazzed up about phosphates and all that crap, so nobody knew all that detergent was scumming up the tanks. And the honey wagon was on the street at least once a week or so, as a result, pumping someone out.

"And we all did the same things," he said. "I don't mean just the cookouts, either, or everybody mowing their lawn on Saturday mornings in the summer, or hanging pots of geraniums beside their front doors and putting out pumpkins in the fall. I mean: we all did the same things, all the time. Monday mornings all the men got out of bed and shaved and showered and got dressed to go to work. And all the women got up and put their bathrobes on and fed the kids breakfast and if it was during the school year, you know, hustled them out the house so they wouldn't miss the bus. And all the men had coffee and read the paper and looked at their watch and said they had to get a move on, and went out to the garage and got in their Monte Carlos or their Mustangs or their Barracudas and drove off to work. And the women during the day did errands in their Pontiac wagons or their Chevy wagons or their Country Squires, and then the sun went down and all the men came home and had one or two martinis and then sat down and ate pot roast with gravy made from onion soup mix, and little boiled potatoes."

He spread his hands. "You see what I'm saying?" he said plaintively. "It was all completely *normal*. Everything was normal. There was nothing that ever happened that was out of ordinary. Nothing ever did. In April it was muddy and in May things warmed up, and in the summertime we drank beer on each other's patios and talked about the Red Sox and how we had a nice time the previous two weeks in the place we rented down the Cape, or we expected to the next two weeks, when we went up to Maine. Nobody got sick unless they were somebody's elderly parents, or one of the kids brought home a case of measles, that then went through the neighborhood, and then a week after it was over, and the last kid was back in school, everybody forgot about it.

"We all got drunk twice a month at somebody's house or other," Brian said, "but nobody had a *drinking* problem, especially not the ones that ended up in AA. Most of us were kind of shocked when the Macklins, when Sally Macklin started offering us a little marijuana with our coffee after dinner, and she gave that up after a while. If anybody went to dirty movies, or was swinging, or down deep was really queer, they didn't talk about it. Nobody got divorced, or died, or found out they had herpes. If any of the women were getting cuffed around, we didn't know about it. It snowed in the winter and it rained on the Fourth of July, and we had our parents over for Christmas dinner, unless they lived really far away, because the kids didn't want to leave all their brand new toys and go out. We didn't know a goddamned thing, in other words—you see? Not a goddamned thing.

"Except for Donald," he said. "Donald knew a lot. And I don't mean that in any wise-ass sense of the word, you know? Like he had a swelled head or anything, because it wasn't that. Not that I saw, at least. He was just a perfectly nice guy, very relaxed, always seemed to be doing well, you liked his company. And if you happened to ask him, you know, what he thought the market'd do next, well, he would tell you, and naturally he would, he might say if you wanted to call him Monday at the office he could look some things up for you and really give you a solid answer, if you were thinking of maybe investing, but no high-pressure thing. And sooner or later, I guess, most of us ended up doing that, calling Don up at the office, because we were beginning to get to the point in our own lives where we were maybe beginning to see a little daylight for the first time in our own financial situations, and also starting to catch on from talking to older people that it wasn't going to be that long before we had to start paying the old tuition ourselves, and maybe we'd better get cracking and start making some plans about that. And where else would you go, huh?

You knew Donald. You liked him. He never tried to straight-arm you into doing something before you were really ready. Somebody had to get the business. Why not someone you knew? "

He laughed. "We were all like that," he said. "If you needed a new car, and you really couldn't afford one of the Volvos they had up at Valley Volvo so you had to get a Ford, well, you might do it, but you'd feel a little guilty the next time you saw Dave Reilly at a cocktail party or something because after all, Dave was the sales manager at Valley and you knew he'd use you all right if you went up to see him, but you just couldn't afford it. And if you had some legal problem, something you needed a lawyer for, well, the first thing you did was talk it over with Jim Macklin, and even if it wasn't something he thought his firm'd be interested in, well, at least you talked to him. You got your insurance from Billy O'Hara and Paul Greeley fixed your teeth, and if you had a trip in mind, you got your airline tickets from Emily Courtemanche. I think about the only person on the street that didn't get the benefit of it was Tom Hastings—he might've been the best gynecologist in the world, but there were some things most of us wanted handled only by people we didn't know.

"So," he said, leaning back in his chair, "in Seventy-one I got the Fleming House account, which is now Distinguished Inns, and things started to take off for me in a fairly big way. And naturally one of the things I immediately do is decide in addition to making the money, and spending it, of course, I would also maybe like to keep some of it, maybe even make it grow. So, after I got the Two-eighty-SL, and opened the Keough plan, and got myself some money in the bank, I called up Donsie Lewis and told him I was interested in getting into the market, in a very small way, maybe doing some cautious speculating, if you know what I mean. And naturally he said he'd appreciate the business, and why don't we have lunch and talk over a few things.

"Which we did," Maher said. "This is coming up on fifteen years ago but I can still remember it clear as if it had been yesterday—the day stuck in my mind. There I was, eight houses up the street from Don, see him every morning in his Lincoln going to work, see him more often than not, coming home at night, see him two out of four weekends, probably, either drinks or dinner party, and now here I am getting into my car and following him into town and going to my office two blocks down the street from his, and I have to meet this guy for lunch to discuss business? It was like a dislocation or something, like I was taking some kind of a step that might turn out to be a mistake, turning this neighbor of mine, that I considered a friend, into a guy I'm doing business with and telling my personal affairs. Which was one thing we never did in the neighborhood, tell each other our private affairs. That was something we didn't do. And I'm having second thoughts, as was my wife at that time, about whether this is such a hot idea we had, letting Donald and naturally his wife, he was still married then, into our affairs. I felt kind of odd, you know?

"Then there was the place he picked for us to have lunch at," Maher said. "I don't know if you guys were around Boston when it was still going strong, but there used to be a joint over on Randolph Street called The Friary. It was down in the basement, the old Russell Building, and they'd done it up so you were supposed to think you were in the wine cellar of some monastery—these big kegs and casks in the walls, dim lights, phony cobwebs, all that kind of stuff—and it had the reputation of being the kind of place you went to if you were looking for a little action and you weren't too particular about what kind you got. The owners were a couple of guys named Joe that were very active around town in various things like sports and stuff, rugby and soccer and road-races, stuff like that, and they were always getting their names in the paper for staging these events. For charities, you know? Crippled kids and so forth. But they also, people sort of shied away from them if they were in positions where they could get hurt if something came out. There were always a lot of young, good-looking women that were in there and didn't seem to have anybody with them, and they had this big blackboard up behind the bar where they had the odds and the betting spreads on various big games, the Vegas line, I guess it was. I remember once I happened to mention to Bart Colby, who you might know because he was in the US Attorney's office then— he's a partner now, in one of the big firms—something about how I'd seen something or heard something about something that was going on at the time when I was having a beer at The Friary, and he got this funny look on his face and said: 'You go in that place? '

"And I said, well, you know how you get when someone challenges you like that—kind of defensive, I guess. I said: 'Yeah. Some reason why I shouldn't? ' Because of course I felt the same way about the place before I went there the first time with Donsie. And he sort of shrugged and said: 'Well, maybe for you there's not. But myself, I wouldn't go in there. 'And naturally I can't leave well enough alone, of course, because I've been going in there quite a lot, at least a couple

times a week, and any time I want to make a trade, or celebrate a
good one that I made with Don, well, that is where we go. And I still,
I still did not feel comfortable when I was doing it. So I have to challenge Bart. And I say, because Bart was always kind of a stuffed shirt,
if you know what I mean, I say: 'What's, the Mob in there or something? That what you're telling me? ' And he sort of shrugs again and
says: 'Well, if they're not, they're the only ones who aren't. ' And
that's all he would say. And then, of course, about six months later the
janitor or somebody comes in to open the place up in the morning and
he finds both the Joes and five women shot to death in the storage
room in the back and there were four kinds of hell to pay in the papers
for the next six weeks about how The Friary was this big clearing-
house for drugs and three of the women were hookers.

"But naturally," he said, "when Donsie first took me there, I don't
know any of this stuff because it hadn't come out then. All I know is
if he decides where to take his customers for lunch on the same basis
I do, I am a cheeseburger-draft beer account, as opposed to a lobster
salad-white wine item. Or else that he's in a position with his firm
where the outfit isn't springing yet for the fancy stuff. Which either
way wasn't very flattering to me, but I will go along.

"Well," Maher said, "I opened the account, big two thousand
bucks, and we go along for a year or two, nothing really major, buying and selling stuff with low price-earnings multiples, concentrating
on shares priced twenty or under so I'm not dealing all the time in odd
lots, and it's working pretty well. Eileen—we're still married at the
time—had a good head for that kind of business, and it gave us something in common we could talk about. Which we needed: she didn't
know diddly-squat about the advertising business, but you couldn't
tell her that, and she was always farting around in my business and
telling me how to run it. And it used to get on my nerves. So, I'm playing nice and conservative, low-key with Don, and in a couple years we
run that account up to the point where I've got about seven thousand
bucks—things are looking good. The business in this office is still
growing by leaps and bounds, and I'm tearing around all over the
place, doing this and doing that, and I'm starting to think: 'Hey, I've
got the hot hand here. I'm a successful man. '

"Which is usually a mistake, when you start thinking that," Maher
said. "You begin to lose sight the fact that partly you're making it
because of luck, which can change and almost always does, and partly because when you started making it, that was all you did. You

weren't out all night, chasing the broads, and you weren't out on the town with the boys. You didn't have the season tickets to the Bruins, which was the hard ticket then, and if somebody that played for the Patriots came into a place where you were having dinner, you didn't know each other. You worked hard, and you went home, and that was all you did.

"Now," he said, "those are also things I didn't know back then. So I'm wheeling and I'm dealing, and I see a lot of Donsie, although not at The Friary anymore, naturally, after the owners get scrubbed, and I decide the way my marriage is obviously going it might be a good thing if maybe I started my own brokerage account, as opposed to the one I've got joint with Eileen. And I'm rolling in the dough here by then, at least by my standards, so I'm going to be the plunger. After all, I'm on a roll. I give twenty K to Don, open up an account in my name sole, and start taking a few flyers. It gets so there's not a day goes by I'm not on the phone with Don, or stopping in during my lunch to have a look at the quotes, and I'm doing really well. I am making more in the market, as matter of fact, than I'm making at my desk. Which also should have told me something, might've waked me up, but naturally did not.

"Now we're up to about the end of Nineteen-eighty," he said, shifting positions in his chair and frowning. "My thing with Eileen is going right down the old toilet. I've got the apartment on the Wharf— it ever occur you why they call them 'apartments'? It's because you get them when you're apart, that's why—and I'm dating this one and that one and flying here and flying there, and going on vacations out of the country all the time. And most of the places that I go, and the people I meet, I am going and meeting with Don. Who is also not living in the neighborhood anymore, and is also in the process of getting a divorce, and is also chasing tail like it's going out of style. And one of the things he was doing was what he always called 'getting a few bob down on the game, ' which in those days usually meant he was betting maybe a couple hundred bucks on regular season games, and maybe a thousand on the Super Bowl or a big fight. I didn't think about it much at the time. It was part of the general image, you know? Few gentlemanly wagers here and there, which I didn't happen to do because it didn't interest me, but I saw nothing wrong with it, if somebody else enjoyed it. We're taking the stews to Nassau, and we're seeing these girls that say they're models but they never seem to have a job, and, hey, all right? There isn't one of them who could get into anything less than a C-cup, and all of them liked their fun. Life was absolutely swell."

He stood up abruptly, jammed his hands in his pockets, walked to the window and stood looking down on the city with his back to the agents. He cleared his throat. "At the end of Eighty," he said, "I had in the joint account that Eileen kept about nineteen thousand dollars' worth of stock. Good, safe stuff like General Foods and Holiday Inns, the kind of securities that maybe weren't ever going to really take off and just zoom, but wouldn't lose you any sleep, either. I had over two hundred thousand dollars in bank accounts, half of which she also got, plus the house, which she got, plus the Porsche which I was able to keep and my sole account with Don. Which was then worth about ninety thousand dollars, if you averaged out the days when it was worth a hundred-thirty with the days when it was maybe under fifty. Very volatile stuff. Lots of puts and calls, precious metals futures, bouncy stuff like that. I took a week off in February that year and went to Saint Thomas for some sun and some nooky. Before I left on Friday morning, I called Donsie, and my account was at a hundred and a quarter. By the time I cut my vacation short on the following Wednesday and flew home, it was down to twenty-nine."

He sighed, turned around and walked slowly back to his desk. He sat down heavily in his chair. "As a result of my hasty and shrewd moves," he said, "the account was down to seventeen by the close of business the following Monday, eleven by Tuesday, six by Thursday and four by Friday. The next week Donsie was calling for margin. I had to borrow against my accounts receivable here. By the middle of the summer I was in the hole for over seventy thousand dollars." He paused. "I have never been so scared in my entire life. My personal net worth, which I'd built up in almost twenty years of damned hard work and great good luck to over six hundred thousand dollars, was down to about forty thousand bucks, and that was in jeopardy.

"I sat down with Don," he said. He laughed. "Sat down with him, hell, it's a wonder we didn't get bedsores, we spent so much time sitting down, trying to figure out what to do. And Don was just as panicked, just as paralyzed, and just as deeply in his own hole as the one we'd dug for me. Don't let me give you the idea he just stood back and paid out the rope for me to hang myself, because he didn't—virtually everything he traded for my account he bought in at least as large lots for his own portfolio, sometimes even more. 'Your guarantee of my sincerity, ' he'd tell his customers. 'You know when I tell you to take a position in something, I'm in it at least as deep for my own account. 'When I went into the tank, he was already in it over his own head, floundering around. I wasn't victimized, or if I was then so was Don.

"We couldn't seem to figure out," Maher said, "either one of us, how to make the bleeding stop. There we were, these two geniuses at playing the market, practically wiped out and completely unable to find a way to get on our feet again.

"Well," he said, "we ended up choosing different strategies. Mine was to pull in my horns, admit I was beat, get out of the situation where I wasn't smart anymore, and go back to concentrating on what I really was smart at, which is what this outfit does. If I was ever going to get back to something approaching solvency, I decided, it was not going to be by trying to outsmart the arbitrageurs in New York or the commodities wholesalers in Chicago—it was going to be by designing advertising campaigns like the ones we did for Distinguished, for Pollux pens and Beacon Life and all those other outfits that you know about today because they hired us yesterday. That's what I am good at, not predicting the next soybean crop, but selling previously unknown products to the common man. And that's all I am good at. All the rest was luck, and my luck had run out."

"That would've been around the end of Eighty-two?" the agent on the left said.

"Well," Maher said, "the fall of Eighty-one, actually. It didn't, it didn't really start to pay off until the fall of Eighty-two. That's when we had this operation back on its feet. When the word started getting around we had the hot hand again. Yeah, I'd say 'Eighty-two' if you were on the street. A year or so before that, if you were in-house, you know? You can tell when the momentum's gone, and then when it's starting to come back. It's like a ballgame, you know? *"Aw right, we're out the slump."'*

"And it was the year after that you took the company public?" the agent on the left said.

"Eighty-four," Maher said. "February, Nineteen-eighty-four. I called the other partners together, and I said to them: 'Look, we're back on our feet. Now none of us're getting any younger, and you, Clyde, have abused every organ in your body, and we got to start thinking about how we're going to take some our profit out of this operation without getting murdered by taxes. And I think the way to do it's to go public and set it up so we can take it gradually, capital gains.

So our kids have something, when we retire, and so we have something before that and after.' And that is what we did."

"Do you recall the initial offering price?" the agent on the left said.

Maher shrugged. "I dunno," he said. "Ten-fifty, eleven? It wasn't there long. I know it closed the first day up six points, and by the end of the year it was thirty."

"So you made a considerable profit," the agent said.

"Not right off," Maher said. "I was healthy enough so I didn't have to sell any of my shares, and I was confident enough so I figured if I held them a while, I'd make more. I didn't start to sell off until the first kid started college. I've still got a lot. I set up that tuition trust for the kids and put some stock in it, and it put one kid through Brown, and one through BC, and the last one's finishing Colgate this year. There isn't much stock left in that trust, but what the hell, it did the job."

"Your other partners, though, did sell," the agent on the right said. "In addition to the stock in the actual public offering, they marketed some of their shares as well."

"Not immediately," Maher said. "Jim got cancer of the prostate about six months after we went public, and the advice he got was to start liquidating his interest. Clyde decided to go back to Providence and start another small operation. So they started selling then."

"And the initial issue was a million shares?" the agent on the left said.

"Uh huh," Maher said. "The partners, we kept sixty percent, so we'd still control the operation, and the rest went out in the market."

"You were equal partners," the agent on the right said.

"No," Maher said. "Jim and I were the founding partners, so we had, of the shares held by partners, he had a quarter and I had thirty percent. Jim and Clyde had twenty percent each. And Michaela Murphy, she's our manager, she had five percent."

"Meaning that the first public offering brought in somewhere around five million, net, after expenses," the agent on the right said.

"A little less," Maher said. "You guys with the Commission tend to underestimate what it costs for lawyers and printers to comply, your regulations. But in that neighborhood, yeah."

"So you personally received an immediate benefit of close to one and a half million dollars," the agent on the left said. "You yourself, I mean."

"'An immediate benefit, '" Maher said, "if you overlook the fact the reason that we did it was to get working capital, mostly. It went, most of it went back directly back, right into the business.'"

"So what you're saying, essentially," the agent on the left said, "is that first you dissociated yourself from Mister Lewis because you were losing large amounts of money in the market, money that you didn't have. And then to make the money back, you concentrated on the advertising business, and not only made the money back but made a good deal more besides. And that you still hold a lot of stock in the company that's worth today a lot more than it was when the initial offering was made."

"You bet I do," Maher said. "I worked hard for that dough. I sweated my nuts off. I don't apologize for that. I was scared, by God, but I didn't buckle, and I'm very proud of that. Everybody I owed money got one hundred cents on the dollar. Ask anyone in town."

"And then the splitting began," the agent on the left said.

"Well," Maher said, "yeah. See, what we wanted was to keep the P/E ratio under twelve or so—makes a hostile takeover less likely, because the more shares there are out, in different hands, the harder it is, some raider corner them. So we split two for one in Eighty-five, and two for one again in Eighty-six."

"So in effect," the agent on the right said, "you've now got nearly three times as many shares as you originally had, and they're worth about three times as much."

"There's nothing illegal about that," Maher said. "We were just, we're just realizing the rewards of hard work. Our hard work."

"Mister Lewis used the same phrase," the agent on the right said.

"About me?" Maher said. "I don't know how he'd know. I haven't talked to him in years."

"About himself," the agent on the left said. "He pointed out to us that even though charges were brought against him by clients charging that he'd misappropriated funds, every single one of the cases had been dismissed. Settled when he repaid the monies. And attorneys' fees."

"Well, I'm glad he did," Maher said. "Donsie didn't have my option. I told him at the time, and this was, what, six years ago, that maybe he could get it back in the market. But I knew I could not, and I was going back to work. But naturally, of course, him being a broker and all, he didn't have something else he could fall back on. Securities are what he does. If he's not good at doing that, picking out what's good to buy, knowing when to sell, what the hell does he have left at all? His ego was involved in a way that mine was not. He had to stay in the game. I'm just glad he won.

"I didn't know about the really bigtime gambling," Maher said. "The illegal stuff, I mean. He couldn't possibly've lost the kind of money that's apparently involved in this mess now, playing at the same level that used to satisfy him with the sports betting. I suppose it wasn't much of a step for him to take, Wall Street Monday through Friday, the NFL and the NBA when the weekends rolled around. And I suppose what appealed to him about it was the idea that after all he's betting against sports freaks who're nowhere near as tough competition as the average stockbroker.

"You think, you know," he said, "when you hear about a disaster like this happening to somebody that you used to know: 'Well, could I have maybe done something that might've saved the guy? And I don't care what it is, whether it's booze, or cocaine like I just heard yesterday maybe another friend of mine that should know better's doing, or what the hell it is. The first thought that crosses your mind is whether if you'd done something, this might not have happened. But frankly, I decided, unless I'd gotten into it with him, I probably wouldn't've even noticed it. He always had a bookie. It wasn't something new for him, to call in for the spread. And if I had known, if we'd seen each other in the past few years the way we used to do, so that I did find out how much he was playing, a different order of magnitude, it wouldn't have mattered to him. Donsie was the kind of man who gives advice—he didn't take the stuff

"It's a tough thing for his kids," he said. "Marcia's remarried now, so she should be all right, but those two kids, same age as mine, they haven't finished college. I don't claim Don was any kind of model father, not by any means, but he always got along pretty well with them. Had a good relationship. Hard for kids like that, even forgetting about the financial part of it that's not going to be easy, hard for them to face the fact of what their father is. Which they will have to live with now. I don't envy them."

The agent on the left cleared his throat. "Mister Maher," he said, "Mister Lewis bought calls on your company's stock each time about a week before it split. Eighty thousand dollars' worth of calls—seventy-five thousand shares at ten-and-five-eighths. He paid for them with the first monies he embezzled from his trust accounts—about eighty thousand dollars. When he exercised the calls, six months later, he paid for the shares with the rest of the eight hundred thousand dollars he stole. He repaid his defalcations with the profits he realized when he sold his seventy-five thousand shares last year at twenty-eight-and-a-half. Two million, one-hundred-and-thirty-seven, five hundred dollars," the agent said, licking his lips around each word. "A net profit to Mister Lewis, after replacing the funds, of just about what you made for yourself on the initial offering. Close to one-and-a-half million dollars. We figure when he did it the second time, he netted close to four million."

Maher did not say anything for a while. "Well," he said, "I didn't know that. I shouldn't be surprised, I suppose—Donald always was a shrewd trader. And he did know this firm pretty well—what our profit prospects might be."

"He also knew," the agent on the right said, "the rules against insider trading enforced by the Securities and Exchange Commission. He broke them, and even though his violations enabled him to restore the funds he 'borrowed' from people who trusted him, he is still going to pay big fines and go to jail. And so's anyone else who's involved."

"I'm sorry to hear that," Maher said.

"Mister Maher," the agent on the left said, "Mister Lewis has made a statement, on the understanding that the United States Attorney will take his cooperation into account when Mister Lewis comes up for sentencing next month. In that statement, Mister Lewis makes certain allegations about conversations that he claims he had with you shortly before each split of your company's stock. He says you tipped him off, and he shared the take with you."

Maher stood up. He hitched up his pants. "Gentlemen," he said, "I don't wish to seem uncooperative, but it really seems to me as though I'd better see my lawyer." The agents opened their briefcases, dropped in their pads, put their pens in their pockets, and stood up in front of the desk. "Very wise, sir," the agent on the left said. He did not offer to shake hands.

LANDMARK THEATER MAY SHUT DOWN

VERNON Goff concedes that what he is doing, selling the Strand Theater, long a regional landmark, carries with it as many fear a strong likelihood that it will soon close down again, this time for good.

"The agreement that I have with Finch Brothers says that they'll make reasonable efforts, consistent with good business practices, to keep it operating. They call it 'a mini-galleria conversion,' so if they do that it'll have to be a smaller version. A sort of midget bijou, boutique theater, vest-pocket size, along with the arcade shops and the café bistro. But they haven't really promised that they're going to do that. They can't. They're not in the same position I've been in these past twenty-three years. They're a big corporation, run properties all over the country, Canada, too. They're closely held, sure; only a few people own shares. But they've still got those stockholders to reckon with, and I don't care who they are, family or not, those people expect their shares to pay dividends. That's how they got to be wealthy.

"I've always been in a different position. I could do whatever I liked. Only had myself to account to; never had anyone else." He laughed. "If I had I probably never would've gone into the business. But I never gave anyone a chance to talk me out of it. ask anyone for advice. It was completely my own decision. I was twenty-nine when I did it, and basically what it amounted to was that I decided one fine day to spend the rest of my life at the movies.

"I knew what I was doing. I went into the kingdom of illusion without any illusions at all. All I could ever really expect to get out of it was a lifetime of hard work and not very much money to show for it. To most people it didn't look like a very mature or a wise thing to do, and even though I've managed most of these years to make a living out of it, maybe they were right. But it made a lot of sense to me at the time.

"Movies'd always been, far and away, what I'd always *liked* the best of everything I did. Anything that had anything to do with going to the movies. The courses that I took in the college about film, its history and so forth: those were by far the ones I liked the best. The people that I guess were my friends at school—I haven't seen much of them since: All of them were convinced William Faulkner or James Joyce was the greatest thing that ever came down the pike. D.W. Griffith was my choice. Him or Orson Welles. And actually *being* at the movies, sitting at them in the dark, but feeling as though where you *really* were was actually with all the people up there you were watching on the screen: that was the best part of all.

"So when the idea of doing it first crossed my mind, the only thing I couldn't really figure out was why on earth I hadn't thought of it before. It was so obvious, you know? Such a perfectly natural *thing*. '*Of course* I should be doing that—what I should've been doing all along, 'stead of wasting my time on all that other stuff.' It was where I really belonged.

"Why did it take me so long? And what brought it on? I would've said then: 'I don't know.' It was Nineteen-seventy-three. I was two years out of law school, UConn, and one day I just said 'the hell with this.' Made up my mind to chuck the whole thing. All the big plans I'd made; the education that I'd worked so long and hard to get: threw it all away. Certainly nobody told me to do it, but nobody tried to stop me either.

"Several were kind enough to tell me," he said, laughing again, "tell me right to my face, that they thought I'd gone out my mind." He winked. "My dear father of unhappy memory: In what I assure you was for him a very rare attack of sensitivity and compassion, he told me I must be crazy.

"But I'd made up my mind. I went through with it. Gave up on the bar exam once and for all. Stopped looking for a phony law job that'd let me sort of *pretend* to be a lawyer 'til I really could become one, provided I'd agree to do what amounted to cleaning latrines for the real lawyers. Put every last penny into it. A little over thirteen grand; what I had left from what Grandpa Peter left me, after law school and the bar reviews. Doesn't sound like much today, but it wasn't small change in those days. And *still* I had nerve enough, on top of that, to go and borrow twenty-nine thousand dollars more from Mason Turner, over at Pioneer Trust. 'Looking for trouble on borrowed money': that's what he said I was doing.

"Good old Mason, though, God bless him. Looked like your classic mean bastard of a banker—and he was that, no question. But behind that stony face was a man before his time. All he cared about was money. Who you were or what you did, or who you did it with didn't matter to him. If you came to him looking to borrow money and he thought what you wanted it for was going to wind up making money for his bank along with you, that was all there was to it. Your name might just as well've been Polly Adler and your business could've been a whorehouse, but if he thought it'd be a money-maker, fine; Mason'd lend you the money.

"Those who didn't think I was nuts thought I was being pigheaded. I didn't argue with them. Forty-two thousand American dollars, to buy an old movie theater that'd gone out of business eight years before that? There'd been a good reason for that: nobody went to it anymore. I was foolish to think that I could ever make a go of it, and when I insisted on going ahead with it anyway, after tons of good advice not to, *well*, that's the sort of conduct that's given obstinacy a bad name.

"Like I say, no argument from me. I thought they were right, the people who told me that. Still do, in fact, far as that goes. Point was, though, that *I* was right, too. It was what I wanted to do."

What he had done with the money was buy, renovate and beautifully refurbish the old Strand Theatre and the stately, white-trimmed, yellow, two-story, wooden building, *1907* carved into the white scrolled oval at the top of the façade, that it occupied on the eastern side of the green in Canterbury. He put in new heat; rebuilt the air conditioning; installed fancy lighting fixtures that looked delicately gilded but were durably-anodized; and reupholstered the seats in stain-resistant red crushed-velvet, vehicle-upholstery grade, a lot tougher than it looked. "If we gave buildings names like we do people, when they reach a certain age, the Strand would be a dowager. A very *dignified* dowager, commanding the utmost respect."

He had gone to all that work despite his knowledge that the day would almost certainly come when he'd find himself "being ushered" unceremoniously out of the movie business—he often called it "show biz," sardonically—a lot faster than he'd gotten into it. "I expected to get the bum's rush," he said. "The only reason that didn't happen was because I've been very lucky finding niches for myself. The way I chose films was by picking movies I'd like to see. That for some reason or other weren't being shown around here. People would come from miles around to see them, up from Connecticut, down from Vermont and even out here from Rhode Island. Because where they lived there wasn't any place where they could see them either. Not even on TV, where they're just not the same; never mind on a big screen like they could at the Strand. Well, *Lawrence of Arabia* was one. In my old ark of a building, I've been able on a regular basis to do something almost no one else can do anymore: I've been able to show Cinemascope, real movies in Cinemascope, the way they were meant to be seen.

"But I never thought it would last forever. The Strand could survive only as long as the big national chains allowed it to. The day their marketing bean-counters saw census figures showing enough people with uncommitted discretionary income in the Canterbury market to justify the cost of a cookie-cutter multiplex would be the day before the bulldozers moved in at Northside Mall. The usual, simple formula; people're all so very stupid, it always works, even, time. Ballyhoo a half a dozen first-run, third-rate movies; show 'em four times a day on tiny screens; twenty minutes after they open in New York; to thirty or forty mindless boobs at a time. Charge those nitwits two and a half or three times what they'll pay to get into my place, plus a buck or two for a big cup of Coca-Cola flavored ice chips and two or three more for popcorn. Nothing to it; park an armored truck beside the ticket window. They'll trample each other to get through the door, and you'll have to vacuum the cash up. Even if I happen to be showing a better movie, *and they know it*, they won't have any money left or time to spend to see it.

"So my days've always been numbered. I've had to scramble like mad; use every gimmick I've been able to think up; grin-and-bear costs going steadily *up* and receipts going steadily down, in order to stay big-screen—and it's cost me. But it's also been the only way I've been able to stay in business: my refusing to put up a partition and divide the house into two—or maybe even *three*—teeny itsy-bitsy screens is what makes my theater different. It's the only reason people still have to come.

"But the question now's become: 'How much longer can I do this?'

It's been hard work, you know? I'm getting a little winded. The fact I knew it'd be hard when I started out hasn't made it any easier.

"In fact one of my friends said the fact that I always knew how it'd end, before I started, and did it anyway, was typical of me, 'Vernon being Vernon, perverse as usual.' I said I prefer to think of it as being contrary. Much better to be a contrarian than a pervert. But the explanation really was that I was no longer afraid.

"My stinker of a father always told me that the man you've got to look out for's the one who's finally discovered that he really doesn't give a shit what happens to him. When he's done that, he's set himself free. He can do anything he wants, and no matter what happens he's sure to have a good time. By the time I was twenty-nine, I'd become that man. I wanted to have a good time. I thought I deserved to have one, after all I'd been through.

"I didn't say that to Mason Turner when I got the loan. I wasn't completely candid with him. To him I talked strictly business. But having a good time was my biggest motive when I lighted up the old barn again." First he'd had to rescue it from the effects of the eight years of vacancy, chill mustiness and damp mildewed neglect. The previous owner-operators, a husband-and-wife team, had grown old and tired, enough so that they'd discouraged each other from gambling the time and money that repairs and improvements too long deferred would beguile the residents of Canterbury into going out to the movies again. "So when they had no luck quickly finding an eager buyer, they'd already primed themselves to conclude sadly that they'd never find one. They pronounced the business dead and closed it down. Retired to Florida."

The price of a business become defunct is a lot less than the price of even an obviously ailing but going concern. Their pessimistic and hasty decision was what put the Strand within Vernon Goff's reach. He said that didn't mean he hadn't been pretty scared when he did it. "But I was turning thirty. I felt as though I had to do something pretty soon if I was ever going to do anything." The Strand had begun to look like what he wanted out of life.

The business appealed to him. It was almost cheap enough for him to buy—"not really in my price range, but if I could resign myself to a lifetime of genteel penury, always *just about* making it, *almost* getting by, it would be close enough." It *might* even yield a modest profit—"if by chance somebody passed through town some day and decided that he simply *had* to have that particular piece of property, just couldn't *live* without it and'd pay anything to get it; someone who in other words was even crazier'n I was. So far that hasn't happened."

Another important consideration—it would always be small enough for him to operate without needing much help or approval from anybody else.

"The first year I was open, Seventy-four, I tried to get kids from the high school to work for me. The couple who'd sold it to me'd done it without hiring any help at all, but when I got in touch with them down there in Florida, they both told me they'd had a hard time of it, and there'd been two of them, keep in mind. So I had to do something. I figured getting the high schoolers'd be the cheapest way to do it, and believe me, that was important. If I could have them run the projectors; clean up around the place every night; sell the popcorn—handle things like that, and pay them the minimum wage. That way I'd be concentrating on the things that go into running the place, keeping accounts and booking the films.

"But pretty soon I had to see it just wasn't going to work, and hire students from the college. I had to pay them more money, but it balanced out because they showed up and did the work. I didn't need as many.

"With the high-schoolers there were 'way too many problems. Very unreliable. Wouldn't show up tonight, they decided they didn't feel like it; no call or anything. And then when they *did* show up? No explanation. I could've *killed* them. I'd look at them and say: '*Well?* Where were you, anyway?' And they'd get this hurt look on their faces and say: 'I didn't *feel* good.' Like that was supposed to do it, was going to be enough. Or they'd tell me their parents put their foot down, didn't want them staying out so late here on school nights. As though what they were now telling me, here, was that if they'd stayed home after supper, their parents would've made sure they were in bed before eleven. Which was ridiculous, expecting me to believe that. And even if it *had been* true, they still could've done it, been home in bed by eleven, and kept their job working for me. If they'd've gone straight home after they finished—as they didn't; none of them did.

"But of course I always suspected, anyway, it wasn't only that— what they said it was, their parents and their schoolwork. It was still a different time, a different climate then. There was more suspicion, a lot more. People had their eye on you; you could feel it. No one ever came right out and said something, but you were conscious of it all the time. You knew it. Always, in the back of your mind. Not that you'd ever actually *done* anything that would've given anyone a reason to stay away from you. Or that anybody ever came right out and claimed you had, either. But that feeling was always with you. The feeling was always there.

"The priest, especially. Several of the kids that I had come to work for me and who later quit, quite soon, on me, not *right* after they were hired but not too long afterwards, either, decided it just wouldn't work out—they were Catholics. Not too surprising, really; this's a heavily Catholic area. But I always kind of thought, well, that that was probably some of Father Mulready's work, over at Saint Jude's. Not that he ever came right out and actually *said* anything to me, anything like that. He was always perfectly correct with me, in every respect. Even when I booked a film he disapproved of and he felt he had to say something from the pulpit, tell his people not to come. He'd always make it a point to see to it that I was informed before he did it.

"Of course maybe what he had in mind was that if he called me first, I might not show the film that bothered him. Might have a change of heart. That thought did occur to me; that what he was really doing was seeing if he could threaten me, intimidate me to the point where I'd get so I wouldn't run anything he didn't like. But whatever it was, he'd either call me up, if he didn't see me on the street, and say to me something like, along the lines of: 'Well, I hope you understand now: I just have to do this. The archdiocese and all. Nothing personal. I know how they say times've changed, but I think we can both agree here, some things never will.'

"Well, as a matter of fact I *didn't* agree with him on that. This was now the Seventies; the times *had* changed, a lot. This wasn't still the Fifties then that we were in, and if he thought it was, well, nobody else did. And especially not where the movies were concerned. The Preminger films—*The Moon is Blue* probably the most—they'd taken care of most of that, censorship and so forth. But of course I always told him that I did, I understood, and that I hoped he understood that when a film came along that I felt I had to show, well then, I had to show it. Even if that meant he had to come out publicly and say he disapproved.

"I don't think he liked me thinking that way, talking like that to him. I don't think he was used to it, having people disagree. But I still came right out and said it to him. I thought I had to, you know? Didn't want him thinking that I was afraid of him. You just cannot ever let people get the idea that you're afraid of them. Even if you are—*especially* if you are. That's just *fatal*, if you ever do that. But then I got so I really *didn't* mind, at all. After the first two or three times it finally dawned on me that when Father Mulready told the people in his parish not to come, it was good for business. Free publicity. And 'forbidden fruit,' it's *sweeter."*

The debt service on the Pioneer Trust mortgage came to $261 a month. Twenty years at nine percent: the total he'd agreed to repay by the end of 1993 for the immediate use of that $29,000 would amount to $62,640. The sight of the figure on the papers that he'd signed hadn't really surprised him, but it made him catch his breath. Local real estate taxes added $85 a month to that. He'd had to sell 58 seats every week, 231 seats every four weeks, at the two-buck price that he charged then (minus 25 percent of gross for the second-run movies he usually featured; 266 seats if he "ran wild and ordered up a first-run film—35 percent of gross") just to meet those building costs, $346 a month.

Every day he had to make eleven dollars and sixteen cents just to hang onto the building. He got up every morning already down that amount before he insured the place or anything inside it, in the event disaster happened and it all burned down, got blown down or condemned before he got it paid for. He was short eleven bucks and change before he turned on a single forty-watt lightbulb or flushed a single toilet; switched on the projector; bought one giant bag of pre-popped corn or anything to butter it; or cooled or heated any space— including the creaky-floored gloomy four-room apartment on the second floor designed into the structure by the man who'd had it built, for the same reason Vernon lived in it himself: to save money; eleven bucks a day.

"The exterminator: Had to have him every month, ninety bucks a month. Vermin love the movies more'n we do. Roaches; mice; silverfish; and every now and then—not too often, though, thank God— you'd have a good-sized rat show up. Run across some woman's *foot*. Grit your teeth and make a few cheerful refunds *those* nights. Course you know what causes it. It's the people who complain about it; your customers attract them. It's way they eat, the filthy pigs, spilling their food on the floor? But you can't *tell* them that, of course—so there's nothing you can do "

His thriftiness came at a price. Regardless of how he happened to feel or what he might like to do of an evening—have a friend over for dinner or even just go to bed early to nurse a heavy cold—he not only had to allow in but welcome everyone who'd come out and paid a small amount of money to spend a few hours in what was not only Vernon Goff's business but also his home; talking loudly in the foyer as they came and went, coughing, moaning and making the seats groan during the movie, tramping up and down the stairs to the basement when they used the restrooms. Some nights when his feature attracted the young crowd from the colleges and the university, the audience took sides and the old building resounded, the kids clapping their hands when the hero appeared, booing and hissing the villain, laughing, whistling, shouting and stamping their feet, cheering when the good guys prevailed at the end.

"The James Bond movies," he said. "Those were never good nights to plan to settle in upstairs with a good book, or try to watch *Masterpiece Theater*. You might as well not bother; it was hopeless. You were sure to have your concentration broken time and time again. I tried to remind myself all those inconsiderate ruffians downstairs disturbing me were paying close to a thousand dollars for the privilege. Closer to fifteen, sixteen hundred, in fact, if it was either after I'd finally had no choice and'd gone up to three bucks all the time—which would've been in Nineteen-ninety. Or before that when I saw a sure sell-out in a new release, like one of those James Bond epics, say, if I booked it first-run and didn't just allow the multiplexes down in Springfield to gobble up my market by default.

"I'd sit there in my office grinding my teeth, smelling the marijuana fumes, hearing the pop-tops when they opened the beers that were making them belch and fart in the dark. I'd be telling myself that by the time those noisy young whelps finished visiting and buying popcorn and candy and Coca-Cola from me, running up my water bill by constantly flushing the toilets, it seemed like continuously, either from seven until nine-thirty, or nine-forty-five 'til around midnight, if they'd filled the joint, I'd have about three thousand bucks more in my pocket than I'd had when I'd finished lunch that day. And I have to say that did help. It helped a lot. But they still got on my nerves, especially if I had the flu the night they thought was theirs to come and howl.

"And it wasn't just the loud kids, either. The older folks could be almost as annoying, in their own sweet way." The aromas of his chicken cacciatores, beef stews, spicy meatloafs and small pork roasts with apples—he'd managed to become a fairly decent cook, if he did say so, living by himself all those years—often penetrated the dry, porous ceilings and partitions, wafting through the building. Obtrusive patrons buying tickets to the early show at 7:00 to his stifled irritation smelled the sauces and the meats only partly masked by the smell of buttered popcorn and detected what he'd planned for supper. Then they snickered knowingly, as though their recognition of the smell of pot roast or whatever proved that they were pretty smart. "They were so damned *smug* about it, you know? 'Ham with honey pineapple tonight, Vern? Getting so you're a regular chef here. Better keep an eye on it, though; don't want it getting dried out.'

"I would've liked to say to them: 'Oh, why don't you go suck an egg, Elizabeth.' But I didn't, for the obvious reason. The people who make movies, act in them and direct them: They can afford to be arrogant, and from all the things you hear, I guess a good many of them are. But people who *show* movies: for us it's a different matter. If we know what's good for us, we keep a civil tongue.

"Not that it's any different for us than it is for any one in any other line of work where the nature of it is that you have to deal directly with the public, personally. You'd best keep your gripes to yourself. Complaining's just not a good idea. Your condescending customers didn't come to hear your roubles—particularly if they're the cause of them. They paid their way into your theater tonight so they won't have to think about their own problems for a few hours. What they want from you is to take their money, give them the right change, and shut up and show them the movie."

His tax bill rankled him each month when he paid it with the mortgage, but he never complained about that, either. It could've been a good deal higher, and he knew it. He'd gotten a break from Alice Cole in the assessors' office. She set the initial valuation at $34,000 when she could just well've made it $42,000, what the public records showed he'd put into the place. That would've cost him twenty bucks a month more—thirteen paid admissions, anywhere from a third to the whole of a slightly under-par weekend night's business—and he wouldn't've had a leg to stand on if he'd moved for an abatement. So when he ran into her one morning soon after he'd gotten the first bill and cursed it roundly, picking up the papers in Gentile's store, he said: "You did me a favor, I think. I appreciate it." She'd smiled, paying Ellen for her morning *Union* and said: "Well, you're a nice boy. Besides, the town should have a theater. And I do love the movies."

He said revivals on free TV must have contented her, if that was so.

When he saw her obituary in the paper, a decade later, it made him stop and think; as best he could remember he'd seen her in the theater no more than four times. Two of her visits, he remembered, came on the same May weekend, in 1981. He'd booked *The King and I* with Yul Brynner and Deborah Kerr. It had been one of the most successful selections he'd made for his all-time best promotional idea: the gratifyingly popular 10th, 20th and 25th anniversary reprises of fondly remembered films not quite legendary enough to have been withdrawn from theater rental for periodic re-release as classics—*Gone With the Wind*, for example; *Snow White* and *Cinderella*—but seldom revived on television or available on demand in video rental stores.

"Those days're *gone*" he said. "The stuff that dreams're made on: all vanished—into thin air. Only one of the reasons behind this decision that I'm making now, but a pretty big one, just the same. Yesterday you got the video store; you no longer had to wait for me to book your all-time favorite film, or hope your local UHF channel would decide to show it. Today the rental stores're obsolescent; you've got the all-movie channels for the oldies-but-goodies I used to bring back, and the pay-per-view channels for the second-runs that used to be my bread and butter.

"That's three big holes punched in the wall of my market niche where I've been hiding all of these happy years. Pretty soon you'll be able to sit in your living room and order up any movie you want from a satellite library, any time you want it. Then my little niche will be rubble, demolished. It won't exist anymore.

"It hasn't gotten quite that bad yet, though I have to admit for a few years now that's the impression I've been trying to give people. Taking a few liberties with the truth; sort of a tradition in show biz. Things're kin-dah bad? Make 'em a little bit worse. Frighten people into thinking if they personally don't start buying at least four tickets from me every week, the Strand'll disappear, and the whole tradition of the theater back at least to John Wilkes Booth'll vanish right along with it. Nothing like a guilt trip to drum up a little trade. They don't really know me. All I am to them's someone who does something or other to do with the movies. So they tell me how much they enjoy the American Movie Channel on their cable service. I look as gloomy as I can and say: 'Oh yes, I know, I know. I guess most people must feel that way. It's absolutely *killing* me, people in my end of the business.'

"It was more like conversation than conviction. Over the years I've gotten so what I believe is that people who want to go out to the movies do it. They go out to the movies. No matter what other leisure-time choices they have, moviegoers will always choose the movies. Always have and always will, no matter how things change. While the people who don't want to go to the movies, well, they just don't. Never have and never will, and nothing will change how they behave either, no matter what anyone does.

"There're probably just as many of the first kind now as there ever were, proportionately," he said, "but there's so many of the mall houses now that they've reached critical mass. They've got me surrounded. The one up in Hampton Pond, for example: in their ads they're bragging they're now 'dedicating,' that's the word they use, like it was a monument or something, one screen—out of eight, mind you: big deal—to the arty first-runs that I used to grab. Shakespeare plays and French flicks, Bergman movies: every single week I could. They weren't my subsistence, no; weren't enough for them for that. But when they came along. boy, they were rich desserts.

"No one else around here wanted them. I used to be able to book them and get what amounted to a regional exclusive. The highbrows and the people who considered themselves intellectuals went bananas. From miles around they came. Every single parking place out front, around the green? VWs in the old days, the beetles and the vans. Then the Volvos took over—Volvos wall-to-wall; grey and maroon station wagons. What wasn't Volvos was Saabs, Subarus and Jeeps.

"The thing of it was that you couldn't depend on them. Never knew when one of those cult films was going to be born, christened, anointed, whatever it was, as something that had to be seen. Usually some foreign film no one'd paid much attention to, and then all of a sudden someone'd give it a rave in the *Village Voice* or some other paper, magazine, all the finer types had to read, and this particular obscure movie among all the dozens of cheap little movies that get made'd turn out to be a sleeper the elite now had to see. *The Long Good Friday* was one. Handmade Films, I think. British gangster movie. Bob Hoskins was in it. He was the head gangster. Couldn't understand a bloody word he said. The people with long earlobes loved it. *Blue Velvet:* another one—dirty movie full of violence for high-minded folks. All the intellectuals went nuts. Simply had to see it. It was like if you missed that film, whatever one it was that month that had everybody up at UMass or Smith talking—a Gerard Depardieu vehicle, maybe; that might do it. *All the Mornings in the World* or a Louis Malle—*Atlantic City* anything he did was always very big.

"I don't know what the hell happened, what they did to you if you were a highbrow and you allowed yourself to miss one. I'm sure it was something terrible, though. They canceled your subscription to the *Times Literary Supplement* or something—*New York Review of Books*. So you had to stay alert, be vigilant at all times. You never knew when one of them was going to come along. And therefore I couldn't tell either.

"The anniversary revivals that I ran were different. You never knew exactly who'd show up, but you knew enough of them would so you'd have a decent house. You could count on it. Alice Cole, a good example. Took it easy on my taxes 'cause the town should have a theater? Four times I saw her in it, total. Half of them were for *The King and I*—Friday and Saturday night, both."

He did say he knew it had been hard for her. She'd already been slowed down a lot by the lung cancer that would kill her two years later, at the age of 74. "Two other times she came. So over the course of ten years she put a grand total of ten bucks where her mouth was. I doubt very much she bought popcorn. A buck a year. Using what amounted to the town's money to keep the Strand open was one thing; spending her own was another. Good thing everyone else in Canterbury didn't feel the same way. I couldn't've lasted a year if they had, much less the last twenty-three."

At Cook's funeral he'd nonetheless mourned her honestly. He calculated her initial tax assessment, the basis of all later revaluations, by then had been worth about three thousand dollars to him, 2,300 average admissions—more than a dozen "near-sellout weekends," as he called any when ninety or more customers showed up for the 7:00 show both Friday and Saturday nights ("Eighty more for the nine-o'clock made it a smash hit. This part of the world goes to bed at a reasonable hour"). In the '70s he'd considered himself fortunate when he logged a dozen in a year, and therefore he was thankful to Alice's ghost.

When she died he was 37, still not exactly sure in his own mind what had happened to him between the fall of '68, when he'd gone down to Storrs for his first year of law school, and the summer of '71, after he'd graduated. He'd started out envisioning a quiet but satisfying and at least comfortable career in private practice in the Springfield area—although he said he would've been entirely willing to relocate to a town in the Berkshires, "if someone'd come along and offered me the right kind of opportunity, working conditions, out in that part of the world. I grew up around here, sure, but I was still flexible.

"The only thing that I was really sure of, going into it, was that what I didn't want, no part of it at all, was a big-city firm. Boston, New York, anything like that—even Hartford or Albany. I'd ruled out all of that stuff. Washington. Even though I realized—and Professor Burke warned me about it, too, made it very plain to me; I have to give him that—that my chances of finding the ideal situation, the kind that I'd have the most chance of being comfortable in, if I wanted to be in a firm, would most likely be a whole lot better in one of the larger cities than they were ever going to be in the smaller ones, like Springfield. And they were going to be even worse in the small towns.

"The anonymity, you know? In New York people don't leave you alone because they respect your privacy—they ignore you and what you're doing because they want you to leave *them* alone. They don't know you and they don't want to. In your smaller city—and the towns're even worse—if they *don't* know you; they *want* to know you. They're determined to know what you're up to. They've always got an eye on you, watching what you're doing. So it's bound to be much easier to keep your privacy in a metropolitan environment. And much likelier, too, that I'd be meeting other people in the city that I might like to get to know. But there wasn't any point in talking about that; I didn't want to do it and that was the end of it. So I knew I might have some problems, but I was resigned to it."

First he'd known he'd have to get the bar exam out of the way, of course, and then assuming that he'd found a job—"the idea that I might not never really entered my mind"—he'd need some time to get settled in. "What I projected when I started law school was that all in all it'd probably take me about five years. By then I'd be having a nice life. Whether I'd be on my own or in a small or larger firm I didn't know, hadn't quite decided. But that could wait—no need to. I had plenty of time. One thing at a time."

He emerged three years later having carried a steady B- average all three years, a C or C+ here and there, a B+ or a few Bs to balance the Cs off. "'The record of a conscientious tortoise,'" he recalls his late mentor, Alan Burke, pronouncing it. Burke in addition to teaching contracts and commercial law was the assistant dean in charge of the placement office. "'Slow but steady wins the race.' It wasn't going to get me a federal-court clerkship, nothing so dramatic, but Alan said a lot of private firms might go for what they thought they saw in it. 'The conveyancers, especially: very partial to that kind of track record. Makes them think all they have to do is hire you, show you where the registry of probate is and what they want you to do in it, find you a place to sit in the office, and bingo-bango, their own long days of drudgery're over.'"

But Goff hadn't been able to locate any of those weary real estate specialists. He sent out copies of his resumé and increasingly plaintive cover letters not only to the real estate "firms that might be hiring" that Dean Burke provided but to virtually every law office between Worcester and the New York line, regardless of which specialty they stated, if any, in the Martindale-Hubbell lawyers' directory. "Most of them never bothered to answer. I suppose they were simply inundated with letters like mine. So after a while they just gave up.

"I had a total of four interviews. One in Springfield, two in Holyoke, one all the way up in Greenfield. I thought that one went the best. The one in Springfield didn't go well at all. And one of the ones in Holyoke, the guy who interviewed me'd been real nice on the phone, real enthusiastic. I was looking forward to it. Solo practitioner, still fairly young, thirty-two or three. Said his practice'd just taken off, *exploded*, and he was bringing somebody else in about five years sooner'n he'd expected. But he got one look at me and I could tell it was over, right off. He became almost hostile. Said I must've misunderstood something he said. He hadn't really intended to hire anyone; he'd just been 'exploring alternatives.' I was out of there in five minutes.

"The one in Greenfield: that would've been a good situation, almost made to order for me. These two maiden ladies, about sixty; they'd known each other in law school. The practice'd belonged to one of their fathers—he'd since died. Always expected his own daughter'd come in with him, but then when she graduated, well, he'd taken her friend on, too. I would've gone up there in a second if they'd made me an offer. Heck, by then I was desperate. Would've relocated anywhere, someone'd made me an offer. But a few days after I was up there, one of them called me and said they'd changed their minds. Wouldn't be hiring anyone new after all. 'Too complicated.' That was what she said."

He said at first he thought the explanation was simply that he'd made a mistake by deciding to defer the job hunt at least until after final exams in May, so as not to jeopardize his class-ranking. And then until after the bar exam in June, taking no chances with that. "But instead of improving my chances, which was what I intended, my rule of One Thing at a Time may have been what did me in.

"And I have to say I also may have it at the back of my mind that if by some bad luck or something I *wasn't* able to find a good job on my own, well, that Alan'd gallop to my rescue. Reach down into this mysterious bag of tricks he always acted like he had—as though he had his hands on all these strings that he could pull; he *loved* to do that—and come up with something simply perfect for me. Not that Alan ever actually said anything, gave me any real reason to think that—I could've been fooling myself.

"Because the chances are there were some firms on that list of Alan's, when he drew it up in March and checked off the ones that he thought I should apply to, that were looking then to add people— maybe even someone like me. There had to've been. Maybe not that many, no, that'd end up actually hiring someone, but still, one was all I would've needed, if it was the right one. But it was July by the time I finally got around to putting my name in. By then those that really needed someone probably'd hired him. So I was left out in the cold.

"They start telling you in first year that if you expect to have a job when you graduate, when it's still three years down the line, the time to get started on it's March of second year. 'Get a summer internship where you think you might like to work, where you hope they'll want to hire you when you graduate. Let them get a look at you, while you take a look at them. That way when you do get out, if everything works right, you'll then have a place to go.'

"That was the first piece of advice I deliberately ignored. You know how it is when you're twenty-one or two; you know so much you can do anything. I could do that in those days, and often did: ignore what smarter people told me about important matters, especially if they obviously knew a lot more about them than I did. But the smaller ones back then that would've interested me: they didn't pay the summer help much. I could make a lot more going back to my old summer job tending bar at the Beach House in Provincetown. I'd gotten to know the owners and the regulars liked me. The tips were very good. I made a lot of friends. It was a lot of fun to be on the Cape in the summer with all the other young sports, goofing off. Much more than it was ever likely to be in some old law office in Springfield, cooped up with a bunch of stuffy old bores and middleaged drones, researching the case-law on pre-termitted heirs and sweating through your shirt.

"Did I know I was taking a calculated risk? Of course I did. What I didn't know was that I'd *miscalculated* the risk, badly underestimated it.

"At the beginning of your third year they tell you that if your second-summer tryout job wasn't quite as blissful as you'd hoped, then you'd better get cracking on the job hunt—'forthwith; all deliberate speed.' I didn't take that advice either. I'd really had to study hard to get where I already was in class-rank, the top of the middle third. I didn't even want to *think* about how hard it'd be to get a job if I started to drop down. I thought if I knew what was good for me I'd better disregard that, too. That was my second enormous mistake. It was deliberate, too.

"I had plenty of time to regret those misjudgments, you may be sure, while I spent the summer after third year waiting for the bar results. What I was doing didn't exactly occupy my mind. When I wasn't writing letters begging people to interview me—'please, sir or madam, even just a crust of bread?'—in the hope that at least they might take pity on me and give me some piecework, then I was doing that dreary work. Most of it was searching titles. Twenty-five bucks a deed—so that the wretch who was paying me to do the work could bill the bank's customer he was theoretically representing oh, about three hundred bucks. It was depressing and humiliating, the worst situation I'd ever gotten myself into in my whole life up 'til then. The only thing that made it bearable was the knowledge it was finite. It wasn't going to last. And I'd learned my lesson. After I'd been admitted to the bar and got a real job, I'd listen to what people said.

"Of course I never dreamed how much worse things could get, and were about to. The bar results were later than usual that year. Everyone was pissed off at the examiners for taking so long and prolonging the agony like that. But in the first part of October it was over. Then we all found out. Didn't we, though—yes indeed. I, especially, and a few more like me: all the other people who had something wrong with them. All of us rejects not only found out then; we'd been found out ourselves as well. Everybody knew. So that was my *third* major mistake. Not passing the bar. Definite oversight on my part.

"When I opened that letter and found out I'd flunked, I was absolutely stunned. No one's ever knocked me down, even as a kid, but I know what it's like. I sat down like someone'd knocked me off my feet. A giant hand came out of nowhere and silently slammed me down. Fortunately I was standing in front of a chair. Otherwise I might've broken my spine. There wasn't any saliva in my mouth. I couldn't inhale. I was gasping; could not take a breath. There wasn't any air. Tears *sprang* out of my eyes, like they do if you yank a hair out of your nose, but more of them. Ran right down my cheeks, *and I didn't know what they were*, what it was that was making my face wet. I felt like I might be going to throw up. I think I probably sobbed.

"I don't know that for sure. I was alone. No witnesses to back me up. I had no one to hear me or help me when I got that dreadful news. There hadn't been anyone, either. I was pretty much entirely on my own that year, entirely by myself. I didn't even have, at that point in my life, anyone that I could really call, or that I would've wanted to, at least, rely on to comfort me. Another thing that I'd put off, until I was a real lawyer, with his own real job. So I had no one I could tell this awful news. Certainly no one in my family.

"My father: of course he was out. By then I wouldn't've called him with *any* kind of news, even if it'd been good. He would've found some way to ridicule me for whatever might've happened. If I'd said I'd just been appointed to the Supreme Court he would've sneered at me for having to take a government job. But this? Tell him that I'd flunked the bar? Not in a million years. And if I'd told anyone else in my family, my mother, either one of my two sisters, they would've let it slip out. One of them would've told him. It would've happened. And then some day or night when I least expected it, he'd call me up and I'd answer the phone, and then he'd just leave me for dead. Like something in the road that didn't make it all the way across before the Greyhound came. No, this thing that'd happened to me: it was something I'd just have to get through the best that I could. I had to bear it alone.

"That was very hard to do. What made it so hard was that I couldn't for the life of me imagine how it'd happened. I literally couldn't comprehend it. Then or later, either. I sat there in my crummy apartment where the only way I'd gotten through the worst summer in my life'd been by making it my mantra that it was all going to end, as soon as autumn came. Now it was fall, October at last, and against all odds I'd survived. The ordeal was finally over. Now I could get started. Except of course I couldn't. Not me: I'd flunked the bar.

"It was *impossible*. I'd taken that goddamned full-time, total-immersion, six-hours-a-day lecture course that you then have to study all night to be ready for the next day—and I'd done it. Taken the merciless pounding the review leaders handed out, driven myself every night harder'n they did in the daytime. Weekends too, you may be sure. The only respite I allowed myself was a few beers on Saturday night. I had one friend from law school who liked me, that I got along with. Older guy, from down near Boston. His wife even liked me. She was from New York. My moot court partner, second year. I'd go over to his place and we would have a six-pack. Each of us would have a six-pack. I don't think Lucy liked it much, but we did that, Gary and I, and she put up with it. For six weeks straight, every Saturday, that was all the fun I'd had.

"Then when it was finally time to take the test, I'd done everything right, just like they said. I'd been such a good little boy. Gotten plenty of rest the nights that led up to it: check. Slept like a log after the first day: check. Up with the larks and fresh as a daisy for the second day: check and double-check. I felt fine. I didn't have allergies. No tummy-ache. No distractions in my personal life—didn't *have* any personal life, like I said; another thing I'd put off.

"Test hadn't bothered me, seemed like it was that hard. I hadn't found the questions *easy*, no; some of them were kind of tricky. But I felt good about them all, how I answered them. In those days the whole exam was essay. This was before the multi-state came in, the exam they all use now. You wrote out your answers in bluebooks. I'd been pleased with the way mine came out. Only one or two of the questions made me hesitate at all, and I was even comfortable with the way I'd finally answered those.

"So I was stumped. I couldn't've done anything more than I'd actually done to prepare for it. I'd made a mistake but I didn't know what it'd been. I couldn't explain it.

"That was why even though I signed up, paid for and sat through another hideous review course, the second one, I passed up the first chance to re-take the exam. It would've been sometime that winter. December; January. Whenever it was, I wasn't ready. I still hadn't figured out what'd gone wrong the first time. That made me scared. My thinking was that I wasn't going to subject myself to the risk of failing it again until I knew once and for all what'd caused me to fail it the first time. And was sure I'd corrected it. Too much was riding on it. My sanity. I still didn't know the next summer, either, the summer of seventy-two, or in time for the winter bar that year. So I didn't retake the exam those times either. In fact, I never did.

"Ten or fifteen years ago, maybe even more recently than that, if you'd asked me why I never went back and re-took the bar exam, that's what I would've told you. That I still didn't know why I'd flunked it the first time, and until I did I wasn't going to take a chance of failing it again. Well, I'm older now and I think I've changed my mind. I think now I do know why I flunked. I may've always known. I think I also know why I deliberately ignored the good advice I got in law school about summer jobs, and job-hunting in third year. I may've known those things all along, too, even though I didn't think so.

"Freud may've had the answer. He said, you know, that there's really no such thing as a mistake. That when something goes wrong, breaks, disappears, gets misplaced—ends, if it's a relationship; well, whatever it is, if you look at it close enough what you'll always find is that the person who lost it or broke it or did something that ruined it, destroyed it, if it was a friendship or a love affair or something else, maybe even a job; it's always because the person that the bad thing happened to either wanted it to happen, or figured it was bound to, and did something to bring it on and get it over with. He made sure. And I now think that's what happened to me. I think I didn't get a job and flunked the bar for the same reason that I bought the Strand twenty-three years ago: because I wanted to.

"Some friends of mine've said I ought to keep the place open two more years. Complete a quarter century I made its revival last, when so many people told me that it wouldn't be a year. I could do that if I wanted to. After all, I'm only fifty-two, and I've been fortunate: my health's still good. But now is when the Finch Brothers people want to buy my building, not two years from now. They've made me a good offer. It won't make me a rich man, not by today's standards, but I've always been careful with my money, and with what they're paying me, even if I were alone now, I'd be comfortable.

"As it is, I'll be fairly well-off—as well as quite happy. Ernest owns the house in Provincetown, for summers, and with what we can now afford to spend on the pied-à-terre we're buying in Key West, I think we'll be quite content. So when people say to me: 'Oh, don't give it up so soon. How can you let the Strand close down? It's been important to us,' well, I know how they feel. But what I have to tell them is that my reason for doing it's the same one that I've always had, for everything I've done. It's never really changed at all. I'm doing it because I want to. I'm still having my good time.'"?

THE HEROIC CAT
IN THE BAG

TWO years before he rescued the cat from the bag, Will Cowens, then 36, found a way to play golf every sunny day from late spring into October. Always an early riser, he found that by scheduling no client-conferences at Wynn & LaBelle, P.C., before 10:30 A.M., and arriving at Grey Hills at first light, when all the world was still, he could tee off by 6:45 and have the fairways virtually to himself. Playing alone and conservatively, to keep the ball in sight and play, and using a cart partly to speed things up—also to avoid badly damaging the turf, wet from dew and night-time watering—he could hole out on eighteen by 9:15. Sometimes he could persuade A. J. LaBelle, 53, a member of his weekend foursome as well as the chief tax man in the firm, to join him and play nine; he had to get the commitment quickly, before A.J. remembered that while he loved golf as much as Will did, he was a good many years older and needed a full night's sleep to do his best work. A.J. was all right; to be pleasant, he agreed in Peter Wynn's presence that Will probably did better work after his mornings' exercise, but since Will worked primarily on real estate development matters concerning Peter Wynn's major contracting clients, A.J. had no basis for his opinion, and Peter Wynn, still disapproving, knew that. "As long as you're sure it's not interfering with what you do here," he said, every time Will slipped and said something about his game. "We're partners in this place, remember. We own each others' days—nights too, when necessary."

The regimen left Will just enough time to shower and change and, by construing all speed limits favorably to the driver, still make it to the office by 10:00 or a little after. Wynn dropped acerbic comments now and then about "those Sunday brunches of yours at the desk, on weekdays," the coffee and the bran muffin that his secretary had awaiting his arrival, but the other people who mattered—Todd Mastro, 44, and Cynthia Dickens, 49, Will's seniors in Peter's sector, and the clients they worked for—were aware that during the colder months he usually opened the office before 7:00 A.M., and in all seasons habitually remained at his desk past 7:00 P.M. And they liked Will; until the day he rescued the cat they deflected Wynn's implied complaints by observing that "Any time I've worked with Will, I've had no complaints. Always does a good job; gets it done right, and on time."

A brief item about the cat in the bag at Grey Hills C. C. appeared in the north edition of the *Springfield Union News* on the morning of the second Friday in May. It proved to be a slow news day in the Pioneer Valley. Late that afternoon a three-person crew from Channel 9 in Springfield visited the club and taped an interview about the incident. Bolo Cormier, 57, the golf pro at the club, and Carla Blake, 31, the on-air talent, rode out from the clubhouse along the path between South Brook and the eighteenth fairway in Bolo's personal golf cart. Chuckie Boyd, 38, the cameraman and driver, and Donna Callahan, 36, the producer, followed in the white Nine/News Ford van with the big orange-yellow sunbursts on the sides. About two hundred yards from the eighteenth tee, Bolo stopped the cart and Boyd parked the van behind it.

From the rear of the van he removed two white molded PVC chairs borrowed from the terrace of the club and placed them in the low rough. Exercising the set-up care that had brought him three regional Emmys, he calculated how long he could play the angle of the sunlight advantageously before it would blind his lens; then he positioned his tripod and camera to capture it dappling the brook beyond the maples along the bank.

Blake used the side mirror mounted on the right door of the van to freshen her makeup and brush out her hair. Then she stepped back one pace and inspected her sleeveless white cotton blouse; she decided to undo the third button.

The producer, Donna Callahan, clipping a lavalier mike to the collar of Bolo Cormier's white polo shirt, also gave him some instructions. "Now you understand when this's actually shown—maybe

tonight, but we're never sure—it won't be anywhere near as long as
we'll spend here this afternoon." Seated in the chair camera-right,
Cormier was deeply tanned; peering down to watch her hands; he
smiled happily and nodded. His bald head gleamed in the sunlight.

Boyd said: "Ah, Donna?" and when she looked his way, pointed at
Cormier, patting the top of his own head.

She looked back at Cormier and said: "Oh yeah." She returned to
the van and took a makeup kit out of the waffled-surface aluminum
equipment case in the back. Cormier looked alarmed as she
approached him with it, but when she pointed to the sky and said
"Your head? The sun? How things look really counts in this business," he nodded ruefully and submitted to the powdering.

They went to work. That night on "Nine/News/5:30" Carla Blake's
fifth voice-over take would identify the compactly muscled man filling the screen as "head golf-pro at the posh private club. He theorizes
that . . ." The sound-track picked up his declaration to her, as yet
unseen. "Out-of-town kids did this to the poor cat. They come up
from Holyoke and Chicopee and they sneak onna the course early in
the morning before hardly anybody's up, snorkel inna water-hazards
for lost balls. We try our best to keep 'em out, but we got over three
hunded acres here. It's like it was fightin' ghosts in Vietnam: they
know we can't guard the perimeter. And even when we do catch 'em,
we might as well not bother—courts just give 'em a slap onna wrist."

Boyd had then zoomed back, so that viewers could now also see
Carla Blake. Behind them the late afternoon sunlight passing through
the stand of maples sparkled on the surface of the brook, at that point
about twelve feet across. Blake said: "And we're about where the cat
was found?"

Cormier nodded emphatically. "Yup. We're about two hundred
yards off the tee here. Most of our members're right-handed and the
ones with the hooks hit a lot inna brook. Could wade, it's shallow this
side, but they've got money and the water's very cold. So it's good ter-
ritory for the ballhawks. Generally work in packs. Prolly three or four
of them're here Thursday around sun-up, all finished divin', gettin'
ready to scoot with the loot." Cormier smiled. He liked that. He said
again: "'Scoot with the loot.'"

Blake forced a chuckle. Nothing Cormier had said after giving the
location would leave the cutting room. Callahan's grim first rule was:
"Let the talkers talk; let the editors edit." That excision from his
remarks would become the first of many made as she condensed the

interview, yielding what her executive producer-director, Bob Metterling, would denounce, but run. "Three-oh-five on the damned wet cat's *still* too fucking long, Donna. Should've cut it more. Especially since we don't have a picture of the fuckin' *cat*. They don't *see* what we don't *show*. "

"The vet wouldn't let us see her," Callahan said testily. "He said he'd given her a sedative and wanted her to sleep."

"Oh, 'The cat was in *seclusion*,' was it?" Metterling said. "Where? At the Betty Ford *Clinic*? At least you could've shot her sleeping in her cage, the luvva Mike."

"The vet wouldn't let us," Callahan said. "He was fucking *adamant*, to use a favorite word of yours—who's always back here bitching, never in the line of fire."

Blake had led Cormier on. "And the cat would've been out here too, at that time?"

Cormier nodded. "Beatrice would've been out here," he said. "She's the cook's cat. He lets her out every morning, prowl around outside a little, after her night's work. Lots of food around any place like this. Mice're gonna be a problem, 'less you keep a cat. Mice're not a problem here. Beatrice's a very good mouser."

"And a *friendly* one, you said," Blake said.

Cormier nodded emphatically. "Well she *was*," he said, "*very* friendly. Dante got her as a kitten, tiny little grey kitten. With stripes. Beatrice is a Maine 'coon cat. Only people Beatrice's ever known 'til now've been the members and their kids, and of course the staff here. We've always been kind to her. She thinks *she's* a member, herself. She sees one of us she really likes, up she comes and rubs herself against your leg, tryin' to get her ears scratched. Noon she's always out around the members on the terrace, tryin' to promote some of their lunch—little crabmeat, chicken salad. Generally she gets it, too, so she's a *big*, friendly cat. But still with the good moves, very quick on her feet."

"And that friendliness would've been her undoing," Blake said.

Cormier's head bobbed up and down. "Uh huh. Not used to mean and cruel kids. She would've gone right up to them, expecting to be petted, and those mean little" the audio was bleeped but his lips read "bastards grabbed her, put her inna bag with all the cut golf balls, ones they couldn't resell, and threw her in the brook. Trynah drown this poor nice cat, just tryin' to be friends. What a rotten thing to do."

Talking into the camera, Blake held up a white mesh shopping bag. "This would be the bag," she said. "It's made of strong, white, waxed twine." She used her left hand to point out the dimensions she described. "It's about three feet from the top of the shoulder strap to the bottom of the bag. Fourteen inches across. The holes between the mesh are about one inch square." She spread one with her left thumb and forefinger. "It looks to be about the right size to hold a day's grocery shopping. We filled it with stones we picked up along the brook and weighed it in the kitchen—it can hold at least twenty pounds."

She turned to face Cormier again. "Now if you'd just tell us what happened."

Cormier looked angry. "Will Cowens—he's a well-known lawyer down in Springfield—likes to get in a round before work. He's finishing up out here yesterday around nine, nine-fifteen. Said he hit his tee shot about one-eighty onna fly; it hooked a little, got another twenny onna roll, ended up on the edge of the rough. Right about here. He's trackin' the shot, see where it landed, he sees something bigger and white start moving away. And he heard this sharp sound, like a baby started crying. He jumped in the cart, came fast as he could, and that's what he found. Poor Beatrice, all wet 'n cold, and freezing and crying, inna bag with the golf balls, eight or ten feet from the brook."

"So this poor animal," Blake said, "hadn't been able to claw out of the bag .

"Well, no," Cormier said. "See, cats' claws're pointed, dig into things, not with edges to cut stuff apart."

"But then not giving up," Blake said, "this really *heroic* cat—and as we all know, cats *do not* like water. I'm not even sure they can *swim*."

"Oh, they can *swim*." Cormier said, "just don't *like* to," vexing her and causing her to frown.

Callahan cut that from the tape shown. The tape broadcast showed her serenely going on without missing a beat. "But apparently she was able to save herself by putting her feet through the holes in the bag, and then what? Swimming or walking, up out of the brook, until she was back on dry land?"

"That we're not sure of," Cormier said. "She might've done that, sort of scrambled around, poked her paws out and then made it outta the brook. Like I say, it's shallow, this side. But there was over a dozen golf balls inna bag with her, fairly heavy, and the bag weighs something itself. She's a pretty big cat, about sixteen pounds, and she looks even bigger, that fur. As cats go she *is* pretty strong. But we're still not sure she could've really done that, dragged herself outta the water alla way up here. Seems more likely one the kids had a change of heart, dropped out of the group, came back and fished her out. Maybe was even gonna untie the bag and let her out, but he heard Will comin' an' screwed.

"Anyway, it was Will Cowens that untied it. He's the one got her out."

The broadcasted tape ended there. Carla Blake, seated at the Nine/News anchor desk, the third button of her blouse now done up again—after Metterling's reprimand upon seeing the raw tape: "Too much cleavage, Blake. I've told you before: This's a *newscast* I'm running here, not a goddamned *tit* show. And put the blazer on, air-time. You know how I feel about sleeveless"—smiled into the camera. "Attorney Cowens declined our request to be interviewed. His secretary told us he says it's no big deal, doesn't want publicity for it. He's just glad the cat's all right."

She turned to her co-anchor, John Wright, four-time Emmy winner, who said: "Pretty refreshing, huh Carla? All the mean jokes you hear about lawyers these days; money's all that interests them. And now here's one who's not only a pretty nice guy but won't even take any bows."

Will Cowens was still at the office when the story aired. He wore a total of ten sterile gauze pads and Band-aids where the cat, by then terrified of all humans, had raked him with her claws while he worked to release her from the bag. He had a large gauze pad on his left jaw and a small one on his right cheek; on his left forearm three dressings; on his right hand and forearm, two dressings and three large Band-aids. Filled with chagrin, as requested he watched it alone with Peter Wynn in the conference room on the TV used to screen taped depositions. "I *named* that fuckin' cat, her first day at the club. There's gratitude for you"

"Will, I told you," Wynn said, resignedly, "I've been telling you for years. When your eggs're in one basket, what you do is watch that basket. Try to cram too many things into every day, sooner, later, you get bitten. Clawed. Something was bound to happen. Your're lucky she didn't get you in the eye."

"Pete," Cowens said, trying to lighten things up, "you don't even *like* to play golf. What you like to do is kill trout, and then *eat* them. You would've thrown poor Beatrice *back*, 'Kind to animals' ain't on your screen."

Wynn sighed. "Will," he said, "this isn't funny. You were over an hour late yesterday morning. And then when you showed up, you were in no shape to handle that planning board meeting last night, looking like you'd fallen down drunk. The whole meeting's on cable TV, for God's sake. All the local news outfits'll be covering, and there's the reassuring lawyer for the Steerforths, looking like a stew-bum? None of the rest of us here could pinch-hit for you on such short notice; this matter's too complicated. The tree-huggers would've eaten us for dinner. So the planning board people give us a break; we get a postponement, a week. Next week Mort and Roger'll come east again, and by then I'll be up to speed. Or Todd or Cindy will."

"Pete," Cowens said, "these're scratches, not stab wounds. My face'll be healed in a week. I know this stuff cold; I raised it from a pup. You don't need to replace me. Next Thursday night I'll bring it home."

"Will," Wynn said, inhaling deeply, "the Steerforths've got twenty-eight mill riding on that Hampden Falls complex. They've got conditional commitments for twenty-year leases on several hundred thousand feet of office and light manufacturing space. The market's finite. If the project doesn't start on time, those commitments disappear. Everything collapses.

"The Steerforths think this's a serious matter. They now think that maybe you don't. You're saving a cat 'stead of thinking of them? They were totally *bullshit* at you. That meant they were bullshit at *me*. That's why I kept you out of my office when you finally did came in. I couldn't get them calmed down. Every time I got Roger cooled off a little, Mort got him riled up again. They would've torn you apart.

"You've been here long enough now to know how sensitive these two guys are. They're not old money; they're straight nouveau riche, still Canadian wildcatters at heart. The way I got their business over twenty years ago was by convincing them, over and over again, that I believed we were equals. I was not looking down on them as a couple of wealthy Alberta yokels I could fleece with fast talk and a smile. They came with me instead of Butler, Corey because they didn't feel like I was *Harvarding* them—their choice of words, not mine. I took them *seriously*. They're the foundation of this firm, the very linchpin. I took on A.J. to deal with their taxes. The three people he's got who're working for him; the three of you on my team; all of the clerical staff, the whole shebang: Everything in this outfit started with them. "Now they've flown their Learjet into Bradley Wednesday night to meet with you here Thursday morning. And you're not only not here waiting for them, they arrive, you don't have a good reason not to be. Not a good enough reason for them.

"These guys understand sometimes things can go wrong. Tornado goes through and takes out a rig; a new gas well explodes: disasters they can understand. Recklessness even, they might tolerate. If you'd come in here late and all bandaged up, because you'd hit a tree hard in a Caddy, or you'd been in a fight in a bar—which you'd *won*—that the Steerforths could understand. And after a few snarls, they'd forgive. But to keep them waiting to rescue *a cat*? That they found extremely offensive. They found it insulting, in fact."

Wynn sighed and his voice dropped. "I'm going to have trouble retaining their business. They've made that very clear to me, Will."

Cowen stared at him. "Good God, I'm history?" he said. "Is that what you're telling me, Pete?"

"No, it's not, Will," Wynn said. "I don't know what the answer is. I won't know for several days. Wednesday morning you're gonna come in and tell me. Either that in fact you *are* history here, or else that you're the best lawyer anyone of us in here has ever met." He reached into the inside pocket of his jacket and pulled out a Continental Airlines ticket folder. "Four o'clock Monday afternoon you start flying to Denver. Alone. Tuesday morning at nine there you're meeting with Roger and Mort, to explain why you should keep your job here. I'd suggest you be there on time. Tuesday night you come back. With your shield or on it."

"Jesus," Cowens said, "after this, I may give up golf."

"I don't think you'll have to go that far," Wynn said. "But if you should see any dogs sleeping out there, I would leave them alone, I was you."

THE LAST WASH OF THE TEAPOT

As Told By Cornelius McKibben, Esq.
A Book for a Play

SCENE

The time is present. It's early evening in New England, late spring or early fall, getting close to dark. I envisioned this as a one-man performance, with a set consisting of a rug, two chairs, some bookcases filled with lawbooks, and a rolltop desk. But it could be expanded to depict Cooper's Store, the bank, and so forth. And the cast could include up to six people.

McKIBBEN (in his law office): The thing about a solo law practice like this, in the sort of place that Greenwich is, is that over fifty or sixty, or in this case, over a hundred, years it tends to become pretty much a reflection of the town. And when you think about it, it seems pretty clear, 'least to me, that it got that way because the men who ran it before you took it over had to've made damned sure it did.

Well, my father, this'd be John McKibben, Junior, was that kind of man. Because *his* father, my granddad, had raised him that way. John Senior came to this country a young man about twenty or so—we're not sure about his actual age; he was always very secretive about it, like he was about most things. Not that he had anything to hide, or anything like that. If he did, he did a fair job of it—we never stumbled over any human bones in the closets, at least, no shallow graves in the yard. Granddad just considered that a man who kept his mouth shut about any secrets he might have was the kind of man that folks'd trust when it came to telling theirs. And he was right, seems like to me.

Granddad read the law in the same office in Northhampton where Calvin Coolidge hit the books, but he saw no earthly reason to go traipsing off to Vermont or some outlandish place like that after he passed the bar. Came right back home to Greenwich and set up his office here. In the course of time, after he'd gotten himself established a little, he married a local girl by the name of Mary Cooper, and settled in for the long haul, right and proper.

He had good reasons. My father used to say that his dad always had some reason for everything he did. And that it was always a good one. He wouldn't tell you what it was, you knew that, of course, and you weren't likely to have much luck trying to guess it yourself, either. And if you happened to strike on it, he wouldn't say if you were right.

Mary was an immigrant, just like himself, but she didn't come here alone. Well, she got on the boat by herself, and she came through Boston herself, but once she got outside of Immigration there, well, her brother was waiting for her. Brought her right back here.

Mary's brother's name was Angus. Turned out to be a senior too, in the course of things. When he finally got married and his wife had a son, they named him Angus, Junior.

Now there were two things about Angus, Senior. One was that Angus and my grandfather knew each other pretty well. Whether they'd been sidekicks in England, before they came here, or they just hit it off when my granddad first rolled in, I honestly don't know. Second possibility seems likelier to me—Angus was a few years older, or so Grandad always claimed, so I'd tend to think they met here, and that's how they became friends. But friends indeed they had become, when Granddad started reading law. And that was one thing.

The other thing was that Angus Senior'd brought a bit of money with him when he came to America. How he'd come by it over there, I really couldn't tell you. His name'd make you want to say he'd been a barrelmaker, sold his business, headed west, but I don't know of any other reason to say that. He didn't make any barrels in America that I know of—he just had a good head for business. Opened a hardware store here, and a cagey move that was.

This was all farming country out around here then—nearest railroad station was the one in Barre, twelve miles to the west, and that was where the stores were. Well, twelve miles out and back was a day's hike in those days. Busy farmer 'd hitch up his team and wagon to make it if he had a crop to ship, apples maybe, or his pigs'd reached their growth and were ready for the market. But he had to have a good reason. He wasn't going to waste the better part, his day, and the wear and tear on his horses, to go all the way to Barre just to get one article. If his claw-hammer broke while he was fixing up his gate from the damage winter'd done, he'd finish up the job with the blunt end of his hatchet, or a stone if he had to, and wait until his next trip to see to a new tool. Same if the woman of the house took a fancy to some drygoods—she never would've asked her husband to make a special trip for that. She'd've waited 'til he was going in, on something made it worth it, and then she'd ride along.

So the hardware store right here in town was a mighty fine idea, from everybody's point of view except maybe the blacksmith's. Knocked him right out of his old sideline of making nails from iron scraps, keeping busy on slow days. Soon as people realized they had a store right here, could send one of the younger boys, their own or one of the neighbor's, to town for something handy that they needed in a hurry, well, they got the hang of it real fast.

And once they started to come in, Angus Senior got himself a good reputation in a hurry. He treated people fair and square, and he'd extend them credit if they were responsible. Sure, his price might be a little higher than in Barre, but if they brought that up to him, he'd say: "Well, I have to pay more freight." And they knew that he was right.

Well, my grandfather was smart too, even though he had no cash. At least not when he opened up. And he figured the surest way to let the people know there was a lawyer here—hadn't been one before him, just circuit riders coming through, and nobody trusted them— was to let them see him and find out.

See, before he started up, the farmers around here all relied on the lawyers down in Barre. Didn't have much choice.

But most of the Barre lawyers were with the banks that wrote the mortgages on their farms, and their equipment loans. Now this was all right, far's it went, but when a man's doing business with some- body who can take his property away from him, he feels a little bet- ter if the other fellow's lawyer isn't his lawyer as well. So Granddad had that in his favor.

And then you had the wills, the deeds, the small contracts for leas- ing pasture land—not much divorce work in those days—and it was lots more convenient, get them all done right in Greenwich. Put a full day's work in and then drive in after dinner. See your lawyer in his office, get that nuisance taken care of without time lost on your job.

So my granddad said to himself: well, the best thing he could do, because at first he didn't have much work to keep him occupied, was to spend a good deal of his time being out where people were. So that they could see him. And that was in the hardware store. Old Angus'd introduce him—"This here's my good friend, John. Brand-new lawyer setting up here. You can trust him—I do." And that helped a lot. If Angus trusted John McKibben, he must be all right. And Grand-dad knew how valuable that testimony was in helping him get trade. He made sure he justified it. He used people all right, and they got so they trusted him as much as they relied on Angus. So Angus never had the slightest reason to regret what he'd told them.

When I was a little boy, and this still in the Depression—which hit people here real hard, too, though they still did have food to eat—a good many of them who had plenty of hard things to think about'd see me coming in this office, pat me on the head. "Your grandfather's word, my young friend, is sounder than the dollar. You should be proud of him."

And there was another thing that came out of those early days, too. In a manner of speaking you could say it was my father, and if it's not stretching a point too much, later on I came out, too. Mary Cooper, you see, clerked for Angus at the store. So back in those days when Granddad was scratching up his practice, spending so much time around there, he and Mary got so they . . . well, let's say they became downright fond of each other.

Now, times were a little different then. Heck, they were different even from when I was growing up. I'm not saying you didn't have an instance now and then where the baby was born on the wrong side of the blanket, or that the first child never came along less'n nine or ten months of the wedding, not by a long shot. But back then it was still unusual, cause for a lot of comment, and it was certainly not the sort of thing that an up-and-coming young lawyer wanted said about his wife—that she'd maybe given him more than just a look at the menu before he ordered the whole meal. And furthermore, Old Angus would've taken strong exception to any man he thought might have tried to take advantage of his little sister. So Granddad spoke to Angus first, after it began to look as though he was established, ready to take on a wife, and got his full permission. Angus was entirely pleased, so John started courting Mary—John and Mary, yes indeed, not a yuppie name in sight—and in due course they were married.

Now I suppose we're saying here about ten years've gone by since John McKibben, Esquire 'd been admitted to the Bar, and come back to Greenwich to try his lot in life. He was doing all right, around age thirty. During the first couple years or so, until he'd scraped together enough money for the down payment on this place—and I do mean he scraped, keeping farmer's hours to save on the lamp-oil expense— Angus'd let him use a desk in the office of the back of his place that he used himself to do his books, gave him his own key to the place so he could see his clients after the store closed. But things'd gone along pretty good since then for John, and while he never talked about it— bragging as another thing he wasn't partial to—at least I ever heard, he had to've been pleased with himself, and how matters'd turned out.

And so did Angus, Senior. He was pretty careful with a dollar, too, and he didn't always have to spend all that extra freight money to pay for actual freight. Got so he could calculate pretty much what he'd need for the next six months of business, and order up large quantities for bulk shipments all at once. Better shipping rates for large lots. Meant he needed more space for his inventory, of course, but since he saw no need to talk about his new freight rates, or the savings in the form of lower prices, he'd built up a cash reserve .

He used it to expand. Added a drygoods section, a small pharmacy— he always called it "the apothecary"—and a US Post Office cubicle, where folks could buy their stamps.

Pretty soon he found that he was running out of room in the building that he had. Well, that was all right. He had courage, and self-confidence, and a bit of vision, too. I don't claim he foresaw exactly how the town'd flourish in this century, of course, the direction it'd take, but he did have faith in it. So he went and he put up his own two-story, solid-brick building with a cement tablet on the front: "Cooper's Store," it said.

That building's still standing to this day. If you were to leave this office and walk three blocks up the street and stand right in front of the bank and look across, you'll see it. Kind of hard to make out the cement tablet these days, of course—the chain-drugstore that took over half the first floor put up one of those damned big white neon signs before I could get the Board of Selectmen riled up enough to introduce a warrant article expanding zoning powers to include sign regulations. Fact, it was that sign that finally did it, made them see what I'd been talking about, 'til I was as blue in the face as that damned big sign is white. But by then it was too late, of course, to make them take it down. Only hope we've got now is that someday they'll pull up stakes and take off and move their eyesore to another town.

But I doubt that's going to happen, in my lifetime at least. The college people, the newcomers, they just love that place. Calls itself a "discount store," so they assume they're getting bargains. And the pizza parlor next to it, the liquor store—"Wine Cask," my foot; if you want booze, call it "booze"—and the auto-parts place, that blasted record store: yeah, I know they bring the trade in, create jobs and so forth, and they pay their taxes, too. And I know if we didn't have them, land around here wouldn't be worth so much, not so many'd be well-off now, now that farming's out of style. And the housing trade'd slump. And that'd cut the bank's business, which would hurt my practice, too. So I guess I' ve got to grin and bear it. But that doesn't mean I have to like it, does it?

Albert Cooper didn't, I know. Said that to me many times. Almost every time we met, right in here or on the street. Never did amount to much, not while he was alive, which my father used to say's the time to do it if you're smart, but Albert did know his town.

Well, I see it's nearly seven, which means Mrs. Hinsdale'll be in, in exactly twenty-four minutes, to review her will again. Mrs. Hinsdale's very prompt, and particular, too. Makes an appointment to come in about this time every year. Says it's her way of satisfying herself that the provisions she's made for the distribution of her estate—she and Ed didn't have any children of their own, and her brothers're both dead, so the personal bequests are all to her nieces and nephews. But I guess those young people're smart enough to know she's got a dollar or two tucked away, in addition to what her property's worth—a goodly sum, I'd guess, by now, at least thirty buildable lots—so they make sure they're very attentive to her. "Keep the old bat happy— she's got a ton of dough." But they've succeeded, I guess—she's never changed any of those articles.

No, it's the charitable bequests that she's always fiddling with. When the pastor of First Parish—that's the Unitarian here—retired a few years back, the church board voted to call a new, young minister. Which was to've been expected, of course, but the new minister they chose is a woman, and right after she got here there was more than idle speculation she's a lesbian, too. Mrs. Hinsdale didn't like that decision at all. She made a special trip in that year, added a codicil that the church probably won't like a lot when the time comes to probate her wishes, but I'd imagine the Society for the Prevention of Cruelty to Animals will be happy enough with it, if they're still among the

Chosen—Mrs. Hinsdale makes her mind up pretty firmly. Once she decides she's mad at you, you couldn't make her change it back if you got down on your knees.

I've had to laugh, just to myself, of course, every time she's come in here and done something like that. And you can bet that there've been a lot of those times, yes sir—every year I can recall since she turned seventy, and that's a good long time ago. I always tell her: "Mrs. Hinsdale, you know, this document's all on computer disc now. We can dash off a new, clean crisp copy in a jiffy. Why add another codicil to this thing? It's beginning to look like a messy copy-book."

But she always refuses to allow that. And she never will give a good reason. Expects that I'll think, of course, that she's being frugal, doesn't want me to charge her for doing a whole new will. Well, maybe it is partly that. But I know what the real reason is: it's anticipatory revenge, maybe the sweetest kind there is. She wants the satisfaction of knowing that after she dies, all the people who annoyed her'll be able to go over to the courthouse and find out how much it actually cost them to get the old lady's dander up. They were in, but they did something, so she put them out. And if they don't think of doing it, going in to read the will, well, you can bet the clerks'll read it, and they'll spread it all over town. Messengers of Mrs. Hinsdale's posthumous revenge.

Well, be that as it may, the fact of the matter is I'd better go through her file again before she comes, so I'll be on top of things when she gets here. If she had the slightest inkling I'd been taking her for granted, why, the next thing that you know she'd've hired a new lawyer, and I would've lost a job. I know I more or less implied I'd tell you about Albert Cooper, and I will, soon as I get this out of the way. So if you'll just excuse me for a little while now. . . .

McKIBBEN: Ah, there you are. Thought I heard you come up the steps. Hope you enjoyed your walk. And you were able to make yourself comfortable out there on that old glider in the dark. Been meaning for years to take it down, get the porch rescreened and so forth, maybe some of that new furniture they make of plastic pipe now. But I never do seem to get around to it.

Partly nostalgia, I suppose. The inertia of nostalgia. My grandfather bought that thing, first year he owned the place. Had it sent up from Worcester. Cushions've been replaced a few times, of course, but the frame's the same. Live your whole life in one place, you get attached to things. Don't like to see change taking place, 'less it's change you can't avoid. Death I suppose, that's the hardest one to take. And the one we absolutely can't do one damned thing about.

Well anyway, we'll go back inside now. Take the night chill off. Had quite a tussle with Mrs. Hinsdale, as it turned out. Bee in her bonnet this year was the Spaulding Library. Named after the fine old gentleman who left the money in his will to the town to build it, back in Eighteen-eighty-seven. Twenty-one-thousand dollars. Lot of money then, and no small change today. Not for most of us, at least. His theory was, as his will said—I know; my granddad drafted it—that he believed a free library was a town's "best ornament, to which all the people, young and old, may repair as they shall wish, and in communal solitude gain Knowledge and Improvement."

Now ever since then that's been a kind of article of faith in Greenwich, at least among a few. It's been a tradition for people who took an active part in town affairs to give some service to the Spaulding. And I don't mind saying it's really paid off—that library's the envy of a good many bigger towns, and a couple of cities I know of, and it's all because Horace Spaulding years ago set that priority for us. Towns're like families and businesses: the first thing you have to decide, no matter how rich or poor you are, is what's most important to you. And that's where you should spend your money. Well, here in Greenwich we believe it's books and education. Or we used to, at least. Still should, in my estimation.

We McKibbens can take some credit for that. My granddad was a trustee for over thirty years, served as president six of 'em. My father followed in his footsteps, a trustee for thirty-eight years, president five terms. And I went on the board, well, I don't like to think about it, but it's over thirty years now. When my father was still there. Ed Hinsdale was a member, about sixteen years, I think, until he took sick and decided that he had to give it up. And Emma, that's her name, his widow, she took Ed's place on the board, and served until two years ago. She said she'd gotten too old for the meetings that run late. Sometimes as late as ten.

Well of course no one believed that. It's common knowledge Emma's up 'til after Johnny Carson, and she follows basketball. When the Celtics play on the West Coast, her light's on 'til close to dawn. It's not a very bright light, Emma doesn't fritter money, but her bedroom's at the front her house, and anyone who has to get up early for his work—the early-shifters on the fire, the police, the long-commuters, they all see it on, you know. And she always knows the score.

No, they all thought what bothered her was certain changes that we made. To keep pace with the times. When we opened up the stacks the first thing, maybe eight, nine years ago, which almost everybody liked—they could go get their own books, and maybe spot a couple more that looked interesting to them. Emma didn't like it. She preferred when she could tell someone to get 'em for her. And then there was the videos. Of course we had to have'em. I don't mean dirty movies, of course—the great movies, like "Gone With The Wind." And home repairs, travelogues—useful things like that. Well, Emma didn't think the Spaulding was the proper place for that. "Libraries are for books."

I knew it rankled her. Another small tradition was for people in this town that took an interest in the Spaulding to leave it something in their wills. Wasn't always a lot of money, not by any means. We've had bequests as small as ten or twenty dollars. But most of them've been between five hundred and a thousand, some earmarked for books, and some for certain kinds of books—generally the kinds of books that the decedent liked. There was one year when we got more gifts to buy mysteries than there were mysteries to buy. I guess as we get older, we tend to favor those. But every dollar that we got earmarked for a specific purpose was another dollar out of taxes we could use for repairs and maintenance, and for salaries, too. So we were glad to have it. Ed left us two hundred bucks, and a generous gift it was—oh, he had a fair amount of money, but his first obligation was to see Emma taken care of, and we all knew that, of course.

But I have to say, we did think, that when Emma went to her reward, the Spaulding could expect to come into a real fine piece of change. And until tonight—I can say this without breaking confidences—it would've. After tonight? Forget it.

I have to say I could not make the head or tail of what was at the bottom of her gripe. As near as I could tell it was that National Endowment stuff, financing dirty pictures. Dirty photographs. I told her that, as she knew, that had nothing to do with us, that we were not involved. But Emma said she didn't care. "Enough is just enough. I pay my taxes every year, and I don't like it, either." I knew that, of course. When I tell her what she owes, she acts like I'm the one who sets the rates and takes her money. "But I have to," she said, "so I do, because it's necessary. But if that's is the kind of thing my tax-money's going for, those awful pictures, then, fine, but they'll get no more from me than what they make me pay."

I did the best I could, but I gave up after a while. My job's to represent the client, carry out the client's wishes. Not to tell the client what her wishes ought to be. At least beyond a point. So the upshot of it all is that the nieces and nephews will be getting their *pro rata* shares of ten thousand dollars that the Spaulding stood in line to get until Emma changed her will tonight.

Now I know I promised you I'd tell you about Albert.

Albert Cooper, that is. I appreciate your patience. But what Emma's told me that I have to do for her, well, that's as good a way as any of beginning about Albert.

Albert was a trustee for over forty years. Never was the president, though—he refused to take the job. Said he didn't think he was up to it. I never came right out and said it, but I thought he was probably right. And it's not that big a job.

You recall I said Albert never really amounted to much of anything, and he didn't. But Albert wasn't really born and raised to amount to much. My father always had a sort of mild contempt for him. Didn't hate him, nothing like that. Didn't ridicule him, either. Just didn't have much use for him. Said he was irrelevant. That the reason he was shiftless was because he'd been brought up to be, had no training for the world. "I'm not saying anything the Coopers haven't said themselves," that is what my father'd claim. "Old Angus told your grandfather in no uncertain terms that the boy was useless—'He's the last wash of the teapot.' That's what your grandfather said."

I've got to go back some here again now—hope you'll pardon me, but it's the only way that I can see to tell you about this town. And Albert, and Albert's things—all that too, of course. Old Angus and his wife had young Angus, only child. Just like Old John McKibben and his wife, born Mary Cooper, had young John, my father. And my father married Rose Brady, very much against my granddad's wishes—in case you were wondering how I got called 'Cornelius,' well, that was her father's name, and a fine man Connie was—best bootlegger in these hills, I'm told, by people who should know. Young Angus'd already married, some years before that. Girl he met in England the year he took his Grand Tour, and after the appropriate interval, they produced Angus the Third.

Now by rights, not to mention family traditions, that should've been the end of that business. My grandfather and old Angus'd started up the bank. My father and young Angus'd gradually taken over. The Coopers had Angus the Third to take his father's place, and young John McKibben could be depended on in his own good time to produce a son to follow him. I doubt many thought my father's son'd be Rosie Brady's son too, but as I said, the times did change, a little bit, at least.

No one was in a hurry then. Everybody knew each other, down to me, when I came along, and already Angus the Third. I was three years behind him in grade school, just as my granddad's been a few years younger'n old Angus when they got here, and my father maybe four years younger than young Angus when they took over. The store was still going all right for the Coopers back then—this was right after World War Two—but they had hired men running it for them. Their real business was at the bank. And so was my grandfather's legal business, and my father's when he took over. It was all very orderly. We'd been a hardy bunch, each generation missed all of the wars, and no one had a reason to expect a bad problem might come up.

But it did, and it was Albert. He'd been born about the time my father married Rosie, January of the year of the Great Crash. Angus Three would've been four years old or so. Albert's birth came as a great surprise to everyone in town. Not as disturbing as what was going to happen to the Stock Market and the country later on that year, but still a great surprise. The Coopers first, of course, because my father told me, they didn't spread the news, but there was a good deal of comment when the pendency of the big event, shall we say, became publicly apparent.

Well, that's the kind of thing that generally inspired a lot of comment in a town this size, back then. Some unexpected event which it really wasn't anybody's business to expect; that could cause a lot of talk. But it all died down after a while. The baby was born, and that revived the subject, but no one could really claim there was something out of line, so that was the end of it.

Now I'm going to sort of skip ahead here, kind of fast, about a quarter of a century, mostly because there wasn't really much of anything that happened that has much to do with this. And if I don't, we'll be here all night, and you never will find out what you came here to find out.

My grandfather died in Nineteen-forty-one. Ninety-one years old, and never been sick a day in his life. He was in here that day, nice

August day, right in this office, working away at that desk, snapping and snarling about Roosevelt, of course—Granddad never did like him. And then that night, it came quitting-time, he quit and went into the parlor. My mother was making the dinner, I was out playing, I s'pose, and Dad was in here at that table. Granddad had the desk. My father worked at the table, until he was fifty-three. Then my mother, Rosie, when dinner was ready, she called us all in to sit down. But Granddad didn't come.

This was unusual. I can't say that granddad was a gourmet, but he surely did like to eat. The dinner-bell rang, he came on like a firehorse, and his plate was clean when he stood up. Well, my dad went into the parlor, and there was Granddad in the chair. Dead. You think about that, if you would. There was my mother, out in the kitchen. My father was right in this room, one wall between him and the parlor. And neither one of them'd heard a sound. It was like he'd just gone to sleep. No "goodbye," no "so long now," no "I meant to tell you." Took all of his secrets with him. Now that's what I call "decorum."

Course of time, I grew up. Boys'll do that, you know. Finished school and then went to college. Same college's as Dad'd gone to. And then down to Boston for law school, of course—times'd changed more since Granddad started out. Meantime Angus Three was right there in the bank, working away with his father, and I came back here—got the table. Sat at it until I was forty-one. Then Dad died, and I got the desk.

By then Young Angus was history, too, and Angus the Third ran the bank. But Albert? Albert didn't do much. Except read. He read a lot. He still had his own room, his same room as always, in the Cooper house, and he had no one to bother. That was because Angus the Third never married—he planned to, very nice girl, banker's daughter, from Wellesley, but other events intervened—and he went to the bank every day. There was nobody else in the house. Albert got up in the morning, after Angus'd left for the bank. He bathed, shaved and dressed, like he was an ambassador. Made his own breakfast, read the newspapers, finished the book that he'd borrowed the day before. Put on his hat, his coat if it was cold, his rubbers if it was raining, and walked down to the library. Took his coat and his hat off, his rubbers, too, put them all on the rack. Returned his book from the day before, and went back in the stacks to find more. This was long before anyone but the librarians were allowed to do that, but it was understood that Albert was different from most of the patrons, and he was "working on something."

Nobody ever understood just exactly what it was that Albert was working on. "Some scholarly project." That was about the best you could get for an explanation. And it wasn't because nobody tried to figure it out, either, because a lot of people did. Angus in fact was one of them. Went over the records of books that he borrowed with your regular fine-toothed comb, and made no sense at all out of it. There just wasn't any pattern to his tastes.

He took books out on weapons, medieval and modern. He took books out on trains, and the West. He took books out on art, and on architecture, and books about emperors and kings. There was one spell when he took out nothing but Prescott, the histories of the conquest of Mexico, and then he veered off to the Crusades. He read all of Dickens, and all of Trollope, and all of Jane Austen, three times. He read Samuel Johnson and Tom Jefferson, Ben Franklin, John Adams and Grant. He read Dante and Ovid, Homer and Virgil, Hitler and Marx and Aquinas. He read Coke's *Common Law* and Grey's *Anatomy*, and he read Edmund Burke and George Berkeley. There was no rhyme nor reason to what he picked out, and it bothered people no end.

It was as though he was doing it for the fun of it. For the sheer hell of it. If he wanted to read it, he read it, and whose business was that, anyway? Of course he went about it very solemnly, always very serious, very grave. "I think I'll take these two, today, please."

But why shouldn't he have, if he wanted to? There was nothing else on his mind. Young Angus, his father, may've been somewhat startled, when Albert showed up after Angus, but he never let on, at least not publicly. He'd made full provision for Albert. Angus the Third was to run the bank, and Albert could do as he liked.

So that was exactly what Albert did. He left it to his brother to run the bank, stayed completely out of his way. He'd liked college a lot, doing pretty much the same thing, and he had an adequate living, so why go to the trouble of changing? From time to time I'd have business uptown, and I'd run into him out on his walks. We'd say "hello" and exchange a word, the state of the world and so forth. Albert had a nice manner about him. Of course he knew much more than I did, about everything but the law. I didn't have time to read all the papers, and study what the stories meant. But he never let on he knew that. He was a true gentleman. And I have to admit, I enjoyed our short talks. I was glad when I ran into him. He kept me abreast of the world.

So was he. I know he appreciated our frequent encounters. I have to admit, I didn't know how much he appreciated them 'til after he was dead and the appraiser came around, but then I found out: a lot. Take a look at that drawing up over my desk. Now I thought it was nothing special. Man on a horse with a lance. Like I said: what the hell do I know? Well, Albert gave me that. We'd had one of our sidewalk discussions one day, he was just back from Europe, and he was all enthused about some artist that he'd just discovered. So he got me interested, and I said I'd like to see some of that man's work some day, and Albert said I would. And the next day, he brought that around. I had it framed, hung it up in the hall. Until I found what it was worth. Although I have to say, when I look at it, it's still looks like a man on a horse.

But that's the point. When I say "the world," I don't mean just what was in the *New York Times* and the Boston papers, or all the books he read all the time, either. Once a month, regular as clockwork, Albert'd get in his "motorcar," which is what he always called it; his Fifty-one, black Cadillac convertible—now *that* was a beautiful car, red upholstery, white top, waxed and buffed to a shine that'd blind you—and drive himself down to Boston. He'd stay four or five days, always at the Copley Plaza, and he'd go to the museums, the Museum of Fine Arts and the Gardiner, to Symphony, a ballgame, whatever was in season, the Public Library, the Atheneum, the bookstores—he had a whole list of regular stops. And twice a year, spring and fall, he'd drive out to Springfield and get on the train and take himself down to New York. He had all his shirts made in New York, so there was that, and he'd go to the opera and plays. Always stayed at the Stanhope, he told me: "It's quiet, and near the museums."

Every five years or so, he'd take the Queen and head off to England, then to France on the ferry, and after that the train to Italy. He had his suits and his shoes made in London, so he'd get measured for them and choose fabrics and so forth. He'd visit the museums and he always planned his trip for some Shakespeare festival. He'd spend some time in Paris, and then he'd hire a driver and tour all the great chateaus—that was when he restocked his cellar, which I never saw 'til he was dead. My God, he'd filled the entire basement, and that's saying something, because that was one big house, case after case after case. The labels meant nothing to me, of course—I'd been to dinner at his place six or eight times, maybe, this was after he got married, and that was another big shocker, but I'm getting ahead of my story somewhat here—and the wine was always good, but I never knew how good it was until the man told me.

After he got that business taken care of, as I say, Albert'd go on down to Italy. Chiefly Florence, I think. He was partial to the museums there. And then he'd come back on some liner or other, trunks of books and so forth along with him. But the only way you'd ever know he'd been away, unless you came right out and asked him, was that you didn't see him for a while, walking to the library, taking his exercise, just being around town as usual, and then he'd show up again, just the same as before. But he was a very cultivated man, a man of some refinement, I believe the saying is, and he'd never bring it up. So while I knew, of course, that he'd been away, the only way I got details was by asking for them.

Same as with the library trustees. Albert was a natural for the trustees, and a valuable addition to the board he was, too. But I had to ask him, or someone else would've had to. He wasn't the kind to promote himself, even though there's no question but that he knew a whole lot more about the place, how it operated and how it ought to operate, than the rest of us all put together. The librarians naturally loved him, thought of Albert as their vote on the board. And I think he enjoyed his years as a trustee. He must've—once he came on, he served until the day he died, and I'll tell you right now, he's been missed.

So that was the way matters stood on that morning in September seven years ago, Albert and his brother, the banker, living in the same house where they'd both been born and'd grown up, everything just going along as usual, nice, sunny day. Albert got up at his usual time and followed his normal routine right up until the call came from the bank. Angus hadn't shown up, and he hadn't called in sick, either. And he hadn't been in at Tom Daisy's.

Well naturally Albert was kind of alarmed. Because Angus Three was just as regular in his habits as Albert was in his. Angus got up at six-thirty every morning, took a cold bath, got himself dressed, had a cup of tea, nothing more, and headed down to Tom Daisy's for breakfast. That's the coffee shop, down there on Main Street. Still there, but new owners. Back in those days Tom and Daisy Cosmopulous owned it and ran it—Tom was the cook and she was the waitress—and so it was Tom and Daisy's, but everybody always called it "Tom Daisy's." Angus'd have the three-egg special, always with ham and two slices of white toast, and he'd gossip a little over the papers, and then off he'd go to the bank. And there were very few mornings he didn't—the Coopers were not a sickly bunch, by any stretch of the imagination.

Well, Albert of course knew Tom wasn't in the bathroom—he'd just been in there himself. So it didn't take him but a minute to go upstairs, and Angus's bedroom door was closed. And so was Angus, as Albert found out right away, soon's he opened that door and went in and saw Angus still under the covers, dead as a haddock. Doctor said he'd died in his sleep. Had a good old-fashioned heart attack for himself, a real lollapalooza. "Probably never felt a thing." Barely sixty years old.

I'm a good deal older than that now, myself, and you start to think about such things. Generally happens when you turn fifty. With some it can be forty-five, and others wait 'til they're sixty. But sooner or later, it comes over you, what you never considered before. Not very pleasant. Kind of cuts down on your cheerfulness.

I find a drink helps, at the end of the day. Be pleased to offer you one. Got some fine bourbon in the other room. Take mine with ice. Hope that suits you. Just keep your seat, right where you are, while I go and wrestle the ice-tray. I'll be back in a minute.

McKIBBEN: Trust this'll suit you. Some years ago I took stock of things, all that health stuff started coming out in the papers, and I'll tell you, I was skeptical. Still am, as a matter of fact. Remember the Big Bacon Scare? Something in bacon causes cancer. Nitrates, I think they said. And peanut butter. Peanut butter also causes cancer. Wonder we elected Jimmy Carter. He grew the damned things, am I right? Would-'ve been just as well, off, we hadn't. Surgeon General's warning: "This candidate may be dangerous to your health." But that would've meant nothing—they all are. I think it was Blaise Pascal, said most of our troubles are attributable to our refusal to sit quietly in our rooms. Lot of truth to that.

Anyway, I never ate that much peanut butter, only have bacon on weekends, so I didn't worry much about that. Especially after it come out they way they found out that bacon and peanut butter give you the cancer was by feeding the stuff to some rats. Now, I've been called one in my time, but I ain't one, as the man said, so I read the story, and it turns out those rats ate about thirty pounds of peanut butter a week. And fifty pounds of bacon. The human equivalent, I mean.

Well now. I think if you were to eat thirty pounds of spinach every week, it'd probably make you sick. Fifty pounds of anything'd likely make you sick. You drank fifty pounds of milk, there'd be calves trotting in from Vermont to take suckle. All you'd be able to say, somebody asked you a question'd be "Mooo," or something like that. Seemed to me the whole lesson of the entire thing was to get rid of impurities. So I did that. I went to a better brand of bourbon, and I think you'll have to agree, this is mighty smooth stuff. Good for the liver and lights.

Anyway, it seems to me that all those doctors're working the preachers' side of the street now. "No back talk here, do as we tell you, and you'll gain eternal life." I've thought about it and I don't believe it any more from them'n I believed it when it came from the preachers. This was something of a disappointment to my father. He was of the same mind, unless I'm mistaken, but he was more diplomatic. Thought speaking his mind'd hurt business. But it still seems to me that if you give up everything that makes life worth living, won't matter if you live to be a hundred—it'll only seem like it.

But I was telling you about Albert. No sooner was Angus Three in the ground than another astounding thing happened. We're not used to surprises in Greenwich. Takes us a while to digest 'em. And now here was another one, right on the heels of the first. We'd barely recovered from Angus's death, when Albert's engagement came out.

Now I've got to be careful here. Don't wish to offend anybody. I realize now there's a different climate, and most people are more tolerant. Don't know's it's a great improvement and all, but that is the way that it is. But nevertheless, in the Forties and Fifties—far as that goes, in the Sixties—a lot of folks suspected a great many things that they never put into words. Wasn't any need to. It's like what I said about my granddad and decorum. People kept to themselves, formed their own opinions, kept their views to themselves and their traps shut.

Nowadays, I presume, someone'd say: "Well, Albert's as queer as a green horse." And most folks would most likely agree. And then Albert would have to make a decision, because he'd be on the TV. "I am not;" "I sure am;" one of the two, and then we could talk about that. But in those days, in this town, nobody said anything. So nobody had to agree. And I must say I think it was better. Of course I do have my own interest here. I never married, myself. Does that mean that I am a queer? I never did anything of a sexual nature, far's I can recollect, with another person, until fairly recently. Of either persuasion. Now think about that for a minute. What difference would it've made, fifteen years ago, if I had? Would I've been a better lawyer for you, or a worse one, if I'd've been running around after women, or making a damned fool of myself with some other man? I don't think so.

Matter of fact, it disturbs me these days when people define themselves according to their sexual preference. When I was growing up, the Cooper men were store-owners and bank men. The McKibbens were lawyers. 'Nuff said. I don't believe any soul on earth, any soul living or dead, could truthfully say that he heard Old Angus get up on his hind legs and say: "Well, I like women, you know." Or Young Angus, either, or Granddad, or Dad. They would've looked silly, if they had done that. It just wasn't called-for. Most knew it.

And I do insist it was better. There was room enough then for the possibility that someone like Albert, or, yes, even me, could just be contented as a selfish, self-reliant, crotchety, grouchy bachelor. "Sot in his ways", as the saying goes. And that he could prefer it to a life with a woman that he didn't love. Or a man he didn't love, for that matter—see, I do know times've changed.

But this is a small town. And the college back then was all-male. When I went to law school down in Boston, well, I really don't know what was available. Didn't have time to find out. The plain fact of the matter is that I've led a sheltered life. I grew up here. I went to college a few miles away. Then I went to Harvard Law, and I graduated, and I took the bar exam, and then I came back here. Did I ever get in trouble? No. I never had the chance. Would I have been a sitting duck for some doxie with big tits and legs that didn't stop? Probably. But I never met one. I just never met a woman who inspired the notion in me, and that, as Robert Frost said about the two paths that diverged in a wood, has made all the difference. I took the one less traveled by.

And so had Albert, until Angus Three died. Oh, there was a brief flurry, that Albert should succeed his brother at the bank, but Albert was firm. He said he knew nothing of banking, never had and didn't wish to, and the best thing the directors could do would be to designate a search committee to recruit a new bank president. There was a sigh of relief breathed, audible in Hartford, and that was what was done.

I guess it was about three, four months later, when Margaret the librarian started sporting the diamond ring. Now I'm taking nothing away from Margaret Miller. She's my client, and before that she'd been at the library for over thirty years. Came here as an assistant right out of Simmons College, and a good little worker she was, too. When Seth Russell finally retired, 'bout five years after he should've, there wasn't any question in anybody's mind, anyone who sat on the Spaulding board, that is, but that Margaret should be the new head. Albert summed it up nicely: "Margaret *is* the library," he said, and of course he was in the place all of the time. He saw Margaret every day. He knew her a lot better 'n we did.

A lot better'n *anyone* else did, it turned out. It was kind of charming in its own way, those two getting together. The kind of development that, when it first gets out, sort of knocks people off of their pins. But once we all had a chance to get used to the idea, the general reaction was: "I'll be damned. Albert and Margaret. Now is that nice, don't you think?"

Well, I did, at least. There was Albert, middle fifties, but still certainly spry enough, by all appearances, all by himself in that house since his brother'd died, not well-fixed, perhaps, but well-off—comfortable. And there was Margaret, late forties, nice-looking woman, in her quiet way, never married, always lived by herself. Bit late in the day to think that there might be children for them to think about, but most seem to think, ones I know, at least, the companionship's just as important, and as you get older, it's more so. Even Emma Hinsdale approved. "I think it's just lovely," she said.

They got married in the summer, August of six years ago. Nothing elaborate, nothing like that. Just had the Reverend Jameson come over to their house and perform the ceremony in the garden—that's another thing Albert did, and like everything, did to the nines; his flowers were just beautiful—and then a catered party on the lawn, under a big blue-and-white striped tent. And I liked the way they went about inviting people. One of Margaret's hobbies was calligraphy, and she did this notice that she pinned up on the community-notices board we have in the library foyer. "Miss Margaret Miller announces her engagement to Mr. Albert Cooper. We would be very happy if everyone who knows us would come to the wedding at our future residence," and she gave the date and so forth, "and share in our happiness."

This was not that many people, really—it wasn't like she was inviting the whole town. The Spaulding's a fine library, but, like I say, Greenwich is a small town to start with, not that many people live here, and by no means all of them or even a majority, use the library. And there really wasn't much way that anyone who didn't visit it would've known either party to the happy occasion. So it was sort of an odd mixture you got that hot Sunday. The trustees, of course, and some people from Boston and New York that thought highly of

Albert, partly because they'd made a lot of money off him, and a couple people from the college, and then all these young people. Children right up to college age. They were all Margaret's friends, going back to the days when she'd checked out *Black Beauty* or *Bob, Son of Battle*, for them, and then later on helped with their term papers. It was a very nice party indeed.

Margaret entered a new world that day, and I'm taking nothing away from her when I say that. Her engagement diamond wasn't all that big—it was just perfect, that's all. The pearls that he gave her for her wedding present weren't showy at all—simply perfect. As far as I know, he didn't arrange for the fireboats to spray when they took the SS *United States* down the Hudson and off to LeHavre, but I know for a fact that they travelled first class. I know because Margaret told me.

"Why I never dreamed," that's what she said, after he'd died of course, "I never dreamed how many people, what people they were, that this quiet man Albert knew well. Why, wherever we went, all these ritzy hotels, they all bowed and scraped when they saw him. The food, the wines, it made me quite giddy. I thought I had known him, this nice, gentle man, studious, quiet, reserved. And of course I had known him, and that's what he was, the same there as he was here at home. But the reception he got there was different. The Berenson Collection opened on a day when it's normally closed, so the curator could take us through personally. The Wallace Collection we saw by ourselves, when we stopped on our way home in London; the director's an old friend of Albert's. There's a small restaurant, up in Montmartre, one of the best in the world, and the owner's the chef and when we came in, he came out of the kitchen and kissed us. Great greasy kisses and torrents of French, and champagnes and my God, what a meal. On our wedding night we went to La Cote Basque, and the owner saw us to our table. I don't have to speculate now, at the Story Hour, when I tell the children how Cinderella must've felt. I know. I got the part."

Her role lasted for almost exactly four years, but as she said when he died, they were great years. We had to put on another assistant at the Spaulding, because Margaret was away so much with Albert. Albert—and this was his decision entirely, no advice from me—recused himself from the meetings and the vote on the subject. He said Margaret'd hate to leave the Spaulding, but they both knew she was away a lot, and they'd talked it over, and the trustees should decide the matter on the merits. And the first time we talked it over, that was the arrangement we agreed on. A deputy chief librarian, to run things while Margaret traveled. But it didn't work out all that well. We couldn't afford the salary it took to hire what amounted to another head librarian, and the young man that we hired began to get itchy after a year—wanted the title himself, since he was doing all the work, and it was hard to argue with him. But Margaret and Albert resolved the problem—they decided to take a cruise 'round the world, be gone for six months I guess it was. So Margaret applied for emeritus status: when she was in Greenwich she'd do what she could to maintain and improve the collection, but she wanted no money or anything like that, and her deputy should be the head. Margaret's as much a lady as Albert was a gentleman. We trustees were all much relieved.

Well, they went to Hawaii, and Hong Kong, and Singapore, Bangkok, Calcutta, Jerusalem, Cairo. They climbed the Acropolis, saw the Pope himself, Capri, Casablanca, Gibraltar. I guess there's a hotel in Africa someplace where they feed the lions at night, and the guests sit and watch over drinks. Albert and Margaret went there, right after the Sphinx and the Pyramids. I've heard it said many times that a person just blossomed after he or she fell in love. Well, maybe it was love, or maybe just the trips, but I'll be damned if both of them didn't. Albert when you saw him walking down the street was as frisky as a young colt in a pasture. And Margaret, well, you could've fooled me, but underneath all those librarian's manners a beautiful woman had hidden. I noticed her one day, and I have to admit, I wondered if maybe I shouldn't 've had my eyes checked a few years before. Right under my nose, my trustee's nose, 'd been this very attractive woman. And I hadn't noticed. Makes you think.

Then came the morning when Margaret woke up and Albert was still beside her. I don't mean he was sleeping. I mean he was *still*. He'd gone through his life very quietly, never making much noise, but any noise he'd been planning to make was out of the question that day. And every day that's arrived since. Exactly the same way that Angus went out—never sick, always healthy, then dead.

Now there was talk afterwards that the English girl Young Angus married must've had a history of heart disease in her family, since all the Cooper men until she got in the act of producing them'd lived to advanced ages and so forth. And then her sons dropped dead in their sixties. But I don't know how much stock you should place in it. Angus the Third was a hardworking man, and he shared my opinion of food: if he liked it, and he wanted to eat it, it was good for him. So he ate it. Well, maybe it wasn't good for him. And judging from what Margaret told me, no French goose was safe when Albert was there, because he did dote on *paté*. He also liked grape juice, as I have said, provided it had fermented. So it's possible the brothers brought it on themselves. And equally possible, it seems to me, that when you come into this world you've got an allotment of heartbeats, but it's kept a secret from you. They run a tally on some machine somewhere, and when you use up your quota, kaput.

The whole question was speculative anyway. The fact was that Albert'd come to room temperature while Margaret'd been fast asleep. The immediate problem, after the death certificate was signed, was to get him in the ground before he spoiled. So we did that. The secondary problem, which I was not looking forward to, would take a little longer to resolve.

You see I knew Albert's financial situation, just as my grandfather'd known Albert's grandfather's and my father'd known Young Angus's, in their time. The McKibbens did the Coopers' taxes, and we drew up their wills. They were good clients—not lucrative, since they figured what we made as the bank's lawyers entitled them to a certain amount of restraint on our billings for their personal business, but good. They always told us the truth. That's the basic definition of a good client. The thing a lawyer fears the most is the lying client. You've got to have a fair division of responsibility in the lawyer-client relationship, as I always tell my clients. "Your responsibility is to tell me the facts and pay me the money. If any lying's necessary, and you've paid me, I'll be the one who does it, to someone else. I'm trained for this sort of thing. You aren't."

The truth in Albert's case was that being of sound mind and testamentary intent, he had spent it all. And that's how Margaret and I found out. . . . well, what brought you here. How Albert without meaning to—despite himself, in fact—had made her a rich widow. Much richer than she would've been, if he'd saved his money. But my drink's gone, and yours could use fresh ice, at least. We've got time for another before dinner—you said you'd stay for that. Braised leg of lamb *Grand Mere*. And I'm sure you'll enjoy the wine.

McKIBBEN: Yes, here we are. Now, as I was saying, we got Albert into the ground—Margaret held up remarkably well, and a cruel thing it was that she had to go through it. All those years by herself, nothing but books, young kids, and a few old farts like me to divert her, and then she'd married Albert and it was as though the sun'd come up in her life. Morning, just before she turned fifty. And then four years later, morning turned into mourning. Hard thing.

But there was more yet to come, which I of course knew when I served as one of his pallbearers, and knew sooner or later I'd have to tell her. Like I said, the McKibbens'd always been the Coopers' personal lawyers, as well as the bank's. So when we buried Albert I had at the back of my mind the fact that he didn't leave her a dime. And that's what I'd have to tell her.

When she came in to see me, I had to, of course. Death'd undone Young Augus's plan. See, once he saw Angus Three all set at the bank, he'd had us arrange his estate accordingly. His expectation'd been, and no one could blame him, was that Angus the Third'd get a good living presiding over the bank, and then retire on his pension. And Albert wouldn't do much at all, so'd he'd have to be taken care of. I don't think Young Angus had a great deal of respect for his younger son—resignation'd've been more like it—but all the same he didn't want the young fella going on the welfare, disgracing the family name, so provision had to be made.

Now that meant doing something that was, well, anathema to people who thought like the Coopers. It meant that they'd have to invade principal, spending not just the interest, but the *funds*. Especially given the way Albert lived. It was classy, but very expensive. Albert was good-hearted, not a mean bone in him, and he did have excellent taste. But Albert consumed. He did not produce. He was not a model of thrift. So what my dad devised was a sprinkling trust of the assets in Young Angus's estate.

That sounds a lot more complicated than it is. Basically it tells the trustees, who were my father and I when Dad devised it, to apportion the income and assets according to the needs of the beneficiaries. Who were Angus Three and Albert. Young Angus'd come to grips with the fact that his second son wasn't likely to develop a taste for honest work in his middle years, since he hadn't in his younger, and cognizant as well of the fact that this meant he wasn't going to have enough quarters of employment to claim Social Security benefits when he got older and started to drool. Or a pension, as far as that went.

But since he assumed, and anyone would, that Angus the Third'd be ripe when he died, and so would Albert, for that matter, the sensible thing would be to devote the trust mostly to Albert. And then there was a catch-all clause—we always put them in, because nobody knows when the Reaper'll come—which was that if Angus Three checked out before Albert, the whole shebang would be Albert's. But nobody dreamed that'd happen.

But it did, of course, and the Cinderella years that Margaret had with Albert got paid for out of the trust. It was a good thing for her Albert didn't hire fireboats—she was damned-near broke as it was. *Depleted*'s the word we use when that happens: "The assets've been badly deplet-ed." Meaning: "The assets are gone. There ain't none. You're dead-busted broke, is what you are." Albert of course'd left everything to her, she being his only live kin, but the trouble was that there wasn't much more than small change in that "everything" he left.

"What will I do?" she said. She had a point. Her former deputy hadn't moved on. He was still in place at the Spaulding, hadn't gotten a better offer, like I'm sure he'd planned to, in no mood to relinquish the job—the son of a buck liked it here. She did have the Social Security, sure, more than enough of the quarters, but she'd been living a notch or two higher than what those monthly checks cover. And besides, it'd be several years before she could claim anything under the Act. And she didn't want to leave Greenwich.

"Well," I said to her, "as much as I hate to say this, I think what you're going to have to think about is selling off what's in that house."

Now I learned early on, from my granddad and dad, that the first thing a smart lawyer does is admit it when he doesn't know it. Admit it to himself, at least. It's hard at first, some never get the hang of it, but those who do stay out of trouble. There's always someone who knows what you don't, and everyone likes to be asked. So I said to Margaret: "What we should do is get an appraiser in there. See what all that stuff is worth."

I think what I most likely envisioned was some kind of a yard-sale. But Margaret looked so desolate, you know, I felt I had to do better. So I said: "There's a man, down on Cape Cod, who knows what old things are worth. My friends say his word is trustworthy. It'll cost you his fee for a day to come out here, but let's see what he has to say."

Well she went for it. And I called him up. And he came out here, and he prowled around. He got this odd look on his face. He spent a whole day, and at the end of it, he said he needed to think. He'd get a motel room and work on his figures, and perhaps we could meet in the morning. I said he could stay here, thinking of money, but he said he'd prefer a motel. "I need to be by myself."

Well, when you hire an expert, the expert decides, or else why did you hire him? The next morning the three of us met in this room and he just shook his head. "The stuff in that house is out of my league. It's out of my customers' league. No fooling, what you've got, Mrs. Cooper, is a treasure-trove for collectors."

We didn't believe him. Literally did not believe him. "Look," I said, "I know the car. The Cadillac has to be worth something."

He stared at me. "How much, do you think?"

"I dunno," I said, "Three grand or so?"

He laughed at me. It takes an honest man to laugh at you when you say something stupid. He isn't afraid of losing.

"Mr. McKibben," he said, "I can sell that Cadillac convertible for eleven thousand dollars tomorrow. And then the man I sell it to will re-sell it the day after for twenty. You know what *cherry* is? That car is cherry. And that's just the beginning. The first editions, the prints and the artwork—have you got any idea of what those suits and Peal shoes are worth? The manuscript copies, the Purdy shotguns, never fired, the swords and the daggers and so forth? Have you looked at the painting over the mantel? Have you ever seen that?"

"Sure," I said, "haystacks."

"That's what I mean," he said. "You're wrong. It's grainstacks. It's a Monet. An honest-to-God Claude Monet."

The only thing you ever learn is that you don't know anything.

"Do you know what you've got, hanging up in the hallway out there?" he said.

"Yeah," I said. "A man. On a horse. With a lance."

"Don Quixote," he said, "a charcoal by Picasso. Signed. An original, right?"

That's when I brought it in here. What the hell did I know?"

Well, that was just the beginning. He said what we ought to do was bring in one of those London auction houses, and we did, and, my God, what *they* said. I couldn't believe my own ears.

Not only did they say it, they backed it up. All of a sudden I went from advising a widowed client who'd been left destitute to advising a widowed client who was in fair way of getting destituted again by the estate-tax laws. I mean to tell you, this was serious money we were talking about here. That drawing up there is a signed Picasso. Those weapons went back to Richard the Lion Heart. Those uncomfortable chairs that Albert'd bought matched the funny-shaped dining-room table—Madame de Pompadour sat on those chairs, and ate custard served on that table. And then the man told me what was downstairs, in that wine-cellar Albert'd put in. Close to a million alone in the basement. My God, a million in wine.

"Well, what will I do?" Margaret said. And I said: "Sell it off. It's worth money. You haven't got any. It's worth a lot. You want to wash down your dry toast with that wine? When some sap'll buy it for plenty?"

She took my advice, which is another way of telling if you've got a good client. That's someone who listens to you. Especially when you've been man enough to admit that you didn't know something, but you went and found it out, and the client benefited. Very often you will find that the client who made out, by taking your advice, really resents you for giving it. But Margaret Miller Cooper was different. She was actually grateful.

So she said to me, after we'd auctioned his clothes—college kids loved those old suits, boy—and there wasn't much left in the house: "Well, now I'm well-off. Well-off and alone. Suppose I should move. Sell the house and go where it's warm.

I said: "You're half-right. You should sell the house. It's too big for you all by yourself. But you shouldn't leave Greenwich. You like it here. And you can do anything you want to do, anywhere that you select."

"Like what?" she said.

"I've got a similar problem," I said. "This house's too big for me, by myself. And like you I've got all I will need. Why not combine forces? Move in with me. We can do whatever we like."

She blushed. Can you imagine that? "People would talk," she said. "I'd be embarrassed. I couldn't go out on the street."

"Not if we were married," I said.

So that's the end of my story. I told you it wasn't exciting. But I can promise you that her braised lamb is good, and we didn't sell all of the wine.

JACK DUGGAN'S LAW

LATE in the morning, the Coupe de Ville—slate grey, black vinyl roof, five years old—emerged from the road in the woods and moved too quickly down the curving highway. There was a building at the bottom of the hill. It was low, one-story, painted white and peeling. It was surrounded by an eight-foot board fence which had been barn red at one time but had not been painted for years. The fence enclosed a trapezoidal area. The enclosure was filled with old tires piled two and three feet higher than the fence. The fence sagged and bulged around the tires. There was a marshland which surrounded the fence. It was crowded with cat-o'-nine-tails and scrub brush.

The Cadillac swung around to the front of the building and stopped with some hastiness. There was an old Texaco gas pump in front, the mechanism exposed from the mid-section to the top, the top crowned by a white disc emblazoned with the Fire Chief hat symbol. There was a sign on the front of the building, above two sagging barn doors. One of the doors was ajar. The sign read: TEXACO. GIFFORD'S. BRAKES. SERVICE. LUBRICATION. The letters had started out black, but had faded to grey. There were old tires scattered around the outside of the fence, and a row of old automobile batteries against it.

The driver of the Cadillac backed it up slightly and ran over the signal bell hose again. The bell rang in the stillness. The driver opened the door of the car and got out. He was in his middle forties. He had dark hair and he was getting thick in the middle. He wore a white shirt with french cuffs and onyx links that were too large. He wore a red tie that was too shiny. He had left his suit coat in the car; the pants were dark blue and well-cut. They did not look appropriate with his brown jodphur boots. He wore wrap-around mirror sunglasses and a Texas Instruments calculator watch. He ran his right hand through his hair, making it stand up. He put his fists on his hips and stared at the garage. He slammed the door of the car and started toward the garage doors.

When the driver was about eight feet from the doors, a very large chow-chow emerged with immense dignity. The dog had a mane and a black tongue. It stood half-in, half-out of the space between the doors and slavered. It looked at the driver with interest, as though it had not had a square meal in some time.

"Nice boy," the driver said politely. He continued to approach the doors. The dog continued to stare at him. The driver reached a point about six feet from the doors. The dog roared and lunged at him, rearing up on its hind legs. It was snubbed up by a chain with half-inch links. The dog sat down. The driver backed up. "Nice boy," the driver said. The dog hung its black tongue out and slavered, measuring the driver.

"Halloo," the driver said to the building. The dog panted. "Halloo," the driver said to the building.

The dog lurched backward, jerked off its front feet, and vanished into the building.

"Is it okay to come in?" the driver said. There was no reply. The driver advanced tentatively toward the doors. He peered around the edge of the one that was ajar. He went inside. The interior was dim and it took him a moment to regain his vision. Dead ahead there was an old man in a khaki cardigan and a dark blue wool ski hat. He was sitting in an old maroon armchair. There was an old floor lamp to the right of the armchair. There was a kerosene heater next to the armchair. It was stiflingly hot in the garage. To the left there was a double rack of new tires. To the left there was a double rack of new batteries. Behind the man in the armchair there was a wooden case, fronted and topped with glass, filled with candies. The dog sat beside the man in the armchair. The dog was still slavering.

"Careful," the old man said. "Grease pit, front of you."

The driver looked down. There was a lubrication pit in front of him.

"Help you?" the old man said. He was reading something, or had been. The magazine was open in his lap. It was open to a double-page spread of a naked woman.

"Yeah," the driver said, "I need some directions."

"Ain't seen you before," the old man said.

"Ain't been here before," the driver said. "What I need's directions."

"No gas," the old man said.

"Nope," the driver said, "no gas."

"Just as well," the old man said. "Ain't got any. Quit pumpin' that stuff six year ago. Damned nuisance."

"Directions," the driver said.

"Directions," the old man said. "Montreal's north. Go to the border. Turn left. You want Quebec, turn right. Simple." He cackled.

The driver did not laugh. When the old man had finished, the driver said: "Ellis house."

"Ellis house," the old man said.

"Yeah," the driver said.

"You from Boston?" the old man said.

"Yeah," the driver said.

"Thought so," the old man said.

"The Ellis house," the driver said.

"Never heard of 'em," the old man said, complacently.

"Bullshit," the driver said.

"Seen my dog?" the old man said.

"Yeah," the driver said.

"Big dog," the old man said.

"Seen my car?" the driver said.

"Nope," the old man said.

"Out front," the driver said. "Big car. Bigger'n your dog.'

"No foolin'," the old man said.

"Yup," the driver said. "I bet I could fire that sucker up and run right over your big dog in about twenny seconds, and peel right outta here and scrape him off the wheels onna first turn."

"Ellis house," the old man said.

"Ellis house," the driver said.

"Third white house on the left," the old man said. "There's a farm pond just before it. It's on the hill."

"Thanks," the driver said.

"I'm Gifford," the old man said. "Dog's Magician."

"I believe in magic," the driver said.

"Who're you?" the old man said.

"Duggan," the driver said. "Jack Duggan."

• • •

Mrs. Ellis was elderly and she wore an apron and she peered at Duggan through thick spectacles so that she resembled the Easter Bunny, but she was not stupid. She sat him down in the kitchen and put the black kettle on the black iron stove to boil, and she gave him a homemade blueberry muffin. The tablecloth was a gingham pattern, but it was done on oilcloth. There was a vase of flowers in the middle of the table, but they were plastic flowers.

"I haven't seen him," she said. "I have not seen Frederick."

"Mrs. Ellis," Duggan said, "of course you haven't seen Frederick. Frederick is in the slammer down in Boston town. It is not an over-time parking ticket. Frederick is in the cooler because the police are under the impression that he went and killed a guy, and they think that they can prove it. If it is not too much trouble, while we are wait-ing for the blasted water to boil, I'd like a few facts here and there."

"I haven't seen him," she repeated.

"I have." Duggan said. "I didn't want to. I was appointed by the court to represent Frederick Ellis on a murder charge because he does-n't have enough money to get his own lawyer. Now I see that his mummy has a whole lot of prime land and a pond to go with it, not to mention some cattle

"Jerseys," she said.

"Frederick," he said. "He can get his own tee-shirts. Tell me all about Frederick, or I will go back into that court down in Boston and recite to that judge that Frederick Ellis may be a thing you might see floating in the gutter, but his family has some money. And then pre-pare to mortgage the cows."

"Jerseys," she said.

"Cows is cows," Duggan said.

• • •

Duggan in the First Session, Criminal, Suffolk Superior Court, waived the reading of the indictment. He stood next to Maurice Morse, a young black man, while the Clerk, Don Sherman, informed Morse that he was charged with the forcible rape of Rose Walters.

"What say you?" Sherman said. "Are you guilty or not guilty?"

"Not guilty," Morse said.

"Counsel?" Judge Shanahan said.

"May I have thirty days to file special pleas, Your Honor?" Duggan said. "As you know, I have the Ellis case to prepare as well."

"Ten," Judge Shanahan said. Sherman wrote on the docket file.

"Your Honor," Duggan said, "I haven't had a chance for a real conference with my client as yet. As the Court is aware, I am presently on trial in a capital case. May I press my request for thirty days in which to file special pleas?"

"You are not presently on trial, Counsellor," Shanahan said, "you are about to be presently on trial. Presently you will file any motions that you may have in Commonwealth versus Morse, *presently* meaning: within ten days. During that time you can press your requests or your pants, just as you choose. You'd look better if you chose your pants.

"The Commonwealth," Judge Shanahan said, "will furnish all statements of the defendant, all material which may be exculpatory in nature, all transcripts of wiretaps, a list of all laboratory tests or other scientific tests which the Commonwealth has conducted and intends to introduce at trial, a list of all witnesses whom the Commonwealth may call at trial, all photographs and other physical evidence, to be inspected at the convenience of defense counsel. So ordered."

"Your Honor," Edie said, getting up, "I scarcely know what the case is about myself. And I also have the Ellis case. I don't know whether there's any of the evidence that you describe. I haven't even seen the file. As the court is aware, I too am currently on trial."

"Work nights," Shanahan said, "same as him. Bail?"

"May I be heard, Your Honor?" Edie said.

"Most likely," Shanahan said.

"This is one of several cases of rape in the same neighborhood," she said.

"Right," Shanahan said. "This is one case. This man is charged with one rape. Go ahead."

"The women in the neighborhood are extremely fearful for their safety," she said.

"Can't help that," Shanahan said. "This man hasn't been convicted of harming a single one of them."

"This is a serious charge," she said.

"Certainly is," Shanahan said. "I'd imagine the defendant would wholeheartedly agree with you on that point. The Constitution of the United States is a serious document. It says the purpose of bail is to insure that the defendant shall appear for trial. Doesn't say anything at all making nervous ladies feel better, no matter where they live. What are you asking for bail?"

"One hundred thousand dollars, with surety," she said.

"Ten grand for the bondsman," Shanahan. said. "Counsellor Duggan, what have you got to say about this?"

"Your Honor," Duggan said, "the defendant has a steady job. He has roots in the community. He's never been charged with anything before. There's no reason whatsoever to believe that he will not show up as ordered by this court."

"Lemme see that file, Don," Shanahan said to Sherman. He put on pince-nez glasses and leafed through it. He looked up over the glasses. "Morse, he said, "Mr. Morse, are you really broke, like you told the clerk?"

"Yessah," Morse said.

"Never mind that plantation talk," Shanahan said. "You broke or not?"

"I can't afford a lawyer, Your Honor," Morse said.

"Mr. Morse," Shanahan said, removing the glasses, "nobody can afford a lawyer. The question is whether you're broke. If you're not broke, Mr. Duggan doesn't have to represent you at huge expense to the taxpayers. If you are broke, he does. You broke or not?"

"I only make a small amount of money, Your Honor," Morse said. "I make two hundred and ten dollars a week, take-home. My rent's sixty a week. I pay maybe forty a week for food and stuff. I haven't got any money or anything."

"You own any real estate?" Shanahan said.

"No sir," Morse said.

"You got a car?" Shanahan said.

"Yes sir," Morse said.

"What is it?" Shanahan said.

"It's just a car, Morse said.

"One of those rectangular things with a wheel on each corner, right?" Shanahan said. This drew a laugh from the regular spectators. "Is there a brand name on it?"

"Yes sir," Morse said.

"What does the brand name say?" Shanahan said.

"Pontiac," Morse said.

"Good," Shanahan said. "Now we are making progress. You own a Pontiac. What model is it?"

"It's a two-door," Morse said.

"That isn't what I asked you," Shanahan said. "Let me try again. What model is it?"

"It's a Firebird," Morse said.

"See?" Shanahan said. "We're making progress left and right here. Let me see if I can speed things up a little more. Is it by any chance a Firebird Tans Am?"

"Yes sir," Morse said.

"Time passes so quickly when you're having fun," Shanahan said. "What is the year of its manufacture? When was it made, in other words?"

"Last year, Your Honor," Morse said.

"Did you buy it new?" Shanahan said.

"Yes, Your Honor," Morse said.

"How much did you pay for it?" Shanahan said.

Morse sighed: "Eleven thousand, three hundred and change."

"Where did you get the money?" Shanahan said.

"From the bank," Morse said.

"Did you borrow it?" Shanahan said.

"No Sir," Morse said, "I took it out of my account, I saved up for that car."

"You don't owe anything on it, then, "Shanahan said.

"No sir," Morse said.

"How much is it worth, do you figure?" Shanahan said.

"I dunno," Morse said.

"Eight thousand?" Shanahan said.

"I doubt it, "Morse said.

"How about seven thousand?" Shanahan said.

"Maybe," Morse said.

"And that's the only thing you own," Shanahan said.

"Well, Morse said, "I got my furniture and stuff,"

"What does the stuff consist of?" Shanahan said.

"My bike and stuff," Morse said.

"Let's deal with the bike," Shanahan said. "We'll get to the stuff as need be. It is a ten-speed bike?"

"Ten-speed?" Morse said.

"Yeah," Shanahan said. "What kind of bike is it?"

"It's a Kawasaki," Morse said.

"Oh," Shanahan said, "when you say *bike*, you mean it's a *motor-cycle*."

"Yeah," Morse said.

"Yeah, Shanahan said. "When'd you get that and how much did it cost you?"

"Last year, "Morse said. "Thirty-eight hundred dollars."

"Borrow the money?" Shanahan said.

"No, Your Honor," Morse said.

"Get it out of that bank account?" Shanahan said.

"Yeah," Morse said.

"What?" Shanahan said.

"Yeah," Morse said, louder.

"I can't hear you, Mr. Defendant," Shanahan said. "You get that money out of your savings account?"

"Say 'Yes, Your Honor,'" Duggan whispered to Morse.

"Yes, Your Honor," Morse said.

"That makes over fifteen thousand dollars you took out of that bank account to buy wheels last year,"Shanahan said. "That's a pretty nice bank account. I wish I had one like it. Where is it?"

"I got the book home in my apartment," Morse said.

"Which bank?" Shanahan said.

"Oh," Morse said. "River Trust."

"How much you got in that account now?" Shanahan said.

"Your Honor," Morse said, "I worked hard for that money and I saved it up."

Shanahan held up his right hand. "Spare me, Mr. Morse," he said. "I'm sure you denied yourself many of life's pleasures in order to prepare for your future. You are asking me to confirm Mr. Duggan's worst fears that he will be forced to represent you for small change paid late by the Commonwealth. This will require Mr. Duggan to deny himself many of life's pleasures in order to represent you. How much money is left in that bank account?"

"I'm not sure," Morse said.

"Take a guess," Shanahan said.

"About nine thousand dollars," Morse said.

"Okay," Shanahan said, "that saves us from going into the value of the furniture and stuff. Mr. Sherman: The Court finds that the defendant, Maurice Morse, is not without resources with which to retain counsel, that he is not indigent. The case is continued for one week so that Mr. Morse may secure counsel. Bail is set at twenty-five thousand dollars, with surety. Case on trial."

"Your Honor," Morse said, as the Court Officer started toward him.

"Mr. Morse," Shanahan said, "you are remanded to the custody of the Sheriff of Suffolk County. Your case is continued for one week so that you may secure counsel."

"I want Duggan here," Morse said.

"I'm sure Mr. Duggan will be happy to confer with you at the Charles Street Jail," Shanahan said. "You will want to discuss a fee with him, no doubt. Mr. Daly is currently on trial. If you want to see him, make an appointment that will suit his convenience. For the time being, you have lots of convenience, at least until you make bail. Case on trial. Afternoon recess."

Morse was led away.

The Judge stood up and marched off the bench. The spectators moved toward the doors. Edie approached Duggan. "Nice, huh?" she said.

"In my next life," Duggan said, "I am going to make my living doing something easy. Brain surgery, I think."

"Yeah," she said. "But in this one?"

"In this one, Duggan said, "I am going back to my office to see Fred Ellis, because thanks to your incompetence, he got out."

• • •

In the early evening, Duggan parked the Cadillac in front of the bait shop at Neponset Circle in Dorchester. The bait shop, which advertised its appointment by the Commonwealth as an official fish-weighing center, occupied the ground floor of a three-story wooden building. The building was covered with tar-paper that was supposed to resemble brick. The window frames and doors were painted cream. There were apartments for single old people on the third floor. Duggan, a bill collector named Mullins who called himself the Commonwealth Adjustment Agency, and the law firm of Kunkel and Concannon had offices on the second floor. Kunkel was over 80. Concannon was Kunkel's daughter. They specialized in divorce law.

Duggan used his key to open the door in the center of the building. He shut it and locked it firmly behind him. The floor in the hall was linoleum. It had buckled badly and he was careful of his footing. It was lighted by one 60-watt bulb. He reached the stairway, which had a curved banister with knurled supports on the right and a dowel banister on the left, and climbed it. The steel treads were loose and creaked under him. At the top of the stairs he turned right, into the corridor leading to the offices. The corridor was lighted badly. The door to his office was half frosted glass. There was scroll painting on it: JOHN F. DUGGAN. ATTORNEY AND COUNSELLOR AT LAW. He opened the door and went in.

There were two people in the reception area. Cynthia, Duggan's secretary, was at her desk, which was synthetic blonde mahogany. Cynthia had an extremely good figure and an extremely slow brain. She chewed gum. Her husband made a halfway-decent living as the manager of a hamburger stand on Morrissey Boulevard, about seven hundred yards west of the bait shop. Cynthia was incapable of conceiving a child. She was 26 years old and she was restless. Cynthia's husband was agreeable to allowing her to do poor work for very little money, so long as it was close by and he thought her boss was harmless. This arrangement was agreeable to Duggan, especially the part about the small salary.

The second person in the reception area was Frederick Ellis. He was sitting on a sofa-bed slip-covered in beige. The sofa looked as though Duggan had slept on it. He had. Ellis had a two-day growth of beard and he did not look good in it. he had dark hair that stuck up and looked greasy, and he wore a denim jacket and jeans which also could have been improved by washing. He looked disdainful. There were two cops seated next to him

Duggan spoke to Ellis first. "You're sitting down already, and you haven't said anything yet. Therefore, keep up the good work." Then he said to the cops: "Whaddya you guys want."

The two cops were in full uniform in Duggan's reception area, along with Frederick Ellis. One of the cops was Panther Ahearn, a stern man in his middle forties with heavy jowls and a permanent expression of exasperation. The other was Roderick Franklin, a man in his late thirties, who sat with his hands clasped in his lap and looked at the floor. Franklin's holster was empty, and the strap which secured the revolver which belonged in it hung loose. Roderick Franklin was black.

"Ahearn," Duggan said, "I needed you like a sore tooth this day. Tell me what is on your mind and make it fast. I've got a living to make."

"Done and done," Ahearn said. He gestured with his head. "Franklin here has got a little problem." He nudged Franklin with his elbow. "This is correct, it is not, Roderick?"

Franklin nodded, miserably.

"Roderick," Ahearn said, standing up and hitching his pants higher, "Roderick shot a fellow last night."

"Shot a fellow," Duggan said.

"Exactly," Ahearn said.

"Where, precisely, did he shoot the fellow?" Duggan said.

"In the chest," Ahearn said. "Just like we are trained. Right below the heart. Three in a circle you could cover with a quarter. Roderick is a damned good shot." Ahearn looked at Franklin. Franklin did not look up.

"I presume there was some reason for all of this commotion," Duggan said.

"There was that," Ahearn said. "There was a silent alarm going off at the all-night grocery, and me and Roderick were dispatched thereto to see if perhaps there might be something going on. When we got there in the blue-and-white, there was sure-God something going on. So we drew out service revolvers and we exited the official vehicle and we entered the establishment and there was quite a lot going on. There were two young gentlemen in there, who had entered posing as customers. One of them had a rather large knife. The other one had a revolver.

"The young gentleman with the knife," Ahearn said, "is a reasonable fellow, and that is why he is still breathing air. As soon as he saw my revolver, he saw the wisdom of obedience to my command to drop the stinking knife. The other gentleman, the one with the revolver, was not as agreeable. He brought it up and pointed it at me. Thereupon, Patrolman Franklin plugged him. Three times. I was very glad of it. Roderick blew him back to last Wednesday."

"Ahh," Duggan said. "I see that Patrolman Franklin does not have any revolver on his person."

"They took it away from me," Franklin said. He did not look up.

"He's up on charges," Ahearn said.

"Charges," Duggan said.

"Departmental hearing," Ahearn said.

"Indictment to follow," Duggan said.

"If the department says he shouldn't've plugged the kid," Ahearn said.

"And?" Duggan said.

"You are going to make damned sure that hearing comes out the right way." Ahearn said.

"Ahearn," Duggan said, "you must be losing your memory. You hate my guts, remember? You told me so. If there was one miserable piece of stuff floating in at low tide tomorrow, it'd be better'n I am. Remember that?"

"That was different," Ahearn said. "That was when you got a little snotbag off on a case that he should've gone to jail."

"That's what I do," Duggan said.

"Right," Ahearn said, "and that is what you're gonna do for Roderick, here." He put his hand on Franklin's shoulder. "You got that, Counselor? You are gonna work your magic in behalf of Roderick, who saved my ever-lasting life. And you are gonna get his gun back for him. And you are gonna see that Roderick does not get indicted. That is what you are gonna do."

Franklin spoke. He did not look up, but he spoke. He said: "I don't want any favors from this honkey."

Ahearn lifted his hand and slapped it down hard on Franklin's shoulder. "You just shut your mouth, Cotton-chopper. I got a wife and I got kids, and they go through groceries like they were lawn-mowers. I'm on the earth this morning, not in it, and that is thanks to you. You did me one, I'll do you one."

"You're gonna pay me, I assume," Duggan said to Ahearn.

"Right," Ahearn said. "Cup of coffee? I'll go for a doughnut, even."

"Nifty," Duggan said.

Franklin looked up. There was misery all over his face. "He don't want this case, Terry," Franklin said. "I can't pay him. You told me already, long before this, what a rat he is."

Ahearn did not look at Franklin. He stared at Duggan instead. He spoke slowly and softly. "He is a rat, Roderick," Ahearn said., "He walked a guy on me the last time I brought in a guy that should've burned, and then he laughed in my face afterwards. You did that, Duggan."

"I did that, Ahearn," Duggan said.

"Roderick," Ahearn said, "this Duggan is the biggest rat in the western world. He bites and he's probably got rabies, too, You need a rat, my friend. You need something that will bite and get the other guys infected. Duggan is your rat."

Franklin looked up again. "I can't afford to pay you anything, Mr. Duggan," he said.

Duggan started to speak. Ahearn silenced both of them. "Nothin' to worry about, Roderick," he said, "Mr. Duggan isn't charging for this one."

"You're not charging?" Franklin said.

"He's not charging," Ahearn said.

"I didn't ask you," Franklin said.

"I'm not charging," Duggan said. "And the rest of what he said is also true."

Duggan then spoke to Cynthia. "What bad things have happened today that I do not wish to know about but people called me about?"

Cynthia snapped her gum. Duggan said: "Don't do that."

She paid no attention to him. She riffled through a stack of telephone messages. "Well," she said, "they're mostly all from people in the court, and I'm not sure.

Duggan interrupted her. "It's after six, for the luvva Mike, I'm at least three hours late, trying to get back to somebody in the courts."

"There was one," Cynthia said, reflectively, snapping the gum. "Said she'd wait for your call."

"There's a happy note," Duggan said. "Who the hell was it?"

"Said her name," Cynthia said, frowning, "said her name was Edie and you'd know her."

"Edie," Duggan said.

"Edie," Cynthia said. "From the DA's office."

"Uh huh," Duggan said. "*Oh*-kay, I'll call Edie from the DA's office."

He turned to look at Ellis. "For your information, Mr. Ellis, Edie from the DA's office is Assistant District Attorney Edith Washburn, and she has got a strong inclination to fit your very large tail into a very small crack. If it is all right with you, I will excuse myself for a moment and call her."

Ellis stared at him. Ellis did not look happy. "You already kept me waiting a long time," he said.

"Put it on my bill," Duggan said.

• • •

The District Attorney was Harold Gould. He was a large and powerful man in a large and powerful office. He was in his early sixties, and he knew what his values were. He also knew that some other people did not share his values, and he resented it. His office in the New Courthouse at Pemberton Square was spare. There was one glass-fronted bookcase which contained a selection of lawbooks that he had not opened in years. His diplomas from Boston College and the Harvard Law School were on the walls, along with his membership certificates in nine organizations. There were two pictures of Harold Gould shaking hands with John P. Kennedy. Harold Gould wore a PT-109 tie-clasp. There were two pictures of Harold Gould with Richard Cardinal Cushing. There was one picture of Harold Gould with Francis Cardinal Spellman. There was a certificate attesting to the elevation of Harold

Gould to the rank of Knight of Malta. There was a large oak desk that was covered with file folders. Harold Gould sat in an oak chair that creaked. His visitors sat in oak chairs that did not creak. Harold Gould, in the early evening, was not happy.

Edith Washburn was uneasy. She was in her early thirties and she had a lawyer's job in a town full of lawyers; she wished to keep it. She disliked Harold Gould, who had appointed her to the job she wished to keep. Once married and divorced, with custody of a son who had not yet seen his sixth birthday and an ex-husband who had managed to elude his child-support payments—there had never been any alimony payments, because she was too proud to accept those or even ask for them—she needed the job that Harold Gould could take away from her if she became too saucy.

"You booted it," Gould said. He had a voice with an edge like a pitted razor blade. "I told you I didn't want that Ellis punk on the street."

Edie controlled herself. "Boss," she said, "I did not boot it. I am not Judge Wilcox. I did not release him on personal recognizance. I asked a hundred thou bail, and Judge Wilcox to let him loose. Judge Wilcox is black. He thinks all defendants're the unfortunate victims of society. That's not my fault either."

"That punk," Could said, "is a murderer."

She sighed. "So I'm told," she said.

"He should be in jail," Gould said.

"So I'm told," she said.

"He isn't," Gould said.

"He hasn't been convicted yet," she said.

"Who's got the case for trial," Gould said.

"Judge Shanahan," she said.

Gould nodded. "Good," he said, "good. Shanahan's a stand-up guy. No continuances. Get that little scumbag in here and convict him and put him in the damned can. Right?"

Edie sighed again. "Boss," she said, "Duggan just got the case. He's gonna want time to get ready. He's gonna ask for it and Shanahan or any other judge's gonna give it to him. The guy's appointed, for God's sake. He's not making any money off this. He's got to eat. He'll be out on the street."

"Who'd Duggan kill?" Gould said.

"Far as I know," she said, "nobody."

"Right," Gould said. "So therefore I don't care if Duggan's onna street. I don't like him, but he ain't dangerous. Ellis is dangerous.

Duggan tilted, back in his desk chair and looked at Frederick Ellis with, extreme distaste. The chair was a tufted Naugahyde Eames model. The desk was a large construction of blond mahogany. Ellis slouched in an armchair upholstered in nubby cerulean blue fabric, and smoked a thin cigar. The walls of Duggan's office were absolutely bare, painted white and somewhat dirty.

"You, my friend," Duggan said, "you are more trouble'n you're worth. That lady is really mad at you, and I think you are going to go away for a while if she has anything to say about it. Which she does."

Ellis tipped the ash from the cigar onto the brown tweed rug. "I can do time," he said.

"So can Big Ben," Duggan said. "Any jerk can do time, just like any clock. Clocks're made of metal. Some of them've got glass onna front. They're *made* to do time."

Ellis shrugged. "Maybe I was, too" he said.

"Maybe you were," Duggan said. He allowed his shoulders to slump. "And in the meantime, I've got to do time for you, because that lady wants to see me. *Tonight.*

• • •

In the remnants of the twilight, Frederick Ellis emerged from the door next to the bait shop, turned right and walked rapidly along Gallivan Boulevard until he came to the International house of Pancakes. He stopped at the entrance to the parking lot and looked around. There was a maroon Cougar XR7 in one of the spaces, pointing toward the street. Ellis approached it, glanced around, opened the passenger door and got inside.

There was another man inside, sitting in the driver's seat. He was smoking a cigar, and the car was filled with the smoke of it. Ellis did not look at him directly, but it would not have mattered if he had.

"I am in the gravy," Ellis said. "I am in the gravy up to my belt-buckle. They are heating up the gravy. I think they are planning to cook me. I am getting nervous."

"Not good," the driver said. "Not good to get nervous. Makes the Man nervous when people get nervous. That is very seldom good for the nervous people."

"Look," Ellis said, "all right?" He turned his body in the passenger's bucket seat so that he could look at the cloud of smoke around the driver. He gestured with his hands. "I got some problems, all right? This guy Duggan that I win, you know what he did? He drove up to see my mother, for God's sake. I haven't seen my mother since the Red Sox won the World Series, for God sake. I can't stand my mother and she can't stand me and he goes to see her and eat one of her damned muffins and now I got that to think about. This guy Duggan takes things *serious*, Franco. He wants to win this case and he tells me he does not think that I am telling him everything I know."

"Umm," the driver said through the smoke.

"It gets worse," Ellis said, slumping back against the seat and facing the windshield. "This broad they got prosecuting me? Duggan makes me think she is another one of those eager types that always plans to win. Between the two of them, I am going to end up at the wrong end of the chain-saw."

"You got problems," the driver said.

Ellis became angry. "Problems?" he said. "I had problems before. I bite my fingernails sometimes and I have been constipated. I borrowed some money off a guy and I didn't have the dough to pay him back. Those, I thought that those were problems when I had them. Now I am looking at all day in the Massachusetts Correctional Institution at Walpole because I borrowed some money off a guy, and you are telling me I got problems? Compared to me, the President has got it easy."

The driver leaned forward and started the car. "I think," he said, "I think we'd better go and see the Man."

• • •

Duggan escaped from the darkness of Tremont Street into Dini's restaurant. The light inside was tinted rose colored, and there were pictures of fish and aquariums in strategic locations. There was a truculent woman in a tight pink jersey dress at the door, with a sheaf of menus. She challenged him. "Yesss?" she said.

"Look," Duggan said, "I had a hard day. I'm supposed to meet a lady here. Her name is Washburn."

The woman clearly did not believe this. "What is your name, please?"

"For God's sake," Duggan said, "have I got to get references to meet somebody for dinner in a place of public refreshment? What difference does it make, who I am? I told you who she is. Is she here? I'm not trying, cash a bum check or anything."

The woman's face grew stern. "I'm merely trying to help you, sir," she said. "There are several ladies sitting alone tonight. I don't know any of their names. If you would give me your name, I could inquire whether any of them is waiting for you."

Duggan sighed. "I got a better idea," he said. "Lemme look around." He brushed past the woman and turned to his right, walking up a slight incline into another rosily-lighted room. It was lined with small booths on the right and larger booths on the left. There was one person in the room. That was Edith Washburn. She was seated at one of the small booths. She was drinking a glass, of white wine. Duggan caught her eye as he walked down the narrow corridor between the small booths and the large booths. She smiled, wanly. He gestured with his head toward the large booth across from her. She looked quizzical. He grinned. When he reached her, he said: "I don't like these tables. When they put me in one of them, I feel like I'm a dog getting into one of those pet carriers the airlines use. Move."

Edith Washburn got up swiftly and crossed the aisle. They sat down simultaneously at one of the large booths. She grinned at him.

"Hard day?" he said.

"An absolute bitch of a day," she said. "Yours?"

"I could use a drink," he said. "Do they have any waitresses left tonight that aren't candidates for autopsies?"

"I saw one a while ago that seemed to be breathing," she said. "I can't be sure, though. Didn't take her pulse."

"Okay?" Duggan said. He put his fingers in his mouth and whistled piercingly.

"Good heavens," Edie said. She started to laugh. "You mustn't have any trouble getting cabs."

"Or birds, neither," Duggan said. "Called in a penguin once, from Antarctica. Walked all the way, poor little critter. Took him to the zoo."

An alarmed and elderly woman appeared at the door leading into the room. Duggan waved her toward them, using the traffic cop's signal.

"How did he like the zoo?" Edie said.

"Wonderful," Duggan said. "We had such a good time, next day I took him, the ball game, Sox lost."

The waitress reached their table. "Just two of you for dinner?" she said.

"That's a quorum, M'am," Duggan said. "But first I would like about a pail of vodka martinis. Put some ice in it."

"Vodka martini on the rocks," the waitress said. She wrote it down. "But if you're not expecting anyone else, I'll have to ask you to take one of the smaller tables."

"Go to it," Duggan said. "Ask away, we're not going to move. There's room enough in this joint tonight for the Second Armored Division. When they show up and the place gets crowded, we will meekly move. Until that happens, I would like my drink and enough space to sit comfortably."

"We do have rules, sir," the waitress said.

"I do have a nasty disposition, begging your pardon and all, M'am," Duggan said. "I am not moving. My drink, please, and the menus."

The waitress hobbled away. Duggan leaned toward Edie. "Tell you what," he said, "you show me yours, I'll show you mine."

She began to laugh again. "You were mean to that woman."

"Okay," Duggan said, "I show mine first. My guy will not plead out. I think he should. If I had a reasonable client, we could belt this thing out on a second-degree in a minute. He is not reasonable."

"He confessed," she said.

"He made a statement," Duggan said. "I have read that statement, which you so kindly provided to me."

"He had his rights read to him," she said.

"Yup," Duggan said. "Signed a document to prove it. Said he'd been to the tidal creek. Said he knew Thomas Monaghan. Said he knew Monaghan was dead. Said he believed Monaghan'd gotten shot by somebody."

"Oh come on, Jack," she said. "He led the cops to the scene."

"Right," Duggan said. "Now you are going to tell me that the cops didn't know there was a tidal creek there until he told them about it."

"No" she said.

"No" Duggan said. "And probably the cops didn't know about Monaghan being dead until they pulled him out of the water, all green and swollen, and he wasn't breathing very much. You are going to tell me that."

"No," she said.

"Edie," Duggan said, "it was in all the papers. Frederick Ellis, my esteemed client, is dumber'n some rocks that I have met. But he can *read*. He can listen to the wireless and he can watch the television. Everybody who ever laid eyes on Monaghan knew he wasn't getting around much anymore. This is not proof beyond a reasonable doubt that Frederick Ellis did him in."

"Jack," she said, "I have some more bad news to improve your day."

"Go ahead," he said. "Everybody else has."

"Gould won't take a plea," she said. "He wants murder one."

The waitress limped down the aisle with Duggan's drink. "Oh good," he said, as she arrived. "That is extremely good. That was just what I needed. I've got an unreasonable client and you've got an unreasonable boss." The waitress set the drink down on the table. Duggan picked it up immediately and swigged from it. "Another one of these little buggers," he said, "and some fried clams, french fries, slaw." To Edie he said: "Order."

"Same thing," she said.

"Martini also?" the waitress said.

"White wine," Edie said. "White wine."

• • •

The Man was short and thin and wizened. He was in his late sixties. He had a shock of white hair that he combed straight back. He wore a white broadcloth shirt with a medium spread collar and a tie made of dark blue silk. He wore a well-cut Ivy-League suit, dark blue, just slightly nipped in at the waist. He wore black wing-tipped shoes. He sat behind an ornate antique desk, made of oak and carved with elaborate scrolling. He sipped at a pony of anisette and then from a cup of coffee. He did not show any expression on his face.

The cigar-smoking driver was in his middle forties, rather flush of face and somewhat overweight. He wore a blue blazer and tan slacks. He sat in an armchair, padded and then covered with tufted leather. Ellis had a straight chair opposite the driver.

"He is worried, Mr. Caruso," the driver said. "Frederick here tells me that he is worried."

Caruso shifted his gaze to Ellis. He spoke mildly. "Worry is bad for a man, Freddie. Worried people tend to die before their time."

Ellis's tone betrayed considerable anxiety. He spread his hands and leaned forward in the chair. He spoke earnestly. "Mr. Caruso," he said, "it is not just me who should be worried. Walsh should be worried and Charlie Carnival should be worried."

"Walsh and Carnival are not around," Caruso said. "They are vacationing and cannot be reached."

"They should still be worried," Ellis said.

"And Francesco," Caruso said, nodding toward the driver, "should he be worried?"

"Probably," Ellis said.

"And I, perhaps," Caruso said, "should I perhaps be worried?"

"Considering what's happening," Ellis said, "you should think about it at least."

Caruso glanced at Francesco. He looked back at Ellis. He leaned forward and steepled his fingers. "You have succeeded, Freddie," he said. "Now I also am worried, and I am an old man who must think also of his health. How can we end all of this worry?"

"The cops haven't got a hard case against me," Ellis laid. "They got all excited when they got the tip and they left a lot of things out."

"Then there is no worry," Caruso said.

"It's the lawyers," Ellis said. "This guy Duggan that I got is some kind of a crazy man, I think, and he is beating all over me that I am not telling him the truth. The DA is this broad that is beating all over Duggan because I will not plead out. One or the other of those damned lawyers is going to get all haired up and that will finish me off. The DA wants Murder One. I do not."

"What could you do, Freddie?" Caruso said it very softly.

"I could run," Ellis said.

"Any man can run," Caruso said. "The question is: how far?"

"I could go on vacation, like Walshie and Carnival," Ellis said anxiously.

"I think that many people would miss you," Caruso said.

• • •

Duggan was in the 99 Restaurant on Pearl Street in Boston. His red tie was loosened from his collar and his speech was some what slurred. He was drinking vodka martinis and he was talking to a small blonde woman in her early twenties who had bleached her hair and gained a little weight since she had purchased her flowered blouse and tan skirt. She had undone the top three buttons of her blouse to avoid getting overheated. "You're married," she said.

"Yup," Duggan said.

"My God," she said, "I never thought I'd see the day when one of you guys admitted it. You still living with her, or what?"

"Yes," he said.

"Yes what?" she said. "When you go home at night, do you go home at night or do you go somewhere else?"

"Yes," he said. "Depends on the night. I do one or I do the other."

"Hot damn," she said. "Which you like better?"

"The other," he said. "Much better."

She linked her left arm through his right arm. "I think we could be friends," she said.

"Until morning," he said, thickly.

"With an option year," she said, "like the other guys who play ball."

• • •

Edie Washburn in the morning met Lieutenant Walter Nolan outside the District One Police Headquarters on New Chardon Street in the Government Center complex in Boston. "Lieutenant," she said, "we have got to talk?"

Nolan was in his early thirties. He wore a plain tan raincoat and a somewhat mischievous expression. "This is so sudden, Edie," he said. He smiled at her and stuck his hands in his pockets.

"Time passes so quickly when you're having fun," she said. She grabbed him by the left elbow.

"Whoa," he said, pulling loose. "Not here in the middle of a public thoroughfare."

"I've got to talk to you," she said.

"Can we have some coffee, maybe?" Nolan said.

"Coffee," she said, taking him by the arm again. "Now, walk, and let's see if we can do that at the same time, we're talking."

They headed up the hill on New Chardon toward Center Plaza. "Look, Walter," she said.

"I have been," he said.

"You're married," she said, "and I like Annie. This's business. I think we have got a little problem with this Ellis guy."

"He should faw down, go boom," Walter said.

"He ain't gonna," she said grimly. "There're two reasons why he won't. There is Harold Gould. The second one is Jack Duggan."

"He drew Duggan?" Walter said. "Son of a gun, I thought Duggan spent most of his time moaning and groaning about his life. He still alive?"

"Very much so," she said. "Not only alive, but very well, thank you."

"He hasn't had a murder case in two, three years," Walter said. "The heaviest thing he's had, I heard about, was a couple smalltime hoods robbed a gas station, and that was about six months ago."

"How'd it come out?" she said.

"Not guilty," Walter said.

"You're a detective," she said. "That a clue to something, maybe?"
"Hell, Edie," Walter said, "it wasn't an ironclad case."

"Is Ellis ironclad?" she said, pulling Nolan to a halt.

"No, Edie, for cryin' out loud," Walter said. "No case's ironclad.
You've been at this long enough, know that."

"Right," she said. "And so's Duggan. And now let me tell you
another thing: Gould won't take a plea."

"Oh, oh," Walter said.

"I am going to have to try this case," she said.

"Sounds like it," he said.

"I have read the file again," she said. "I do not feel cheerful."

• • •

Mrs. Ellis was waiting in Duggan's office when he arrived in the morning. She was wearing a nubby pale violet coat and a black pillbox hat
and black sensible shoes. She had curled her hair. She sat clutching her
black vinyl purse on her lap. As Duggan entered the office, she was
glancing surreptitiously and disapprovingly at Cynthia.

Cynthia was drinking coffee from a paper cup. She slurped it. She
was chewing gum at the same time and reading the paper.

Duggan looked dreadful. He had not shaved. He was wearing the
same clothes he had been wearing the night before. He had not gotten
much sleep and his eyes showed it. So did his expression. He closed
the door. He stared blearily at Mrs. Ellis. "Mrs. Ellis," he said.

She pursed her lips. She looked him up and down. Cynthia paid no
attention to either of them. Mrs. Ellis said, "I came to see you."

"So I see," Duggan said. "I don't recall inviting you, but I see
You're here."

"I'm surprised you can," she said, sternly.

"Oh, Mrs. Ellis," Duggan said, "there are many things I cannot see
this morning. One, for example, is the money to defend Frederick on
a murder charge. You will recall, we had some discussion about that.
You weren't interested. Another thing I cannot see is your appointment at this ungodly hour."

"You didn't have an appointment to see me," she said. "You came
anyway, at your convenience."

"You are not defending my son on a murder charge," Duggan said.
"And losing your shirt on it."

Mrs. Ellis surveyed him again. "Your son might do better if I did," she said.

"Would you like to talk about sons, Mrs. Ellis?" Duggan said. "Do you really want to do that? I'm willing if you are. I ain't perfect, but until one of my kids gets hauled up on a murder charge, I'm 'way ahead of you. And if one of my kids does, I'll pay for his defense. No welfare for Duggan, no sir."

She paused and looked down at her handbag. Then she looked up at Duggan. "I want to talk to you," she said.

"So I gathered," Duggan said. He looked at his watch. "It is nine-oh-five, Mrs. Ellis. I am due in court at eleven. I can get there in twenty minutes if I'm lucky. That gives us almost two hours. You must've left home early. Go get something to eat and come back at ten."

"I don't know this area," she said, with a whine in her voice.

"Walk around and get acquainted with it," Duggan said. "You won't like it. No cows. Now beat it."

Her lower lip trembled.

"I mean it," Duggan said.

She stood up and straightened her coat. She headed for the open door.

"Cynthia," Duggan said. Cynthia looked up. "Did I wake you?" Duggan said. She gazed at him as though she had just noticed that he was in the office. "of course I did," Duggan said. "Go and get me a fried egg sandwich with two strips of bacon inside, and two large coffees."

"You want toast?" she said, chewing the gum.

"I would like the sandwich on toast," Duggan said. "I do not want the sandwich and the toast on the side."

"I haven't got any money," she said.

He reached into his pocket and pulled out a crumpled five, which he threw on her desk. He stalked to his office.

"What about the phones, Mr. Duggan," Cynthia said.

"They'll be here when you get back, Cynthia," he said.

He was taking off his jacket loosening his tie and pulling it down, and unbuttoning his shirt as he walked.

• • •

Duggan entered the Fifth criminal Session of the Suffolk Superior Court through the swinging oak doors. The benches were empty and the high windows spilled sunlight into the courtroom. There was one court officer on duty, a heavyset man about fifty. The officer was smoking a Salem.

"Not supposed to smoke in Court, Bailey," Duggan said. He was clean-shaven. He wore a clean yellow shirt. He wore a grey hopsack suit and a blue-and-gold tie.

Bailey looked at Duggan. "My, my," he said, "and what a fine fig-ure of a fellow we're cutting this morning."

"Clean living," Duggan said, "that's what does it."

"Got a shower in your office, huh?" Bailey said.

"Nope," Duggan said. "Complete wardrobe, though, and a men's room with running water, sometimes hot."

Bailey shook his head. "I wished I was a lawyer," he said. "Way is it, I got to work for a living."

"Lemme know when you start," Duggan said. "Judge in?"

"Judge Shanahan?" Bailey said. "Oh, Judge Shanahan is in all right. He's been in since eleven, when you were supposed to be here. So's Edie." He got up from his chair and started toward the judge's cham-bers. Over his shoulder he said: "Hope your shaving lotion's nice."

• • •

Judge Shanahan had a rosy, pudgy face, a roly-poly body, sparse grey-ing hair and an unfiltered Lucky Strike. He was short and he had an executioner's sense of humor. He was seated behind the scarred desk in chambers and regaling Edie and defense counsel Sam Waldstein when Duggan entered. He gave Duggan a perfunctory greeting and continued.

"So," Shanahan said, "this jerk Cangelosi gets up on his hind legs and asks the cop when he first wrote down someplace that the defendant was suspected of being a drug dealer. Now there is a beauty. You can see the cop cocking his bat already. He looks like Ted Williams, up against a slow pitcher. And the cop says he wrote it down a long time ago.

"Now," Shanahan said, "even I know this. I read the damned reports. They are full of the most scandalous gossip you can imagine. There is stuff in those reports that would be enough to hang the Pope if you could prove it. The trouble is that Gould can't prove any of it. And if Edie, for example, offered all that hearsay, I would take her head off. But the DA isn't offering all that hearsay, and for some reason or other, the DA is not objecting to Cangelosi bringing it in. I think I know what the reason is, but that is beside the point. I leave him do it

"Well," Shanahan said, leaning back in the chair and blowing smoke rings, "Cangelosi asks the cop when he wrote it down. And the cop says he wrote it down in the same damned report that Cangelosi's waving around like a damned flag. Which, of course, he did. And Cangelosi demands to have the cop show him where it is written down. And he throws the report at the cop and invites him to read from it.

"So," Shanahan said, "the cop does. He does it slowly. He considers every word like it was cole slaw and he had to chew it, so as to get all the flavor.

"It was in the report, all right," Shanahan said. He was grinning. "*Everything* was in the report. The report said the cop knew the defendant was a dirty, rotten, no-good, lousy, miserable dope pusher. It said the cops had good reason to believe he was a pimp who beat up on his ladies. It said there was no question that he carried a gun and used it to pistol-whip the people that he didn't find it necessary to shoot. It went on and on. The jury was eating it up. It was really good stuff.

"In the middle of this recital," Shanahan said, leaning forward, "Cangelosi *objects*. Now, that was a new one to me. I never had an objection before from a lawyer who was asking the question. 'You're objecting to your own question Mr. Cangelosi,' I said. He tells me he is not objecting to his own question. He is objecting to the cop's answer to the question. I can see why he might. It is blowing his boat right out of the water. The trouble is, when you ask the question, you don't get to object to the answer."

"'He is putting in hearsay and undocumented evidence,' Cangelosi says. 'He certainly is,' I smartly reply. 'He is able to do that because you invited him to do it.' Well, there was a great tussle, and in the meantime the prosecutor is sitting there with a grin that the Cheshire Cat would've envied."

Shanahan rocked back in his chair and clasped his hands behind his bead. "And that, ladies and gentlemen," he said, "is today's lesson in trial practice. Sam, you are excused."

As Waldstein arose, Shanahan stubbed out his Lucky and lit another one. He surveyed Duggan critically. "You look reasonably good today, Jackie boy," he said. "What did you do, go through the car wash on foot?"

"No," Duggan said, "I went to your embalmer and told him I wanted the same discount special you bought."

Shanahan began to laugh. "No respect for the court as usual, I see."

Waldstein pursed his lips and gazed disapprovingly at Duggan.

"Hiya, Sam," Duggan said. "Didn't notice you before. Course, you're easy to overlook."

Shanahan guffawed.

"I don't think . . . " Waldstein said.

"I know it," Duggan said. "You should try it some time. Whyncha beat it now, so I can talk the judge. Okay?"

Waldstein glanced toward Shanahan, who only smiled. Waldstein left chambers. Duggan took his chair.

"Tell me about this twerp Ellis," Shanahan said. "We gonna belt this out or what?"

"Or what," Edie said. "Gould wants a Murder One."

"Wonderful," Shanahan said. "Duggan?"

"Ellis says he's innocent," Duggan said.

"Trial, then," Shanahan said. "Confound it. Blasted nuisance." He pulled his calendar over and studied it. "This's a pain in the neck, you know."

"Life's full of hardships, Your Honor," Duggan said.

• • •

Duggan was at his desk. He was speaking urgently into the phone and the door to his office was closed. He said: "Look, Honey, I'll be there by five-thirty. I will really be there. You can count on it. I am not going to let you down."

• • •

Frederick Ellis emerged in the darkness from the Sheraton Boston Hotel. He was wearing a leather car-coat and an anxious expression. He stood in the doorway and gazed at the street. The maroon Cougar came into view. It pulled up at the entrance. Ellis opened the passenger door and climbed in. "Francesco," he said.

"Frederick," the driver said. He was smoking a cigar. The car was filled with the smoke.

"Francesco," Ellis said, "where the hell're we going?"

"Frederick," the driver said, "the Man is concerned. He is worried. Just like you wanted. He is just as worried as you are."

"Now I am even more worried," Ellis said.

"You must stop worrying," Francesco said, Putting the car in gear. "In the position you're in, when you get worried, everybody else gets worried."

• • •

The Cadillac slowed to a halt in the driveway of the yellow colonial garrison house in a western suburb of Boston. The side door, leading to the breezeway, immediately opened. A girl about nine years old came out. She was prancing. She wore a blue melton coat with red embroidery around the button holes and sleeves. She wore white knee socks and black Mary Janes. She had long blonde hair and she wore barrettes. She began to run toward the car, but she had breath enough to scream. She screamed: "Daddy."

Behind the girl there was a boy, about three years older. He came out more slowly, ushered by a woman who remained inside the jalousied breezeway, and shut the door behind him. He put his hands in his pockets and studied the sky for a while. He wore a tweed overcoat and L.L. Bean boots.

The girl embraced Duggan exuberantly. He was only halfway out of the car and he was off-balance, but he recovered himself and picked her off the ground. He hugged her and swung her. He carefully concealed from her the tears that came up in his eyes. He made his voice gruff and said: "Mark."

The girl said: "I'm so glad to see you, Daddy."

Duggan said: "Right. Get Mark." He turned away from her.

The boy came down the walk very slowly. The girl ran up to him and took him by the left hand. She skipped. He lagged. She brought him up to the car.

Duggan said: "Hi, Mark. Hungry?"

Mark stared at him for what seemed like several minutes. Then he said: "Can I have steak?"

"Sure," Duggan said. He was forcing heartiness. "Gino'll make braciole for you, we ask. Politely."

The boy pondered that. He nodded. "I would like that," he said.

• • •

Gino Ferraro was holding court at his restaurant, close by the Boston Garden. He wore a blue blazer and tan slacks and a red-striped tie. He needed glasses and he had had them made in gold-filled aviator frames. When Duggan and his kids came in, Gino was effusive. He said: "Annie. Mark. So good to see you." They shook his hand. Gino said to Duggan: "Table for three, Jack?"

"Please," Duggan said.

Gino clapped him on the back. "It's good to see you, my friend," he said. "When're we goin' the track?"

"Tomorrow is out," Duggan said. "Police hearing. You hear about that guy Franklin?"

"Poor guy," Gino said. He shook his head.

"I got him," Duggan said.

"Poor guy, you," Gino said. "He got any money?"

"If he has," Duggan said, "he's hangin' onto it."

"Ahh," Gino said. He ushered them into the dining area.

He spoke to Mark. "And you, young man, are you goin' the game?"

"Steak," Mark said, as he sat down.

"Ahh," Gino said, "braciolettine. And for you, Mr. Duggan?"

"Gimme a beer, Gino," Duggan said.

"It's a pleasure, Jack, see you with the kids in here," Gino said.

Duggan slumped. "Out on dates," he said. "Out on dates with my own damned kids."

Gino patted him again. "It'll get better, Jack. It'll get better."

• • •

Harold Gould had been to morning Mass and had a cup of coffee. He was dressed in a grey cheviot suit and he was madder than a hornet. He slammed his fist on the desk when he sat down in the creaking oak chair. He shouted at Edie Washburn. His face was inflamed and his veins stood out.

"I dunno," she said.

"He isn't here," Gould said.

"He isn't here," she said.

"Can't fool you, can they?" Gould said.

"Nope," she said.

"Find him," Gould said.

"Okay," she said.

"Find him before noon," Gould said.

"This may be hard to do," she said.

"Struggle," Gould said. "Life is very hard."

• • •

In the early morning, Walter Nolan stood with his shoulders hunched under the tan raincoat on the macadam launching ramp at the marina. There was some cold grey sunshine. There was an object floating in the water. It was Ellis. Edie Washburn stood next to him. She wore a tan raincoat.

"This," Walter said, "does not look like a plea bargain to me, under any circumstances."

"The defendant appears to be dead," she said.

"Terminally dead," Nolan said.

. . .

Duggan showed up at his office fairly early in the morning. He did not look good. Cynthia snapped her gum and snapped at him. "Hard night, Counsellor?"

"Very," he said.

"You should go home at night," she said.

"I did," he said.

"Frederick Ellis is dead," she said.

Duggan sat down fast in the reception area. "Dead," he said.

"Dead," she said. She snapped her gum again.

"Cause of death?" he said.

"Gunshot," Cynthia said. "He's on the slab. Southern Mortuary."

Duggan did not say anything for a while. "I appreciate the address. I don't think I care to see him."

"He didn't pay ya, did he?" Cynthia said.

"Nope," Duggan said, getting up.

"Then the hell with him," Cynthia said. She went back to her coffee, and her newspaper.

"Exactly," Duggan said. "Exactly."

. . .

The hearing room was windowless. The walls were walnut panelling, halfway up. Above waist level, the walls were white. They needed paint. The commissioner and two uniformed officers sat behind a long oak table. The commissioner wore a grey flannel suit and a stern expression. He said: "Mr. Duggan. Have you any more questions?"

Duggan turned and glanced at Franklin. Franklin shook his head once. Duggan turned back to the commissioner. "I have nothing further," he said.

"Would you care to be heard?" the commissioner said.

"Actually," Duggan said, "I think I've been heard enough at this proceeding. I can talk some more if you like, but I don't think I'm going to add much to the supply of human wisdom."

The commissioner did not cover his grin quickly enough. "That will be fine, Counsellor," he said. He rapped the gavel. "The hearing will be in recess while we deliberate." The spectators began to shift in their chairs, collecting coats. "We will deliberate right here," the commissioner said. "No need to leave unless you wish to."

The commissioner leaned to the officer on his right and spoke behind his hand. He nodded and turned to the officer on his left. He spoke behind his hand again. He nodded again. He rapped the gavel. "The board is agreed," he said. "We find the charges against Patrolman Franklin to be without merit, and that he acted with prudence and discretion in protecting the life and safety of a fellow officer. Anything further?"

"Nothing further," Duggan said.

The commissioner banged the gavel again. "Hearing is adjourned."

Franklin stood up very slowly. Ahearn came out of the spectators' section and shook his hand. Each of them had tears in his eyes. Ahearn took Duggan by the hand. "Thanks," he said.

"Yeah," Franklin said. "Thanks."

"Nothing to it," Duggan said. "Lead pipe cinch."

"See?" Ahearn said. "I told you he was a rotten louse."